Beyond the God Particle is revealed
a world of splendid, blinding beauty,
but one to which our mind's eye
will adapt."

Leon Lederman
Recipient of the Nobel Prize in Physics 1988
in
The God Particle

ELOHIM
MASTERS AND MINIONS

Winston Trilogy Book II

A necessary sequel to
One Just Man

A novel by
Stan I.S. Law

INHOUSEPRESS
Montreal—Canada

Second paperback edition 2015
http://stanlaw.ca

Published in Canada in 2008 by
INHOUSEPRESS
http://www.inhousepress.ca

Cover design after a sculpture by
Bozena Happach

This book is a work of fiction.
Names, characters, titles, places and incidents are either the products of the author's imagination or are used fictitiously.

LIBRARY AND ARCHIVES CANADA CATALOGUING IN PUBLICATION
Law, Stan I. S
Elohim : Masters and Minions : a necessary sequel to
One Just Man : a novel / by Stan I.S. Law.

I. Law, Stan I. S. . One just man. II. Title.
PS8623.A92E545 2009 C813'.6 C2009-900216-7

Second paperback edition 2015
ISBN 978-1-987864-04-5

Printed and bound in the USA

At any given moment, life is completely senseless.
But viewed over a period, it seems to reveal itself
as an organism existing in time, having a purpose,
trending in a certain direction.

Aldous Huxley
(1894-1963)

Contents

Prologue

He wrote, 'Call me Ishmael.' And with those three words Melville set his quill on a fragment of immortality. It was easy for Herman. Not so for me. I have no name. Call me Nobody? A Nomad? Or even Petrus Latter? Or Lazarus? Some might remember the body I wore as having belonged to a man named Peter, the original name I carried from my baptism to the day when my hands became blessed with the power of healing. Not I, please note, my friends, just my hands. I was cursed. My medical career destroyed. My future...?

People will tell you that anyone who has the gift of healing realizes that it is a spiritual phenomenon. That it is not the hands, but the power that flows through them. Not so, my friends. I felt no power. No transfer of spirit, no flow of energy, no sense of elation. *Nothing*. No spiritual phenomena of any sort. Just my hands. Cool, listless, virtually unwilling, they were the instruments of an agency that chose to remain beyond my senses, beyond my understanding.

Even in Rome I couldn't... but that comes later in the story.

Believe me. I had nothing to do with the effect my hands had when they came in contact with people. Whatever took place was not the result of my will, nor even the consequence of my medical knowledge or the skills acquired at great effort and sacrifice over many years. Yes, in those early days I had been known as Dr. Peter Thornton, FRCSP, a fresh inductee into the society of the Fellowship of the Royal College of Surgeons and Physicians.

Somewhere in the hoary past.... Another time, another lifetime.

Now? Now I am once more Nobody. I've spent considerable effort trying to maintain my anonymity. Sometimes successfully. At other times...

Three times I've left my lair. Three times I'd been accosted.

Then came the separation from the world. I crawled into a hole and pulled the covers over me. I died. In every sense but physically. We all do at times, only few of us realize it. Even fewer of us ever come back to life.

"When did it all start?" I asked Smith, in the hope of catching him off-guard.

For a while Winston continued to arrange crystal glasses, upside down, in a stainless-steel cradle suspended from the ceiling on long rods. It seemed to absorb all his attention. When he stopped, he faced me with a vaguely amused smile. A funny smile that was hardly visible, yet lightened his deeply lined face.

"About twelve billion years ago, some say further back, Sir," he said, slowly stressing every word. "About the time Elohim created the world," his eyes smiled, but his face remained serious. "From that moment on, we were each given a choice, to be gods or minions."

At the time I took it as a turn of phrase. It never crossed my mind to take his words literally.

"To put it a different way," Winston continued, apparently changing the subject, "when matter came into contact with antimatter... or really separated. When the conversion of energy into matter was of such magnitude, well... scientists these days call it the Big Bang. We, you and I, are one half of that explosion. The other half remains locked in the hearts of the countless black holes. None had existed before the world came into being. When the two were still one there was only one reality—omnipresent, single, without differentiation. A Single Soul, not individualized. To this day, some people call it God."

So much for catching Winston Smith off-guard.

According to Smith, it was then, in that evanescent instant, that I was born, even as we all were, into a reality of contrasts, of black and white, of hot and cold, and of good and evil. Into the world we all live in. At least we think we do. The world of illusion, of Maya. The world we all perceive as real.

For a while, apparently an extremely long while, I served the illusive reality. I served Caesar. As we all do. And then? And then my life took a different turn. I got caught up in a vortex of forces that refused, and still refuse, to let me go. Don't even imagine that we, humans, are granted the so-called 'free will'. It is there, but it is coiled up inside us like the many dimensions the scientists are talking about. Quantum mechanics, they call it. Go look it up! Go on! You can read all about it on the Internet. It's all coiled up, invisible. Held in abeyance. Free will, as we think of it, is the greatest fallacy religions have spread to the people of the world. We are puppets. We can oppose the currents carrying our vessels for a little while, but soon, all too soon, we will be swept up again and taken to our destination. Some to heaven, some to hell. Others? Most others just onto another joyride on the eternal carousel of life.

I still believe that it all really began when I joined the seminary. I mean, began for me, in this particular cycle. I had the best of intentions of becoming a priest. To serve my God and His people. Ultimately, to earn my place in paradise. It seemed like the right thing to do. Later? Later I seemed to have contracted a severe case of cold feet. The hunger remained but the will waned, dissipated in a reality that denied the invisible, the intangible. The world was too solid, too hard to pierce with ideas, or with ideals of the ephemeral.

I escaped. I suppose, I've been running ever since. A year after the seminary, I decided that if I couldn't serve my soul, I would do my best to serve my body. Or anyone's body. I took up medicine.

I was lucky. My brother died. It sounds callous to equate my luck with my brother's death. But if it hadn't been for his untimely demise, I would never have moved to his house, never taken up residence in Westmount to look after Ruth, his widow, never enjoyed the company of Jonathan and Moira, Jo and Mo. But most of all, I wouldn't have met Winston, the sublimely normal yet still enigmatic *majordomo* who's affected my life in a way that to this day remains quite unpredictable.

After five years of medicine at McGill University, and four years of residency at the Montreal General, I finally passed my Fellowship exams. I became Dr. Peter Thornton, MD., FRCSP. Something to be proud of. That's as high as you can get in my... in my ex-profession. I lost the license to practice medicine due to a technicality. I lost my credentials thanks to my "gift". I discovered that my touch, the touch of my hands, healed people. Not my strenuously acquired medical knowledge, nor my years of burning the midnight oil, nor even the four years of residency at Montreal's best teaching hospital.

Just my hands. Or whatever used them.

I felt like a second-rate TV evangelist administering the 'touch' of the Holy Spirit on the sinners. On the sinners, abusers, perverts, or just the unfortunates who'd lost their way. Only there was no 'spirit', no invisible or visible light emanating from my palms. I didn't wield the Bible in my hands to add weight to my actions. I touched them and they recovered. Rather like the rays of sun healing you, or an aspirin removing your headache.

There was no point in pretending to be a doctor any more. Again, I escaped.

I wasn't a doctor anymore, I was a freak. Some men, some women, become magnificent poets, some produce immortal works of art, some play a music that stimulates your soul and mind to greater things. I healed. Or my hands did. I became an instrument of something over which I had absolutely no control. Nor could I refuse to heal anyone. I could not touch them and let them remain sick. The diseases eased, the bones mended, as though invaded by an onslaught of stem cells that rebuilt the injured organs, arms, or legs in an amazingly quick time. I was a nobody with a gift.

I still am, I suppose. A Nobody.

Immediately following the discovery of my curse, gift to some, Ruth gave me a home where, thanks to her generosity, I managed to escape reality and hide from the hordes, or at least from quite substantial crowds, who followed me in the hope of a miraculous cure. Later, but more secretly, I continued to practice my gift until the exhaustion of trying to serve too many too quickly nearly cost me my life. I'd forgotten about Buddha's admonitions about the middle path. About not worrying about tomorrow. I took my patients' maladies upon myself. I wasn't ready for such a burden. I was a doctor of medicine, not a saint.

Winston, the ever-enigmatic majordomo, saved me. Cathy did the rest.

Cathy…

Even as I write this, her jade-green eyes, as dreamy as they are piercing, draw me into a forbidden garden of Elysian promise. She is the only one who seems to understand my soul when I lose control over my own inner being. She may be across the ocean, the vast Pacific, yet her eyes, shimmering behind my own eyelids, draw me into the mysteries that churn within her own soul, lapping the very limits of my consciousness, enticing my dreams, my desires. Like magic.

I owe her my life.

Things happen. Things over which we have little control. Events swept me to Gdansk, where the expectation of my healing ability put me face to face with Lena, the most fascinating woman I've ever met: Lena Walesa, the granddaughter of Lech, the famous founder of the Solidarity movement. She was then, even as she is now, running Solidarity International, the organization that, according to Ruth, has two billion members. Some organization! It recognizes no borders, no national identities; it crosses oceans with equal ease. Last year, Ruth, once its staunch opponent, had a change of heart. Now, she's committed her life to Lena's ideals.

And then there was Rome. No words can describe what happened there. Suffice it to say that the Holy Roman and Apostolic Church would never be the same. Never. It cannot. Not with Lena looking after its worldly domains with the Last Pontiff's blessing.

It is a strange world. If it hadn't been for Cathy's mother, who tried to recount those events in her book, *One Just Man*, I would never have believed them myself. Judge for yourself.

When, last year, Cathy, Ruth, and I returned from Rome, I thought that, at least for a short while, I could hide out in Ruth's cabin up north, perhaps, once again, with Cathy for company. I had memories there. I also had fresh memories to sort out. There was so much we had to say to each other—Cathy and I that is. She's such an incredible woman. She gives without ever expecting anything in return. Perhaps there are other people like her, but I haven't met any. Completely selfless. She's the sort of person Winston alludes to when he points to humanity's future.

Ah, yes... Winston Smith. The man-mountain. A teacher, friend, sage, and all this while hiding under the sombre mask of our majordomo. He carried me to safety when I went too far, when I'd diluted my life-force too much. When I was little more than a beginner on the eternal climb to my ultimate destiny.

Ultimate?

"There is no end to infinity," Winston would say. More than once.

Somehow our psyche refuses to accept that there can be existence without a beginning and, therefore, without an end. We are born, we live, and we die. We fool ourselves that there is a hereafter. Not so. There is no beginning that we know of.

"You sound like an atheist," Ruth remarked, probably afraid that I might impart my pagan philosophy to her children. This exchange happened only a few months ago, before I learned to keep my thoughts to myself.

"If you define your God, you'll limit Her by your definition," I replied softly. "If you don't, what am I to believe in?" I had been thinking of Spinoza's admonition.

"It is the here and now that matters," Winston would murmur in a voice that could penetrate walls. A deep basso that could attain fame and fortune on any stage of the world. With his six-foot-six stature, an overpowering dramatic presence, he could have become a star in Hollywood overnight. Or in New Delhi. Or Beijing. There are no barriers that could constrain Winston. Not the Winston I know.

Not that I really know him. A man as cryptic, as enigmatic, as obscure as what had happened to me, way back when, at the General Hospital. One day I was a promising member of the teaching staff, the next, a has-been with healing power flowing from my unwitting hands.

"It doesn't flow from your hands, Peter," Ruth told me. "The power flows through you!"

How come people who never healed anyone know so much? "When I kiss them, or kick them, no one gets healed," I barked, and immediately regretted my temper. She meant well.

I cursed the day when it happened. I don't any more. Nor am I grateful. I am simply resigned. I've learned the meaning of submission. Islam—isn't that what it means? Submission? Only I still have no idea to what. Or to whom? I've learned that it is completely useless to resist or oppose the power that's taken over my life. I had ample evidence of it in Rome. And since.

And then we were back in Westmount.

At the time, I didn't know how long I would be allowed to remain in Ruth's home before the leeches, grasping for my inimitable power, caught up with me. If and when they did, I told myself, I shall no longer be Nobody. Once more I would become a Nomad.

I admit it. I was scared. I've been scared for a long time.

I no longer left the house. I didn't dare. We couldn't have stayed up north any longer, either. Cathy had her work. In the meantime, I had to gather my thoughts. I had to attempt to understand what had happened to me. In some ways, it all still remains beyond my understanding, though most events have begun to fall into place. My eyes are being opened. Slowly. I now know that it will be a long journey.

I refused to be just a thing, an instrument over which I had no control. None at all. I felt an overpowering need to learn who I was. What was my purpose. Indeed, what was the purpose of humanity. Winston would help me, I knew that even then. And, in quite a different way, so would Cathy. I can't claim that I knew it, but I felt it. It's quite amazing how many things I just feel even now. It is as though I have become an observer of my own life unfolding on a course over which I still have little control. Right now, I tell myself, I must go to sleep. When I wake up, perhaps all the problems will have gone away. They never do, of course. They probably never will. Never.

I thought that I should have undergone plastic surgery on my face and should have bought asbestos gloves to keep me from affecting anyone. Asbestos gloves and a veil of invisibility. I was fecting anyone. Asbestos gloves and a veil of invisibility. I was tired of being exploited. By anyone. By distraught mothers, by drunks with pickled innards, by smokers with cancerous lungs, even by the Gdansk henchmen of the most fascinating woman in the world. Or, for that matter, by the Holy Father himself, though I very much doubt he had much to do with what happened at the Vatican. Finally, I refused to be exploited by the power within me. Whatever it is.

I developed a single profound ambition. To be like other people. I wanted a white picket fence with Cathy and myself raising a dozen children. Just the two of us. Far, far away, at the end of the rainbow, in a long-forgotten corner of this wonderful world of ours. I wanted time to see it. To dip my fingers in lakes and rivers, to dive into their caressing waters and... to forget. It was all moving too fast. Much too fast. I needed time to grow old. Like other people. To forget about the power in my hands.

***

Genetics

If the Universe is the Answer,
what is the Question?

Leon Lederman
[In 1988 he shared the Nobel Prize for physics]
with Dick Teresi in
The God Particle

1

The Reunion

"I suppose the lines will be a mile long," I said, clipping my hair even shorter. I had to. Otherwise my wig just wouldn't fit. I don't go out very often. Hadn't for nearly a year. For crying out loud, I've been a prisoner.

Winston looked as if he were about to say something.

"No matter," I continued, providing my own answer. "The show will be running for the next four days."

"After the matinee performance you are attending this afternoon, Sir, there is enough time for at least one more show later this evening," Winston affirmed as though declaring the secret of the ages.

He was right, of course. Each performance took about two hours, a thirty-minute break, and *da capo al fine*. After all, there were no 'live' singers. It was all illusion, like the rites they performed in the Cathedral until a year ago. The latter were merely symbolic, now—holographic images. Really, only the actors had changed.

"I believe the parking is underground, Sir," Winston offered, settling the question of lines.

New parking only just finished for Lena's visit. Ruth had also told me that the architects had contrived to triple the number of seats in the nave.

"Mrs. Thornton tells me that the Cathedral is freshly renovated with Solidarity funds. She says it is like new, a temple to behold, Madam said. The Last Pontiff would have enjoyed it." It sounded as if Winston were trying to divert my thoughts from my frustration.

I took a sip of water. In spite of the humidity that seemed to permeate my room from the outside, my throat felt dry. I used to love autumn. All the colours... the mysteries of the descending fog… the peace I felt just before falling asleep. But watching the droning rain through widows streaked with meandering rivulets of pollution did not fill me with an abundance of joy.

I managed a weak smile. The Last Pontiff. That was how everyone referred to His Holiness. He seemed such a nice man, way back when… When I was more than a vegetable gracing Ruth's house.

More water. What I really needed was a shot of Scotch. I was nervous.

Only the Last Pontiff didn't have any money. Nor did anyone else in the church. What with the billions and billions of dollars' worth of art to protect, to insure, to maintain at the right temperature, humidity, plus the buildings themselves... it was just too much. And with the hundreds of thousands of churches to look after... the buildings often crumbling thanks to the scourge of the modern era, the pollution, the corrosive smog, the acid rain…. The Church or really the Vatican, went bust. Bankrupt. The *Instituto per le Opere di Religione* went out of business. It would have been sad had it not been for Solidarity. Had it not been for Lena. And she was such a good Catholic. Aren't all Poles? As for the Last Pontiff, I wondered where he'd been passing his time since our meeting in Rome. The shortest meeting with the greatest consequences. I knew he was all right. Physically. Or mentally for that matter. Part of me will for ever be with him.

I suddenly realized that I must hurry. Lena would be here soon, and I still had to shave, otherwise taking off my false beard would be too painful. My first outing. Suddenly I felt a cold shiver.

I was scared. I hated that.

I remembered the Cathedral *Marie-Reine-du-Monde* well enough from way back when I too called myself a good Catholic. Originally designed as an exact one-third replica of St. Peter's in Rome, down to a copy of Bernini's *baldacchino* over the main altar. Indeed she reigned well over the whole of Quebec—back in 1894—when the building was completed. Funny that. Cathedral comes from the Greek *kathedra*, a seat. The seat of a bishop. Whatever happened to His Eminence? Where is he sitting now?

I saw Smith's reflection in the mirror. He'd just finished laying out my dinner jacket and trousers on the bed. The dress-shirt with a starched collar was ready too. Ready to jump into. At least it wasn't a monkey suit, I thought.

"Is the old bishop still alive?" I asked, hardly expecting an answer. There was no reason for him to have died. Unless he rejected the new order. Some fundamentalist priests just couldn't take it. Especially those who thought of the Church as a career. The last Encyclical issued by the Last Pontiff came to them as the shock of a lifetime. The Church's possessions taken over by Solidarity, an International Union. The Church itself? People weren't clear. Some priests ended up in the Douglas Hospital for the insane. Others were luckier. They found jobs as teachers, in hospitals, libraries. There hadn't been that many choices. Those that became priests to serve others continued to do so. There had been many who didn't accept the Last Pope's cathartic dissolution. People still wanted to have their babies christened, the elderly hoped for the last unction. Still others thought that a marriage ceremony without a priest's presence was little more than a glorified premarital agreement. It wasn't a marriage at all. Ruth told me that the ex-clerics had not been turned out into the street. Lena had offered the unemployed priests a saving grace. They were allowed to remain living in their parsonages, vicarages, or manses, the often opulent surroundings to which they'd become accustomed.

"I can find out for you, Sir," Winston said, sounding slightly embarrassed. He'd acquired a reputation of knowing just about everything.

"What? Ah, yes, the bishop..." I was lost in my thoughts. That happened a lot to me lately. "Not that it matters," I absolved him. I didn't really care. I was tired of caring. For too long I cared too much. It almost cost me my life.

The old Cathedral of *Marie-Reine-du-Monde* was a particular favourite of Lena's. It reminded her of her new home, the Vatican, where she'd taken up residence on the day the Last Pontiff had dissolved the Church. Well, not dissolved really, but made it in the image and likeness of what the Lord had intended. At least, that was what he'd said at the time.

"Let us call ourselves brothers and sisters," he'd said *urbi et orbi,* his white flowing robes aflutter in the window of his apartment. "Let others call us Christians. Let others call us brothers who love one another."

It didn't go over very well with the evangelists.

He'd said it only last year... God, how time flies...

I turned to the clothing laid out on my bed. The dress-shirt was a perfect fit. Smith got it for me. He does just about everything for me these days. And he still has time for the children.

I had to get a move on. It wouldn't do to be late. Not for our reunion. Not for my first outing. I kept saying that to myself while all along trying to play it down. Nerves, I suppose. And I knew the bow tie would give me problems. That was when Ruth came in without knocking. Yesterday I would have snapped at her.

"Let me do it for you," she said.

She was so patient with me. I must really try harder to be nice, I told myself, letting her grab the ends of my bow tie from behind. She'd always tied the bow for my brother. It was like riding a bicycle—things you never forget. Women are like that. They remember. And they do the seemingly impossible with such ease. Like tying a bow tie.

"Will there be parking?" I asked changing the subject. I meant in the new underground garage. I was being stupid. Of course there would be parking. Lena was coming with us.

"Yes, Peter, now hurry," she threw over her shoulder and was gone in a whisper of silk.

Then I remembered. Immediately west of the Cathedral, under and around the statue of Sir John A. Macdonald (one of the remaining echoes of English culture in Quebec), the remaining bones of the long dead and surely by now forgotten, had been moved to the mausoleum built in front of the old Sunlife building. The land was then cleared and excavated down to six levels, providing parking just for the Cathedral alone. The trees had been replaced even if fifty years younger from their ancient predecessors. All thanks to

Solidarity. In the past, such work would have blocked traffic for months if not years, and the contract would have been extended by a couple of strikes. Now? Now, Solidarity had completed the job in well under a year.

Modern miracles?

The days when the old bishop could hardly fill the Cathedral pews were also long gone. Well, gone for a good few months—ever since the first performance took place with free entry. I think it was the Genesis, a performance that would make Hollywood proud. Or even jealous. The Cathedral had all the state of the art audio and video gimmicks. I'd heard that what you saw and heard was more real than nature itself. Since the New Year, the various churches in Montreal had given twenty-four religious performances to packed audiences. The church was flourishing like never before.

"The wonders of modern science," I murmured, lost in my thoughts.

"Indeed, Sir," Winston agreed.

After another sip of water I began emerging from my self-imposed apathy. Things concerning the world were coming back to me. Slowly. Like this parking business. They charged an arm and a leg for each car, but the entrance was free. Good, if you could walk from wherever you lived, and a clever way for Solidarity to break even. But then, Lena Walesa was one of the smartest women I'd ever met, and that includes my own Cathy. What a team they would have made if only Cathy weren't such an affirmed individualist. An intellectual, emotional, and practical libertarian. And today, Lena was flying in for the Command Performance. Like royalty. She commanded and they performed.

Royalty? Lena, the Goddess descended from the Olympus to rule over her people.

"Will there be anything else, Sir?"

Winston stood by the door. I glanced at the mirror, scowled, shrugged, and I smiled my thanks. At least I managed not to snap at Winston. I don't think anyone ever snapped at Winston. He was just too big. Unsnappable.

My thoughts returned to Lena. I'd never had such mixed feelings about anyone. Man or woman. Lena was a mixture of traits as overt as they were enigmatic, as seemingly frank and personal as they were politically motivated, as beautiful as she was impressive with her uncompromising acumen. No wonder she runs Solidarity International with such ease. Though still based in Europe, where its ranks continued to swell at an unprecedented rate, they'd also begun swelling across all the continents. Except the USA.

The USA. The world's only superpower. The *überpower* without an empire. At least, so they claimed. With a clout they could not use. They needed cooperation, not submission. Yet they resisted the Solidarity movement with all the means at their disposal.

"Hurry or you'll be late," Ruth interrupted my meandering thoughts. "Lena's always on time," she added unnecessarily. As if Lena could do anything short of perfection.

Lena was going to visit us at home and then we would drive together to the Cathedral. I'd never seen the new version of the Bible, as staged by the latest technology. In the past one could hear oratorios performed in the Cathedral, or Notre-Dame Basilica or Christmas carols at St. Joseph's Oratory. But an opera? I wasn't sure I wanted to go. I don't mean I was scared to leave the house, but, well, the years I'd spent at the seminary still had a vague, undefined hold on me. Was the House of God really a theatre? Even for staging the scenes from the Bible? Is this progress?

"Coming," I replied, adjusting my bow tie. Ruth left in a bit of a hurry.

I made final adjustments to my false beard, pressed on my bushy eyebrows and inserted an insole into my left shoe to give me a 'natural' limp. I hoped that would be enough. I couldn't recognize myself in the full-length mirror. The front door buzzer sounded.

"Darling!"

"Darling!"

"Mo! Jo!"

"Aunt Lena!" Moira and Jonathan exclaimed at the top of their voices in perfect unison. Who needs opera, I smirked.

It was time to go down.

One more sip of water and I was *almost* ready to face the world. To be completely ready I would have to drink a gallon and then pee for an hour. For a long, redeeming while. Just to gain time. Instead, I left my room and stood silently in the shadows at the top of the gallery, taking in the scene below. I could just see them all from the top of the curved stairs that led down to the entrance hall.

I couldn't help wondering how women, even the most powerful woman in the world, could remain and act in such an intrinsically feminine way. From my vantage point I observed both of them simultaneously kissing the air about ten centimetres outside each other's ears. Then they looked each other up and down, nodded in obvious satisfaction and added, "Darling, you look fabulous! Absolutely fabulous!" univocally, emulating Mo and Jo. Smith seconded these assertions with a deep bow. Somehow he was already downstairs being the perfect majordomo. Good for him, I thought grudgingly. Good for them.

My feet were glued to the carpet.

Dark green silk seemingly wrapped haphazardly around a tall yet ethereal silhouette, and black velvety softness clinging to voluptuous contours of mother earth.

A study in contrasts.

Why must I go down?

Ruth—the one in green. Dark, slim, almost slinky, an epitome of quiet, sublime elegance emerging directly from an expensive beauty salon. Not that she had, she just looked like it. Fiery ruby earrings and the necklace I bought her when I could ill afford them embraced her elegant, slim neck, underlining the gentle oval of her face. They were a gesture she'd received from me, once, in my moment of weakness. An old story. Her lipstick was a perfect match, a lustrous echo of the precious stones. My brother Andrew had been lucky to hold a woman that beautiful even for a few years. She was so much more than most men could hope for.

And then there was Lena.

As glorious as Ruth looked, she stood next to the personification of the elemental forces of nature, compressed into a vital form. Exuding life, vitality, exuberance, crowned by an abundance of blond hair, pinned up on the top of her head like a crown of the realmdom she so richly deserved. Her black dress descended from a wide collar around her neck. No décolletage, front nor back, no frills or decorations. No jewellery of any sort. Even her arms were hidden by sleeves descending to her wrists. Just smooth, flowing velvet. As usual, she wasn't wearing any make-up. Or didn't appear to be. The sapphires of her eyes flashed rays of blue light imbued with a strange amalgam of love and power. The seemingly impossible. Isn't power the very antithesis of love? Yet in those eyes they seemed to abide in perfect equilibrium.

Unwittingly, I couldn't help comparing the women to Cathy. Not just physically, but as people and women of substance. I realized, almost at once, that I couldn't define Cathy in the same terms. My images of her were just those, images. There was the Cathy of the Ritz-Xentung. The mystery, the directness, the slim body bereft of the clinging yet so superbly restrained Qi Pao, a pure silk tapestry of phoenix motif in the diamond frame.... I still remembered that night. Dr. Catherine Mondellay, the daughter of Dr. Bartholomew Mondellay, the man who put the first Chinese man on Mars. The complete absence of protocol, of acting, of pretense. Disarmingly so. And then that very slim body that was mine to take... to embrace in the never-ending tango till the early hours... on that very first night.

Later Cathy up north, bringing me back to life.

Then Cathy in Rome, in the Vatican…

I didn't see those images. I felt them. I experienced them anew, fresh, unspoiled by time. Perhaps she too was immortal? No, I couldn't compare Cathy to anyone. How I wished she were there, that night.

I shook my head. I didn't belong down there. Not any more.

Lena was under the impression that I'd saved her life—in Gdansk, over a year ago, when an army of handpicked physicians couldn't wrench her out of a coma. Under my touch, she emerged unscathed. Dear Lena. For a short while she'd drawn me into a whirlwind of life that I had no idea existed. That was long before I slipped into my depression. If I were still practising medicine, I would have diagnosed myself as suffering from a neurotic phobia. Of people. Of almost anybody. That was why, today, Ruth had put her foot down.

"You can continue to feel sorry for yourself but I cannot allow my children to see such personal abnegation," she said. "When Lena comes, there will be an army of security agents crawling everywhere, including around our house. If you don't come with us, then I hope you won't be here when we return."

Ruth had never spoken to me like that before. She meant what she said. She was my sister in-law but she was also the Canadian Chief of Solidarity International. I'm sure she was right. I'm pretty sure that I needed to get out. But there and then, at the top of those stairs, I was in a bad way.

Weren't my fears real? I wanted to remain upstairs, just looking. I've grown shy of people. Any people. All people.

I bit my lip and slowly pushed one foot forward. I made my way down one step at a time. Not gliding down the balustrade like Mo and Jo. Not even descending at a trot as I used to. As young people do. But I made it. Lena embraced me warmly. My head only just cleared her ample pulchritude. She was that much taller than I. I swallowed hard. Suddenly my throat was dry again.

"Peter, darling Peter. You are my strength. My life," she murmured, for my ears only. "How are you, my friend?"

I didn't feel strong at all.

I hadn't seen her since Rome. She'd visited Ruth once or twice, but I'd pretended indisposition. I'd forgotten the effect she had on people. Overwhelming, including on yours truly. "I don't change much, Lena. I just am," I replied, and for some reason I had the impression that she knew what I was talking about, which often was more than I did. I was really losing control, not only over my hands, but over most of my senses. "I mean, I am fine, Lena. Just fine...."

She released her embrace but continued to examine me with a steady gaze.

"Is he all right, Ruth?" she asked, still looking at me.

Ruth smiled. I glanced at my sister-in-law. Her eyes said, *He will be. Give him time*. She knew Lena's ways of gathering information.

"He is still incognito, if that's what you mean. He'll *remain* in this get up, I suppose?" She was referring to my eyebrows and beard, which hadn't fooled Lena for a second.

"I dare say he will," Lena agreed. "If they don't look into his eyes...." And then she swung towards Ruth. "And where's Winston?" she asked.

Winston had, as usual, managed to make himself invisible. He melted into the non-existent cracks of the rich floor-to-ceiling palisander panelling lining the entrance hall. And now, just as mysteriously, he emerged at Lena's side.

"I'm at your service, Madam," he asserted with quiet dignity.

Lena embraced the giant with firm conviction. "It is so good to see you," she said planting a kiss on his cheek.

I caught my breath. This was the first time since I'd met Winston Smith that I saw him embarrassed. I could swear there was a gentle hue of pink creeping up from behind his starched collar. And yes, he was definitely at a loss for words. Can you imagine that? Winston Smith at a loss for words?

***

2

The Decalogue

We left within five minutes. Ruth and I in the back seat, with the children squeezed between us. A uniformed security guard at the wheel looked like Winston's brother. Somehow the width of his shoulders failed to add to my waning confidence.

I wished Winston himself were with us, but he'd declined. I suspect he would be busy with the 'post-mortem' dinner. The man was a jewel. In the front seat, Lena looked and sounded excited. She kept telling us how wonderful it was to see us all at home, in Westmount. I listened with one ear, while keeping my other ear open for any unfamiliar sounds. I had no idea what I was expecting to hear. Police sirens? Evidence of some car chase? I also kept stealing glances at the two limousines, one in front and the other behind us. I knew them to be Lena's escort. Just as when a high-level politician comes to town. Not that I'd seen many. Always too busy, I suppose.

"I do not have a home, Ruth," Lena said, glancing at Ruth's children cuddling up to their mother. "Not a real home like you."

Something in her tone told me that she didn't expect to have one. Ever.

Lena had decided to sit up front, next to the driver, just to see more.

"In the States they don't let me," she smiled wistfully. "Security and all that," she added.

Now that made me feel much better. I imagined a hail of bullets coming at us any minute. But I remembered that I was not afraid of death, only of recognition.

"Here, in Canada, you must be the most peaceful people in the world," Lena said, staring out of the window. "Not much has changed..." she murmured.

"Wait till you see the Cathedral," Ruth put in.

Usually the kids were reasonably well behaved, but with Auntie Lena's arrival, they seemed determined to impress her. They were determined to point out, through the rain-drenched windows, all the interesting sites en route to our destination.

"And that is the church of St. Francis of Assisi," Jo said, his finger jutting in front of my nose to a stone building I once knew and loved.

"And that is where the architects have their museum," Mo would not be left behind.

Lena had to acknowledge each building or site, or else it wouldn't count.

"Look, look, Aunt Lena, look..."

I also looked. *We are not being followed...*

Gradually the dryness in my throat subsided. I was as ignorant as Lena of the latest townscape. Not that much could have changed in a single year. Perhaps the longest year of my life.

We were only followed by Lena's escort car, its headlights on just in case. In case of what, I wondered?

"At least we don't have to go out in this rain..." Ruth murmured.

Fifteen minutes later, a state-of-the-art elevator, 'lift' as Lena called it, deposited us up in what used to be the choir. A tiny anteroom, which opened onto a single line of eight chairs, a loge designed for the very, very VIP. Visiting presidents, prime ministers and their immediate entourage, whose security was of paramount importance. And, of course, for Lena Walesa. A liveried man led us to our seats. The red velvet upholstery was as regal as the Vatican chairs had once been. Only the glutei imprints had changed. Over the last year many bishops and other princes of the church had retired. Those who remained faithful to their calling had returned to the ancient traditions, when you could recognize the elders by their behaviour, their wisdom and kindness, and not by the attire they wore. They had returned what was Caesar's to Caesar. They'd shed their regalia, their imposing appurtenances, and donned the simple clothing of the men to whose spiritual welfare they'd originally dedicated their lives. These were strange times, indeed.

"Would you care for some refreshments, Madam?" the uniformed man asked. He looked uncomfortable in a toned-down version of a Vatican guard, with the sword and lance replaced by a small stun gun. Certainly more effective even if less deadly.

Lena looked at Ruth questioningly. It was too late. By now Ruth, as evidently all of us, had her eyes riveted to the space in front of us.

"Perhaps later," she replied. Here, she was the host.

Even as I looked down, the columns began to dissolve into palm trees, the statues of saints gradually assumed shapes of Arabs going about their business. Even the elevated ambo metamorphosed into a crag of rock breaking down the monotony of sand and the occasional small outcroppings that appeared out of nowhere. And in a few short minutes, the desert stretched all the way towards the distant horizon. Hundreds if not thousands of people, who seconds ago were sitting in the pews, shimmered, and also dissolved into a rocky terrain.

I shook my head. I'd had occasion to experience the wonders of holography during some medical demonstrations while still at the General Hospital, but this was of quite a different genre. This went way beyond Hollywood.

Moments later I was looking at a desert that was moving towards me, slowly, yet inexorably, with the mountains on the horizon growing ever closer. I learned later that the activation of the holographic images had been designed to coincide with Lena's entrance. I wondered what the old bishop would have to say about all this. On the other hand, was it any more profane than using the House of God for an Oratorio?

"Mommy, look!" This was Jo pointing down, towards our left.

There, a group of people emerged from behind some rocks and moved slowly, evidently tired after a long journey, towards the approaching mountains.

"*Let my people go,*" a really deep *basso profundo* intoned from a great distance. Perhaps from behind the mountains?

"*Let my people go,*" the basso repeated.

Apparently, by some hook or crook, or by the magic of technology of the middle 21st century, people sitting in the nave below were enjoying the same images. The wonders of holography, I whispered. No one heard me. The scenery was riveting. The multitude of people, dressed in long abas such as we are used to seeing on the paintings of old masters depicting the Exodus, accompanied by livestock and hand-pulled carts, seemed oblivious to us. Yet I found them strangely unsettling. They were too close, within touch, yet seemed lost in their own reality, their own time.

"Aren't we all?" I murmured to myself. Aren't we all lost in our own time, our own reality?

"*Let my people go,*" the basso repeated. His voice was still distant yet it reverberated in the large space of the nave. It seemed to echo from the distant mountains and return with renewed force. "*Let my people go... go... go...*"

I took a deep breath. Other than the basso and the creaks of the carts, the people moved in deadly silence. They seemed on the point of utter exhaustion. Perhaps they were. I'd never crossed a desert. I'd never even been in one. Yet even now, though I knew it was just an artificial effect, an illusion, it had a hypnotic effect on me. I felt drawn into the grotesque shadows, expecting something to emerge from their depth. The artistic directors of the opera had done an incredible job. If there were people here, who have never had a spiritual experience in a church before—here was their chance. The atmosphere was eerie, ephemeral, intangible yet commanded one's whole attention.

As I looked up, again I held my breath. The ceiling had disappeared, as though rolled back, and the starlit sky, serene in its mysterious splendour, stretched from one horizon to the other. A small, perfectly round moon showed the pilgrims their way. Ever eastward, toward the mountains. How did they do that? How on earth do they get such effects?

"*Take my people home....*" The sonorous voice was getting closer.

Silence stretched.

And then the voice filled the church, reverberating from every corner.

"*I AM THAT I AM... I will bring you up out of the affliction of Egypt unto the land of the Canaanites, and the Hittites, and the Amorites...*"

The list went on. Even as the litany continued, the chorus of people began to supply background affirmations of the promises. The male and the female voices, tenors, baritones, sopranos, and mezzos mixed in a euphoric plea that could not go unanswered. This was history, of course. It was the promise God had once made to Moses before his favourite servant began his long journey.

A dozen voices, all deep, singing as one in a commanding monotone, semi-aria, semi-melody: "*Take my people home...*" the behest repeated. It seemed to come from all quarters, the side aisles—now stretches of sand, from above—the shimmering stars... from everywhere. A roll of thunder, no lightning, just an ear splitting thunder rolling from one horizon to the other.

The command to be obeyed.

At the head of the long procession of abas, a man taller than all the others raised his staff signalling obedience. "I shall," it seemed to say. "I'll make sure Your will shall be carried out." It wasn't spoken, nor sung, but the import was there. Unquestioning, abject obedience that translated into the power of leadership.

At the same time, in direct contrast to the sonorous basses and the response of the staff, a chorus of voices, seemingly thousands of them, initiated a forlorn dirge. It flowed along the sands, echoed from the dark outcroppings, and drifted like fog to cover the whole desert with a blanket of sorrow. A dirge of good-byes to the land now left behind, to the security it offered. It was a farewell to childhood, a painful weaning of men and women coming of age.

"*Let my people go...*" The mountains echoed for the last time.

The dirge stopped suddenly. The Cathedral, the desert was filled with eerie silence. The throngs came to a halt. They were facing a mountain that mysteriously materialized before them, its majesty as forbidding as it was unyielding. It barred the people's way. It was the end of a long journey. The end of an era.

"Mount Sinai," I heard Ruth whispering to her children.

Mo and Jo hadn't moved. They were as frozen as the public must have been down below, in the desert. Indeed, as I was. Of course... Mount Sinai. The way station where the Hebrews had to make a decision. The old ways, or the new... Don't we all? Don't we all face Mount Sinai, periodically, throughout our lives? Each time I escape from any reality, I take a turn in the desert. I face the new, the unknown. This is what those people had faced. The unknown. For most of us, the greatest fear of all.

This was the essence of the Exodus. A change. A change in consciousness. From slavery to freedom.

A large group of elderly men detached themselves from the crowds and approached the man holding the oversized staff.

"The seventy wise men," Ruth whispered.

I didn't know Ruth was so well versed in the Old Testament. Was it Winston's influence? He seems to invoke hunger for the esoteric in all of us.

Moses detached himself from the group of seventy. Slowly his moonlit contour walked up the incline. Then only a shadow followed him as he came in and out of our vision. Once again a deadly hush enveloped the people....

Then somebody laughed.

There followed a wave of movement among the throngs. They turned and twisted. Voices emerged, tenors, baritones, sopranos... sextets interpolated with octets, choruses answered with ever growing vigour. Fires were lit. Some women began dancing, their lithe bodies twisting, undulating, in progressive passion. Men clapped their hands in rhythm.

The silence had turned into a wild Saturnalia.

Dionysus would have been proud of them. Wine flowed easily. Individual voices rose in mounting octaves praising the merits of ecstasy, of love and passion of Eros and euphoria. What began as an innocent diversion for people wearied by extended travel in a featureless desert grew. First slowly, then with increasing intensity, into a wild orgy of unparalleled proportions. It grew spontaneously. Music, stimulated by whirling tambourines, accelerated its rhythm. Many a comely maiden shed her clothing, revealing contours only just swelling into womanhood. They whirled in wild abandon. Sparks of the nearby fires danced their own wanton patterns on their skin glistening with sweat. Here and there a young man would dive into the writhing confluence of flesh, followed by shrieks of consummate delight..

Seemingly, this night would never end…

In sudden alarm I glanced at the children. Both had their palms pressed into their eyes, the way they did when playing hide and seek. Reaction to the last clap of thunder? Hopefully. Thankfully these were only holograms and not the real thing.

As time went on, a strange mist descended over the desert. The mountain dissolved. The main altar was now visible. The desert faded and revealed pews filled with people, believers, practically cringing in their seats. The image of the Bacchanalia was gone and the voices were dimmed. And then the eerie silence was filled with a collective sigh. It was nearly a minute before people joined their hands. Not to pray, but to show appreciation.

End of Act 1 of the Decalogue. The Ten Commandments, of course, were still to come. I glanced at the program. The words had been embossed, or possibly engraved, in gold letters on a single piece of plastic that looked like a stone tablet. That was it. No explanations, no commentaries, no credits for the libretto. People were expected to know their Ten Commandments. Presumably, the presentation was intended to be self-explanatory.

THE DECALOGUE

Opera in Three Acts

Music by

JOHN BROWN

Act I

Escape

Act II

The Commandments

Act III

Liberation

The name of the composer struck a bell. John Brown. Cathy had mentioned him. Some twenty years ago, an extraordinary musician, a violinist unparalleled in the history of music, had swept the world. Her name was Ann Howell. She'd married a physician named Brown, Dr. Brown, a strange mixture of a physicist and physician. That is how Cathy knew of him. She'd told me that their son was the composer of a number of operas, The Decalogue among his earliest. What a shame Cathy couldn't make it tonight. She was giving a lecture at the Science Museum, freshly opened in Ottawa. It had been named after her father, Dr. Mondellay, the eminent physicist responsible for popularizing portable nuclear generators, the solution to many of the world's problems. Not all, however.

The attendant who'd originally shown us to our seats approached us again, this time bearing a tray with glasses. There were three slim flutes with bubbles dancing in the soft light, and wider glasses, evidently with fruit juice, for the children. In the middle of the tray there were two small plates with *amuse-gueules*. They were tiny, elegant, and proved most appetizing.

Lena smiled her thanks.

As we were finishing our champagne, the lights began to dim. Once more, the Cathedral dissolved into a mass of clouds. They grew in density until they became almost palpable. I wondered how people in the pews felt. Perhaps they had different effects altogether.

Moments later, sweet strains of a dozen harps resonated among the disappearing walls. Next, the sweet voices of a great many children, reminiscent of the Vienna Boys Choir, emerged from the convoluting clouds. No people, no children, just the voices, sweet, angelic. The effect was quite unearthly.

Against this background, a single ray of light flashed across the clouds. It hovered, hesitated, and then wrote something on the vapours. The chorus and the harps gave way to the original chorus of bassos intoned in a Gregorian monotone:

I am the Lord your God, who brought you out of the land of Egypt, out of the house of slavery, you shall have no other gods before me.

The simple monophonic, unaccompanied music of the Middle Ages. Memories of my seminary days. They too seemed centuries away. There was too much accompaniment around these days. A constant soundtrack. Drums, percussion everywhere. At all times. I longed for the simplicity of just voices.

And then the moment was past…

The choir picked up the words and raised them into a beautiful melody. This was a command but also an assurance, a promise… there was joy in the children's voices. Even as the melody died down, the lightning flashed from east to west, across the length of the firmament. Jo curled up under my arm while Mo hid her head in Ruth's lap.

You shall not make yourself an image, whether in the form of anything that is in heaven above, or that is on the earth beneath, or that is in the water under the earth. You shall not bow down to them or worship them: for the Lord your God, am a jealous God….

Even as the bassos delivered the dire command, the lightning grew in intensity until the whole church seemed filled with flashing lights. I pulled Jo a little closer. I found the effect somewhat overdone, but I could well imagine the effect it had on the 'masses' sitting below me. The powerful composite voice articulating every word, every note, against the background of the lightning extravaganza.

The Decalogue continued.

You shall not make wrongful use of the name of the Lord your God….

Remember the Sabbath day, and keep it holy….

Honour your father and your mother….

Each commandment was picked up by the angelic voices. What had been delivered by the bassos as an unquestioning commandment, was raised to the level of joy, of celebration. The commandments became gifts to be cherished, to be grateful for when sung by the boys' angelic voices.

The next commandment exploded as a roll of thunder and terrible lightning.

You shall not murder….

The silence that followed was deafening. I felt icy fingers on my spine. You shall not commit murder. Thou shall not kill. No matter how phrased, the command was uncompromising. There was no, 'Unless in self-defence,' or 'Except when defending your country, or your goods, or even when defending your family, your children.' Thou shall not kill for it is murder….

You shall not commit adultery…..

The basses delivered this message in a more tempered tone. The children echoed the sentiment.

….neither shall you steal, nor bear false witness against your neighbour….

Who were my neighbours? The people next door? I had no next door. I'd spent most of the last twelve months locked up in my room, rereading all my books, searching for the meaning of my *gift*. I'd found no meaning. No sense. No explanation. Or was Lord God referring to a different sort of kinship, a less literal neighbour. I was snapped out of my musings by the next stanza. This time the bassos and the children mixed in an interpolating melody, as though the young voices intertwined with the power and gave it a sense of innocence.

You shall not covet your neighbour's house….
You shall not covet your neighbour's wife….

These were the bassos alone commanding absolute obedience.

Nor male or female slave…. Now children joined the male chorus, *nor ox, or donkey, or anything that belongs to your neighbour*. In the last phrases the boys' voices took pre-eminence, making the whole message more human. The lightning receded towards the far horizon, the clouds parted revealing the stillness of the night. The boys' voices continued, softly, moving away, slowly with the receding clouds.

And then there was silence.

I glanced at Ruth and Lena. They were both staring straight ahead. Mo and Jo remained curled up on their seats, Mo desperately trying to hide under Ruth's arm. Jo was peeking at me from under my elbow. As I winked, his face emerged cautiously as though making sure it was over. Mo and Jo were too young for Mr. Brown's concept of heavenly power. They should have stayed at home. It was too late. No matter. I had a strong suspicion that they would remember this evening for a long time. And there was another act to come. For their sake, I hoped it wasn't scary.

I wondered how the people, those down below, could see the performance. I know that all pews had been reoriented towards Bernini's baldacchino, but still, they had to have dozens of projectors to let all people enjoy the opera equally. Of course, the sound was easier to control. The speakers could be installed anywhere and everywhere. Probably the latter. On the other hand, the holographic video must have looked different from each side, which could make it even more interesting. Perhaps you might see the same opera four times, and always see a new version.

I was never good at technology.

Minutes later the lights began to dim until abject darkness enveloped all of us. From below I could just discern distant sounds of flutes piercing the night air. Little flames winked in and out, here and there, until they grew into fires set in the same desert that we had left at the end of Act I. Only now there was much more activity.

The music grew in volume. Male and female voices intermingled in a choral symphony that matched the frenzied movement of the people. Then I saw it. As a dozen strong men lifted, at arm's length, a large golden calf, it glittered in the reflected light of the mass of fires. A collective ‘ooooh’ escaped a thousand mouths; the audience probably mixed with the actors in the desert. The dancing women were nearing a dervish frenzy, jumping and leaping up and across the lying bodies which had already given themselves to sexual orgy.

For an incongruous moment I found myself hoping that Mo and Jo were still shielding their eyes under the protective arms of Ruth and myself.

In the midst of all this the clouds gathered lower and lower over the desert. The contours of the mountain disappeared inside the descending mists. A sonorous ramble rolled, slowly, ponderously, from all sides towards the middle. The frenzied dancing reached a mad crescendo.

And then it struck.

A single bolt of lightning split the golden calf in half. There followed another clap of thunder, this time immediately overhead, and a large stone smashed itself over the central fire. The sparks shot everywhere, like meteors that pierced the desert atmosphere. People collapsed onto their knees. They hid their faces in their hands.

The scene split in two, horizontally.

Below people remained in an apparent stupor of fear, while above, separated only by the clouds, Moses sang a dirge of his own.

“*Lord, my people have sinned a great sin... and have made them a god of gold... yet now, if you forgive them their sins....*”

The aria was filled with pathos worthy of the occasion. The libretto was taken directly from Exodus, word for word. Moses seemed desperate but still trusted that his people might be forgiven in the Lord’s infinite mercy. As the male chorus of voices filled the Cathedral, he knew he’d succeeded.

“*Whosoever hath sinned against me, him shall I blot out of my book. Go now and lead the people unto the place of which I have spoken unto thee. My angel shall go before thee...*”

There was not a whisper from the audience. The unison voices of God hovered in the air, as though suspended beyond time and space. It was an awesome moment.

"*I will send my angel before thee, and I will drive out before you the Amorites, Canaanites, Hittites, Perizzites, Hivites and Jebusites…*"

As the recitation went on, the desert people moved to establish the tabernacle. Some of them pitched a tent just outside the camp. Even as others gyrated in the desert like an aimless river, Moses returned, seemingly placated. It was all very dramatic, and yes, even beautiful. Regrettably my own life had turned me into a sceptic.

How very convenient, I thought. What God was really saying was blame Me, since I can do no wrong. No wonder the people in the desert began to lift their heads. The Lord's last words were echoed once again by the beautiful children's chorus, then joined by sopranos, the mezzos and other voices. The harmonies were, nevertheless, inspired. John Brown had earned his title of Master Composer, as was amply proven by the last thunder, this time that of applause.

I took a deep breath. In my mind I could hear my brother's slow, confident voice: 'The structure of the opera was definitely interesting. I am reminded of Moussorgsky. In Boris Goudonov, the only real struggle is between the Tsar Boris and the people. All else is peripheral. Here too, God and the people are the main characters. Even Moses plays second fiddle to them.'

Dear Andrew... he would have loved it.

"Is God really angry?" This was Mo tugging at my elbow. "Is he?" He really needed to know.

"God is never angry, Mo. He just pretends…" I did my best.

"But he smashed the calf and cut it in half," Jo insisted.

"He did, but that was just to show the people that they shouldn't worship any idols," I tried again.

"So he wasn't really angry?" Mo wouldn't let go.

"God is love, Moira. Love is never angry."

This seemed to satisfy her. I took a deep breath. The Hebrew God sure sounded angry, I thought. Boy, was he ever!

I glanced at Ruth just as she seemed to be wiping off an errant tear. My sister-in-law looked sad. "What is it, dear?" I whispered.

"Oh, it's nothing," she said, a tiny smile denying her momentary weakness. When I didn't look away, she murmured, "You know how Andrew loved opera?"

She didn't say any more. It had been almost six years since she'd lost her husband. My brother had loved opera, a lot more than I ever had. Poor Ruth, I mused. Yet somehow, in an inadvertently selfish manner it was good to hear that other people also had problems. That I wasn't alone, struggling, angry, frustrated. And I had left the house and survived, and Ruth wasn't going to kick me out.

***

3

Post-Mortem

We filed out quickly, hoping to avoid the crowds. We almost succeeded. A half-dozen men saw Lena and insisted on bowing low, in the process blocking our passage. For a dreadful moment I was sure they were after me. How presumptuous of me. I was nobody. At least, next to Lena.

My anxiety passed as quickly as it occurred.

Out of nowhere, two burly characters stepped in and gently but firmly moved Lena's admirers aside. Within minutes we were all safely tucked inside the Solidarity limousine. Throughout all this, Lena smiled angelically, as if she had nothing whatsoever to do with any of this minor fracas.

"Can we come to see the next opera, Auntie Lena? Can we?"

I had to smile. Don't children ever have enough? Jo was twelve and thought it immature to succumb to emotional pressure. He was also growing very protective of his sister, a mere year younger. Still, the opera was definitely a traumatic experience for all of us, particularly, I thought, for the children. At least Mo seemed to have tacit reservations about a repeat performance. Her face was set into a brave mask of courage.

"We shall see, darling. We shall see," Lena assured them, having no idea if and when the next show would be.

"So how did you like it?" Lena turned to Ruth who was once more sitting with me in the back seat.

Ruth was too worried about the effect the spectacle might have had on her children to reply at once. Lena's eyes turned to me. "And you Peter?"

"I would have let them stay in Egypt a little longer," I said. "They didn't seem quite ready to displace other nations with their own folly."

"Peter! Why must you be so serious? This was an opera. A show. Nothing more," Lena smiled, but her smile didn't carry much conviction. She must have been aware how close the libretto had run to the original script.

"Our life is little more than an opera, a show, Lena. Until we grow up. Then… but I don't have to tell that to you, of all people!" My chuckle was even more forced.

"I think I would like a Martini," Ruth volunteered a change of subject.

We didn't talk much until we reached home. There was something very pensive about the opera. Not just the words, and the promise from 'above', but the music itself. *I will drive out the Canaanites, the Amorites….* This was as bellicose a statement as any in the entire Bible. Whatever happened to loving thy neighbour? The Hebrew god was a little too eclectic for my taste. As for Brown, he was still young when he wrote the music, but he was definitely mature beyond his years.

Just as the burly driver pulled into our driveway, mysterious shadows flitted out of his way. Those mysterious intruders seemed unaware that the lights had been set on automatic to illuminate an approaching car.

"It's started," I whispered miserably, all my fears returning.

"Don't worry, Peter. It's all right…." Lena put her hand on my shoulder.

I took a deep breath.

The long walk down the slope in a bitter cold, rainy night, an escape to below the tracks, a forlorn tavern on an incongruously brightly lit street... the sign Gaston Brown, propriétair, then darkness inside, forbidding yet strangely inviting... deep bowl of soupe à l'oignon or steaming, thick bouillabaisse, placed carefully on chequered cloth, whichever was the spécialité de la maison on that day. Then the stench upstairs, overpowering... finally the stint in the shabby inn with a never-ending procession of unfortunates making demands on the power emanating from my hands.

It all came back in a rush, disjointed flashes. Images of pain…

…a fat woman with a dozen children feeding the youngest milk laced with gin, the man who couldn't quit, whatever it was... then killing a woman to sate his craving... the mechanical, robot-like walks in the rear courtyard under the starlit sky... twenty paces to the left, twenty forward…

"Peter?"

"What is it, Gaston?"

"Peter!" Lena was tugging on my sleeve. "We are home…"

We were parked in my garage. Our garage. None of this belonged to me. At twenty-nine I was still a Nomad, remember? As I had been in the tavern. The inn half-way to hell. Mostly just the sicknesses, the diseases, remained in my memory. They were all mine. Mine to keep. Mine to deal with, to take upon my shoulders.

"I'm sorry. I was far away," I said.

"Welcome back," Lena whispered. She looked worried, concerned.

"I'm all right now. I'm sorry, Lena. It comes over me, now and then. Lately, less often…" I lied. Actually, lately the images haunted me most nights. I had to do something. I couldn't just sit and hope they would go away. Gifts like mine are not given to be buried, like talents, below the ground.

Europe had been different. There, no one knew about me. Not even the cardinals and other eminencies in the Holy Father's entourage. He'd asked them to step out when that strange exchange took place. I still don't know what it was. I wonder if I ever will.

The driver cut the engine. For a brief moment we all sat in silence. After the overpowering music, then the noisy humdrum of Montreal streets, the absence of any sound was kind to my ears. Even the children seemed to take a deep breath. The silence seemed almost necessary. Was it the opera, I wondered, that left such a lingering sense of disquiet? Did it remind us that for the last three and a half thousand years we hadn't made much progress? That we still killed, stole, fornicated and worshipped money, power, and other idols? Did it remind us that it was really time for us all to grow up?

The moment passed.

Winston opened the door to the garage with a slight bow. We were back in the land of the living. Even I managed to drop my morose reminiscences. I helped Ruth out of the car, then walked around the back of the limo to assist Lena, to find that she was already leading Mo by the hand towards the foyer. The security guard was already blocking the entrance to the garage, his hand resting gently on some sort of firearm. Probably a stunner that had become fashionable lately among the private sentries.

"Dinner is ready, Madam," Winston announced, the moment Ruth stepped into the hall. I could hear his stage whisper though still in the garage. "Whenever you're ready," he added, with his usual politeness.

"Children, hands, please," Ruth admonished.

I was the last to leave the garage. As I came in, I looked past Lena and Ruth, toward the sitting room. There, curled up on an armchair was Cathy—her face turned up on the armrest. She was sleeping. I tiptoed towards her and planted a gentle kiss on her lips.

"Johnny, darling, is it time to get up?" She stretched luxuriously, but her voice was much too sleepy to be real.

"No, Barbara, we have another hour or so," I replied.

"Pig," was her next retort.

"Oink, oink," was the best I could come up with.

And then pandemonium erupted when Mo and Jo, displaying their haphazardly washed hands, saw Cathy. She also began her Thornton career as Auntie Cathy but had since progressed to first names. "Auntie makes me feel old," she'd confessed.

Cathy had a way with children. Actually, all guests had a way with Mo and Jo. Perhaps it was the children who had a way with people.

At dinner, unavoidably, we discussed the opera. Cathy, who'd managed to fly in from Ottawa on an early afternoon plane, had missed us by only a half-hour. She'd considered trying to catch up with us at the Cathedral but thought better of it.

"I really hate when latecomers stomp all over my feet," she said. "Anyway, I can see the performance at any time during the next four days, right Lena?"

"So I am told, though they don't tell me everything, you know?"

I couldn't picture Lena not knowing something she needed to know. Evidently, this wasn't one of those things. "So what did you think of it, Peter?" she continued.

"I am not an expert on music, but I was impressed with the libretto," I mused aloud.

"I dare say Moses did a fairly good job on it," Ruth put in with unaccustomed sarcasm. I noticed that attitude often among Catholics. They seldom had anything good to say about the Old Testament.

"That is not quite what I meant," I countered pretending to take her comment seriously. "What I meant was that seldom does English sound so good in an opera. I like my librettos in Italian, or even Russian, not English. But Brown pulled it off. And anyway, the young Maestro took liberties. The I AM THAT I AM, comes from a different chapter of the Torah, and a different mountain. Mount Horeb was, I believe, where Moses enjoyed his interchange with the Burning Bush. What I really meant was that I was struck by the actuality of the libretto, if I may call it that. It hasn't diminished over thousands of years."

"Sorry, Peter, I don't know what got into me," Ruth sounded contrite. "But I see what you mean. Perhaps that's exactly what made me aggressive... some sort of subliminal sense of guilt?"

In spite of Winston's unquestionable culinary skills, he'd opted, I am sure drawing on Cathy's advice, to order dinner from Ritz-Xentung, which in recent years had extended its specialties to cover Cantonese, Jiangsu, Shandong and Szechuan cuisines, all available for home delivery for feasts of up to fifty people. What today's gathering lacked in numbers, it made up for in quality. Cathy made sure that the eclectic menu complemented itself superbly. However, Winston had refused to make use of the usual complement of waiters that R/X provided.

"It is not often that one is privileged, Madam, to serve such distinguished guests," he affirmed with great gravity. Actually, Winston delivered most statements with such gravity that he managed, on occasion, to obscure his deeply entrenched sense of humour.

On that particular day, I am sure he felt that Ruth's guests, Lena and Cathy, would feel much freer to talk without outsiders listening in. As usual, he was right. The intimacy of the home atmosphere was what attracted Lena to our place in the first place. That and the people, including the children. As for Cathy, it was in her honour that Winston had opted for Chinese food. Not that Cathy didn't enjoy international cuisine, but she had a weakness for most things that reminded her of the home she hardly knew. She was born and raised in Montreal. Her mother was French Canadian, but she was proud of her Chinese origins from her father. Hardly surprising since her father was not only one of the richest but also best-known scientists in the world. Mondellay was a name he'd adopted in Canada. It was the nearest he could get to literal phonetic translation of the Mandarin original.

"How come everyone around me is famous and I am still struggling?" she asked, the last time I saw her. There was no jealousy in her voice, just wonderment.

I hardly knew how to answer her question. "Just lucky, I suppose," I quipped.

I got a little kiss for that.

After a dessert of Peking Dust, a gooey concoction featuring fresh chestnuts and whipped cream, Mo and Jo bid us goodnight and raced upstairs to their respective rooms. Frankly, the Chinese do not overly indulge in desserts, preferring to satisfy their sweet tooth between meals, especially when entertaining. The children, however, thought the large dessert most appropriate.

"Ten minutes and I'll tuck you in," Ruth called after them.

We lingered at the table over coffee. Ruth eventually went upstairs to check on the children. The rest of us moved into the lounge to enjoy the fireplace. We settled into the comfortable chairs.

"Stop! Drop it!"

We froze. The curtains had been drawn but the sounds of feet were unmistakable.

"I'll drop mine if you drop yours," came the reply. It sounded very close just outside the window. The voice was harsh, threatening.

We all stood up. Silent, frozen.

There was a popping sound followed by a scuffle. I hoped it wasn't a gun with a silencer. The next moment something was being dragged along the ground. Then silence.

I saw Lena press her index finger to her ear. She must have had some sort of listening device implanted inside, so deep, as to be unnoticeable.

"It's all right," she said, calmly. "No one was hurt."

"Just how do you know?" Ruth was up on her feet. She glanced at the stairs, probably thinking of the children.

"It's all right, Ruth. Relax. There were two of them but my men took care of everything. It's all right, now," she repeated as calmly as though she were describing last year's weather.

"B-b-but... but," Ruth was looking at Lena, her eyes still wide with alarm.

I glanced at Cathy. She was actually smiling. She saw me looking at her.

"I just love watching people," she whispered.

"Weren't you worried at all?" I asked.

"What, with the most powerful woman in the world sitting in our midst?"

"You mean you are used to this sort of thing?"

"My father has had two armed guards following him for years. Ever since somebody tried to force him to give up the formula for cold fusion at gunpoint."

"And?"

"Dad is, was, I suppose, the equivalent of a black belt in the ancient art of Chinese unarmed combat. All three men were arrested an hour later. One suffered a broken neck. Father couldn't forgive himself. That was why he hired the armed guards. As a deterrent mostly."

"Dr. Mondellay practised martial arts?" Somehow I couldn't picture the distinguished, grey-haired gentleman hurting anybody.

"Kung Fu, Wushu or Ch'uan Fa, depending where you come from," she answered innocently. I preferred not to ask if his daughter had inherited any of her father's skills.

Ruth was back in her armchair, with Lena smiling reassurance.

"This sort of thing happens wherever I go, darling. It is nothing to worry about. They don't mean to harm me. They're just curious...."

If she wasn't speaking the truth, then she was a magnificent liar. I was nearly convinced myself.

"But what if...?"

Lena cut her short. "Ruth, dear. Now that we work together, you must learn to rely on experts in every field. Haven't you noticed that for the last six months my men have been following your every move?"

"Men? Following me?"

"Men, following you. And staying out of your way. The house has been under constant observation."

"I never... six months?" There was abject disbelief in her voice.

"Of course you didn't. Had you spotted them, they would also have been spotted by those from whom they were protecting you. They are professionals, Ruth. Even as you are."

Ruth was busy trying to restore her breathing to normal. She was not used to the cloak-and-dagger stuff. Her life, apparently until now, had been orderly. An open book. Except for the incident with the children which took her and me to Gdansk a year ago. So many things had started happening that year that still bore fruit even now.

Finally, Ruth managed to return to normal.

"More coffee, anyone?" She was a real trooper.

By now we were all back to our chairs, comfortably disposed around the fireplace, a welcome sight after the drizzly weather outside. You expect rain during the Canadian autumn, as during any other autumn, I suppose. Not that we experienced much of it. These days, people travelled from a heated garage at one end to similar comfort at the other. Climatic changes were almost incidental. Unless you liked walking. But I, I kept reminding myself, had been confined to indoors for some time now. I was ready to escape the city, the country, the world if necessary, to regain my freedom. Freedom of anonymity.

Freedom to remain in my self-imposed prison.

I had to snap out of it. Had I really become that neurotic?

The glow of the open fire took me back to the countless fires burning in the desert, at the foot of Mount Sinai.

"A lot has happened since I was a churchgoer. I suppose, people no longer pray in churches. They enter their closets and shut the door... or go up a mountain, apart...." I probably misquoted Matthew's gospel on both counts. It's been a while.

"Isn't that what we are supposed to be doing?" Ruth sounded unsure of her ground. She missed the old order, the apologetics, the rituals, rites, even the liturgy, more than any of us. She was a through and through Catholic, of the old, traditional order. "The Holy Father..." she began yet her voice wavered. There was no Holy Father telling her what to do any more. On the other hand, she could no longer be *plus catholique que le pape*.

"Poor Ruth," Cathy whispered in my ear. Cathy didn't have such problems. Lao Tsu satisfied her inner needs.

"Think of the first Christians. They had no churches, no Cathedrals or basilicas. They just prayed when they felt the need to pray," Lena said.

"And not even on Sunday," I murmured. "They still obeyed the Sabbath day."

Lena knew exactly what she wanted. She'd taken on the Vatican's wealth in the worldly realms. She had no intention of touching the spiritual side. As far as she was concerned, the Last Pope had done the only thing possible.

I was beginning to feel sorry for Ruth and decided to come to her rescue. "Yes, Ruth, dear. That is exactly what brothers and sisters are supposed to be doing. We have entered a new age, the Age of Aquarius, and, to quote another scripture, 'I make all things new.' John, I think. But that is not the point. The point is that after being led by the hand for over two thousand years, the Christians, Catholic and Protestant alike, must stand on their own two feet. They must come of age."

"And this justifies turning the churches into theatres?" she asked, wistfully. "What of the Holy Sacrifice?"

"How many times must He die for our transgressions?" I asked quietly.

"The Holy Sacrifice, as you call it, the Mass or the Holy Mass is intended to commemorate the Last Supper. There is no reason why all who want to cannot celebrate this memory each time they sit down, at home, to their dinner."

"And the Holy Eucharist?"

"The Body of Christ or the body of Jesus?" Cathy asked hardly above a whisper. For her the whole compendium of mysteries of the Roman Church was just that, a compendium of mysteries. Her job, as a scientist, was to unravel mysteries, not envelop and inveigle them with traditions.

"W-w-why... both, I suppose?" Ruth stammered.

A sharp crack in the fireplace sent an arc of sparks into the air. Then, a few little wisps of flame appeared from behind the offending log. The wisps were strangely reminiscent of candles, such as were, once, equally disposed at the back of an altar.

Hoc est enim Corpus meum. Hic est enim Calix Sanguinis mei, novi et aeterni testamenti: mysterium fidei....

How I'd practised these words.

I saw a boy in a short surplice kneeling on the red carpet, on the steps of the altar. Towering over him the priest, a man just an arm's length away from God, was offering him the Body of Christ. I closed my eyes, opened my mouth, and desperately prayed for a miracle to happen. Any miracle. A miracle of understanding, or of unquestioning faith, or of deep conviction in the righteousness inherent in the teaching of the Church. His Church. The One, Holy and Apostolic Church. The Infallible Church. I prayed for a miracle that would tie me, enduringly, permanently, to my God, my Church, my Faith.

I accepted the wafer on my tongue, pressed it against the palate of my mouth. Nothing happened. I wondered, incongruously, how long it would adhere there. The Body of Christ sticking to my palate.

"In the first case, it is a symbol, in the second?" Cathy spoke slowly, her voice questioning.

No one dared to say cannibalism. The concept of the Holy Communion was still very dear to some. Especially to Ruth. No one wanted to hurt her sensibilities.

"It's not easy," Ruth whispered.

"It never is," I admitted. "Perhaps this is what the Holy Father intended when he advised people to go back to the concepts of early Christianity. To being brothers and sisters to each other. To unite..."

For a moment I wished I had such problems as Ruth had. Decisions that dealt with where and/or how to pray. How about if God's grace manifested through you against your will? Can great artists refuse their talents? Can great musicians refuse to play their instruments? Can they pray, 'God, stop this folly?' Or escape to the old, tried *non dignus sum?*

Ruth still looked lost, vaguely bewildered. Perhaps that was how I felt when I'd decided to leave the seminary. It hadn't been easy.

"No, it never is easy..." I confirmed with such conviction that Cathy looked up at me.

"What is it darling?"

"Well, no offence, Ruth, it's just that people want their lives to be easy. Most of them long for early retirement and a long, passive, insipid, stultifying wait for death. What if you're immortal? Wouldn't you rather opt for a challenge?"

"I never wanted to retire, Peter. Never." Ruth snapped out of her apparent depression. She glanced at Lena for confirmation.

Lena nodded. "The Hebrews also snapped out of long years of a passive, insipid, stultifying wait for death. Moses saw to that. In the third act!" She brought us back into the present.

"And how!" I challenged. "With an angel flying ahead and clearing the way." I tried to keep sarcasm out of my voice.

"How I wish I had such an angel..." Ruth murmured, dreamily.

We were all growing tired.

It had been a long, emotionally charged day. For all of us. Lena and Cathy had flown in from afar, Ruth had been working since early morning, and I, well, I'd taken my first step towards growing up. At least, I hoped I had.

Lena had her own bedroom, upstairs, once Andrew's study. She loved her room. She called it her home away from home. "I'm so tired of the impersonal hotels," she admitted in a rare moment of weakness. Cathy would spend the night with me. It wouldn't be the first time.

"Will there be anything else, Madam?" Winston filled the archway leading to the dining room. For some reason a great hush followed his innocent inquiry. Ruth shook her head.

"You have, darling..." I muttered softly, looking up at our inimitable majordomo. "You have...."

The great angel withdrew from the archway into the land where only angels dared tread after a sumptuous dinner for six. The kitchen. Ruth followed him with grateful eyes.

"Perhaps you're right, Peter. What would we do without him?

***

4

Solidarity

From Solidarity's point of view, Canada presented a bridge between the European and the USA influences. A sort of Pons Varolli between the East and the West hemispheres of the world. A bridge not just between the two diverse civilizations of Europe and the USA, but the second largest country in the world where they could touch, intermingle, and each emerge none the worse for wear. There was more to that cauldron. It had been hoped that Canada, since Quebec's separation and eventual re-assimilation together with three of the northern ex-USA states into the body politic of the Confederation, would provide a broader link between the Far East and the West as a whole. Chinese influence in Canada had become sufficiently significant for this to happen.

"It hasn't been easy," as Ruth liked to say. Yet it was principally her job to accomplish the task.

And as you can imagine, there were many problems. The three principal elements—Europe, the USA, and the Sino-Indian block—took it upon themselves, for reasons best known only to the highest echelons, to direct their resources into divergent areas of research. Not to the exclusion of others, but they each found their true, natural expression in distinct fields of science, technology, and even philosophy.

Europe was well established as the seat of Solidarity International, which held at the forefront of its philosophy the elimination of classes, other than those resulting directly from personal accomplishment. Even then, the incomes of the men and women at the top were not allowed to exceed a multiple of five over the national and later the Solidarity average. Also, with its new headquarters in the Vatican, Solidarity International became the heir to the cumulative heritage of world cultures. First the Cathedrals, the basilicas, then even the most humble parish churches came under its generous aegis. Solidarity provided the funds that were needed to maintain the priceless jewels of man's patrimony, of man's efforts to rise above the ordinary, the mundane.

From the scientific point of view, Europe, and thus Solidarity, supported the development of genetics: not to alter man's biological form, but to enhance it in a manner that would make us all more perfect specimens: what we were surely intended to be. I suspect that there was a tacit undercurrent of a fundamentalist 'image and likeness' lurking at the root of this choice of research.

The USA, which over the years had swallowed up what used to be Mexico and all the Central American republics down to the Panama Canal, had a mind of its own. While still placing individual man's rights at the forefront of its social policies, it placed no restrictions on the accumulation of personal wealth. For some reason, it still worked there. In terms of averages, a typical American was still richer than any member of any other society in the world.

The people at the top, however, thought that in order to maintain America's financial supremacy, they had to develop the means of being independent of countries which heretofore had provided cheap labour. The only way this could be accomplished, they reasoned, was through the development of robotics, which led as a direct consequence to the development of Artificial Intelligence, usually referred to as AI.

Dubious logic at best. Their desire for independence from the vagaries of foreign labour had obvious advantages, but it also reduced the numbers of the affluent clientele who could afford to buy the American product.

And then there was China and its close ally, the Indian Federation, also known as the Sino-Indian block. There the philosophies remained as mixed as they had always been. Apparently, one cannot tell some 2.5 billion people how to think. What you can do is to assure that those in power could remain there. And those in power decided that the best way to accomplish this unspoken ambition was to dive, head first, into nanotechnology, microscopic robots that worked inside the human body. It had been hoped that, in time, those minute pseudo-organisms would not only enhance the efficiency of the human species generally, but would also be programmed to influence not only the automatic response, but even the thinking patterns of their carriers.

So there we were. Genetics, AI, and nanotechnology quietly gathering their forces, each endeavouring to prove their superiority over the other two. Ruth sat, so to speak, in the middle.

Though she was busy with Solidarity which, these days, was taking up much more of her time, my self-imposed solitude demanded that I spend evenings talking to her on subjects that occupied the long hours of my idle existence. We talked Solidarity, its impact on the social and psychological structure of society, but also, and quite often, on Ruth's views on religion. While officially the Church of Rome had accepted Solidarity International as the overseer of all the Vatican's wealth, most Europeans, and indeed a good number of Canadians, were still deeply entrenched in religious fundamentalism. This trait was imbedded so firmly in their psyche that, rather than listening to the Last Pope's admonitions, they continued to attend churches, demanding that at least some of the old rites be maintained.

"Love one another. Love the font of goodness that wells within you, and all else will be taken care of," he said, a phrase reminiscent of the sentiments expressed in the New Testament.

This advice might have been good if only people understood what the pope had been talking about. The well of goodness? For the life of me I couldn't find much compassion for the world around me. People continued to be greedy, chasing after the almighty dollar, and thought nothing of taking advantage of their position to exploit other human beings.

What came much more easily to them was accepting a good theatrical performance, inspired and based loosely on biblical themes, like the Decalogue, in lieu of the Holy Mass, or the other sacraments that few if any had ever really understood anyway. It was a sort of fundamentalism of the New Age, an oxymoron if ever there was one.

"How can you reconcile the two?" I asked Ruth one evening.

"How do you reconcile medicine with your healing power?" she countered.

"I don't!" I said.

But I understood. One cannot reconcile fire and water, nor can one deny the existence of either. We live in a dualistic reality and contrasts, indeed the opposites, were here to stay. Somehow this very premise always gave me a sense of dissatisfaction.

There must be a reality that lay beyond duality, a way, an actuality, an existence, something more than the uncompromising cruelty of nature. Could we draw life force, life energy directly from the atmosphere? From the air; the Universe? From cosmic rays?

I've heard of some people who don't eat at all. I don't mean some fakirs in forgotten Indian villages, or that Nepal Buddha boy, who some years ago went on for months without any food... sitting cross-legged meditating. I mean normal people. People like you and I, who simply persuade themselves that food, physical food, is not necessary for their physical well-being?

I've heard of people who call themselves 'breatharians', that is relying on air, on breath only, to sustain their bodies in perfect health. While some of them, periodically, nibble on a piece of chocolate, a cookie, some cheese, or suchlike, or even drink some water or tea, they do so to satisfy their sense of taste, not to sustain their bodies. Should they in the process of non-eating lose weight excessively, they disqualified themselves as breatharians. I'm not convinced that air would be enough for me.

Over the course of our evening discussions it became apparent that Ruth was having real troubles adapting to the New Way, in some ways the Old Way, in which the Last Pope had ruled we should conduct our lives.

"Lena has done more to improve man's relation to man than the Church did," Ruth said. There seemed to be a festering anger in her for having been told to stand up on her own spiritual feet. Not that I blamed her.

"Perhaps we should have listened during the last two thousand years," I mused.

"To the Church's teaching? I couldn't have. I haven't been here that long," Ruth said, in exasperation.

"You still discard the concept of reincarnation?"

"I don't discard it, I just don't know anything about it," she said weakly. "How could he have left us all alone..." she blurted out angrily. "I have children," she added now full of sadness and fear.

Children but no husband, she could have added. But her complaint was directed at the Last Pope, not at Christ himself.

"I rather think they are in good hands, Ruth," I said. "I am sure Smith will not let them come to any harm. Physically or mentally."

"And what of spiritually?"

"That most of all..." I said, this time feeling as much at sea as she must have been.

I'm sure I already mentioned that Winston Smith was a most enigmatic fellow. Brought into the household, into Ruth's life, at the expressed wish of my brother, Ruth's husband, Winston was responsible for more unexplainable events—you might say visions—in my life, than anything or anyone in my thirty years. Not that he'd imposed any particular philosophy on any of us. The giant was too mild-mannered to impose anything on anybody. A Buddhist by behaviour, a mystic by his attitudes, the best of Christians by the way he treated others. Yet, whenever I touched on the subject, he seemed completely irreligious.

"Religion is the process of re-linking us to our source, Sir. I do not feel that I've ever lost the connection," he said once at the time when I'd complained about the overt agnosticism of my colleagues in the hospital. This was way back, but it's stuck with me.

I looked it up one day. Religion, from Latin, of course: *religare*: to bind, to bind together again. Most things in the church came from Latin though the first teachings had been recorded in Ancient Greek. Even so, the Latin Vulgate, or the 'common translation' produced by Jerome, was accomplished from Hebrew and Aramaic, though only later, around the years 382 and 405. Some claim that the Gnostic version dates back to the first century of the modern era.

As for the re-linking... just how did Winston know such things?

I'd spent some years in the seminary and I was vague about the concept of religion. There was Buddhism, and Hinduism, and a dozen other -isms, but I had been told that our religion was right and everybody else's was wrong, so there was little point in pursuing the matter.

And then came the doubts. Not the original disenchantment that made me leave the seminary, but the very principle of compassion pouring at us from up above in a never-ending stream. If only we'd asked. I saw people begging their gods for respite, only to observe countless patients dying painful, apparently meaningless, deaths. Day after day. It was hard to bear witness to virtually continuous human suffering and to maintain undying faith in the omnipresent compassion of the 'most high'. Or even the Most High. In God. Perhaps people were praying to the wrong god. Or perhaps Buddha was right when he said that life is suffering. At least he found a way out. I was still looking.

At other times I thought that perhaps I had it all wrong. That perhaps Ruth and Lena were right in their beliefs. Perhaps we were meant to enjoy theatrical performances in our churches, enjoy the music and the art. After all, wasn't art in all its forms also a manifestation of the Creative Force? Did it not all emanate from the same Source? From God, if you must?

I could see myself making a tour of the Montreal churches, false beard, eyebrows and a light limp in tow, and feel the better for it. I knew I never could. I would feel such a charlatan. I would be the Hebrew in the desert paying homage to the golden calf. There had to be more to it all, more to life, more to being a human than just paying homage to other people's ideas. No matter how inspired. If God was omnipresent, then I didn't have to go anywhere to find Him. Or Her. Or It, for that matter. Is not God, God by any other name? Or was it a rose…

According to Zen Buddhists it didn't matter much, either way.

Since Lena's visit, we all became acutely aware of Solidarity men lurking in the dark corners of our garden, cars breaking down directly opposite our address, and requiring prolonged repairs, then and there. Suddenly our street became a haunt for heretofore rare tourists taking snapshots of the autumn colours that were now in full glory. Few seasons can compete, in Canada, with autumn. Poems have been written about it.

Strangely enough, all those men who we suspected did their inconspicuous best to give us a sense of security had the very opposite effect. They brought to our notice the uncertainty of our existence.

About a week after we noticed the security measures, I became obsessed with the idea of getting in and out of the house without being spotted by the spotters. Or, if I couldn't do that, to at least sneak out and come back as a complete stranger and dare the goons to stop me. Perhaps 'goons' was a bit too strong a word, but you get the idea. I had remained in the house by an act of my own will. I had not been restricted in my movements by anyone else. At the time I hadn't realized that I'd spent all that time incarcerated indoors precisely because of what I expected from others. No matter, my mind was made up.

But first, I had to practice.

I began by inviting Jo and Mo to the back-yard for a game of cricket. Not that I could play it, but I hoped that they would be even worse than I. Three reasonably straight sticks made do for the wickets and a baseball bat, that seemed much too wide for such a small garden, served as a substitute for a cricket bat. The object was to limit runs, not to multiply them. The ball, however, was a real cricket ball I had inherited from my brother. He'd actually played cricket in school.

After our second outing, I became a reasonably proficient slow bowler, giving my delivery a wicked off spin. No pun intended, though I did rather like it. Winston, time permitting, was the referee, standing behind me. Jo and Mo opted for batting.

"Out!" Winston announced, when my ball kissed the off stick. There were no bails to fall off. There was no need to complicate things.

Jo had already scored five runs, all singles, and it was high time for Mo to take the crease. The same five runs later, Winston looked at his watch.

His finger went vertically up in the air.

"LBW," he announced gravely. "Leg before wicket," he explained as Moira looked up in disbelief. She knew what the finger meant, just not why it was stuck up in the air. Mo didn't quite agree with the judgment but it was time to go in anyway.

"Please, Uncle Peter, one more over, pleeeease!" Once again the plea was delivered in perfect unison.

We had two more overs before going in.

The next day, I put on my best disguise, designed to confuse everybody, and made my way to the kitchen. I peeked outside, into the small backyard, and seeing no one, I vaulted the fence to our neighbour's, sneaked through their leaf-covered lawn, and emerged on the other side of their house. The next moment I was walking down the street, rather full of myself at having evaded the trained professionals.

Still, my hands were trembling, there was a strange prickling at the back of my neck, but I'd done it. I'd overcome my fear. I'd left the house alone for the first time in just over a year.

I had no other objective than to test my theory of being fully qualified to become an international spy, an agent of expert disguise, of unparalleled stealth and guile. Half an hour later, by then only slightly perspiring, I decided to come back by the front door, just to see if anyone would dare to stop me in my tracks. I was almost ready to enter the gate when an elderly man who was trimming the hedge looked up from his work, seemingly to stretch his aching back.

"Did you enjoy your little walk, Doctor Thornton?" the man asked in halftone.

There was no danger of being overheard but I was as angry as I was disappointed. Apparently my attention to detail hadn't paid off. My skirt must have been too long, or too short, perhaps my shoulders too broad, or just my make-up a trifle overdone. I walked past the man deciding to leave sleuthing to sleuths. I was glad, however, that my folly had not been spotted by amateurs, who might have recognized me for who I really was and thus forced me to leave Ruth's hospitality.

This was my first and last such escapade. I guess I'd just have to return to the much more familiar job of trying to sort out my place in the scheme of things. From that goal I was as far away as ever. But no one would, nor should, do it for me.

I mentioned my escapade to Ruth. She was in shock.

"Why did you do such a foolish thing," she looked at me with wide eyes.

"I told you, I don't like to be constrained. I thought you felt the same…."

"But I am not constrained. Those men are there to make sure that I can come and go as I please!"

"It won't happen again," I said meekly. And when she continued to look at me as she would at Jo for having forgotten to wash behind his ears, I added, "I promise."

It all would have ended there if it hadn't been for the night that followed.

I heard a single scream from the garden just below my window. I rubbed my eyes. 3:35 a.m. The next minute there was a crash followed by a heavy thud and another scream more agonized than the first. I thought quickly. Someone must have fallen from a considerable height onto a bed of roses.

As quietly as I could, I peeked from behind the curtains. A man of considerable bulk was indeed lying prone atop the now defoliated rose twigs, an experience I wouldn't recommend to anyone. Two men were wielding electric torches into his eyes. In the moving light I saw that the lying man's leg was bent at an unnatural angle.

"Cut that light," the culprit shouted threateningly. "You're blinding me!"

He was still in shock. Once that wears off the pain from the leg would be excruciating.

The two men standing over the fallen body didn't say anything, but with obvious agility turned the man over slipping handcuffs over his wrists. Next, one of the two guards—for they must have been Lena's men, stuck something into the man's mouth and tied it around his face. He did it quickly, expertly, but not before a gasp of pain escaped the felon's throat through clenched teeth. I was right. The leg was not only broken but the misbegotten son of a wayward mother must have torn some ligaments.

All this took no more than one or two minutes, at most, but it was enough to make me realize that my holidays were over. I strongly suspected that the handcuffed man was a member of the distinguished press corps who had been giving periodic reports about my apparent disappearance.

"STILL NO SIGN OF THE HEALER" and similar headlines appeared about once a month on or near the last page.

A knock on my door took me away from the window.

"It's all right, Sir," Winston's voice was calm as ever. "It's all taken care of. Good night, Sir."

"Good night, Winston," I replied still looking outside.

I walked to the door, but the corridor was already empty. I'll thank him tomorrow, I decided, and pulled on my pants, covering the top of my pyjamas with my dressing gown. I returned to the window and opened one side.

"Wait there for me," I called out, quickly closing the window. The night chill gave me instant shivers.

I tiptoed down the stairs, making sure not to wake the children, and walked out through the kitchen door. The two guardsmen had already extinguished their torches but held them at the ready, as if they were about to fire their weapons. I wondered if they carried firearms.

"I'm sorry, sir, but it wasn't our fault. He just sort of sneaked up on us."

"Bring him into the kitchen," I said ignoring the lame excuse. Lena can deal with them later. Actually, for all I knew, it would be Ruth who would mete out their just punishment. My interests lay elsewhere.

It was nine months since I'd practised my black magic on anyone. If the power had left me, I would be a free man. The reporter could report all he wanted, till he was blue in the face, and it would do him no good. I would be free. If not, however, this was my chance to see if I still had it in me to do the right thing. If the man recovered, my fate would be sealed. Ruth might give orders to hold him a day or two, but after that I would be a Nomad again.

"Put him on the floor," I said.

The man had fainted. I was right about the pain. Torn ligaments are the worst. Much worse than bone fractures.

"Leave us alone," I said.

"But Sir...."

"Now," I said. For some strange reason confidence was returning to me at an alarming rate.

I didn't raise my voice but the two men obeyed. They turned on their heels and walked out into the chilly darkness. Perhaps they thought that allowing a man to lean a ladder against a building they were supposed to have been watching was bad enough. Upsetting the ladder and thus bringing the man down in a most unfriendly manner obviously wasn't enough to make up for their omission.

They must have been dozing.

For a moment I hesitated. Staying with Ruth these last few months was the first real holiday I'd had since I was a little boy. The five years of medical studies, the four years of residency at the General, took a lot out of me. Then came the 'gift' that nearly killed me. I spent time up north with Cathy recovering from one thing or another. First from total exhaustion, the second time from my experience in Rome. For some reason, my meeting with the Last Pope had a draining effect on me that grew and manifested fully only some months later. It must have had something to do with some sort of internal readjustments. It was as if my whole body had been torn into little pieces, shaken, and put together in a marginally different way. As an example, after my second stint up north, I discovered that I was ambidextrous. Completely. I had absolutely no preference for left or right hand or leg.

I looked down at the man lying at my feet. He was in his late thirties. Like most people these days, he ate a little too much, didn't exercise enough. 'You can talk,' I scolded myself. I might mention that, at the time, after just three short games of 'cricket' in the back garden, I could hardly move. My back ached, my bowling arm hurt; frankly, I ached all over. Months of sedentary life did nothing for my physical wellbeing. As for the man prostrated at my feet, that much was obvious. He was knocked out cold. Had to be the pain. What remained less visible was what exactly had happened to his left leg. It stuck out practically at a right angle directly away from his side. Knees are not supposed to bend like that. Not if the man is still alive.

"You're lucky you fainted, my friend," I mumbled under my breath.

I couldn't let him remain like this. In my mind I bid my silent farewells to Ruth, Mo and Jo, and to Winston. Then I knelt down beside the man. With a kitchen knife I cut the man's pant leg along its length. Slowly, using the medical knowledge that still lingered somewhere in my subconscious, I straightened the man's leg into a semblance of a natural position. The ligaments and muscles didn't want to return to normal. They'd stiffened in the new position, like a spring that you bend beyond its limit of elasticity. I had to pull hard but finally succeeded. Yet this was only the outward dressing, like putting on a new pair of trousers. The insides were still all scrambled.

"Here goes nothing," I sighed, and bent over the man's body.

I placed both my hands on the man's knee. I expected some sort of effect. A surge of energy, or a light or heat to exchange between our bodies. Between his leg and my hands. As usual, there was nothing. There never had been anything. Of the hundreds of people I healed in the tavern, the people I helped in my travels between different motels, nothing ever happened. No outward sign that I had anything to do with anything. I could never understand that aspect. How can physical change take place without physical influence?

"What happened?" The culprit blinked repeatedly at the kitchen ceiling light. "Hey man, what am I doing here?"

"You fell off a ladder," I told him. "You must be more careful," I offered.

"What ladder?" And then his voice changed. "Aaaah... that ladder...."

I got up, opened the door to the outside, and called the guards in. There was no reason to tell them what had happened.

"He's all yours, gentlemen," I said, and directed my steps toward the dining room. "And don't forget to shut the kitchen door behind you," I threw over my shoulder.

They didn't like that but right now, I didn't care very much. I'd just destroyed my freedom, the warmth of family life, the sparkling fireplace.

I didn't sleep well that night. I'm not sure I slept at all, though I did have chimerical visions of the pope lying before me, struggling with each breath. And then a voice whispered in my inner ear.

Looking at me through physical eyes, I am eternal, omnipresent, all powerful. I am whatever anyone wants me to be. Looking through my own eyes, I am no more than a spark of consciousness floating in an endless Ocean of Love.

I'd heard those words before. Once—long ago. In Rome? I had been speaking to myself, if I recall, only it didn't make sense at the time. Even now, I've only just begun to sense the meaning of the tantalizing words.

The next morning we had a private tête-à-tête. Ruth had already spoken to the senior officer in charge of security for our house. Later, with breakfast coffee still on the table, Ruth, Winston, and I met in a Council of War. At least that's what I chose to call it. I wished that Cathy could have been there. No matter.

Solidarity security confirmed that a reporter from the Montreal Daily Press had been arrested for attempting to gain entry into the house. Apparently he knew, or at least suspected, which was my bedroom, and carried with him a digital camera with which he hoped to make a killing in the media by revealing my whereabouts. By some means which best remain undisclosed, the Solidarity squad managed to induce the man to divulge all this information without resorting to painful forms of persuasion. In fact, the security guard said that the man, once caught, sang like a canary. An expression I hadn't heard since early American films.

I don't think I've heard a canary sing…

Ruth said that they could hold the man for forty-eight hours, but after that, since no actual harm had been done, apart from the bed of roses, the authorities couldn't refuse the man bail. Once he was out he would be free to talk.

"To sing like a canary!" Ruth actually said.

My sister-in-law didn't fit into the cloak-and-dagger scenario. She may have been the top Solidarity person in Canada, but she was busy with policies, liaisons with provincial heads, easing tensions with other organizations. And she was good at her job. Few people managed to remain angry at Solidarity manoeuvres while meeting Ruth face to face.

"How is his leg?" I asked innocently.

"Whose leg?" Ruth asked. "No leg was mentioned while..." she pulled short. "Did you get up last night, Peter?"

Winston smiled as though saying, 'I did my best Madam.'

"The intrepid reporter fell off the ladder," I replied, leaving the consequences to be guessed at.

"So the man knows?" Ruth looked crestfallen.

"He fainted. He might not be aware of what happened."

"And he sings like a canary?" Winston joined the conversation.

Ruth and I couldn't help it. Despite everything, we laughed. He sings like a canary coming, straight-faced, from Winston was just too much. We laughed. Winston smirked and couldn't help it either. A moment later deep booming thunder filled the room. As I looked at him, I was glad he was laughing with us, not at us. A deep booming laugh. How God would have sounded had He laughed at the Hebrews, rather than threatened them with extinction.

Or worse, Sparafucile.

Or Mephistopheles.

Or the devil himself.

***

5

Cathy

Cathy joined us around nine in the morning. She looked fresh, elegant, and beautiful, in direct contrast to my dishevelled hair and dressing gown over my pyjamas. At the same time there was concern in her eyes, a certain disquiet that rarely ruffled her feathers. I was still drowsy although I wasn't sure if it was from lack of sleep or from the forced return from my self-imposed retirement. At least, that's how I thought of it. The question was what to do next.

Cathy offered me her parents' home as haven from the probable publicity. She had her own quarters, a bachelor apartment downtown that was no more than a *pied à terre*, but she thought it too small for two people to live in comfortably for any length of time. And, after all, though neither she nor I was of the church-going persuasion, we weren't 'married'. There still were some priests who went through the motions of what used to be marriage vows, but those became mere symbols of once dogmatic sacrament.

We wouldn't, of course, have a legal ceremony. Not in the old-fashioned way which still held some people, like Cathy's mother, under its spell. About twenty years ago, the minorities of various lifestyles, first the polygamists who claimed their rights on religious bases, then the gay people, then even some far-reaching group configurations of two men *and* two women, or even more of each had all been granted legal status under equal-opportunity legislation. Which was fine for a while.

But then, Ottawa went further and issued a new decree.

Henceforth, it said, there would be no civil institution of marriage, of any sort.

The parents would have tax deductions for each of their children up to the age of eighteen, and death duties could only be avoided if your satchels were donated to whomever you chose no less than three years, barring accidents, before your demise. If you didn't trust your own children, or whomever you regarded as your life partner, well, too bad.

The government has made a killing.

For a while there were sporadic street demonstrations demanding the re-institutionalization of marriage. Mostly various Assemblies of Baptists who claimed that Jesus personally attended the wedding in Cana, and therefore marriage should continue to be a legal institution. The Federal spokesman replied that the government had no objections to anyone inviting Jesus or anyone else to their wedding. However, regardless of the invitee, the government would not impede on the separation of church and state, and thus would not partake in anything resulting from a purely religious celebration. Marriage was out—death taxes were in.

Cathy offered to let me have her 'escape', as she called her digs, all to myself, but I couldn't possibly accept. She'd already done so much for me.

"But they wouldn't find you there, Peter. At least for a while…" she added lamely.

"That's not really the point," I said, thinking aloud. "Nor could I possibly impose on your parents. More important, I don't believe I'm meant to hide my, ah... abilities any longer. Things happen that take control of our lives…"

"Everything has a purpose," Winston nodded in solemn agreement.

"I don't know what you…" Ruth began.

I knew exactly what he meant. During the last year or two, whatever had happened in my life had always led to the next phase with apparent inevitability. There was a sequence of events that seemed as sweeping as the torrent of a mighty river. And now, hardly through choice, I'd discovered that my previous abilities remained intact. Could I possibly waste them?

I looked at Winston. Uncharacteristically, he seemed lost in thought. His eyes half covered as I'd seen him on a few occasions when he seemed to be engaged in deep contemplation. Only a moment had passed, but somehow I felt drawn into his realm. I tried to resist but....

I need the cessation of your ego. I need the faith that you gave me in Rome... that 'let it be thy will' but spoken with equal conviction to that which it took to give you healing power... this submission-resignation-humility empowers me to enter your consciousness....

I'd heard those words before, or something very close to them, in the Vatican. I'd heard them just before I decided to relegate my ego to virtual non-existence. It happened just before my consciousness had united itself with the ailing Pontiff. And here it was again. A demand for total commitment. The absolute negation of selfhood.

"...you mean." Ruth completed the sentence. All that thought, all that memory in a blink of an eye. "I really don't know what you mean?" she repeated, her eyes searching first Winston's, then my face.

I'd noticed that before. Whenever I entered a different reality, there was a total suspension of the laws that govern the Universe we live in. Time and space seem destined to serve only the five senses we use in everyday life. Yet I had repeated evidence that there were other universes, other realities, other laws that govern them...

"I mean, Madam, that all things that happen to us have a purpose even if it is not always apparent at first sight," Winston explained.

His words were directed at Ruth, but meant for me. But I already knew the answer. *I've been running too long. No more escapes. I must act.* I must meet my fate regardless of the consequences. *Otherwise my uncertainty would just drag on and on, and eventually I would give up anyway.* What I'd found so difficult, at least at that stage of my development, was to suspend my thinking, my analytical abilities, as well as to suspend all logic and commit myself not to instinct but to intuition. I had to learn to act in areas completely new to me. Perhaps new to all of us. With the possible exception of Winston Smith.

It would be a lot easier if I had some idea what my fate was.

Even as I mulled over these thoughts in rapid time, I caught Winston's eyes on me. There was a guarded smile in those eyes. There was also something that I could only describe as love. The sort of love one feels for a new-born baby. Was I that naive?

Cathy left soon after. She told us that she would arrange to take time off and be at my disposal. She'd done it before. I wondered if that was why I loved her so much. It wasn't just her beauty, nor even her sparkling intelligence, but her willingness to change direction in mid-tack to help another human being. To help a man in need. The paradox was that, at the time, I had no idea what my needs were.

I saw her to the door.

"I have to visit MIT next week, but apart from that, I'm yours," she assured me.

"Promises, promises," I said. She gave me a naughty wink.

God, I loved that woman. In every way imaginable. I still do.

I was beginning to think that we all take ourselves too seriously. There had been healers before me. Men or women with unusual gifts, and... somehow they survived. Actually this wasn't strictly true. They survived for a while.

Bruno Gröning and Jose Pedro De Freitas better known as Arrigo, hadn't done so well. They were both ostracized, Bruno was virtually murdered for what he did, which was healing people with little more than his very presence. Arrigo was a more complex problem for the medical establishment. Excision of tumours, attachment of loose corneas, extraction of bleeding ulcers, even malignant cancers scraped out with a pocket penknife were not looked upon kindly. Particularly not by the members of my previous profession. The kitchen knife I used that night to cut the reporter's trousers shimmered before my eyes. I decided, there and then, not to resort to any kitchen utensils in my future intercessions on behalf of broken legs, torn ligaments or any other internal abrasions. Who could tell, someone might be watching.

Cathy was true to her word.

She called back that afternoon saying that we should meet to decide on the appropriate course of action. Ruth assured me that they could hold the trespassing reporter incommunicado, under some pretext or another, for another day or so.

"But that's it," she insisted. "I'm not even sure if such a short time is legal."

"I wonder why we are always so preoccupied with rights of the law-breakers to the detriment of the innocent party." I must have sounded a bit peeved. "There is something wrong with our legal system."

How I wished I would stop snapping at Ruth. I owed her even more than I did Cathy. It must have been some sort of subliminal guilt complex. Maybe I should at least play with the children more often. Be of some use to her.

"That's as it may be, but I am no longer a private person," she said.

Cathy was in a different field altogether. From early childhood, most likely inspired by her illustrious father, she'd been fascinated by physics. She studied patterns of things rather than people. By the time she was six, she could recite more of the laws of physics than most high school students. Then Einstein filled her field of vision. He was then replaced by quantum physics, which began with the distinction between particle and wave phenomena. She'd found her passion. She re-examined Newton, who had used both approaches to analyse different aspects of light. She moved on to Dalton, studying his Law of Multiple Proportions. Then came Boltzmann with his gas-theory based on atomistic concepts, Max Planck and his famous constant. Hertz led her to Lenard, who led her to Bohr, or more accurately to the Bohr-Sommerfeld model that introduced the quantum condition.

There have been more but I don't remember them all.

By the time she was twenty-five, Cathy'd earned her Ph.D., garnered a string of medals, and won a number of other awards.

One afternoon we were sitting on the settee, she leaning against me, but rising when she wanted to make a point, or to show how exciting some detail was. In those moments I didn't care what she was talking about. I just listened to her voice.

"...the advanced solution to the problem came in 1923 from Heisenberg and Schrödinger who published an alternate solution using complex wave functions. Two years later Dirac showed that both formulations were in fact equivalent. Broglie, Davison, and Germer completed the cycle."

I am sure that for my sake she omitted a number of other, less prominent names. Nevertheless, she was up on her feet again and had just stopped for breath. Her eyes were shining. I nodded dutifully, not wanting her to stop.

And now, here she was, asking me virtually the same question.

"You do see, don't you, Peter?" she asked frequently, hopefully.

"Yes, darling. Of course I do."

I didn't. I understood her fascination with the subject, not the theories she was expounding. I don't think anyone understands quantum mechanics. Not even today. If anyone says otherwise, they are lying. Except for Cathy, of course, although she stopped short of actually affirming her comprehension. I think she was fascinated precisely by its mystery or, better still, by its intangibility.

She was standing by the fireplace studying my face from above. A glorious smile lit up her face. I must have looked dumb and worried.

"Peter, darling. If you don't understand, don't worry. Richard Feynman once said that if he could explain it to, forgive me, an average person, he wouldn't have been worth the Nobel Prize. Physicists are like that. And quantum physicists more so."

I smiled my gratitude. Peter Feynman?

This took me back almost a year. We'd just returned from Europe. Cathy had given me a little book by David Lindley, with the preposterous title: *'New Scientist's Guide to the Quantum World'*. It was a tiny edition produced by New Scientist, with an equally tiny Foreword. In it the author asserts that: "...the only way to come to grips with it is to suspend disbelief." Suddenly I found kinship with Cathy's quantum mechanics. I had considerable experience in suspending my disbelief.

Cathy and I were the only two people I knew, not that I knew myself that well, who were prepared to go through life in a state of suspended belief. Or disbelief, for that matter. On the other hand, it did not advance my problems with my waning faith in an all-powerful, compassionate, forgiving God. Perhaps there was a time, at the beginning of human civilization, when a wondrous and kindly Being had helped us along on our meandering way. Some good many millennia ago. An aeon or two. As for now, as for the so-called modern era, it seemed to me that we simple folk were more or less on our own. Isn't this, more or less, what the Last Pope had told us?

"The answers lie within you," he'd said.

I wondered if the same applied to quantum physics.

As for Cathy's inner needs, those not fully satisfied by her infinitely small and unpredictable particles, she relied, at least in part, on the Old Master, known in the West as Lao Tsu. We all travel by our own individual path, she'd said when I tried to explain to her the religion of my youth. If electrons travel an unpredictable path, can we do any less? I couldn't argue with that. Conformity was definitely the weakest link in all the major religions.

Cathy leaned down and poked a charred log that was in danger of slipping from the cast-iron grating.

"Listen to what the Old Master had to say about the road you travel." She recited from memory:

When people hear of Tao, the highest minds practice it;
The average think about it and try it—once in a while;
The lowest minds... laugh at it.
If they did not laugh at it, it would not be the Way.

"The Old Master tells you to go, but he does not impose on you the direction. That you must discover on your own. Isn't this a better way than being obedient to someone else's will? Or being an obedient sheep for that matter..." she added, under her breath.

Time retreated into the glowing embers of the dying fire. For a while I stared fascinated by a single, flickering flame. It held me in a hypnotic spell. Then a sharp crack was followed by a lone spark that flew off in an elliptical orbit only to smash into the black side of the hearth. Like her atom smasher, I mused.

As for the sheep, she need not have worried. I'd left the flock some time ago, although I still suffered from occasional pangs of guilt.

The next day we met was in a small restaurant just off *rue Ste-Catherine*, on Green Avenue, where we'd first had a rendezvous about a year earlier, just before I gave up my promising medical career. It was small and cozy, and there was a sparkling fireplace in the coffee room. The chairs were comfortable, the lights dark enough to offer a warm, informal atmosphere and me a semblance of anonymity. Even the tablecloth reminded me of home rather than a public place. A small candle held in a tall container of reddish glass, on each table, complemented the decor.

It was only my second outing since the Decalogue, if you didn't count my idiotic jaunt in full disguise. Or my cricket games in the back garden. For the first few minutes I felt acutely uncomfortable. I felt people's eyes on me, mostly on the back of my neck. I expected someone to approach me at any moment and beg me to save his or her ailing son or daughter or some other member of their family who, for all I knew, was not worth saving.

Strange, that. I strongly suspect that very few of us are really worth saving. Yet, I can't help wondering if, at the depth of our being, we don't all hold a certain potential, even if I'm not sure what that potential really entails.

Ad majora natus sum, I recalled from my youth. Did it apply to everybody?

A year ago such a thought would never even have entered my mind. I was becoming judgmental. I wasn't going forward, I was regressing. I needed a strong effort of will just to relax. I was definitely becoming neurotic.

Cathy seemed to have noticed my struggle and smiled her encouragement. Dear Cathy... it was her idea to come here. And, of course, she was right as usual.

Surreptitiously, I glanced around.

No one came near us, no one seemed to have so much as looked in our direction. Apparently only some unique or at least retrograde members of the press were still trying to whip up business by digging up old stories about me. There was indeed a time when I wouldn't have been able to appear in public without being recognized and pressed for some sort of assistance. People used to follow me from motel to motel, even as I was trying to elude them.

We had coffee and dainty almond cookies. For the first time I actually enjoyed the feeling of unwinding the spiral that seemed taut for the last twelve months. I suppose I was at least partially responsible for it being so strained. I had acted like a megalomaniac, a self-centred egoist imagining that the world spun around me.

"Do you still want to leave town?" Cathy asked, her green eyes looking enticing in the flickering light of the candles.

"Why do you ask?"

"They asked me to go to Cern."

I continued to stare at her eyes. They seemed to be emanating gentle flames of their own, perhaps picked up from the candle between us. Her words didn't quite reach my awareness. "Sern?" I raised one eyebrow.

"CERN, European Organization for Nuclear Research" Cathy sighed. "It's just outside Geneva. It is a twenty-seven-kilometre-circumference tunnel in which they are colliding protons at seven times the energy level of the American Fermilab's Tevatron, which is a mere seven-mile accelerator." Again she said it all on a single breath. She did that often with physics.

"What's the hurry?" I asked, for the want of something better to say.

"They are looking for the god particle. The Higgs boson, believed to bestow mass on all other particles. Theoretically the Large Hadron Collider has the capability to find it. They've been trying since 2007. They think they are doing something wrong."

"And that's were you come in?"

"I'm sort of interested in... God," she said. Her eyes were now reflecting the flickering light of the fireplace.

"Me too," I admitted. Then I smiled. We both knew that we were thinking of entirely different concepts. Cathy and I may have travelled in the same direction, but our starting points lay miles apart.

"They're also studying antimatter particles," she added.

"Isn't that rather dangerous?"

"Only when they come together."

Suddenly I sent up an ardent prayer to whoever created the god particle that should Cathy ever visit Geneva, He, She, or It would not allow the opposing particles to come together. Not even for…

"It's all done with magnets," she explained.

I would rather it were mirrors.

We ordered a second coffee.

"I'll stick around and take my lumps," I said, answering her original question. "Will you be away long?"

The waitress came back with what looked like a Ming dynasty pot and topped up our cups. She hesitated at the table as if she were thinking of something, then slowly walked away still confused. Cathy and I sipped our fresh coffees. Before I'd had my second sip, the waitress was back. Her eyes were wide and seemed empty, lost. She stared at me, and as I watched she raised a small sharp knife. She hesitated just for an instant, and then with a single decisive stroke she slashed her left wrist. Blood spurted all over our table.

"My husband left me," she said, in a steady, emotionless voice. "I have nothing to live for."

She stood there bleeding and I sat frozen while milliseconds ticked away.

"Peter!" Cathy's eyes screamed at me though her voice reached me as a throaty whisper. "Peter," she repeated weakly.

I reached over and took the woman's wrist in my hand and squeezed. There is a lot of blood in the human body and I felt this woman's pulsing out between my fingers, dripping onto the floor.

I kept my eyes on Cathy; I didn't want to see the waitress' eyes. After some ten seconds I let go of her arm.

"Why?" she asked, staring at me.

I couldn't avoid her eyes any longer. She hadn't come to commit suicide; she'd sought me out to heal her. Not her hand, not even her severed veins. Her soul. Her aching heart?

"Go home and be grateful for the life that is yours to enjoy. You have a lot to live for." I don't know why I said it. It just seemed like the right thing.

Cathy was up on her feet. I wiped my hands on the tablecloth, left a $20 bill on the table and made for the door. Cathy followed me without a word. The whole affair took no more than thirty seconds, and luckily no one in the café seemed to have noticed the ordeal.

"So much for anonymity," I murmured. "So much for...."

I felt slightly drunk. It was the feeling one has after getting up from a longish stay on deeply bent knees, when blood rushes away from your head to feed the starving lower extremities. I wasn't used to this sort of thing any more. We all commit suicide by the choices we make, by the way we lead our lives. But we extend our self-mutilation over many years. Like people who eat too much, or drink to excess, take drugs, or even don't exercise. No matter how much we deny those foibles, they are all forms of suicide. But those methods are not so drastic. Not so immediate.

"It's all right, darling. We both knew it would happen. You just had to make sure," she said quietly.

I realized that she was right. I never really believed that I could get away with being completely anonymous. Invisible, like Winston. People have long memories and, at the time, my face had been in all the papers. Mine or the fellow called Doctor Peter Thornton, FRCSP. A brilliant young physician with a promising career.

We drove to the lookout on Mount Royal, pulled up and cut the engine. The panorama of Montreal stretched before us. Four million people nestled beyond the fringe of autumn's slowly depleting colourful skirt. Nature's gift to man. God's gift? Isn't everything? I tried to erase the reality I saw in the young woman's eyes. So much pain, so little life. I thought that life is the opposite of pain. Life is order and harmony that something within us wrenched out of the universal chaos. Sometimes it manifests as beauty that we, the all-knowing apes, are trying so often to destroy. Ultimately, we all succeed.

For a while we sat in silence. Then Cathy unlatched her seat belt and leaned her head on my shoulder.

"Kiss me," she said.

But why me? What gives me the right to interfere with the order of things? To manipulate reality?

"Kiss me...."

I couldn't stop thinking about the waitress who'd decided that I and I alone had the right, the gift that could contradict the laws of nature. Perhaps God's laws as well. Only cutting one's cephalic and the median antibrathial veins simultaneously would produce that much blood. Had she really wanted to commit suicide she would have cut her throat. No. This was only a desperate cry for help. Still, without me there, she would have died. Did she know that? On the other hand, without me there she probably would not have cut her veins.

It was a strange world.

"Kiss me, Peter," a small voice at my side whispered. "Kiss me now... please."

I must have been crazy. I was sitting next to the most fascinating woman I'd ever met and was indulging in the rationalization of human behaviour.

Her lips were a wondrous, enchanting, mesmerizing way to divert my attention. For a while I thought of nothing else.

"I love you more than I can say," I whispered.

"Kiss me again," she replied.

The newspapers reported the incident on the fourth page. Most people don't usually read past second or third. A short note followed the relatively small headline.

HE'S BACK

> Dr. Peter Thornton, the eminent physician at the Montreal General Hospital who gave up his medical practice after discovering healing powers in his touch, has returned after an extended absence from the city. It has been reported that he was instrumental in stemming the blood flow from a waitress who

> accidentally cut herself at the Café Papillion, a favourite haunt of the rich and famous. It is hoped that the good doctor will no longer avoid his responsibility of sharing his gift with those who need him most.

That was all. A short and bitter condemnation of my actions with little regard for what actually happened. Good for them, I thought. They could have put me on page one. They could have published my address and my description. They must have discarded all the old photos. After all, it is seldom indeed that public interest in anything other than global war can be maintained for more than a week. Ten days at the most. I was passé. Old hat. There must be a god after all. I might have had to be on the run right now.

Ruth saw the newspaper at breakfast.

"What does this mean, Peter?" She looked only slightly shocked. Imagine, she seemed to say, after all that happened over the last twelve months.

"I suspect she'll be all right," I assured her, thinking of the waitress.

"Why did you, ah... touch her?"

"Wouldn't you in my circumstances?"

This brought her back from wherever her mind had wandered. My gift, or whatever it was, was not firmly established as part of her reality. Ruth had never seen me performing my ministrations. For her it was all hearsay. There may have been some truth in it, but, well, you know, people like to talk. No, it was definitely not integrated into her reality. Nor was it in mine, really, not down to my inner being. The gift remained something foreign to me. Not part of me but imposed on me against my will.

"I'm sorry," Ruth said. "Of course," she added without looking at me.

It was this averted gaze that made me realize that the strain I was putting on her was more than she could handle. She had problems of her own. Her high position in the ranks of Solidarity International was drawing on all her reserves.

"I've been asked to go to CERN. Near Geneva," I lied. Cathy hadn't actually asked me, but I suspected that her hint could be construed as at least an implied invitation. Cathy may have thought that I had other plans.

"We'll all miss you," Ruth looked me in the eyes again. I sensed that she was sincere. "Especially the children," she added.

Except for the children. For some reason I didn't allow them to enter the equation of my complex life. Yet they were my late brother's children. And my partners in the game of cricket. I was the only uncle they had, and Ruth was keeping late hours in her office.

"I didn't tell her I'd go. Cathy I mean. But it might not be a bad idea."

"You must do what you consider best," she replied, her voice uncertain.

Ruth had too much on her plate. My brother's untimely death left her with two children to bring up. Andrew's death itself remained a mystery. There was talk of an explosion, of unsavoury characters assaulting him on one of the construction sites, even of some Chinese equivalent of voodoo being cast on him. I asked Winston, but he only said that it was the right time. No amount of prodding would force him to say any more. I didn't feel like raising the subject again and again with Ruth. She seemed reconciled to her present fate.

Ruth had already been well established at the United Nations, when Lena coaxed her to take over the cause of Solidarity. After the initial trial period, Solidarity began paying her the 5x multiple of an average salary. As high as they went with anybody. But there still were the children who needed their mother. Winston was a gem of exceptional quality, but he couldn't provide the warmth that only a mother could give.

"It wouldn't be for long," I said. "Unless you really want me to stay," I murmured lamely.

"I do want you to stay. You're family. But I also need you to be fully convinced that what you do is right." This was the old Ruth. Logical, positive, uncompromising.

Cathy repeated her offer that evening. She dropped in after work. She did that frequently. It was what kept me going.

"I think you'll be freer to think there," she said. "At least for a while."

We began making plans. We decided to take an apartment together, and to hell with gossip. We'd been together for more than a year. We never actually discussed 'marriage', but that was only because Cathy's work took her all over the place, and my future was steeped in uncertainty. We both had to settle down, physically, mentally and even emotionally. As Matthew commanded in his gospel, we had to say 'Yea, yea, or Nay, nay.' A commitment to each other. That's what the Old Pope would have said. Not that we weren't certain of our emotions for each other. It was our relationship to the rest of the world that left a lot to be desired. Cathy loved Ruth for what she was, not for the work and allegiance she now held. As an affirmed individualist, Cathy couldn't stand the common denominator that Solidarity continued to introduce into our lives. Or into other people's lives.

"We'll find something overlooking the Lake," she said.

"And we'll buy a yacht and escape from everybody," I purred dreamily.

"And... and we shall be together each and every night..."

***

6

Genetics

The call came at six-thirty the next morning, the time of day when normal people are trying to squeeze in another little dream.

"Good morning. Will you hold the line for Dr. Brent?"

Winston had answered. He didn't reply but held the line.

"Hello?" the woman's voice inquired.

"To whom does Doctor Brent wish to speak?" Winston said after a little while.

"Why, Doctor Thornton," she replied. There was almost an 'of course' following the name.

"I shall put you through, Madam."

"I am sorry. I am Dr. Brent's personal secretary. Perhaps it's inconvenient?"

I overheard the one-sided discussion from upstairs. I had to smile. A year ago, by seven a.m. I was already finishing my morning rounds.

"Not at all, Madam. My name is Smith. I shall see if Doctor Thornton is available."

I was already up. I'd showered and was getting ready to shave. I'd decided to take better care of my personal appearance. People in Geneva might be more demanding than Ruth and Cathy. I was about to become a normal person. A sort of cross between a Peter

Thornton and a Nomad. Something between Nobody and, hopefully, Somebody.

I picked up the receiver.

"Peter?"

"Doctor Brent?" It had been over a year.

"John, remember? We had dinner together."

That was the last time I saw him. I'd been invited to his house following the unusual events that occurred on my ward. Too many cures, the Old Man had called them. Patients had recovered too quickly, he'd said. And then, at his house, he was kindness itself.

"I do remember, ah... John," I nearly stammered. It isn't easy to address an ex-god by his first name. "Of course I remember. How is Mrs. Brent?"

"Lucy's fine, thanks. Look, Peter, I want to see you. Can you make it today?"

"At the hospital?" I dreaded the thought. At the General everyone knew me. I must still be regarded there as a freak.

"I think we'd better make it at home. You remember the address?"

He repeated the street and number. I still remember standing outside his door for an hour, not quite daring to press the doorbell.

"May I ask what it's about, ah, John?"

"Dr. Tsan and I had an idea. You might help us, if you agree."

Dr. George Tsan was the President of the Royal College of Physicians and Surgeons. He was the one who officially welcomed me to the congregation of Fellows. Dr. Tsan and Dr. Brent went way back. In fact, they'd studied together.

I was a little taken aback. What would the two top physicians in Montreal want with the likes of me?

"Peter?"

"Yes, sir. I... I would be..."

"Around seven?"

"Yes, sir."

I still found it difficult to say no to my ex-boss. Not that he really bossed me. He just carried an aura about him that commanded obedience.

I called Cathy. She was out. I left a message.

I took a cab and waited outside until my watch showed exactly seven o'clock. I thanked my lucky stars that it wasn't raining. For some reason I pressed the button a little nervously. I was about to re-enter my past. The same apron-clad lady whom I met a year ago opened the door. She looked as though only days had passed. The same hair rolled up in a severe, tight bun. The same shade of silver that I also remembered on the Chief of Medicine's aging head. Ah, yes. And the same penetrating eyes.

"Peter!" Her voice belonged to a woman half her age. "How are you? You look great. Really great. We've been so worried. Why didn't you keep in touch?"

I returned her warm hug.

"There are many things I should have done these last twelve months, Lucy."

Addressing Mrs. Brent by her first name came more easily. Of course, she was a lot less commanding. And prettier too.

Neither one of us noticed John Brent standing behind me. He neither moved nor said anything. As I turned, for a second or two he remained silent. Then he embraced me as I imagine a father would a prodigal son.

"Come in, Peter. Come in my son."

Those few words re-established our relationship. Of course, a man of his seniority could well address most people my age as 'son', but it didn't sound like it. There was a quiet conviction in the term he'd used. A feeling of intimacy. I knew that he had a soft spot for me, but I was not aware how deep it went. He led me to the fireplace, and made his own way to the cabinet. He poured two dry Amontillados, and repeated, I could swear, the words he'd spoken a year ago.

"Lucy won't mind if we start without her."

For a while we both stared into the fire, reminiscing. Last time I was there, we talked about my gift, which, at the time, I thought was in about the same vein as voodoo. After all, it had ruined my career. A year ago, Dr. Brent had confessed that had he known a man with my particular talent, as he'd called it, he most probably wouldn't have lost the only child he'd had. There and then, he made me feel guilty for disparaging the gift that had been thrust upon me. It was also at that moment that I felt a wave of deep affection that seemed to sweep both of us into a different relationship. He was no longer my boss. I was facing a man who cared about me—not as a promising young member of his staff, but as a man. A human being.

After dinner, we returned to the armchairs strategically placed in front of the fireplace, so as to shut out the world outside. The curtains had already been drawn and the room, much smaller than Ruth's, looked as intimate as a private den. It was as far away, as different as it could be, from the messy yet sterile conditions of the office Dr. Brent occupied at the General. They belonged in two different worlds. He seemed equally at ease in both of them.

"I had a strange phone-call last week," John Brent began once he removed his shoes and stretched his feet out towards the warmth of the fire. "I think you've met her," he added as if watching the effect his words had on me.

I waited.

"She was introduced by her secretary as Lena Wałęsa, pronounced Valensa, I believe. She made a very strange suggestion."

"It's a small world," I murmured.

"Indeed. She said that you are an extraordinary human being." For the first time John Brent raised his eyes from his stockinged toes and looked directly at me. "Not physician, you note, not healer, but a human being."

There was little I could say. I thought she was more than extraordinary. She was utterly unique.

"She also said that you were unique." John was watching me intently. "Do you know why she would form such an opinion of you?"

I assumed this was a rhetorical question.

"She is a very commanding lady," I said instead.

"Yes, persuasive also. Even over the phone, although we did use the video link."

So my old friend and boss had met Mother Earth. The Goddess herself. I wondered where it would lead.

"She told me that in Europe they've made considerable advances in the field of genetics. Now I, as you know, am not a geneticist, but she insisted that some of the advances they'd made might be of great interest to us."

I still had no idea what he and or she might be leading up to.

"She further suggested," Dr. Brent continued, "that you would be ideally suited to act as liaison between the European and our own research group. Now, tell me, Peter, why would she pick you for such a job?"

Normally I would have replied, 'Because of my big blue eyes', or something of that sort. But one didn't talk like that to the Old Man. To the Chief.

"It may be that she doesn't know too many people with a medical background?"

"Or ones she feels she can trust?"

At this Lucy joined in. "Don't you men ever stop talking business?"

As I recall, at the risk of sounding chauvinistic, to Lucy anything that strayed too far away from her favourite roses, or the beauty of Canadian autumns, or any of the wonders of nature was business. And now, that it was too unpleasant to go out and actually participate in it, the least one could do, apparently, was to talk about it

"It's not really business, dear. It's more like solving little puzzles that affect us both. I mean Peter and myself. It's just a friendly discussion. You are welcome to join us," John assured his wife. He next gave her a quick résumé of what we'd been talking about.

"She is the Solidarity bigwig, isn't she?" Lucy asked.

"Very big indeed. There are none higher," I replied.

"And she wants you to do what precisely?" Lucy asked looking at me.

"I have no idea. A sort of liaison, apparently. Not that I know that much about genetics," I said.

John cleared his throat. "Before calling you Peter, I had a look-see." John Brent was full of quaint expressions. "I found that in Europe they are thinking of immortality."

If I was supposed to be impressed, I wasn't. I always thought of myself as immortal, even if my definition of 'myself' differed from the usual self-centred nomenclature. Not that I was any authority on self-centredness.

But then there was that phrase from the Decalogue delivered with such force, such conviction, by the sextet, or perhaps an octet of deep bassos, only a few days ago: *...you shall have no other gods before me*. Not even immortal gods made out of clay or flesh and bones. Will the last idol we give up be our ego? Our own creation that we all admire daily in the mirror. I suspect this was the idol Solidarity wanted to immortalize.

Nevertheless my ears pricked up.

I wondered what had really stirred Lena's juices. Did she really want herself and her members to become the masters of the world? A sort of super-race of immortals? Spectres of past *ûbermenschen* and other attempts at supremacy had failed miserably. Only this time, it wasn't a question of nationality or some chauvinistic stirrings. Solidarity was as international as you could get. Her attempt to enrol me on her payroll was proof enough.

Regrettably, I had but a smattering of knowledge about genetics. No more than a physician would, which was next to nothing. I knew that Watson and Crick started the ball rolling back in 1953. They described the structure of the DNA molecule as a double helix. If I remembered right, they said that it was a pair of strands of polynucleotides. I also knew that by the beginning of the present century they'd finished transcribing the genetic code. That was about it.

"That's a pretty long time," I quipped. In a physical sense, the idea of immortality was too idiotic to even consider.

"They are quite serious, Peter." My ex-boss continued to study me from under his bushy eyebrows. "I rather thought that your, ah, ah... your special abilities wouldn't interfere with such a work, while your medical background might come in handy."

I rolled that around in my mind. Recently I was a hanger-on. Not financially, but in every other way I was bleeding Ruth and Cathy and even Winston with my real or imagined problems. It was time for me to stand up on my own frustrated feet and not wait for Ruth to put the emotional food on the table. The only way that could happen would be if I got busy. Really busy. If my grey cells began to spin not just around my own self. Lately, I hadn't even chipped in my fair share of upkeep. Not that Ruth ever said a word.

But frankly, it was getting embarrassing. I always managed to come up with a convincing excuse for myself.

"I'll do it, John," I said, "whatever it is. You're quite right. My years of training might finally be of some use." I couldn't quite keep a touch of bitterness from my voice.

"Now, if I understand correctly, you help people one-on-one. If you advance the knowledge of genetics, you might help thousands, perhaps millions simultaneously."

I nodded. The Old Man was right, of course. If I had a chance to help humanity, it would be inhuman to refuse. Yet somewhere, at the back of my mind, there was a nagging voice telling me that this was all wrong. That there must be another way. Another direction for the human race to pursue. And then, John raised his head up and allowed himself a deep sigh.

"We missed you, son. We…" he didn't finish.

Lucy came up behind his armchair and gently stroked his grey hair. Her gesture alone spoke volumes. 'He missed you, Peter. He missed you badly,' it said.

A son they'd lost so early in life.

I swear that I never realized that Dr. Brent harboured such personal feelings towards me. He wasn't a man who carried his feelings on his sleeve. There had been sighs, now and then, but, well, it was all so long ago. And it was also all so hygienic, so... impersonal. A walk along the deserted, sterile, insipid corridor where the lights never dimmed; the all-pervading smell of antiseptic; the gathering around the various beds, patients prone, some propped up on their pillows, all freshly washed, many with sponges… Nurses in primly starched uniforms stepping aside... Dr. Brent and I in front, the interns and the junior residents in a semicircle, filled with awe. Then snappy questions.

"Brown, Kimberly, McNeil... how would you diagnose the…" There followed a half-dozen diseases, some with complications, which the residents were expected to know by heart. Often they didn't. Except for me. My photographic memory never let me down. At least not when the Chief was present. Apparently he noticed that, even then.

I smiled sadly at the memory. Even then I danced to a mysterious tune, intoned in the distance by an invisible piper. Didn't Einstein say something like that? How did he know?

"I'm sorry, sir. There was nothing...."

"...you could have done. I know, son. But somehow, it did not make things any easier."

I saw it in his eyes. He could have said, Not then, not now.

"Yes, sir. I know. I really understand..."

"I know you do. And somehow that makes it even harder," he said, and looked at the smouldering fire. Little more remained to be said.

"Shall I call you tomorrow, sir?"

"Yes, Peter. Do that. Tomorrow."

I left quietly. This time Lucy did not see me to the door. I was wrong. They'd both aged during those last twelve months. Perhaps we all had. She stayed with her husband stroking his hair. Ever so gently.

After leaving the Brents', I realized that I'd forgotten to ask for whom I would be working. Or where, for that matter. I left quickly. After all, it hadn't been a dinner invitation—more like a job interview. We might have started talking about the old days. Would have been painful for both of us.

I wondered what the future held for me.

Would I automatically become a card-carrying member of Solidarity? For some reason I couldn't explain, I hoped not. Like Cathy, I loved my freedom. Not that I had enjoyed much of it lately. At least in my soul I was free. Free to dream, to think what and how I wanted to. Would that change?

I picked up the viphone to call Dr. Brent and ask him. Then, I took a deep breath. "Whatever is to happen—will," I whispered under my breath. Whatever happens I shall continue to serve 'myself', my true self, the self I met in Rome. Not some other idols. Not even golden calves or burning bushes. For the first time in months, I slept well that night. In the morning I called Cathy. In a few words I told her about my interview with Dr. Brent.

"That's wonderful," she exclaimed, when I was halfway through.

"Are you so happy we shall be apart?"

"Peter, the European Centre for Genetic Research is in Geneva. A twenty-minute drive from CERN."

I felt as if I were emerging from a deep hibernation. I was stunned. I was reminded, for the umpteenth time that, indeed, what must happen—will. Cathy and I were definitely meant to happen.

Two days later I drove her to the airport. There were no tears. Just a warm embrace until the depersonalized voice announced boarding time.

"I'll call you the moment I get there. And I'll look for an apartment big enough, just in case."

However, not all dreams come true. At least, not immediately. Some are there just to teach us to hope, and keep hoping, no matter how unattainable the horizon appears to be. For now, I was not to travel with her to Geneva.

The Royal Victoria Hospital, affectionately referred to as the Old Vic, was impressive. The heads of the various departments sounded like the Who's Who of medicine. Leaders in research and theory. I began to rub shoulders with people I'd previously only read about. What the Old Vic discovered today, the General, my old hospital, utilized tomorrow.

For now, my own office turned out to be a decent room, larger than I'd expected, with an antechamber for my secretary. It was located right next to the library. It was there that I found the privacy to do my work. No one knew me. No one had ever heard of a Peter Thornton, let alone Dr. Thornton. They were all much too busy doing their thing. And things there were many.

I realized only then, that most of the people who, in the past, benefited from my 'gift' were the poor. The poor, the lonely, the discouraged. Those whose life, or vitality, was at the lowest ebb. Others, apparently, could cope on their own.

My first job was to familiarize myself with the research done so far. The titles of the briefs read like a dream that a surgeon would find breathtaking.

Reversing Degenerative Disease
Overcoming Cancer
DNA Mutations
Mitochondrial Mutations
Toxic Cells
Combating Heart Disease
Gene Chips
Somatic Gene Therapy
Cell Loss and Atrophy

And after a list another twenty titles long, came the *pièce de résistance*.

Human Somatic-Cell Engineering
Human Cloning

And finally a question followed that must have stirred dear Lena's juices: *Can We Really Live Forever?*

Would we want to? Would anyone really want to live in the same house, the same furniture, wear the same clothing forever? Is our body any more than that? More than a house, a place we stay for a little while. Don't people realize how long 'forever' is?

No matter.

I started going through the files. Apparently, the intention was for me to become sufficiently familiar with them to visit Cathy, I mean Geneva, and compare notes with their achievements as some kind of expert. Not at research but at assessing its efficacy. Then and only then was I to venture into the United States, and ultimately into the Sino-Indian coalition. I must admit that once I got engrossed in the files, they captured my whole attention. I forgot about my reservations, about the philosophy underlying the research, and merely soaked up the knowledge. For as long as I can remember, knowledge, information as such, has always fascinated me. This was no exception.

A week later I was sitting at my desk when my private line rang.

"Thornton," I snapped. I was in the middle of something.

"Lena," came a soft reply, the single word oozing charm and femininity.

I was fairly stunned. "Lena? Is it really you?" It could have been a prank.

"How are you, Peter?" There was concern in her voice.

"Never better," I said, "in no small measure thanks to you," I assured her.

"When will you visit us?"

"Us?"

"I am in CERN, with Cathy. We were just talking about you. Hold on…?"

"Hello, darling. Isn't she nice?" Cathy was bubbling. The initial reservation she had regarding Lena was obviously dissipating into thin air. "Lena tells me you'll be coming over soon?" As much a statement as a question.

"I guess she knows more than I do!" I must have sounded a little frazzled.

"She says it's all up to you. That you are in charge of the project."

It had never crossed my mind that the whole aspect of liaisonship, if there is such a word, had been left up to me. On the other hand, since the moment I began, no one ever expressed any interest in my progress. Also, I've never been in charge of anything. Except the patients on my ward, of course, but there and then, there had been an army of staff to back me up, if necessary. Now…?

"I'll call you back, darling. Love you," I said, and rather rudely hung up.

I had to reconnoitre. This was principally a Solidarity project. On the other hand, I had been given an office in Canada, in a Canadian institution. My first cheque hadn't arrived yet, and I didn't look at my account to see if there had been any retainer placed there. For all I knew, I might have been working *pro bono*. I didn't think so, but it was possible. I could call Dr. Brent, but I hated imposing on him. I'm sure he was as busy as ever, and I was already indebted to him from way back when. In addition I carried a debt of gratitude for the job I was doing. John was a true friend, I mused pensively.

I decided to talk to Ruth. After all, she was Solidarity Canada. She had to know something, if not everything Solidarity was doing. She was in the kitchen when I got home.

"Am I working for you, Ruth?"

She laughed. "What gave you that idea, Peter?"

"I don't know who my employer is," I replied.

"I thought Dr. Brent hired you, didn't he?"

He did. But... but it was Lena who appeared to be calling the shots. She'd more or less defined my job by phone that very afternoon. And John Brent hadn't called even once.

"What's the matter, Peter?"

I didn't answer. Ruth studied me for a little while before expanding on her previous statement. "All I know, Peter, is that your job is of the hush-hush category. We don't talk about it. We don't discuss it. And don't ask questions. I have no idea why it is so hush-hush."

I weighed that for a moment.

"With Lena, one is never told much detail. She's very careful in the selection of her team, if one can call it that. Having made a decision, she leaves people alone until something happens that requires her input. That's the way my own job is run. Even when she and I meet, we seldom discuss business."

I was beginning to get the idea. What I'd started had not been attempted before. It was a new idea to unify the world research under one coordinator. Well, to coordinate the knowledge, so to speak. While John Brent opened the Canadian institutions for me, Lena, or Solidarity, opened the European doors that would normally be closed. Being a first, Lena could hardly tell me what to do. She must have assumed that I would know more about it than she did. Or would, very quickly.

"That's a very strange friend you have, sister, dear," I said.

Ruth smiled. She smiled quite often lately.

"Tell me about it," she said. "If you can..."

And then I remembered what John Brent had said, 'She also said that you were unique'. Was Lena collecting people? Or was it her way to equalize her apparent desire to bring everyone to a common denominator of Solidarity International. Whichever it was, I was right in telling John that Lena Walesa was herself a very unique lady. And mysterious, too. Why else would she have given Ruth the impression that the work I was doing was so very hush-hush? Perhaps she didn't like competition. Or gossip. Or it just may have been a way to keep her interests in separate drawers. It can't be easy to give direction to over two billion people.

And counting…

What if my job, in her eyes, was to improve the minds of the working class through genetic manipulation? What would become of the others, those left behind? If the members of Solidarity ultimately become, well... even relatively immortal, what of normal people? Not that Solidarity members were anything but normal. But what of Jane and Joe next door? And then I remembered that Solidarity never barred people from joining the ranks of their organization. The only disqualification was if they wanted to earn more than 5x the Solidarity average. Other than that, the sky was the limit.

***

7

The Basilica

I've never been to Geneva. A year ago, after flying from Canada to Gdansk to Rome in a little over two weeks, I'd criss-crossed Europe. Cathy and I lingered a little longer, but somehow we seemed to have avoided Switzerland.

"Would you like to come with me?" Ruth asked one day. The question came out of nowhere.

I looked up from my papers. In spite of long hours in the office, I still took some work home. There was so much of it, so many details, and a lot of it was quite unfamiliar to me.

"I am flying to Rome next week. You might say hello to Lena, and then take a break and pop over to see Cathy. It's only an hour's flight from Rome."

For two months I'd been working like a slave. Cathy and I talked two or three times a week, but she seemed as consumed by her work as I was by mine. At long last I could definitely afford the trip. I was getting a retainer from the General equivalent to a full-time staff member. At last I had made the financial class of which I'd been dreaming for some ten years. Not that I had much time for dreaming. I was too busy enjoying myself doing the work I'd quickly learned to love. In genetics, I found a new interest as one does in anything once one digs a little deeper. Ignorance may be bliss, but it's a boring kind of bliss.

"The children will be all right with Winston, for a day or two," Ruth continued, when apparently I continued to stare at her in near disbelief.

"I've never popped over anywhere," I said at last.

Ruth must have taken that as tacit agreement. I imagined the soft, yielding body pressing against mine, right there, at the International Airport in Geneva.

"What time?" I asked, my mind still wrapped around Cathy. "What time do we leave?"

Ruth smiled. "You were thinking of Cathy, weren't you." That was not a question. I must have had an inane smile on my face.

"And what makes you think that?" I inquired, in all innocence.

"I know how you love flying, Peter."

There was no denying that Ruth's logic was impeccable. She must have been thinking of my first contact with Solidarity. My many years of studying, during which I hadn't had time nor inclination to travel much anywhere, had been terminated by a forced flight to Gdansk, under false pretenses. It had been suggested to Ruth and myself that if we ever wanted to see Mo and Jo in good shape again, we should board a plane, immediately, and proceed to an unknown destination that turned out to be Gdansk. The whole affair had been vastly exaggerated and once Lena learned about it, she promptly fired the culprit from his senior position. She would never allow such shenanigans to be carried out in her or in Solidarity's name.

Nevertheless, the Gdansk affair had forced me to travel for the first time in years. Till then, my trips had been limited mostly to Toronto and Johns Hopkins in Baltimore, always to hear some lectures. And now, a year later, Ruth was suggesting another trip, virtually for pleasure only. I was perfectly aware that millions of people flew every day of the week, that thousands of Canadians went south for part of the winter, that business men and women, like Ruth for that matter, thought that a flight was no more than an extended taxi ride. For me it meant being shut in a metal container like an oversized sardine, breathing recycled, stale air, which other passengers exhaled for my benefit. That, and to listen for interminable hours to the drone of the engines from supersonic jets that expelled as much pollution from their innards as a small town in a week; and that's just at takeoff. Perhaps more so: while the town got its energy from practically pure fission converters, the planes still relied on the old jet fuel. Some things apparently were never meant to change.

I spent the next two days putting my papers in order, making a list of priorities and items of my particular interest for possible discussions with my counterparts in Geneva. Then I called John Brent, whom I hadn't seen since our dinner, to thank him, belatedly, for his part in my new position.

"You deserve it, my boy," Dr. Brent assured me. "Make sure you stay in touch." He hung up before I had a chance to inquire about Lucy. John Brent has been a busy man for as long as I can remember.

I realized that I was surrounded by people who seemed determined, and even committed, to help me in any way they could. This included John, Lena, Ruth and, of course, Winston, even if his infrequent advice was in a different category all together.

Of late, Winston had been rather silent. Not that he'd ever been a chatterbox, but he had volunteered, on occasion, some advice. It seemed to me that, at least for now, Winston was more interested in Mo and Jo, probably realizing that both Ruth and I were short of time. The children seemed none the worse for it. Each time I returned from the Old Vic, they greeted me in their wonderfully boisterous way that dispelled, within seconds, any tension I may have accumulated through the hours of intense work.

"We visited Mars, Uncle Peter," Mo would exclaim. Or, "We've been playing hide and seek in the rings of Saturn...." This would be Jo, who would never allow himself to be upstaged by his sister.

I'd forgotten that Winston could create such vivid imagery in his stories that the children could well imagine that they were actually there, wherever *there* was.

I may be repeating myself, but it bears repeating that in some ways I missed those early days, just after Winston had extracted me from my misguided need to share my elusive gift with as many people as possible. Not that he ever told me what to do. Yet, in his own inimitable way, he would point out the consequences of certain actions and leave it to me to draw my own conclusion. I can honestly say that I've learned more from Winston about the essence of life, than from all the years I'd spent in the seminary. I don't mean about the biological progression but the real essence that seemed to permeate Winston's Universe, in a way that was hard to understand, let alone explain. Winston seemed to have his being as much in our mundane reality as in any other he chose to adopt. His mind, his very presence, seemed to oscillate between some parallel intangible realities. And, on occasion, he allowed me, and apparently Jo and Mo, to catch a glimpse of those elusive worlds.

Winston was not an ordinary man.

"In one hour we're leaving for Mirabel, Peter," Ruth announced.

I was already packed and ready. I went downstairs to say good-bye to Winston. I was hoping for some last-minute advice. I was deeply tempted to ask him what he thought about my present job, about my trip to Rome and Geneva, about all sorts of things that still gnawed at my disorderly mind.

"It seems to be unfolding rather well, don't you think, Sir," was his enigmatic comment.

When practising medicine, I knew exactly where I was going, and why. Lately I'd been groping in the dark. I was reminded of an old quotation that, at one time, had given me a smattering of an answer regarding the influences that seemed to have taken over my life. The quotation was from John, long ago my favourite evangelist: *The wind bloweth where it listeth, and thou hearest the sound thereof, but canst not tell whence it cometh, and whither it goeth: so is every one that is born of the Spirit.*

At heart, I was still a scientist, trained to use my mind in the most logical way I could. Yet, since the 'gift' took control of my life, few things had obeyed the laws of logic. I seemed to have repeatedly stumbled on a predetermined order of things, or events, and only when I resisted the course they outlined I knew, subliminally, that I was exercising my ego, which was not supposed to come into my life. At least not more so than absolutely necessary to sustain my body and soul in a reasonably symbiotic relationship.

Had I stopped resisting whatever it was that was taking me on a trip that ultimately led far beyond Rome or Geneva?

"Yes, Winston. I think it is," was the best I could come up with.

"Please be good enough to pay my respects to Miss Mondellay and Miss Walesa," he added with a grave face. This profound facial gravity worked better on other people. I'd already learned to detect the sparkle in his eyes, which seemed to negate taking anything too seriously.

Nevertheless, coming from Winston it meant that the two ladies had an intrinsic role to play in the unfolding of my personal Universe. I didn't expect to get much more out of Winston. He was already going upstairs to get Ruth's baggage. He came downstairs precisely when the front doorbell announced the arrival of the Solidarity limousine that would take us to the airport.

"Ah, there you are, you two. Don't forget Jo's math, Winston, he must practice it daily."

Jo much preferred imaginary trips to faraway places than the cold equations.

"No, Madam. The young master will practice it daily."

Ruth knew she could trust Winston. Even an excellent private school couldn't cater to all the individual children's needs. For some reason she couldn't quite understand, neither of her children had been known to ever question any of Winston's instructions. The peculiar thing was that I don't think I had ever heard Winston raise his voice, or even use anything but the gentlest persuasion.

That was Winston. He coaxed, he cajoled. Or maybe it was Black Magic.

My next pleasant surprise occurred at the airport. In fact, a series of surprises. Remember, I'd hardly left home during the last year or so, and I certainly was not used to VIP treatment. Our limousine entered by a side gate, which cut a virtual tunnel in the mounds of snow that had fallen last week. The first true Canadian winter storm. Today, at long last, we were blessed with blinding sunshine that glittered and sparkled on the ubiquitous luminous blanket that made the whole world look fresh and clean. I'd forgotten how beautiful winter could be. I'd forgotten a great many things. Only the chill reminded me that we must always pay our dues. Even for beauty.

We continued along what looked like a private road to a hangar built well west of the main building. The gate opened as we approached and we drove right in. I had a *déjà vu* of people being kidnapped in just such a manner.

I needn't have worried. A uniformed officer with Solidarity insignia on both lapels opened the car door and asked us to follow him. Ruth did so immediately, with me following her, my neck craning in all directions. We were led to a lounge where another uniformed gentleman asked us if we had anything to declare.

"Only my brother-in-law, George," Ruth replied, gracing the man with a disarming smile. She was getting very good at that. Charming men, I mean.

"Very good, Madam," the man saluted and turned towards me. "And you, sir?"

I decided to play the game. "Only my sister-in-law, officer," I said, half expecting to be arrested for playing hanky-panky with the security guards.

"Please follow me," the man replied without another word.

We passed through three doors that were evidently needed to shield us from the main hangar where a streamlined beauty was already warming up. This time I really did experience a stomach constriction. The supersonic jet looked like a twin sister, or was it brother, of the airplane that I remembered from my previous experience of flying with Solidarity. Only now nobody's pocket seemed to bulge over a concealed weapon.

"Have a pleasant flight," the man said saluting.

We stepped on to a platform that whisked us forward and up to an aperture that was already opening. We entered the plane from underneath, not from the side as I was used to. Correction. As I'd done the few times I'd flown in my life. And the plane was the latest model, after all.

"We can use it to evacuate in case of unforeseen problems," Ruth explained making the unorthodox entry perfectly clear.

"They just kick us out?" I asked feeling none too witty.

"Something like that. Inside capsules that absorb the supersonic speed."

I never thought of leaving a plane flying at supersonic speed. I suppose that 007, or probably a 0007 by now—the films never ceased—would have used such a method in lieu of an ejection seat. For some reason the knowledge that we might be called upon to jump out at 15,000 meters did not help my waning confidence.

"Do you expect trouble?" I asked, hoping for a strong negative answer.

"Solidarity has over two billion members. And almost as many enemies," Ruth said. Then she looked at me. "Peter, I fly, on average, at least once a month. As you can see, I am none the worse for it. Just relax and enjoy it. We are much safer here than in any commercial aircraft."

Now I was really worried. So commercial aircraft were unsafe? I suppose we have firing power to repel any enemy aircraft. All my aspirations regarding my destiny, my presumed or hoped-for destiny of helping humanity at large seemed to pale at the thought of my personal safety. For some reason I had never experienced fear, not even when walking in the middle of the night through districts of Montreal known to harbour the most unsavoury characters, but ending my existence so far in the air left me with a feeling of dread.

"A Black Label for my brother, and a Clamato for me, please?" I heard Ruth saying.

We were already sitting, facing each other, in the luxurious seats of this business executive airplane. I had no recollection of walking down the aisle and reaching my seat. As I looked around, I noticed that there was no aisle. The cabin was designed as a small conference room with a seating area at one end. Ruth and I were the only passengers.

"You *are* a big-wig, aren't you?" I cocked my eyebrow at my sister-in-law.

"Ask Lena. I just do my job the best I know how."

By the time my Scotch arrived, the plane was moving out of the hangar and gathering speed along the runway. Farther away, the white fields began to race in the opposite direction. My seat began to swivel to face the front. In the next few seconds it began to change the angle in relation to the floor, even as the bird rose effortlessly towards the blue sky. We were on our way to Rome, to

Geneva, to Cathy. Somehow the butterflies that whirled in my stomach minutes ago landed on some inviting flowers. I was calm, I was happy. I was filled with a profound feeling that the world was continuing to unfold itself just as it should.

"Cheers, Winston," I murmured, downing the Scotch. I'd never downed Scotch in a single gulp. On the other hand, I'd never been a VIP flying in a private jet before, except for that time on the way to Gdansk to meet Lena. But with Lena strange things were bound to happen, as I was about to find out all too soon.

The Aeroporto Leonardo da Vinci di Fiumicino was exactly as I remembered it. Not that I saw much of it the first time. Ruth and I looked out through the portholes, then at each other. We both laughed.

"No snow!" we exclaimed in unison.

Winter was more forgiving in Rome. Our jet continued to taxi until it disappeared in another hangar. There, we were transferred to an elevator that took us up onto the roof. The next moment we were airborne again. The helicopter, more like a utilitarian taxi, took us towards the Northeast, and in no time at all we hovered over Città del Vaticano. The rotors gave a strained sound as we landed at the tiny heliport.

Time retreated by a few centuries. We walked through the gardens, slowly, trying to pick up the scent of the flowers that were long gone, imagining the immaculate lawns still evident in the winter months, enjoying the feel of the ground under our feet. Minutes later a uniformed guard, still sporting the red, yellow and blue papal colours, opened the doors for us at Solidarity International Headquarters. On his left hip he carried a lengthy dagger, perhaps a sword. His right hand rested lightly on a much more lethal weapon. He may have represented the heritage of the Church, but he protected Lena Walesa.

We'd left Montreal less than six hours ago. There was the time change, of course. At the Vatican it was already evening. As we stood at the door to her office, I saw a voluptuous figure detach itself from the oversized desk and float towards us. In the fading light, with just two directional lamps washing the working area with diffused light, Lena moved like a wave of charm and delight.

"I thought you would never get here," Solidarity's boss approached us with open arms.

"Head winds, Lena," Ruth murmured, as a way of an excuse. "I brought you a surprise," she added.

Ruth had a lot of gumption. Even I knew that the prevailing winds over North Atlantic were westerly. No matter. At Mach 3 or 4 it hardly came into the picture. I kept my brilliant knowledge of climatic air currents to myself. As Ruth stepped through the door, Lena saw me cringing behind her.

"Peter, dear Peter. I'm so glad you could come!"

She really had no idea what I was doing. I truly was on my own, master of my own time. "Wanted to pop up to Geneva," I said, "The European Centre for Gene...."

"To see Cathy!" Lena exclaimed. "How wonderful. I always knew you would come."

This whole meeting was unreal. Here was the most powerful woman in the world, a woman who controlled a budget that nearly equalled that of the United States, rejoicing in her hired help taking time off to see his girlfriend. Perhaps she's an ardent feminist, I wondered. Sticking to woman's rights above all else?

"I was rather hoping to find time to see her," I lied lamely.

"Of course you will. Come in. I'll be with you in a few minutes."

At this, Lena's face, posture, her whole persona underwent a complete change. The effusive hostess looking after her guests metamorphosed into a precise, almost mechanical Commander-in-Chief. Having returned to her desk, she pressed a number of buttons with her left hand, as though playing a harmonium. She issued instructions of ten words or less in four different languages while, with the other hand, she was typing some other data on one of her computers that mysteriously rose from the polished surface of her desk, only to withdraw again the moment she finished working on them. She seemed to be doing the equivalent work of a dozen men and women put together. Ruth and I waited and watched. Well, I watched amazed. Ruth seemed unfazed.

"There, now we are free to enjoy our evening," she announced, a beaming smile once more lighting her face.

From the day I saw the Decalogue inside our humble, one-third replica of the *Marie-Reine-du-Monde* Cathedral, I had had an overwhelming desire to visit, once again, the full-size original. On the way to Lena's private quarters where we had both been invited for dinner, I excused myself. I took a detour, on my own, just to recapture the awe I'd experienced when I first saw the enormous space of the nave, the ceiling that seemed to hover half-way to heaven, the baldacchino in all its glory.

I wasn't disappointed.

One cannot visit the Vatican, cast one's eyes inside St. Peter's, and not see the Pietà. That was what I really wanted to see, again, Michelangelo's masterpiece. Such incredible beauty in such unbearable pain. You might call it the Ecstasy of Anguish. I was almost afraid that, by some miracle, the Pietà would not be there, that it might have been lifted to a higher reality by angels jealous of her splendour.

I entered the Basilica by the doorway leading to the Scala Regia, just next to the Tomb of Countess Matilde, and proceeded past the monument honouring Gregory XIII to the main nave. To my right, the colossal Papal Altar, crowned with Bernini's baldacchino dominated the whole central space. Three times bigger than our humble replica in Montreal, its columns spiralled upwards, ignoring the simplicity, elegance, of earlier days, perhaps omens of later decadence. Mainly bronze, partly gilt. Four giant angels, two pairs of *putti*, Cupid-like children... Saint Peter's keys... sword and book... emblem of Saint Paul... Perhaps it was Paul's rightful place. Had it not been he that really assembled the Church?

The baldacchino was staggering. I remembered it reached up over twenty-eight metres. Towards heaven. Yet, in the context of the Basilica, it was just a fragment. Almost tiny. The left and the right transepts extended to the altar of St. Joseph on one side and Saints Processus and Martinian on the other. They were still both etched, vaguely, in my memory, yet now they seemed far, far away. As for the length of the nave, the Filarete Door looked miles away.

Yet the Main Altar was still as impressive as ever, especially when one stood up close to it. So much work, so much sacrifice to erect this monument to human endeavour. Or was it to God?

Alas, right here, the link with the culture of early Greece and Rome had been severed forever. No wonder some named Pope Julius II the father of materialism. At the time, the late 15th century, this was the biggest and greatest theatrical extravaganza in the civilized world. They just didn't have holography to enhance their effects.

I tried to imagine how the Decalogue would look, indeed, sound, here, in St. Peter's. I tried to imagine Mount Sinai—three times as high, the meeting Moses had, above the clouds, like the ceiling itself, where the Commandments had been etched with the blade of a laser beam, god's finger, onto the stone tablets. It would have been so much more breathtaking. More impressive, convincing. Modern technology made the myths of the past tangible, acceptable. It made them real. You no longer had to rely on an act of faith. You could see what 'really' happened.

"Look, dear, the angels are flying..."

"Look, dear, the Christ has risen... see the stone moving...?"

"Look dear, God touches Adam with his finger..."

"Look dear, look..."

Our faith had been transformed into a series of visual images, an assembly of symbols substituted for spiritual reality. Is there such a reality? Reality of Spirit? The Last Pope thought so. He insisted that we retrace our steps and find it. Or at least try.

For a dreadful moment I wondered if they'd also done 'justice' to the Sistine Chapel. Surely they wouldn't do that. It is one thing to allow the artists to create their images of myths, another to bastardize the images themselves. There was nothing really wrong with the holographs showing us inspired scenes from the distant past. After all, is this not what artists had done throughout history? Is this not what Leonardo, Michelangelo, Raphael, Titian and many other great, immortal artists had done?

Isn't this exactly what Solidarity International was there to protect, to preserve?

What a pity that we did not have other organizations that would make an equal effort regarding the art of the Egyptians, Phoenicians, Assyrians, not to mention the Far Eastern heritage? Alas, even the mighty Solidarity was not omnipotent. Lena may have been sitting on the throne of the Vatican, but, as far as human heritage was concerned, her influence was limited to what the Last Pope had appointed her to do.

It was after visiting hours and the great church was empty. I walked to the ends of the two transepts, then on, around the Main Altar, past the statues of St. Bruno, St. Helena, and St. Elias. Behind me loomed the Altar of Saint Peter raising Tabitha. It was right opposite the monument to Clement X who created a See at Quebec, whose bishop was to depend directly on the Holy See. I remembered that still from my days at the seminary. How selective is one's memory. We remember details that have no bearing on our lives. None at all.

I walked on.

Art, priceless art everywhere. No one could ever afford to recreate such works, much less to maintain them. Protect them from the ungodly… I was surprised how well I remembered some fragments from my last visit. Some were etched in my mind—others seemed new to me.

I reached the end of the nave. I was standing in front of steps leading to the Main Tribune that holds the Cathedra Petri. It is framed by the monuments to Paul III and Urban VIII on the right. St. Peter's Throne. That's where it all began. I looked up.

O Pastor Ecclesiae, tu omnes Christi pascis agnos et oves

"Pastor of the Church, you feed all Christ's lambs and sheep." On my right there was the same inscription in Greek. For Paul's sake?

The Throne looked impressive. Worthy of the First Pope. And what of the Last one? Will his chair be equally as impressive? His Cathedra? Will anyone bother to honour him?

I am within you. And without you. I am also everywhere and nowhere.

The words sang in my ears. Within you and without you. I'd only once heard those words. Here in Rome. At the Vatican.

I am a state of Consciousness. Your soul. Your salvation. Your immortality. Your Lord. Your Master. I am also your friend, your mate, your benefactor... I am Alfa and Omega, the beginning and the end—yet I have no beginning and I have no end.

"And who am I?" I'd asked once before. Who am I, I repeated again.

You are nothing, an illusion. You are a journey, a vehicle, a way, Tao. You are a means of self-realization. You are that which enables me to be that which I am. You and I are one.

"I do not understand."

I know. Nor can you, ever. Trust me.

It was a replay. Word for word. Like an old-fashioned CD, playing in my mind, my heart. Round and round. Where are you, I asked? I heard small laughter. "I am always with you," I heard again and once more that chuckle. "Look behind you."

I spun on my heels.

Before me stood a smallish man. He wore a grey suit, no tie, his hair hadn't been cut in a while. It was that beautiful colour of grey we all hope to have, one day. Slowly recognition dawned on me. I was facing the Last Pope. The man with whom I'd once shared my innermost consciousness. Probably still do.

"How are you, Peter?" he asked. His voice sounded younger than I remembered it. Of course, then, a year ago, he was dying. A year and two months.

"I am fine, Father. I'm fine." For some reason my eyes turned misty.

"I am an old friend, remember? Call me Vincenzo. There is only one Father and he is up in heaven." He looked into my eyes. "Or perhaps down? Or within?" He chuckled again. "Come, let's sit down."

He beckoned me to sit next to him on the steps leading to the Main Apse, the Triune.

"So, my boy, really, how are you?" he repeated as if not satisfied with just pleasantries.

"Don't you know?" I asked.

The Last Pope smiled but didn't say anything. Then he nodded.

"We know each other," he said. "We always shall. I wanted to make sure that you know how you are."

***

8

An Old Friend

"I haven't been here for over a year," the Last Pope mused. The sweep of his arms embraced a lot more than just the last twelve months. He seemed to embrace the centuries that it took to assemble this priceless collection of art and architecture that surrounded us.

Vincenzo Magnani, the Last Pope's original name to which he'd reverted after his abdication, sat on the top step, his eyes sweeping the Basilica with an aura of wonderment. He pointed to various monuments, paintings and sculptures of saints and people of renown, smiling to some of them as though recognizing old friends. To our right, he pointed to the Altar of St. Peter healing a Cripple.

"You were not the first, Peter. Your namesake learned the trick before you," he said, the chuckle never leaving his voice. "The altarpiece is also called the Curing of the Paralytic, a mosaic reproduction of the original by Franceso Mancini. It seems so easy," he murmured wistfully.

"It is, in a way. Only it wasn't Peter who was curing the paraplegic. It was he who is…"

"…who is within him?" This time his laughter echoed in the immensity of the empty space. "I wonder when we will learn that we, of the dualistic reality, must also be of a dual nature. For some reason, we seem bent on suppressing this fact."

I gazed at Bernini's Cathedra Petri, the Chair of St. Peter. He had denied thrice the call of the spirit. The rest of us deny it practically all the time. We reject its very existence. No wonder Jesus called us dead.

Vincenzo must have been reading my thoughts. "Let the dead bury the dead," he said softly. "Luckily we can come to life."

"And then what?"

"And then search, for understanding."

"And if we don't?"

"Then we shall revert to our previous, dormant condition."

Then we shall be dead again, he could have said. There was great sadness in his voice. After all, he'd catered to the dead most of his life.

"I set them free." Again he seemed to be reading my thoughts. "I died. For two thousand years we flooded their minds with rules and regulations, tied their aspirations with liturgical knots, to keep them from finding the truth... Yet the truth shall make you free," he quoted again.

"But what is the truth?" I couldn't help myself.

"You are the truth. On occasion it manifests through you. When you heal. When you lay your hands on them. When you give someone another chance to find what they seek..."

"But it is not I," I protested weakly. "It is the power that... that..." I was embarrassed to use trite words to explain my lack of understanding.

"Peter, my friend. You and the power, as you call it, are one. You and I are one. We are all one. Is this column apart from the Basilica? Remove it and the roof will fall down. That is why life is so precious. Each time one of us dies, dies without understanding, we delay the joining. The unification. You must find the way."

"Me?! Why me?"

Vincenzo lowered his eyes from the ceiling, and once again swept the vast space with his arms. "I will give you all this if you bow before me."

Jesus' temptation in the desert. The devil offered him the world, and Jesus rejected him outright.

"You cannot serve two gods, Peter. You must pursue what is in your heart. Always."

What was the man talking about? Was it about my new interest in genetics? My withdrawal from the mission of healing the sick? Was genetics but an escape from my real purpose? Whichever it was, Vincenzo Magnani, the Last Pope, knew more than he let on. It was evident, at least it seemed very probable, that somehow he was reading my thoughts. For what reason?

There was that theme of duality. The way he put it, we were body and soul. The elemental duality. How do we unite the two into that which is one? Was that my mission? The unification? But why me? I never asked for the healing power to be manifested through me, or through my hands. And what did it have to do with duality?

Then I remembered the short span of time when I travelled from motel to motel, trying to convince people that the healing power lay within them. That once they believed in a particular reality, it became manifest. *If ye have faith as a grain of mustard...* I believed I could heal people as a physician. I worked day and night. I absorbed all that modern medicine had to offer. I really wanted to cure them. And I did. Ultimately with my bare hands.

If ye have faith as a grain of mustard...

I heard a chuckle behind me. I turned slowly. There was no one there. I was alone in the vastness of the Basilica. The vastness of space created as a monument to human faith.

What a waste, I thought. What a waste....

I looked at my watch. I had no recollection at what time I'd entered the Basilica. Time had indeed lost its meaning. Still, I had to hurry. I hoped Lena and Ruth weren't waiting for me. Surely, they were asleep by now. What a shame, I thought later. I'd completely forgotten about paying homage to Pietà.

The next day I met Vincenzo again in Lena's office. I'd spent the morning visiting Pietà, after all, and then wandering around the Vatican's countless treasures. Later I had a snack on my own. Now I'd only dropped in to touch base and apologize for last night. Also to see what, if anything, had been scheduled. Vincenzo was sitting quietly, to one side, while Lena and Ruth were engaged in a heated discussion by the window. Yes, that same window where, in the past, so many pontiffs had appeared to bless the crowds. Urbi et orbi. The gentle gusts of almost non-existent wind wrapped the flowing tulle curtains around both women. For a moment, they looked ethereal. Since they seemed so preoccupied, I turned my attention to Vincenzo. He didn't allude to last night, nor to any part of the discussion we had. I was too uncertain of what was going on to volunteer mentioning it myself. I sat down next to him. In my eyes, the Vatican was still filled with magic. That elusive magic that transcended time, where the past and today met in quiet congruence.

We talked generalities. Vincenzo praised Lena and Solidarity for the great job she and her people were doing protecting the heritage.

"It leaves me free to pursue my passion," he confided.

I looked at the old man. He seemed much older in daylight. He must have been in his nineties. Only his smile remained his usual benevolent hallmark.

"Miss Lena has allowed me to earn my keep in the library. You can't imagine the riches that the Church has accumulated there. For countless years they were kept under lock and key. A lot of the writings could prove invaluable to men and women of today."

"Truth doesn't age," I said.

I was looking at the two women by the window overlooking the Piazza San Pietro. I wondered if Lena ever had time to take advantage of the environment she was working in. Even her own office, particularly in daylight, seemed stripped of the otherwise omnipresent treasures. A simple desk, four renaissance paintings on the walls facing each other, and a dozen chairs disposed in front of her desk and against the walls. That was all. This was a work place, not a museum.

"But what of new truth?" Vincenzo murmured at my elbow. "Once we thought of a geocentric world, then heliocentric. Now? Now we spin around the centre of our galaxy. Tomorrow?" He spoke as though discovering yet another truth.

"The truth doesn't change," I insisted. "Our understanding of it advances with time."

Vincenzo smiled. He looked pleased.

For a while we reverted to more down-to-earth subjects. I said that Lena had told me that while Solidarity was putting its faith in genetics, the Americans were making enormous strides in robotics. She was worried, I told him, that in time the robots might put the members of her organization on the unemployment list. Robots are coming into their own, she'd said. She also claimed that in the States, they need just one man to produce three hundred cars. The rest of the working force was robots. Even in Japan they couldn't match that, she'd insisted

"Then," I told him, "she lowered her voice to a conspiratorial level and told me that what really worried her were the advances in artificial intelligence."

"You could have told dear Lena that AI is an oxymoron. Intelligence is a natural defence mechanism against oblivion. Our will to survive is part of it. Also, we all are little more than robots. In my case and yours, we've developed our bodies to find expression in this reality. It is a temporal..." Vincenzo graced me with a hardly perceptible wink, "ah... temporary arrangement. The art is to learn to enjoy it," Vincenzo said, the twinkle never leaving his eyes.

If I didn't know better, I would think that the Old Pope had decided that life is just a bowl of cherries. A sort of merry-go-round where everyone was allowed to join.

Again I looked up at our hostess and Ruth. How rude, I thought. They're acting as though they were alone. As if Vincenzo and I weren't here. I know that business must come first, but for as long as I've known her, Lena had always been a perfect hostess. Till now. Well, two, or four for that matter, can play this game. With Ruth and me probably leaving early tomorrow, I decided to enjoy my old friend's company while I could. I moved my chair to face him. He seemed quite unperturbed.

Vincenzo had another unnerving characteristic. Each time he opened his mouth to say anything, anything at all, he was shedding some twenty or thirty years of his life. His grey hair, even his deeply lined face, seemed to light up with inner life. Perhaps that was the intelligence he was talking about.

"Are you suggesting, Vincenzo, that we, or at least the members of Solidarity, shouldn't worry?"

"From what I gather, Lena believes that artificial intelligence is a threat to..."

He didn't finish his sentence but I began to feel uneasy. I had a fleeting impression that Vincenzo had access to future knowledge. That was impossible, of course, but... I was too young to be upstaged by a computer. Or a man thinking like one. I still remembered when a computer took on all comers in a game of chess—until Yuri Kovaloff beat it five times in a row after drawing the first match. Later Kovaloff claimed that in the first match he had to learn how the computer thinks, and then, he, Kovaloff, stopped thinking at all. At least that is what he claimed. I doubt this could happen today, or during the last five years or so. The evolution of AI, from what I've read, was progressing on an exponential sequence of growths, separated by short periods of relative stagnation. The knee of the curve had been passed about three years ago. No one could predict where this exponential curve would lead.

Again I glanced at Lena. I could see that her qualms hadn't dispersed after Vincenzo's assurances. She still wasn't listening. She behaved as though she hadn't heard him. Her face retained the usual smile, but her eyes were no longer sparkling. Lena was worried. The strange thing was that her worry seemed directed exclusively towards her people. Could I be reading her thoughts? Or perhaps emotions? Was that possible? That was how she thought of them. Her people.

Let my people go... I remembered from the *Marie-Reine-du-Monde*. Let my people go. The question was where. Apparently I, among others, had been chosen to provide the answer. I had been entrusted to find time enough for the people to survive whatever AI could throw at them. I had to give them longevity to reach their destination. Whatever that might be. I wondered if Lena knew. One thing was sure—anything that denied the supremacy of human being over all machinery or electronics was, in her eyes, a danger to the dignity of the human being.

"I've got to get to know my enemies," I murmured.

Not so much my enemies as the technology that might threaten Solidarity and its workers. But what of the admonition 'sufficient unto the day is the evil thereof'? Was Vincenzo putting those thoughts in my mind? Perhaps AI was the evil of the day. On the other hand, what of, 'I say unto you, that ye resist not evil'?

Why was I preoccupied with biblical sayings? I hadn't practised my religion for years... It must be Vincenzo's presence? I looked at the old man.

Vincenzo smiled and a moment later got to his feet.

"Duty calls," he said over his shoulder, and the next moment he was gone.

For a little while his smile lingered before my eyes. Then, all too soon, the room seemed to have lost part of its light. It seemed half empty. I found this quite incredible. Usually when Ruth, let alone Lena, was around, I was deeply aware of their presence. They invariably filled the room, whatever space they occupied, and managed to harness the energy in that space to the exclusion of other people. Here, an old man, walking with a slight stoop, always speaking in half-tones as though not wanting to interfere with the flow of the world, shut the door behind him and left a vacuum.

I wondered what had happened to him last night, in the Basilica.

Surely, I told myself, surely he must know every nook and cranny to have pulled off his disappearing trick. Why not? He lives here. For years and years. But why wouldn't he mention anything about it today? And then I felt that vacuum again. It was as if he took part of me with him.

"Peter, I'm so glad you could come!" Lena embraced me with her usual smile as if I'd just entered her office.

"Ruth asked me to touch base..."

Frankly, I wasn't sure what I was doing there.

"I reserved our plane for eight tomorrow morning," Ruth said, at long last also turning from the window. "I'll spend the rest of the time in meetings with Lena, and then, around seven, we can have dinner together. Would you like that?"

"You reserved a plane? An airplane?" I would never get used to being included in the ranks of the high echelons.

Ruth smiled. She looked vaguely amused. "Around seven?"

I nodded, waved to Lena and left.

I had a day to myself. I wondered if I could sneak into the Vatican Archives and see Vincenzo again. There seemed to be things that still remained unsaid. Under the orders of Pope Paul V, the Archivum Secretum Apostolicum Vaticanum, the Secret Archives, had been removed from the Vatican Library and, until the late 19th century, were kept absolutely closed to Vatican outsiders. Adjacent to the Vatican museum, I found access through the Porta di S. Anna in via di Porta Angelica. There was a guard at the door, but he merely waved me to come in. I wondered if my face had been circulated on the audiovisual intercom that Lena had installed throughout the Vatican. I'd read somewhere that the Archives were estimated to add up to the linear length of some eighty-five kilometres of shelving. I wondered if I had the slightest chance of finding Vincenzo in such a labyrinth.

For a while I sauntered around on my own, unwilling to disturb the ten or twelve men and women I saw bent over their work stations. About an hour later I found the Last Pope hiding between stacks of parchments, literally hidden from anyone approaching him.

"Pull up a chair, Peter," he said, without turning.

The only person with that much sixth sense I'd ever met was Winston.

"*Buongiorno ancora,* Father Vincenzo, am I bothering you?" It was still before noon. Soon it would be *buon pomeriggio*.

"Vincenzo," he corrected again. "I am too old to be bothered. Nothing I do will affect the future of humanity."

He'd already done that, a year ago. Nothing *I* would do would ever affect humanity as much. But there still was an aura about the man that I could sense even as I approached him.

"You came to talk about your work, Peter?"

Was it that obvious? "Yes, Vincenzo. I need your advice. Do you think I should continue working for Lena?"

"I do," he replied, a chuckle returning to his voice.

Soon we all shall, I wouldn't wonder. "What I meant is that I have this, you know, this knack for healing people. But I don't seem to have any control over it. I can also help them in other ways. At least I used to be able to. What I meant to ask you... is it my duty to use the talents I have, or can I let them remain dormant and take a different road?"

"To where?"

"That is, sort of, what I meant to ask you..." I must have sounded either lost or dumb.

"Why do you think I resigned, Peter?"

"So that we could stand on our own feet?"

He didn't say anything. Then he straightened up his back that till now had been bent over some old manuscript and leaned against the back of the chair.

"Peter, everyone travels an individual path. If it were otherwise, all by one path would be redundant. That would exclude billions of people from the journey. As it is, they are indispensable to the Whole. As for your work, you must ask yourself, always, where is it that you are going? If you can answer that, the rest becomes clear."

"Where are we all going?" I murmured under my breath. He must have heard me.

"All to the same place, only few of us realize it." Those last words carried overtones of sadness. "You of all people should be aware of your mission. After all, you were confident in your actions a year ago."

"That wasn't me, Vincenzo," I said. "That was..."

"Yes, Peter? Who was it?"

I had to sit down. My legs refused to support me. The images of our meeting in the papal chambers, His Holiness working hard to catch his breath... and then that voice...

I, your consciousness, cannot experience anything in the phenomenal reality without an instrument through which such an experience is made possible. It is rather like a photon. The vibrations in the gross, physical Universe are very slow. A photon cannot exist in such a reality. It cannot travel slowly, let alone be at rest.

You have convinced yourself, which means that you have programmed your subconscious, that the physical body is immortal. Well, no reality can deny the rules of a particular plane of perception, but as long as the basic rules are not broken, those same rules permit a great deal of latitude.

"…so we need our bodies to find expression… to advance… I must talk to Cathy, the photons… we are made of quarks and leptons, she said… our bodies are…"

I had to see Cathy. I am not my body, but my body is the means of discovering my way. My road. My Tao.

I looked at Vincenzo. Once more he seemed lost in the yellow parchment he was studying.

"Thank you, Vincenzo," I said softly so as not to disturb him.

I was already some twenty feet away when I distinctly heard a soft, caressing voice saying "You're welcome, Peter. You're very welcome." I spun on my heels. There was no one behind me. Vincenzo must have hidden behind another stack of manuscripts. I have to get some more sleep, I thought. I'm beginning to hear voices.

This made me think of yesterday evening in the Basilica.

It struck me that talking with Vincenzo, yesterday or this morning, or in the library for that matter, neither of us mentioned the word God. Or the Lord. Yesterday he spoke of some saints, important people, but not God. Or any divinity that looked kindly upon our daily struggles, demanding and/or rewarding us for our efforts. Ordinarily, this would be of little consequence, but on all three occasions I had been talking to the Last Pope.

Once again, I met Ruth in Lena's quarters, where the Spartan furniture contrasted strangely with the splendour of the architecture. The coved ceilings, an array of old masters adorning the walls, marble sculptures in recesses flanked by alabaster columns, all spoke of a bygone era. I couldn't see the table; a simple white tablecloth covered it, but the functional fibreglass chairs belonged more in a business conference room than in the splendour of the Vatican. I was willing to wager that the original chairs had been replaced in order to protect them from wear and tear. Apparently Lena took her job as the curator *extraordinaire* very seriously.

Ruth looked tired. It seemed that Lena was a very different person when working. She demanded absolute effort of herself and no less from her lieutenants. I wondered when my turn would come. Yet as she entered the dining room, she'd evidently left her work in her office. She looked perfectly relaxed, practically radiant, as though just returning from an outing, a picnic in the Vatican gardens. The latter was negated when she began eating. Her capacity belied her contours. She had a statuesque body, but apart from the usual accoutrements of womanhood, she carried no excess fat. Her waist would be the envy of any woman half her age, or half her height.

By the time we sat down, there were eight people at the table. Lena's closest entourage, I gathered. Ruth already knew them all and took care of the introductions. They seemed nice enough. Quiet, overtly confident, knowing their place, or presumably their particular expertise. They were the best of the best. I was hoping to see the Old Pope. No luck. Perhaps he'd retired early. He deserved it. He was old enough.

I was seated at Lena's right hand, Ruth at the left. It was evident that we both were her guests of honour.

I felt flattered. I started observing the diners more closely. No one reached for a glass, fork or anything on the table until Lena initiated the dinner. She was the host, but also the queen of the gathering.

While she ate with restraint, she didn't pick and choose. Her plate was left perfectly clean. Her intake of liquid, however, was limited to a glass of water before she started, a half glass of Chablis with the sole Waleska, and another half glass, this time of Burgundy, with an assortment of Italian cheeses. She had no dessert.

I'd never eaten anything that good. The fillets of sole were served in mornay sauce, garnished with lobster and scallops, served in a nest of duchess potatoes. Had I not felt embarrassed, I would have asked for a second helping.

"So, Peter, how are you enjoying your new profession?"

The question came in the middle of the serving of cheeses, when I was convinced that I would get away without having to report on my work.

"In many ways, I find it fascinating, Lena," I said cautiously. "In others it presents a challenge that has philosophical connotations that I haven't quite resolved."

I could have heard a pin drop, had one done so. No one touched their plate. No one raised a glass, or even swallowed. This was my performance and I was the new kid on the block. They were all curious.

I gave a run-through on all I'd gathered to date. The past achievements, the present trends, and finally about the possibilities for the immediate future.

"As I am sure you already know, our way differs from that taken by the USA or the Sino-Indian interests. The USA has chosen to give priority to robotics, with the accent on so-called Artificial Intelligence. There is only one possible outcome from such research. It will make man obsolete. When robots endowed with super-human intelligence are achieved, man will become subservient to his own creation. In minor ways, we already are. Even in everyday life we can no longer function without airconditioners, heat-exchangers, cars, aeroplanes, all sorts of automated machinery and, most of all, without computers. Our children cannot cope with simple arithmetical problems without the use of their calculators. And this is only the most primitive though intrusive aspect of how robotics have taken over our life."

There was some nervous stirring among my captive audience. One or two opened their mouths, swallowed air, and thought better of it. Lena's lips displayed the gentlest of smiles.

"Go on, Peter, we are all ears..." she added unnecessarily.

"Then there are those who have opted for nano-technology," I continued. I was surprised how much confidence Lena's words of encouragement had given me. After all, I'd only researched certain aspects of genetics, so far. I wondered if my thoughts outside the defined field would extend my mandate. I took a sip of water and ran my eyes over the eight people surrounding the table. Somehow, they didn't look so 'intellectually' threatening any more.

"Well, I am not very conversant with the field, but it seems to me that what the Americans are attempting to do from without, nano-technology will do from within. Rather than displacing man 'in toto', they will invade our organisms from within, with countless minute robots, the nanobots, that will invade our blood, manipulate our biological system and all it entails and, eventually, affect the way we think."

Now the stirring was more pronounced. I wondered if some of those present didn't know a great deal more about the subjects I raised than, at this stage, I knew myself. What they were missing was the big picture—the overall analysis of the consequences of the liberties that scientists were taking with our bodies, which nature had taken a few million years to develop.

Yet no one volunteered to add anything to what I'd said. Suddenly I felt on the defensive. I was criticizing matters I knew very little about.

"And we, Peter," Lena's voice was hardly above a whisper. "Are we, Solidarity International, just as guilty?"

I welcomed the interruption.

"We, Lena, we at Solidarity, are no longer concerned with healing the sick, the Alzheimer's patients, or even the paraplegics. The hospitals do that. What our researchers are working on is the improvement of the healthy. Those that are well but want to do better. To improve not only our bodies, but our minds, our ability to absorb and retain new information. Ultimately..."

I stopped short of the subject of immortality.

"Yes, Peter?" Lena coaxed, again, hardly above a whisper.

"Well, ultimately they are determined to conquer death...." There was a more lively stirring among the guests. Only Lena and Ruth remained perfectly still.

"Is that where you have philosophical reservations?"

I nodded. I was thinking that had this happened sooner, the Last Pope would remain with us for years to come. Perhaps forever.

Slowly the hum of conversation returned to normal. Most present hadn't heard about the latest research in genetics. They were impressed.

"What a pity you didn't invite the Last Pope; he would have had something to say on the subject," I said.

Lena looked at me with a quizzical gaze, shaking her head from left to right.

"What a strange thing to say, Peter. The late Pontiff died earlier this year. He asked to be cremated quietly in case someone wanted to make relics out of parts of his body. Didn't Ruth tell you?"

***

Robotics

The more the universe seems comprehensible,
the more it seems pointless.

Steven Weinberg
1979 Nobel Prize in Physics

9

Geneva

Already in bed, I switched on the TV just to check on tomorrow's weather. My stomach doesn't take kindly to rough stuff, especially over the Alps. When I flew from Gdansk, one of the passengers, a nun, began to recite her rosary, aloud, over a particularly wobbly part of the crossing. It did nothing for my stomach.

The weather forecast had been pre-empted. Splattered across the whole screen were the American Stars and Stripes, with a sign, flashing on and off, that announced:

L'AMERICA LAVORA PER TUTTI

This sort of thing began some years ago when the United Nations withdrew its backing from the American armed invasion of a minor, what was once called, African banana republic, to pacify the local warlord and stop them from performing mass executions of the 'disloyal opposition', which had been duly elected by the citizens of the Republic.

The USA had decided to get rid of the power-hungry junta on their own. They accomplished their end with their usual efficiency. The army barracks had been razed to the ground in a single overnight air raid. Early on the succeeding morning, the military junta had promptly left the abused country.

Two weeks later the UN offered, in compensation, to pay for the financial burden that the US had borne on their own. Later that year, a motion was unanimously carried: only the USA had the military clout to carry out 'police actions' in troubled areas of the world, and the UN Security Council would limit its backing to a democratic majority vote, and not a unanimous agreement as had been necessary in the past. Also, the motion stated that while the US would carry out the military actions on their own, the financial burden would be borne equally by all member nations of the UN. Once again, the vote was unanimous. As for the financing, well, what's another point or two added to the already overtaxed citizens? At least they didn't have to dip their fingers in blood and could look the other way with a clear conscience.

This motion had only been passed after many years of mostly failed attempts to create coalitions that would take care of nations indulging in disorderly conduct. The concept of coalitions was perhaps unfortunately buried in stacks of bureaucratic paper. Some written reports ran into more than a thousand pages, all of which had to be translated into all the official UN languages. By the time the politicians finished reading, discussing, and cogitating what action to take, the problem had usually spread far and wide, forcing much wider and more expensive actions than what would originally have been necessary.

With the passing of the motion, the UN had decided, at long last, to occupy itself with the aftermath of such actions, not with the initial surgical incisions. For that only one nation had the necessary clout.

The US officially became the World Police.

Strangely enough, the moment the UN was absolved from the 'police' functions, it became a vastly more efficient organization. It handled its assumed responsibilities with alacrity and precision. The UN had finally come of age.

But the annoying, flashing sign on my TV was not what caught my eye. Such announcements always preceded statements pertaining to forthcoming military actions by the US. Below the

Italian title affirming that America Works for Everyone, there were a series of buttons that enabled one to listen to the news in the language of one's choice. Or at least the dozen official languages of the UN. I clicked English and listened, my disbelief growing with each word.

...the first time in history, the requisite relief action will be fully automated, with the human component staying back a safe distance from the enemy lines. Further...

While the word 'relief' was used loosely, the sentiment was well understood. At any rate, for me that was enough. Lena was right. The robots were displacing their human counterparts. Had she already heard about this before she spoke to me? Was she attempting to jump the gun? I still had no idea why she'd chosen me to act as her adviser. Frankly, I didn't like this one bit. By nature I am a loner. I like to keep to myself and the closest possible circle of friends. Public domain lies outside my interests. On the other hand, I did need a job. Any job.

I don't get depressed very often. In fact, with the sole exception of the time when Winston rescued me from my near catastrophic sojourn at Gaston's and brought me back home to Westmount, I don't remember ever falling flat on my emotional face. Actually, there was that one other time. The day I'd discovered my healing power and the consequent requiem for my medical career. But that was about it. Usually I thought of myself as reasonably sane.

I liked that—reasonably sane. Rather than unreasonably.

And now this. The USA playing soldiers. With robots?

I spent the night tossing and turning, unable to find peace. Paradoxically, I also felt myself restrained in a straitjacket, unable to move. I woke up in total darkness. My hands were still bound, painful. I discovered that I was lying on my stomach, squeezing the life out of my pillow with both arms. I turned over and tried to reason things out. I didn't get very far.

Did I really imagine all those meetings with Vincenzo? Should I put myself in psychiatric care, neatly wrapped in a strait-jacket for my own good? My own protection? Had my dream been an omen? A message? My subconscious trying to drop me a hint? What if I were driving a car and started hearing voices telling me to turn left or right, or smash into the oncoming traffic? I was no longer a reliable driver of my own vehicle, my life. Of my brain, my body.

I had to escape.

I had to escape from any environment that inspired such a state of mind. Did the Vatican bring about such images? Or did I merely permit myself to wander, to let my mind look for its own satisfaction, to make up for the long-carried sense of guilt for that original escape? The escape from the church of my youth?

Questions. I wished Winston were here.

Last night, on the way to my room from a walk on the Vatican grounds, I saw a man staggering along, then leaning against the wall in obvious pain. I turned toward him and then, for a reason I couldn't understand, I held back. What gives you the right, I listened to my own thoughts, what gives me the right to interfere with the man's karma? Who is to say if this was the last payment he was making on an old debt, perhaps from an incarnation or two back, that would free him to advance to a different reality, a different world that we all, at one time or another, seem to be searching for? There had to be different realities.

I had to escape.

When my gift began overriding my free will, I was losing part of what made me human. I was merely reacting, not acting as a free agent. I was becoming a spiritual cowboy, sating my own needs, not helping others to find their way. I had to learn to wait and see. To help when asked—not to volunteer. I'd already learned the hard way, back at Gaston's, not to cast pearls before swine. It had cost a woman her life. Somehow I'd gotten away with that. I might not, the second time.

I had to escape.

The question was where. Or how. I wasn't even sure what exactly I was running from, but my whole being, my psyche, was in a state of utter rebellion. I wanted to shout, 'No, I will not!' *Leave me alone... let me be... let my people go*. Was this how the Hebrews felt before they left Egypt? Restrained, rebelling? *Let my people go...*

I switched on the bedside lamp. It was three a.m. Today I'd see Cathy. Dear Cathy. I would make love to her until I reached a state of total oblivion. Until my body, the body itself, took over all my mental and even emotional functions. Until I was no longer able to think of anything but her beauty, her sweetness, the softness of her breast, her mouth.

Dear Cathy. *Please, please help me to escape....*

My holiday was over. We were up at six for a final briefing from Lena. I felt as though I were escaping from a reality I couldn't handle. The Last Pope, Vincenzo, rattled me more than I cared to admit. I also felt like a bit of a fool. If it hadn't been for Lena's obvious fondness for me, which apparently included my quirkiness, if such it was, I would surely have been dismissed from her immediate entourage. As it was, Lena seemed not only to have faith in my sanity, but ascribed my esoteric, if not psychotic meetings with Vincenzo to my secret talents. I was not prepared to argue otherwise.

"We are all clear on your Canadian procedures," she said to Ruth, one hand on her shoulder in trusting assurance.

Ruth nodded.

"As for you, sir," she turned towards me, "I was very impressed with your report on genetics, as were my lieutenants. I'm sure you'll advance your research still further with the European scientists, and report to us in due course."

I breathed easier. After my comments about Vincenzo, I wasn't sure she would take my efforts seriously. On the other hand, I hadn't been told about the Last Pope's demise, and there was no real harm in pleading my ignorance. Yet for the next week or two, I would thank my lucky stars that I hadn't shared with anyone my joy at having met Vincenzo on three separate occasions. I'd been told that Solidarity had the best psychiatrists on call, but I didn't feel like being taken under their wing. Anyway, no one mentioned the matter again.

And then I noticed that Lena was looking at me in a strange, slightly embarrassed way. Well, here it comes after all, I thought.

"I wonder if I can impose on you a bit further, Peter," she said. "I really have no one to whom I can entrust this matter..." She looked pensive and slightly lost.

I marvelled how this magnificent vision of womanhood, this personification of Mother Earth, managed to look like a little lost girl.

"It's robotics, Peter. They worry me. I really need someone of your abilities to look into it. Ruth will give you a few names you might contact for me. I am sorry, Peter, I know you are already busy..."

I wasn't busy at all. I had been *busy* studying for my Fellowship. I had been *busy* when healing people in a forgotten tavern in the middle of winter. Now? Now I am coasting in neutral, I mused, though I kept my thoughts to myself.

"I'll be happy to look into it, Lena. It will be my pleasure," I assured her.

The little girl was gone, an effusively grateful woman returned.

"I knew I could count on you, Peter. I'm very grateful."

With a final embrace, a kiss on both cheeks and a surprisingly strong squeeze of my hand, she was gone. So much for a little lost girl, I thought.

"I thought she handled you rather well, my brother," Ruth giggled softly. "She did that to me about a year ago. I've been working for her ever since."

It was a smaller jet, the business executive class, and not even supersonic. After all, we were only hopping a few hundred miles. Even so, the business executive offered a lot more than a standard Y class on a commercial traveller. The seats were wider, they reclined lower down, and there was a footstool that slid from under the seat to support my outstretched legs. In front of me there was a TV that slid miraculously down from the ceiling. It was equipped with touch selection choices. But I wasn't about to waste my time flicking the channels when the view through the oversized side window offered the snow-capped Alps in all their glory.

"There's nothing on," Ruth said, seeing my eyes glancing at the screen. "There seldom is anything, these days," she added.

We had breakfast on board, then relaxed looking at the mountaintops. The eastern slopes were awash with morning sunshine that stopped only at the dark line of conifers marching upward in their Sisyphean effort. The western sides of the mighty Alps still hid mysteries in their deep valleys. The peaks sparkled the brightest, with just occasional rocky crags denying the snow any foothold. The world was a beautiful place. I found it hard to believe that so many people managed to create so many problems for themselves. Often for others. We seem to create problems and then strive to overcome them.

For a moment I sat back to rest my eyes.

Apparently, Solidarity wanted to outlive everyone, while the Americans were determined to outdo the rest of the world in making money. And China and India wanted microscopic robots. Everything was directed at our bodies, at our physical enclosure, or at the very least at adding comfort to our mundane existence. Not that I was against such a sentiment. I liked comfort as much as anyone. Yet somehow... it just didn't seem enough.

"So how did you like Lena this time?" Ruth butted into my thoughts again.

"I cannot but admire the woman," I said. I meant it. Lena was in a league of her own.

"She *is* rather special," Ruth confirmed, looking through the window.

I pressed a button and my armchair lowered itself to a near horizontal position. Yes, I thought, there is nothing wrong with physical comfort. I glanced at Ruth, who did exactly the same. We exchanged smiles.

My thoughts returned to my previous meandering. Didn't anyone believe any more, I wondered, in that thing called soul? And if the soul, by whatever definition, was just an old wives' tale, then what of that esoteric power emanating from my hands? What of my meetings with Vincenzo? Perhaps I'd been imagining both. Perhaps I shall straighten up in my chair, wake up, and discover that I'd had a fascinating dream. Or, also just perhaps, I'd realize that I had visited an alternate reality that is there, ready-made, waiting for us—intelligent apes—to enter when we are finally ready.

"Is there anything I can offer you, Sir?"

I died and went straight to heaven. This wasn't the same girl who'd served us breakfast. This was an angel in her private realm hovering over the Alps.

"No, thank you, Miss," I purred.

"Captain Costello," the angel corrected. "At your service, Sir," she added, seeing my stupefied expression.

Eighteen months ago I'd have suggested joining the mile-high club. Now? *Ad majora natus sum*, I murmured. And Cathy, I scolded my disorderly thoughts.

The Captain moved away with a gentle sway of her hips. I closed my eyes. So much has changed... So much has changed since I left the General. So much since I'd walked out from the seminary.

I was long past believing in the Big Juju, in a benevolent, or for that matter merciless, God of the Old Testament, but I couldn't accept that there was not more to being us, to being human, than just our body. Cathy insisted that we are made up of quarks and leptons. Perhaps. But what keeps them together?

Whatever kept the Captain's legs together was doing a marvellous job. From my deeply reclined position, I noted that the angel had calves descending with a gentle, elegant swoop towards two perfect, slim ankles.

I liked legs. I liked them a lot.

What made those legs, ah... those subatomic particles come together in a form resembling a human being? A God named Evolution? If we were created in the image and likeness of that which some still call God, were they referring to God's body? And if not, what was it that we were emulating? And even if we were made up of just quarks and leptons, isn't the whole greater than the sum of its parts?

And what a body...

It was the intangible, the elusive that held me in its spell. What was more, that which from a scientific point of view isn't, which literally does not exist, was repeatedly manifesting itself in my life. *Visibilium et invisibilium omnium.* The church had thought of that long before the scientists invented the electron microscope. Or the cyclotron, for that matter. Dear Cathy. *She, too, had a marvellous body.* There had to be a reason.

And talking of bodies, I mean reason, I wondered where Cathy fit into the scheme of things. While I was quite happy knowing her exclusively for her charm, her beauty, her sparkling intelligence, the touch of her fingertips, the smoothness of her skin, the... *And her ankles weren't half-bad either.* I began to suspect that all these might well be just icing on the cake. Cathy was so much more...

Also, there had to be a reason that fit into the destination towards which, according to Vincenzo, I was advancing. Continuously. A destination to which I was determined to take Cathy. Or at least a reason according to my vision of Vincenzo.

Perhaps to a field that lay beyond the doing right and doing wrong.

The eastern sun continued to kiss the tips of white crags. They shimmered, sparkled, seemed alive. For whom had such beauty been created? Who looked at those peaks before man learned to fly? I pointed to them even as Ruth did the same to me. Her eyes were full of disbelief, as, I suspect, mine must have been.

Intelligent apes?

On the other hand, Vincenzo held that we are all progressing, even if apparently at a snail's pace, toward the same end. I always preferred to think of it as advancing towards a beginning. The church used to call it, Life Eternal. They called it *vitam aeternam,* but their vision implied a status quo. An Eternal Stagnation. An achievement that could not be exceeded. In my vision, the beginning was just that—the Beginning. Like in the Revelation of Saint John. *And I saw a new heaven and a new earth: for the first heaven and the first earth were passed away.* For some reason the apocalyptic verses I once studied were coming back to me. *And there was no more sea,* John had continued.

I closed my eyes.

Sea, in biblical symbolism, usually represented our mental aspect. The subconscious, to be more precise. Thus, this New Life would not be hampered by the dross we'd accumulated over millennia of evolution. A fresh start characterized by spontaneity. Life to me always represented change, and change meant excitement.

I opened my eyes. I would hate to end up in a religious heaven where I would sit for eternity gazing at my own navel. *There was so much more one could gaze at...* Or even God's navel, no matter how big or divine.

"That's Lake Geneva," Ruth said, putting away her notes.

And for now, I would rather gaze at Lake Geneva.

Cathy was at the airport. She looked radiant. Radiant but, on closer examination, there were signs of fatigue in her eyes. The sort I used to get from staring for endless hours at my computer screen. They hadn't invited her to CERN for her beauty, only for her brains. Although they would have done pretty well on either.

"They must be nuts," I murmured.

"Who, darling?" She tilted up her mouth for another kiss. We had a lot of catching up to do.

"Never mind. Is there room enough for Ruth in *our* place?" I asked, stressing the word 'our'. I knew about Ruth's plans, but I wanted to show off.

"Even if we make it a *ménage à trois*," she winked at Ruth.

"With my own brother?" Ruth looked utterly shocked.

They both chuckled. Ruth had previously told me that she was leaving Geneva that same day, as her next meeting in Montreal had been scheduled for ten the following day. It turned out that she had meetings today, also, in Geneva. After a cup of coffee at the airport, Cathy dropped her off at the United Nations building, the UNOG. With more than 1,600 staff, it was the biggest United Nations duty station after the Headquarters in New York. She referred to it as the Heart of Europe.

There we said our good-byes, and, for the first time in months, I had Cathy all to myself for as long as I chose to stay.

It turned out that Cathy did not rent a romantic apartment overlooking Lake Geneva. She had been spending so much time at work, that the best she could do was to accept a single-bedroom *pied à terre* on the French side of CERN. She walked to and from her laboratory every morning. It would have to do.

Over the second espresso, Cathy described to me the function that Geneva still played in the world.

"There are more than fifteen million passengers landing and taking off from the Geneva International Airport every year, but the operation is as smooth as the proverbial Swiss watch," she said. "Fifteen years ago Switzerland threw her lot in with Europe, but there is still an atmosphere of neutrality about the country. If the USA or China or Russia or India or any of the African countries want to make unofficial inquiries about any of the European facilities, they still drop unofficial hints in Switzerland."

"And Zurich?"

"Zurich is the centre of business. Banking and law mostly. Geneva is the political hub of the World. The offices of the United Nations, the Advancement of Human Rights, and a goodly portion of international research into vast areas of pure and applied sciences, still prefer the implied neutrality that Geneva offers. Even as national boundaries come down, individual cities gain in importance."

"Not to mention CERN," I smiled.

"It is the world's biggest, and the best," she admitted. "And the work we do is sponsored by 183 nations. Both financially and in terms of manpower."

We went for a long walk around the CERN installations. There was practically no snow, and what little there was seemed meticulously cleared from all the paved areas. I told Cathy a little about the Vatican and mentioned my experience with the Last Pope.

"I wish you'd been there. In the end, I made a complete fool of myself suggesting that he should have been invited to our farewell dinner."

"Didn't he die earlier this year?" she asked.

Apparently I was the only one who had been kept in abject ignorance. I promised myself that I wouldn't shut myself away from the world, regardless of the work I was doing. My total commitment also meant total exclusion of everything that was not directly connected with my work. And before that, I seemed to have been in a semi-dormant condition, both mentally and emotionally.

"Got your God particle yet?"

This was meant as a joke, but Cathy's face turned serious. "The Higgs? We're close, Peter. Very close..." There was a dreamy quality to her voice.

In the years I'd known her, I'd never seen Cathy so completely engrossed in her work. Except for the casual remarks about Geneva and the beauty of the surrounding country, her mind was turned inwards. There were moments, even during the first hours of my arrival, during which I felt that I was interfering with her work. I knew the feeling she had. I'd felt the same way when I was working on my Fellowship.

"And then?" I asked.

"I never thought about the 'what then', Peter." She paused. "I suppose then we shall know what God is made of..." she said slowly.

"Quarks and leptons?"

"No, Peter, that's us. God is way smaller...." she mused.

"What a funny way to describe God," I laughed. "Usually people think of Him as enormous. In fact, infinite."

"If you get enough quarks and leptons, you also get close to infinity. But seriously. Wouldn't you like to find the link between energy and matter?"

"Is that what the bozo is?"

"You're a bozo. I am looking for boson, with an 's'," she corrected with a straight face.

Her eyes were shining, filled with the divine energy that she was seeking. She must have felt the way I did when I was talking to Vincenzo.

"I don't care what I am, as long as I am close to you..." I murmured. I felt like a robot singing the same tune.

She ignored me. "Do you think that there is something beyond energy and matter, Peter?"

"Is there something that we cannot measure you mean?"

"What a strange way of putting it. Well, I suppose... yes."

"Then my answer is also a resounding yes."

"I wonder... Do you know, Peter, that they have mathematics to support the idea of parallel universes? Of universes that wink in and out of existence in the blink of an eye?"

"Is that good?" I didn't follow her reasoning.

"It means, Peter, that there are countless realities that our religions have touched on, naming them heavens or some other esoteric form of existence, and... well, they may have been right."

"*I knew a man in Christ, about fourteen years ago... such an one caught up to the third heaven,*" I quoted from Corinthians. Cathy looked impressed. "You never told me you knew your scriptures by heart."

"I don't. Sometimes some of them strike a chord in my memory. For no reason."

"Perhaps there is a reason," Cathy mused.

She seemed awfully dreamy for a scientist. Perhaps she was searching for the same destination that I was. At least, according to my friend Vincenzo. Or my image of him. Maybe he, too, was suspended in some parallel Universe that permitted him to make himself known to me.

"Tell me about your boson," I changed the subject. I loved watching her when she talked physics. And also I needed something to distract me from the robots that kept forcing their way into my mind.

"Well, it's not really a particle, not yet, at present it is a field..." she began, her eyes drifting towards the horizon.

My mind reeled... *beyond the doing right and doing wrong there is a field....*

She talked for a while. Hearing her voice was enough. God, how I loved that voice. A total commitment, absolute absence of doubt, absolute conviction that her work, her research was necessary to advance the human race.

"....properties like ripples on the surface of a pond..."

For Cathy, physics was akin to poetry. She didn't just like it, she loved it. It was the world in which she found her fulfilment.

"....to give particles mass, we need a background field that becomes locally distorted when a particle moves through it."

I had little idea what she was talking about. I didn't care. I listened, and I looked and I was replenishing my resources. Even as an engine needs fuel, I needed to be with... to hear Cathy talk.

"....in all respects that matter, the field is indistinguishable from empty space, yet it invades all space and endows it with its presence..."

She could be speaking of the Holy Spirit. Perhaps that was why they called it the God particle. Invisible, indistinguishable, yet all-pervading. Was it science or religion that she was preaching?

She talked for an hour and I listened. By the time she stopped, I realized that, for now, there was no room for me in her life. Hopefully, just for now. Also, the news last night had put pressure on me to initiate my work on Artificial Intelligence. It was no longer a matter of science fiction. It was here and now, and it was here to stay. At least for as long as the USA remained the police of the world.

"It's all so beautiful," she said. "Do you know what a famous physicist once said? I think it was John Lederman, the recipient of the Nobel Prize for physics towards the end of the last century. He said that, one day, when people discover God, He'll turn out to be a beautiful melody. That's how I think of physics. It's a beautiful melody where all the notes fit precisely in the right place to create a most beautiful harmony…."

She could go on like this for a long time. Perhaps forever. Like the Universe. Or like God. Or like my love for her that I knew wouldn't diminish with time. It would go on and on, and on, until it permeated the very space I live in. Like Higgs field. Forever.

I decided to fly back with Ruth. Cathy saw me to the airport. She had so much work, she couldn't stop talking about it. She said that she would be back in Montreal early next week. Or the week after. My amorous designs would have to wait. After all, Lena herself had commissioned me with new work. I held Cathy in my arms for a long time. We no longer needed to talk. Yet, for some reason I couldn't explain, I became convinced that she and I were definitely advancing towards the same destination. Whatever it might be, we would get there together. And live together. Like in a bedtime story—happily, ever after.

***

10

Almost human?

A single call to Ruth's office introduced me to the Solidarity chief expert on Artificial Intelligence.

"His name is John Robb, known to his friends and enemies alike as JR, not that he has any enemies...." Ruth's secretary rattled on. I often wondered how Ruth managed to put up with her. Finally, one day, I asked her. "Why Janie?"

"Why Janie?" Ruth repeated, looking at me in disbelief. "Janie knows everybody," she affirmed indignantly as if that qualification alone made her indispensable. Perhaps it did.

My own secretary, Miss Dibbs, a lady of very few words, nodded, knowing of JR the moment I mentioned his name. An hour later, she admitted him to my office. I was looking at a tall man, lanky, with long dangling arms and a thin, horizontal moustache of the straightened-out handlebars variety, from which his arms seemed to hang down to his knees. If he was an example of advances in artificial intelligence, let alone of robotics, then they hadn't done a very good job on him.

And then he smiled and all previous reservations vanished. The unsuccessful robot turned into a delightful man.

"I'm told you met Miss Walesa," was his opening line. If his mouth broadened any wider, it would crack.

I got up and shook his hand. A warm, firm handshake. I wish I could have said that she'd sent her regards.

"She asked me to get in touch with you," I said, instead. At least this was partially true.

Apparently meeting Lena, personally, was regarded within the Solidarity ranks as something akin to a private audience with royalty. Mr. Robb was obviously in awe of my stature within Solidarity to have met Lena face to face. The sum and substance of my trip to Gdansk and Rome, last year, had not been advertised. The Walesa guest list at the premiere of the Decalogue, however, was easily accessible. After all, we had sat in the front row of the 'royal box'.

"But, yes, I have met her a couple of times," I said. This was not why he was here. "Sit down, JR. May I call you JR?"

He looked surprised. "Everybody else does."

"I want you to assume that I know nothing about artificial intelligence and tell me all about it." This was as close to the truth as I could get without actually pleading acute ignorance.

"All?" His left hand made an enormous arc as it swung up to scratch his head.

"The basics?" I corrected. "Isn't AI about simulating human intelligence?"

The smile reappeared.

"Not usually or even not often. More than anything it is about pattern recognition—not that we are not endowed with this ability, even if most of us are not aware of it," he looked pensive. "You know, Doctor Thornton, no one's ever asked me this question," he managed to look grotesquely amazed. "They should have...."

I waited for him to gather his thoughts. His eyes narrowed as though inspecting something microscopic suspended in front of his face.

"If we, humans, had as many megabytes in our heads as an average computer, we would overheat and probably explode. Our heads, I mean. The reason we are still ahead of the computers, at least in some areas, is that we can eliminate superfluous information, which does not fit the *pattern* we're formulating. Does this make any sense?"

He looked a little embarrassed. I waited.

"We are not trying to replace the human mind with a computer. Rather, the researchers are attempting for the computer to complement the human mind. To do things that we find difficult or even impossible."

"Are they hoping for some sort of symbiosis?"

"That's the word!" This time both his arms swung into orbit. "That's as close as I could make it with a half-hour lecture. Symbiosis," he repeated, a deep satisfaction widening his smile beyond the usual human capability. Perhaps the man was a cyborg after all.

"What's a cyborg?" I asked.

"In sci-fi or in real life, Sir?"

"Let's stick to real life," I had to smile. The man was capable of grinning and looking worried at the same time. He also used the title 'Sir' selectively. I think he limited it to questions that he regarded as inane.

"A cyborg is a cybernetic organism which adds to or enhances its abilities by using technology."

"That's a Wikipedia definition?" I'd already looked it up myself.

"Well, yes. But it's the correct one."

"Start at the beginning, would you? Pretend I've never read science fiction," I coaxed.

"Well, Sir, as you know, there is a gradual and inexorable progression of men from biological to nonbiological. A great many of us already enjoy neural implants designed to improve our functioning. Many advocate a direct connection to the brain to add to our intelligence. When that happens, we shall all be cyborgs."

For some reason he wasn't smiling when he said that. He looked deadly serious.

"You mean when our brains and the computer are permanently connected?"

"Nothing is really permanent in this world, Sir. But as permanently as we can make it." This time JR did smile.

"Something funny?" I wasn't amused.

"The funny part is, Sir, that I have no idea how on earth we would ever tell them apart."

"From us?"

"From anybody."

I let that sink in. The more I heard, the less I liked it.

"Do our friends, down south, have cyborgs?"

"We all have them. I have personal friends who have artificial limbs, internal organs, even eyes. Cyborgs have been around for years."

I had never thought of the advancements in medical science as producing cyborgs.

"So it's a question of degree..." I was thinking aloud.

"Degree of intelligence," JR butted into my thoughts. "Once we replace or enhance the human reasoning power without recourse to an external source of energy, we will have created fully-fledged cyborgs. In the sense originally conceived by the sci-fi authors."

"And just how far are we from such a... such a creation?" I had to ask.

"Our southern friends, as you call them, probably have one already. Hopefully not an army of them. What we don't know is how operational they are. How reliable. Don't forget that a cyborg is not intended to replace the human race, just some of the tasks that humans, at present, find difficult."

So Lena was right. The members of Solidarity, the workforce, were already threatened. And then I wondered why JR had used the term 'at present'. I asked him.

"While the Americans are working on the practical version of a cyborg, their objective is to create something to perform tasks that most humans not only cannot, but will never be able to do. But I am told that in India, or the Sino-Indian coalition, they are enhancing human capability with nanotechnology. We really do not know who'll get there first."

"There...?"

"Who will produce a superman first, Sir."

While I'd been giving all my attention to internal medicine, the future had arrived. Apparently, in those few years, half of the world had passed me by. As for my last year or so, from the scientific point of view, it was a total write-off.

"Are you saying that there is some sort of competition going on?"

"Why, yes, of course. We are trying to make man as good as he can be. The Americans are trying to make man invincible, and the Sino-Indians are trying to let their man outwit both—us and the Americans. It's quite a game."

He didn't look worried; if anything, there was excitement in his eyes. I was not equally amused. I had to advise Lena on how to protect her people. My God, I thought, I was beginning to sound like a preacher. Lord, Lena, Father... protect my people. Let my people go....

And then I recalled that headline plastered across the TV screen in Rome. L'AMERICA LAVORA PER TUTTI. The Americans had to be invincible to do their job. But what if they decided that the scope of their influence should be enlarged? According to Ruth, the USA was the only segment of the world where Solidarity could not gain a foothold. What if they thought that the best way to assure their military hegemony was to remove as much of the opposition as they could?

"What do you know about Mgambia?" Mgambia was the recalcitrant republic where the US had decided, surprisingly for once with the UN's approval, to restore the democratically elected government.

"That's a bit different," JR looked pensive. "I am not an expert on military logistics. But developing a cyborg with superhuman powers, I mean a robot really, but with the appearance of a human being, would come in very useful in such circumstances."

"Are you trying to tell me that that's possible?"

"The Pentagon seldom makes public announcements. These are released by the White House press office. But what they admit to is often some years behind the experimental models."

And such a robot would bypass any qualms the UN may have about human rights, I thought. I kept this idea to myself. After all, in the not too distant past, the US of A had often chosen to ignore human rights when it suited their purposes.

"Thank you, JR," I murmured. "You've been most helpful."

For now, we left it at that.

On the way home, I passed by a medical clinic. In spite of the purported advances in genetics, indeed, in all branches of medical science, there were still never-ending lists of patients waiting for medical treatment. The problem would remain for as long as the governments continued to subsidize the physicians, or the establishment, and not the patients. More than two years ago, Dr. Brent had told me that if only the bureaucrats helped the poor to cover their medical expenses and allowed the reasonably well off to buy their own medical insurance, they would be able to cut the taxation in the Province by half.

"By half, my friend," he'd insisted. I recall my old mentor pounding his desk to drive the point home. "By half!" He gave his desk one last wallop. This was very unlike my old friend. The rest of the time he was the gentlest of gentlemen.

As I walked past the clinic, I could see through the floor-to-ceiling windows that the waiting room was filled to the brim, so much so that the last six or seven people couldn't even get inside. They were queued outside, leaning against the window of the CSLC, stomping their feet and hugging themselves to stave off the cold. I felt playful. I pulled my hat over my forehead, raised the collar of my raincoat, and joined the line. Then I put my hand on the shoulder of the man in front of me, and asked if he had a smoke. A safe question, as I hadn't met a smoker in at least a year.

"You're kidding, right? What, right here?" he said, pointing at the clinic. The man looked so offended that I suspected he thought I was asking for a reefer. While tobacco had gone out with the continually rising taxes, marijuana had recently been rising in popularity.

After a brief moment the man stretched his shoulders, left and right, then he shrugged in pensive disbelief, looked at his watch, and left the queue. I repeated the exercise five more times, asking alternatively for a cigarette and inquiring what time it was. I held their arms for little more than a few seconds. Each time, within moments, the person before me left the queue and went on his or her way.

I was toying with the idea of going inside the waiting room and moving around until most if not all people recovered sufficiently to decide against waiting any longer. My ex-colleagues of the medical profession thought nothing of being late, of keeping the sick, the infirm waiting, often for hours.

I glanced again at the tired, coughing, sick group inside.

There had to be a better way. Yet, was this not what I was supposed to be doing? Healing the sick? Restoring order and harmony? Besides, the walk-in clinics only removed the symptoms; they didn't cure their patients. I shouldn't feel bad for helping those people. Standing on the street in the middle of winter, with the wind whistling and a penetrating cold and a biting sleet that cut into your face, would do little to help their diseases, whatever they might have been. Yet even a dozen men with my 'gift' would not be able to change the system.

When I got home, I told Ruth about my experiment.

"I just wanted to see if the touch still worked," I said looking at my hands. For some reason I felt a little guilty. It sounded as if I were checking on a machine that I hadn't used for a while, like a heater or an air-conditioner.

"It doesn't seem right," she said, confirming my own reservations.

"But what harm was there in it?" I really needed to justify my behaviour.

"I don't know, it just doesn't feel right. It may have something to do with casting pearls before swine..." Ruth had been getting quite religious since she began working for Solidarity. The old-new style people. The biblical values with modern theatrical performances.

"And I am which...?" I asked.

"Don't be flippant, Peter. Your gift is precious and unique," Ruth was not amused.

I didn't like that. I used to be a physician, and I never thought of attempting to cure people as casting anything before anybody.

"And what of the sun that rises on the evil and on the good, and the rain that falleth on the just and the unjust?" I quoted from memory. I must have been making mincemeat of Matthew's admonitions.

Ruth didn't notice my goulash.

"Perhaps you are right, Peter," she admitted. "I never thought of your gift in quite those terms."

Later that week, Cathy confessed that she drove back from the Geneva International Airport in a rare state of rejection. Her tone was frustrated, but even on the tiny screen of the viphone, she looked dazzling. Her despondency, she told me, was partially my fault. She had been dreaming of my dropping in, of the two of us strolling through the park along Lake Shore Drive, of watching the sailboats coming in and out of the harbour like white butterflies skimming the water... safe, protected by total anonymity. She knew how much I longed to be lost in a crowd. At least she said she knew. I think she only imagined....

"But, darling," I tried to cheer her up. "Surely, there are no sailboats on the lake this time of the year?"

"You know what I mean," she insisted. "And when you finally came, instead of asking about your work, about your new interests, I kept blabbing nineteen to a dozen, about my own stupid bosons."

I smiled my understanding. I, too, had been lost in my work on occasion.

"Why must I be so stupid!" she scolded herself.

The first time we'd met outside of Canada, she had been swept up by the magic of the history of science. She dragged me to the University of Rome, where Enrico Fermi, at the tender age of twenty-five, became a professor of theoretical physics. She just wanted to stand where he had stood, to touch the blackboard on which he'd spent hours in his futile attempts to discover nuclear fission.

"If he'd only used a thinner foil to cover his sample of uranium..." she'd purred dreamily, "...he would have discovered fission there and then."

I suppose even then my ego had suffered because she wasn't hanging on my every word. Not that I'd had that much to say, but Cathy had always been my sounding board. I could never fool her. I needed her for that.

"I swore to myself that the next time we met, I would not utter a single word."

The following week, when I picked her up at the airport in Mirabel, she was almost true to her word. She kept silent for so long that I had to pull up on the service road and ask her what was the matter.

"I want to listen," she whispered. "I want to know all about you," she added, her voice even softer.

"But that's exactly what I want. I want you to tell me more about the bosons, and god particles, and a beautiful melody called god."

"You remember all that?" she looked up slowly, a slight shimmer fogging her eyes. "You really listened..."

For the next few minutes neither of us said anything. Our lips were busy. God, how I'd waited for this moment. Then I drove her directly to the hospital to see her father.

Lena was working at her desk at the Vatican. Towards the evening, her private secretary delivered to her a sealed envelope, stamped FOR YOUR EYES ONLY. This was not the first time such a courier arrived at her desk. She dealt with matters of great sensitivity and a degree of secrecy had been imperative on a number of occasions.

Minutes after I left Cathy at the General, my phone rang. Ruth's secretary told me to come to the Solidarity offices and see Ruth at once. I did.

The audiovisual connection in Ruth's office was already on. I was looking at Lena at her desk, in her Vatican office.

I saw Lena press a button on her desk, presumably her own scrambler. The image shimmered, became absurdly distorted and then stabilized. Her mood seemed pensive, a single vertical line etched on her forehead. She confessed that she'd experienced an unaccustomed feeling. She'd felt fear.

"No one can tamper with the contents of such envelopes," she assured us, and then continued. "For a moment I couldn't believe my eyes. It looked like a badly put-together spy story or some feeble attempt at blackmail. I refused to take it seriously."

Ruth and I still didn't know what exactly had happened. Something was definitely wrong. This was not the Lena we knew, yes, and loved. She was still composed, but the digital camera refused to lie. There was strain in her eyes. Running Solidarity alone did not affect her as did the content of that envelope.

"Inside the manila there was a single, paper-thin CD." She looked straight into the lens of the viphone. "More out of curiosity than anything else, I slipped it into my computer. Soon I was looking at myself, going about my business, answering calls, talking to people. Just then I had an important message to take, and I switched off the CD, to examine it later, if it proved necessary. I still had no idea why anyone would send me such a disc. I've seen myself on hundreds of occasions, performing hundreds of tasks. Perhaps someone was polite enough to send me the disc before it was released to the press. I put the disk away."

"And that's it?" Ruth looked slightly complacent. She'd dropped out of an important meeting just to hear Lena's message. "There was also an eight-by-eleven photograph of some men with me sitting at the head of the table. I was looking at people I knew, people I'd met on a number of occasions. It was a Madame Tusseau gone wrong, a nefarious wax museum. Some of the faces were twisted, showing great surprise. I had no idea why until it hit me." She took a deep breath. "I was looking at the photograph of the United Nations' Security Council, with me at the head of the table."

With that she allowed the camera to glide over the photograph, then to enlarge each face to a life-size image. The images were perfect.

"But you don't sit..." Ruth sounded lost.

"...at the Security Council," Lena finished for her. "Nor do the Presidents of China, India or the United Europe. The only major absentee was the President of the United States."

What followed was a prolonged silence. At last, Ruth smiled feebly.

"A Photoshop composition? They can produce marvellous effects with the latest software."

"I had the same thought, but my experts examined the disc and the photo. They tell me that both are authentic."

"Any ideas?" I asked.

"We have our people at the Pentagon, of course. They may have gotten off the pictures and the CD, but were somehow hampered from including information in the same envelope. To date, I haven't received anything more on the subject. Our people may have been eliminated."

Ruth and I kept silent. Lena sounded as though she were referring to her own people as procuring and passing on to her the information. As for the 'elimination', in Pentagon lingo this meant only one thing. The man or woman who got hold of the CD must have been caught and terminated. The USA were the world policemen, but no one policed the USA.

"But why…?" I murmured. The USA were supposed to be the good guys.

There was little either one of us could add.

"It's as if I were kidnapped, drugged, filmed in these situations and then returned to my offices without anyone knowing anything about it. It just doesn't make sense."

"And you weren't away…" Ruth started lamely.

"No, Ruth. I haven't been away even for a moment." She then turned to me. "The other possibility is that it's not actually me." She paused, thinking. "Peter, I want you to keep working on the AI angle. The more we learn the better. It seems that our friends are more advanced than we thought. But there must be a reason for the particular direction their research has taken. Assuming the photographs are of real people, so to speak. I still don't know much about cyborgs."

Nor did anyone else. If Lena had read my reports, she knew almost as much as I did. Cyborgs are exactly as we are, but with considerably enhanced potential through the introduction of artificial limbs, organs, and other parts. But none of this explained the faces that belonged to people who could not have been in the pictures.

"But Lena.... cyborgs…?" Ruth sounded nervous.

"Lena, is there anything else in the photo, anything that doesn't look right?"

Lena looked down at the photo in her hands. Ruth and I waited.

"The photograph of my grandfather that I keep on my desk. I haven't moved the photo from my desk since the day I moved to the Vatican. In Gdansk, I kept it on the shelf behind me. It's not on my desk in the photo."

"And that's it? Just the photo of your grandfather?"

The famous Lech Walesa on whose early work Solidarity International had been built.

There was no rational explanation for any of it. My mind was still reeling with the possibilities. If it hadn't been for some stuff I'd read recently, it all would have sounded like science fiction. Extensive plastic surgery, or perhaps they'd picked up a strand of Lena's hair in a public washroom and cloned her exact copy? And if they could do that with her, they could do it with anyone. I wouldn't put it past them. The possibilities were staggering. First clone a person, then enhance him or her with bionics, then program them with software embedded in their brains, or in whatever the creatures used for thinking.

If the US wanted to scare the top echelons of Solidarity International, they were succeeding. And if so, it meant that the US were scared themselves, and that meant they were becoming dangerous.

"Right. I have to go show this to my people. Unless the danger is immediate, use only the scrambler in Ruth's office. We know it's safe."

Without so much as bye-bye, the connection went dead. Lena was like that—socially, the most perfect hostess you could imagine; in business she was cut and dry.

It slowly dawned on me why Lena hired me. No matter what the individual expertise of any member of her stuff, what really mattered was trust. She knew she could trust me not to sell myself to the highest bidder. That was worth more than any professional expertise. One could always learn, but one could not become more honest. You either were or weren't. A little like with polygamy. You either were or weren't faithful to your spouse. You could not be a little or even fairly faithful.

There was something else nagging at the back of my mind. By the time I got back to my office it was gone. It came back on my way home with a cold shiver, which had nothing to do with the weather. I was thinking of human clones.

Cathy called me later that day. Her father was already better. "Nothing serious," she said, "but at a certain age parents appreciate their children showing their concern."

Dr. Mondellay had a benign lump removed from his neck.

"He'll be home by tomorrow," she said sadly.

"Isn't that reason enough to celebrate?"

"Of course, Peter, but I was sort of hoping to be in Montreal for a few days."

"And now?"

"And now I can fly back tonight."

"Make it tomorrow?" I almost begged.

It's strange, I thought. Nowadays children expect to be pampered and spoiled by their parents for as long as they live. Cathy was of the old school, or it could have been her Chinese heritage. In China, parents, and not just your own, are objects of respect and devotion. She may have been madly in love with me—almost as much as with her bosons—but should her mother sneeze, she would fly over the Atlantic, to pass her the tissues. Cathy was like that.

"I'm booked on the midnight flight. I have a conference tomorrow…."

"Love you," I said.

"I know... that's why it's so hard to go back."

But she did.

***

11

Winston Smith

Whatever was happening in this big round world of ours, little left a mark on Winston Smith. A colossus himself, within his personal orbit he was the sun around which the earth turned, the earth in which human foibles spun in repetitive gyrations. Winston remained static, even as he moved at speeds that few young men could match. Time and space seemed to have little effect on him. One could not be sure of his age, and other than being a very large man, physically, he often managed to be virtually invisible.

So much for his material attributes.

There was yet another Winston who remained as enigmatic to Ruth and myself as many of the statements he made with apparent ease, or lightness, and profound conviction. He was definitely well versed in various myths, particularly those of India, the ancient India, although he neither broadcast nor even shared his acquired knowledge unless asked a specific question. On one occasion he let it slip that he spoke fluent Sanskrit, as well as the Pali language, in which he read the original canon from which, he claimed, he drew a vast storehouse of knowledge concerning the rules of conduct governing his daily affairs. He also amused himself with *ad hoc* translations of Teluga poems, which he asserted were the most succinct expressions of a great philosophy of life. This must have been close to the truth, because, as far as I was concerned, Winston had never been wrong.

"Each reality has rules that must be learned in order to be fulfilled," he declared.

At the time, I had no idea what he was talking about.

At the personal level, Winston—in the days when I still addressed him as Smith—had saved my life. As I may have mentioned already I, more or less, mostly more, collapsed in the tavern, in the seedy part of Montreal, below the tracks, run by my old friend Gaston. Winston, by means completely beyond my understanding, sensed that I needed help. He came to my rescue.

My stay at the tavern had been a sort of marriage of convenience. While I remained completely passive in my ignorance of what was happening to me, my hands healed people, as a result of which Gaston got extra customers. The ale flowed, big bowls of steaming *bouillabaisse* or *soupe à l'oignon* were slurped daily from early afternoon till past midnight, in vast quantities. Gaston's inn, or tavern, became the Mecca of the poor, the sick, and the thirsty. I took care of the first two, he of the latter. The symbiosis worked well, until the strain of taking upon myself the diseases of so many people had proven too much. Some call it karma, I call it the law of nature. According to Cathy, it is also the law of physics. At the time I didn't know that nothing in this world could ever disappear.

"Except into a black hole," she murmured.

But while both Ruth and I greatly benefited from Winston's presence in our home, his real contribution, particularly of late, was directed at Jonathan and Moira. Within two days of their father's, Andrew's, funeral, Winston had presented himself at the Thornton residence with an envelope addressed in Andrew's handwriting. Apparently Andrew had met Winston Smith in China, where my brother had been building a number of dams across the Yangtze river, known locally as the mighty Ch'and Chiag. I learned later that Winston had performed some sort of considerable favour for my late brother, but I never managed to get any details about it from our majordomo.

"I did what anyone would have done," Winston had assured me at the time, about a month after his arrival, dismissing the matter out of hand. Judging by how he'd helped me at the tavern, this must have been the understatement of the year.

I can still picture, or rather hear, the moment of our first meeting. There was Ruth, slim, tall yet somehow petite at the same time, introducing Winston in her soft mezzo-contralto. The next moment Winston confirmed her introduction, affirming his name in the deepest basso I'd ever heard. He would have made a marvellous God in Brown's Decalogue, without the need of a backup octet. From day one there was a mystery surrounding Winston, which in no way dissipated over the years. At one time, he was even a frequent visitor of my dreams, a feat that no one else, with the exception of Cathy, had ever accomplished.

And now, with Ruth and myself being kept busy by our commitment to Solidarity, or really to Lena, he alone looked after the children. He was their guide and protector; he not only looked after their physical welfare, but somehow became their intellectual, if not spiritual, mentor. At one time Ruth, who had been brought up in a strictly Catholic tradition, expressed her reservations about the set of beliefs Winston appeared to be imparting to her children. I recall one particular exchange.

"Are you trying to teach them about perpetual reincarnation, Winston?" Ruth had asked. Such concepts were at odds with the Catholic teaching, wherein on dying you go to heaven, hell, or a stint in purgatory, which, by the way, has never been explained to my satisfaction. I always held that the earth is our purgatory, and if we don't fulfill our obligations, we shall simply continue hereafter for as long as it takes.

"Not at all, Madam," the basso rumbled in quiet confidence. "I am attempting to teach them how to avoid it."

This is as near as I can remember it. It was so very 'Winston': always unexpected, always beyond the simple, the trite, the ordinary. Winston was not enigmatic, he was an enigma.

In spite of Ruth's reservations, the children were growing up famously. They were joyful, balanced, well versed in social graces if that is not too fine an edge to assign to ones so young. But most of all, the children exuded happiness. Whatever influence Winston wielded on them, it resulted in two happy, well-behaved, exceptionally bright children. They both attended a small private school, where Winston delivered them each morning while arranging for one of the parents living nearby to bring them back. Mo and Jo enjoyed fun and games, but I often caught them sitting with Winston, hardly talking, apparently sharing something that could only be some sort of spiritual communion.

As I never tire of repeating, Winston, in so many ways, was himself an enigma.

One evening I returned home some minutes earlier than usual. It had been a particularly tiring day, filled with meetings with a throng of experts in every field remotely connected with AI, robotics, as well as genetics. As I stepped out of the lobby, I found Mo and Jo sliding down the balustrade, then racing upstairs at breakneck speeds only to repeat the downward glide. The game was accompanied by the euphoria of ear-splitting screams. Winston was standing at the bottom of the stairs, a stopwatch in hand, apparently conducting the escapade with stoic detachment. Was the man deaf, I wondered? Only when he wants to be, I supplied my own answer. I was always jealous of those rare men and women who could exclude noise from their lives. Presumably mothers raising their children can. Or baby-sitting grandmas. Lena's also like that. I am not. I can close my eyes, but I cannot close my ears.

I stopped dead in my tracks.

Before I could say a word, Winston raised one hand, and Jo stopped in mid-step on the way up. He must have had eyes in the back of his head. Mo, already sitting astride the balustrade—too late to withdraw from her turn—continued to slide down, in a ridiculously slow motion as she endeavoured to brake her descent with both hands. Occasionally a squeak escaped the friction between her little palms and the polished balustrade, but otherwise she came down in complete silence. The cacophony of shrieks that I'd heard from the vestibule had vanished into thin air.

At the same time, a long arm intending to take my coat blocked my passage.

"I am happy to announce, Sir, that Miss Mo has bettered her record by point six of a second. She is very promising indeed, Sir."

I stood there flabbergasted.

It was in moments like this that I was brought back to reality. Be ye like little children, I mused. It wasn't just a question of Mo and Jo, but apparently Winston was just as involved, taking the game with all the gravity it deserved. There were god particles, quantum mechanics, genetics, robotics, artificial intelligence, the possible existence of humanoid cyborgs or even clones, and also there were children who were just having fun. And, of course, there was Winston, who would not allow the children to forget that life was supposed to be fun.

"If we forget how important we are, our experience of fun grows exponentially," he once told me. Only now I think I understood what he meant.

The deadly silence lasted at least three seconds.

"Uncle Peter!"

The usual unison of voices accompanied by two bundles of energy reached me at the same time. Had I not been braced against the door and bolstered by past experience, I would have been lying flat on the carpet. The children were not only growing in wisdom, but in bulk and muscle.

Winston, having taken my coat, disappeared, only to return with an extra-dry vodka martini, a taste I had developed, quickly I might add, on my first trip to Europe.

"I forgot it's Friday," I nodded my thanks. While I enjoyed my Martini, Winston limited his bar service to Fridays only. I wondered if he was thinking of my predisposition to do almost everything to excess. This included my medicine, my stint at the tavern, and apparently my present research for Lena.

"You really need a more balanced life, Sir," he repeated from time to time. A year-and-a-bit ago he would not have presumed to comment on my personal habits, but fourteen months ago, he hadn't as yet saved my life.

I stretched out in front of the fireplace. This was as close to luxury as anything I could imagine. A warm home, a crackling fireplace, and a Martini in my hand. Ah, yes. And children who were seen but not heard. Right now, they weren't even seen. After greeting me in the hall, they had disappeared upstairs, probably to take care of their homework. I couldn't help wondering why, people such as Ruth and I, and certainly Lena as well as most of the people she employed directly, lived in a self-induced, or self-imposed, rat race. Nothing would persuade me that one could impel others to work the way we did. Certainly not your average Jane and Joe of the Solidarity ranks. In fact, we slaved so that they might not have to. What a strange inversion, I thought.

Perhaps Winston was right. Perhaps I did need a more balanced life.

My rambling thoughts were interrupted by Ruth's return. She went upstairs to check on the children and, evidently satisfied, came downstairs to join me at the fireside. Winston served her a dry sherry—as strong a drink as Ruth ever indulged in. Of course, neither of us recognized wine as alcohol. The nectar of the gods was an integral part of any decent dinner. Remember Cana, Ruth mentioned frequently. What's good enough for Jesus should be good enough for us.

For a while Ruth seemed lost in her thoughts.

"Shouldn't we be playing tennis, or golf, or do some sailing?" I asked.

"I did once. Now, I suspect, I'll rest when I'm dead."

"I don't know. I haven't spoken to many dead people lately," I mused. "Why don't they appear to us and report on the life style in heaven? Or in that other place that looks pretty cozy this time of the year...."

We both turned at the sound of throat clearing.

"If I may, Sir, Madam. On the subject of the departed. It is not the dead who retain their bodies and allow some mortals, such as us, to afford a glimpse of their existence. It is us, the living, who can develop the ability to reconstitute the characteristics of the dead, that are spread across the matrix of the Universe."

After a moment of silence, Ruth stunned, I pensive, I decided to question Winston hypothesis. A futile attempt at best.

"And just how would we go about it, Winston?"

The majordomo allowed himself the vaguest of smiles. It looked as if he were about to say 'oooo' and changed his mind.

"It is only individuals who are capable of individualization. The Whole forever remains Whole." The two Ws sounded definitely capitalized.

Go figure, I thought. Winston always gave precise answers, it was just that most of us could never understand them. The next time we looked, Winston was gone. Mild sounds from the kitchen told us of his whereabouts.

"I wonder what he's cooking," I murmured, my stomach beginning to show signs of life. I had had no time for lunch that day.

"Something for the living, I hope," Ruth made her interests clear.

And then it struck me that I had never talked to Winston about any of my work. Perhaps I assumed that such would be completely out of his reach. After all, he was an excellent majordomo—the best—but I could hardly expect him to hold opinions about internal medicine, let alone artificial intelligence, or for that matter, on genetics. The awkward thing was that whenever I'd underestimated Winston in the past, he'd proven me wrong.

After dinner we played some games with the children, then raced them upstairs to see if we could match Mo's new record. It remained safe after Ruth had problems sliding down the balustrade hitting each upright, while I hurt my knee on the first turn.

Ruth and I, both invalids, decided to retire in front of the fireplace and lick our wounds. We were both too lazy, perhaps too tired, to climb the stairs and go to bed. For a while we just sat there, hardly speaking. Then I picked up some reports I had brought home with me, while Ruth dozed off in the deep armchair. Winston was judiciously absent. After a while, Mo and Jo came down to kiss both of us goodnight and returned upstairs. Quietly. In fact, the whole house seemed to grow very quiet.

"How do you know when you're being followed?" Ruth asked, without taking her eyes from the flickering flames.

"How would I know?" I wondered why Ruth would come up with such a question.

"You must have been, you know, when you still…"

"…practised my witchcraft?" I smiled at her discomfiture. "Not really, I usually managed to evade them, whoever them might have been at the time."

"I have an unpleasant feeling at the back of my neck... even when I walk around in the office…" she said slowly.

"You have security people?"

"It could have been one of them."

"Why would anyone want to follow you, Ruth?"

I was sure she was imagining things. I really couldn't think of anything one could gain from following my sister-in-law, other than having a very nice rear view, so to speak.

"I thought you might be able to tell me," she sounded disappointed.

We left it at that. Moments later we went upstairs, and I, for one, had a very good night. Ruth couldn't say the same thing next morning. I told her to speak to her security people and see what happened.

The evening following that chat, Ruth ran into the sitting room as though followed by a stampede of elephants. She managed to look even more pretty than usual, as the telltale marks of a bad night vanished into thin air.

"I've made it," she said, smiles all over.

"Nice to see you, too," I replied.

"No, really!"

"Yes, really!"

"No! I mean I made the circuit!" These were all verbal exclamation marks.

I had no idea what she was talking about, and I said so in no uncertain terms.

"You've been drinking Tse Tung during office hours, right?" The Tse Tung was *le dernière cri* cocktail in Montreal. Cathy had told me. She was quite proud of its Chinese name.

"No, silly, I've made celebrity status!" she said, still all a-twitter.

The fact that my sister-in-law was a very bright person did not stop her from being very much a woman. For as long as I can remember, celebrity status was, and is, the secret dream of every woman I've ever met. With the possible exception of Cathy, who always was and most probably will for ever remain a celebrity. And not just in my eyes.

On the other hand, I recently developed an aversion to all celebrities, particularly those related to positions of authority, and, with the exception of my old friend John Brent and Lena, I held most other celebrities in low esteem. Ruth, on the other hand, was a confirmed authoritarian. She thrived on the rules and regulations that, in her opinion, made the world go round. I suppose a certain celebrity status unavoidably goes hand in hand with those wielding power.

I shrugged, giving her agitation the contempt it deserved. I hated crowds, hated celebrities, I even hated being singled out in public for any reason whatsoever. Anonymity was my strong suit, at all costs.

Just as suddenly, Ruth changed the subject. At least I thought she did.

"I saw him," Ruth continued undeterred. "You know that feeling I had yesterday of being followed? Well, I was!" she finished triumphantly.

"And?"

"And what? Oh, yes. I saw his reflection in the glass door. He was taking my picture. A film, I shouldn't wonder. And then, later, there he was again, this time in the cafeteria. I like to be seen by my staff, you know. Good for their moral. Equality and all that. Anyway, when I saw him, he pretended he was repairing the lens or something, but I am sure he was making some sort of record of me."

I kept quiet, but at the back of my neck I felt the slight prickling I sometimes feel when all is not right.

"Did you ask him why he was taking your picture?"

"Well, no. When I got up, he was gone. Very fast on his feet."

"And you think the same man was doing the same thing yesterday?"

"And two or three days before that. I didn't say anything because I wasn't sure. Not that I can really be sure even now, but...."

"Celebrities are never sure. They just take it for granted," I murmured.

"Do you think so?" Taking my words of wisdom seriously, Ruth looked pleasantly aghast.

I gave her a minute or two to settle down from the Olympian heights of celebrityhood before asking the next question.

"How well do you know people in your office?" I already knew the answer, but I wanted to bring the reality of her work to the forefront of her mind.

"Well, there are dozens of them. But for the most part I know them by name. First names mostly. Why do you ask?"

"Was there anything familiar about the man taking the pictures?"

"Why, no. You're right. He must have been a member of some celebrity magazine... or something," she added pensively.

"And do people have free access to your offices?"

"Peter, there are over four hundred employees at Solidarity International Canadian Headquarters. We handle the inquiries of millions..."

"So anyone can wander anywhere in the building?"

"Only if he carries Solidarity identification," she said. "You know that?"

Since about the first quarter of the present century, Solidarity identification consisted of an implant that worked rather like a fingerprint, or a retina scan. It projected directional micro-radiation that triggered a response in a scanning device. Your individual serial number not only confirmed your identity but identified your credit rating. A member of Solidarity International could travel world-wide, without having to open his wallet. It also enabled you to enter spaces designated for members of the Solidarity only. I refused to have anything to do with it. Ruth, after a period of objections, succumbed.

Convenient and secure, she'd said at the time.

And obviously, not secure enough.

“But the man’s face didn’t strike any bells?”

“Well... no. But there is nothing to stop almost anyone from becoming a member of Solidarity. In fact, we encourage it. *In Pluribus Unum* is our motto. We rely on diversity.”

There was an almighty stink when Solidarity, in those early days just in Europe, had adopted their motto. For some reason, no one had checked the use of Latin on the other side of the Atlantic. This very motto, ‘in pluribus unum’ had been used on American coinage for generations. Hardly anyone knew it. After all, whoever bothered to read all the stuff on a bank note, let alone on a quarter or a dime? And what was more, the best way to make the Solidarity motto acceptable internationally, especially in Europe, had been to use Latin. Nowadays, no one identifies the phrase with the coinage. Solidarity won.

After dinner, during which we never discussed business in front of the children, as usual we returned to our armchairs. Happily the children preferred their own room for fun and games, and we were both too tired to impose our presence on them.

Winston cleared his throat. “Might I interest you, Madam and Sir, in a nightcap?”

During winter months we sometimes took a cup of cocoa or a small glass of Porto before retiring. Ruth didn’t answer, probably milling over the events of the day. I didn’t think she was in the mood to talk unpleasant business. I smiled my thanks and shook my head.

“I think we won’t be staying up very long, Winston. Thank you.”

His bulk loomed over me, appearing even bigger while I was sunk in the embrace of the soft leather armchair. What a marvellous cyborg he would have made, I mused. Already powerful, there was so little one would have to do to make him super-human. And then I met his eyes. No way, I corrected my previous supposition. Not in a million years. In that moment I was deeply convinced that Winston was super-human already.

***

12

Escape

Her 'things' caught me off guard. Cathy sounded out of breath, more excited than I'd heard her since she scribbled her name on the Fermi blackboard, in Rome, a full twelve months ago.

"We got it," she practically screamed. "I just had to call you."

"I love you too," I replied.

"We got it, darling. We got the evidence of things not seen!" she twittered. Not at all like a Ph.D. in physics and special delegate to the CERN laboratories.

"I'm delighted to hear it," I commented dryly. "But Paul got it before you." I had to say it.

"What!!!" If it hadn't been digital audio, the circuits would have burned out.

"The evidence of things not seen," I repeated.

"What!!!"

This was becoming tiresome. "Paul wrote to the Hebrews, I forget where exactly, but what he said was that faith is the substance of things hoped for, the evidence of things not seen," I explained.

Cathy started laughing half-way through my exposé. Finally she got hold of herself.

"How wonderful," she said, still tittering and then promptly ignored my remark. She didn't care much for the Bible and western traditions. "We were hoping for the results, believing that we would get them against all odds, and now we see the evidence of their existence without actually seeing them. Wonderful!" Her voice was rising again.

"Care to explain?" I prodded.

"Well, it was like with the quarks. We didn't see them, exactly, but when we smashed the proton, we saw the trails the quarks left behind. Little curves like those from exploding fireworks."

I remembered that part. That was years ago. "And now *l'histoire se repet* with the boson?"

"Precisely. The trails are different, of course, but they follow our mathematical projections exactly. We expect to know more with each hour. The computers are humming, the staff is excited, oh, I love you, Peter," she blurted out at last.

I was glad to be included with the bosons, the quarks and the excited staff. Not to mention the computers.

"And I love you, darling," was my relatively prosaic response.

"Must run, now. Love you," she repeated, again, and the line went dead.

So much for romantic farewells.

So there really was a god particle? That of which all other fundamental things are made? Even smaller than leptons and quarks. I wondered what happened to the strings. To the Superstring theory, otherwise known as the Theory of Everything. Weren't those vibrating, two-dimensional bits of energy supposed to be the fundamental building blocks of... everything? In my younger, pre-seminarian, dinghy-sailing days, duct tape was binding everything, not strings or gluons or whatever the scientists had come up with since.

I sighed deeply. Those were the days of innocence.

No matter, Cathy chose me to share in her joy. That's as good as it gets, I mused. And then it struck me. If bosons were the smallest particles of the manifested god, then was the Higg's field the essential aspect of the unmanifested god? Was the field that through which god manifested itself? I'll try to bounce that off Winston, even if I have absolutely no idea why he should know. But really it was the large version, the one created in His image and likeness, that was giving me problems lately.

The Montreal Neurological Institute, which over time had swallowed the Old Vic, is just the other side of Mount Royal, hugging its gentler slopes. I left the office and started out on my usual brisk walk of some twenty minutes back home to Westmount. On occasion, in the full of Canadian winter with her attendant sleets, snowstorms, and generally obnoxious weather, I cheated and took a taxi, but so far the winter had behaved itself. And anyway, global warming was giving us, in Quebec, the extra few degrees we'd all hoped for, and also appeared to have extended all seasons at the expense of winter. Which, we all agreed, was as it should be. Except for the avid skiers, of course.

I was walking at my usual pace, thinking of the fireplace that, hopefully, Winston had already laid out. And then I became aware of a prickly feeling on the back of my neck, that telltale sign that all is not as it should be. I wondered if I'd forgotten something at the office, some work or some instruction I was supposed to give. I racked my brains to no avail.

Since my return from Geneva, there hadn't been a single case of my being followed by any ambitious press agent, looking for a headline. If fact, people appeared to have almost forgotten about my 'hands'. For better or for worse, these last few weeks I'd lived like a normal, reasonably anonymous, unobtrusive human being. As far as the world at large was concerned, I'd achieved my ambition. I was a nobody.

Nevertheless, there was that prickly feeling...

Assuming it was a tail, as they are prosaically referred to in detective stories, I veered down to Sherbrooke Street, where, emulating Ruth, I was hoping to get in front of some window panes, which would show me the reflection of anyone lurking behind me. I was sure that if I just spun on my heels right there, along Pine Avenue, the delinquent 'whoever-it-was' would duck into the evening shadows and I would never find out who he or she was.

In less than ten minutes, I found my window pane.

The experiment worked.

We were long past the technology in which a flash was required to take pictures in the dark. The celebrity hunters still used them mostly, I suspect, for effect. Celebrities always liked to face the flashing cameras. But the super-sensitive digital camera equipment had no need for extra light. They could recreate contours from minute differentials.

I stopped.

The man was standing on the other side of the street. I couldn't see him too well, but he was holding something that looked, from afar, like a telescoping lens aimed at me.

I walked back up the hill without bothering to look behind me.

Winston was waiting for me in the hall. He looked at me with a raised eyebrow, then relaxed seeing my expression. Somehow I think he must have sensed that I had been under a different kind of stress. We all experience such feelings on occasion. Winston just seemed exceptionally good at it. Fine-tuned, if you will.

"It is the total pattern, Sir," Winston said, as if that answered any questions I might have on the subject.

"What pattern?" I asked. I often wished he wouldn't make such cryptic remarks.

"You are more than your facial expression, Sir. It is the whole picture from which I draw my conclusions, Sir."

"You mean the way one moves, walks, sits, breathes and such like?"

"Those, too, Sir. The whole picture."

"Not the aura?" I asked facetiously. Winston liked such quirky expressions.

My majordomo smiled and went to hang my coat in the wardrobe. "There is nothing paranormal in the Universe, Sir, except our inability and unwillingness to understand nature," he said when he returned.

He said it in the same tone of voice as he would describe the menu for supper or comment on inclement weather. I sensed that the 'unwillingness' part had been directed at me. I, as an ex-physician, was a bit of a stickler for materiality, which made me quite an inordinately unsuitable candidate for the healing gift. If I couldn't see it, measure it, or otherwise perceive it with my senses, then even if it existed I would have little use for it. It was a question of practicality.

As usual, he read my thoughts. "Like love, Sir?"

That shut me up for a little while. I sat for a few minutes just watching him prepare dinner.

"Can anyone acquire the art of seeing auras?"

"Of course, Sir."

Now *that* I found cheerful indeed. But I knew nothing would induce him to teach me the trick—if trick it was.

"Everything in the Universe vibrates, Sir," he said. "Some scientists now believe that, in essence, everything *is* vibration. Hence the string theory." He stressed the verb 'is'.

So now I had to contact my Cathy to learn about the string theory to learn about the aura, to learn about how to learn to perceive it. I wondered if Winston had enough of a sense of humour to be having me on. But then I thought of Cathy. She did say once that the strings were two-dimensional units of energy vibrating at different frequencies. Or something like that.

"Not just matter, Sir. Our thoughts, even our consciousness, are just vibration. Hence, since we, as such, all vibrate in a similar fashion, we are composed of similar particles of matter. What aura indicates is the response our vibrations have to external stimuli."

"Electromagnetic?" I had to ask.

"I am not a physicist, Sir. But I would hazard a guess it has something to do with electromagnetism and photons."

Which left me exactly nowhere.

"And just how would one learn to see such an aura?" There was no harm in trying.

'There are exercises, Sir. We must learn to perceive colours outside the normal range," he said.

At last that was something I knew something about. Our eyes can sense a very narrow range of frequencies, usually between 0.3 and 0.7 micrometers, from violet to red. Beyond that spectrum we need instruments. But how can you change the human eye to see more than it was designed to?

"With practice, Sir."

I wished he would wait till I asked. No matter. I knew more. Our eyes have photocells that can perceive only three colours: red, yellow and blue. It is our brain that mixes them into an infinite number of intermediate shades and intensities. Strange though it may seem, that's what TV and computer screens exploit. Mixing pixels, or the three primary pigments in different proportions, we see different colours which are not really there. We assist in cheating ourselves.

"And just how would we benefit from such an ability?"

"When the aura, particularly around our head, does not agree with what the person is saying..."

"...then we know that person is lying." I finished for him. This was an affirmation rather than a question. It was fairly obvious. It would give the aura-reader an obvious advantage. One could make inroads in politics if nowhere else.

"Then why don't people learn it, Winston?"

"I was hoping you might be able to tell me that, Sir."

Ouch! That hurt. Because we are lazy? Stupid? Time wasters? Unbelievers? Set in our old ways? Unable...

"There are many reasons, Sir," Winston came to my rescue. "I am sure you'll learn it when you feel the need for it."

"Ah, yes. We don't feel the need for it...." Or because we are lazy, stupid, time-wasters... I've already been through that.

"Will that be all, Sir?"

"What, lazy, stu... ah, yes. Thank you Winston. Thank you very much." I preferred not to ask any more questions just then.

My ignorance in the matter of auras was simply the last straw. I'd escaped from the seminary, from the practice of medicine, then from exercising my healing power. After living off Ruth for a year, I accepted a sinecure from Lena. Having gotten nowhere very far with genetics, I tackled the artificial intelligence angle with the attendant robotics, yet couldn't do so fast enough to protect Lena, and now apparently my own sister-in-law, from some undercover characters imposing on their private lives. I considered myself as close to being an abysmal failure as I could possibly be. The depression I'd experienced during the previous twelve months was knocking on my door again, with renewed force.

I had to snap out of it.

If the guy who had followed me wished me harm, then I wished he'd succeeded. I wasn't doing anything useful with my life. Nothing that would leave a mark on humanity. There was an Indian saint, a man known as Sai Baba, who'd once said that man lives for the sole purpose of leaving the world a better place—for having lived.

"For no other reason was he born, for no other reason did he live," the sage declared.

And here I was. Pushing thirty, with nothing accomplished. By the time he reached my age, Mozart had left a vast heritage of music. Other artists, Anne Brontë, Christopher Marlowe who rivalled Shakespeare, Percy Shelley and John Keats, whose poetry still delights us... scientists, mathematicians as great as Niels Henrik Abel, Frank Ramsey, Ferdinand Eisenstein... all left legacies behind them by the time they were my age. By the time she had died, the twenty-four-year-old Thérèse of Lisieux had achieved sainthood. I, an ex-physician, an ex-healer, an upstart geneticist, a semiliterate expert on artificial intelligence... had already achieved failure.

I wanted to escape. Only no longer from other people—just from myself.

By the time I stopped feeling desperately sorry for myself, it was getting close to midnight. I was in my room upstairs. Appropriately, I was sitting in the dark, curtains half drawn, dark thoughts convoluting in my mind. My back to the window, my eyes followed the senseless filigree of shadows swaying across the wall in front of me. The bare branches and twigs moved left and right, and left again, repeatedly, senselessly, at the command of the whistling gusts.

It was all senseless. The wind, the shadows, my life.

What can I do, I asked myself? What can I possibly do to turn back the flood of discontentment that fills my heart?

And then there was Cathy. A woman as bright as any man could dream of. As beautiful as any man had a right to hope for. As nice, as generous... oh, Cathy, won't you help me? You always did in the past....

Precisely. You always helped me in the past. What have I ever done for you? I couldn't even offer Cathy a home, security, a nest to raise a family. I had no home. Not a place I could call my own.

Winston... Winston are you there....?

The night was as dark as it was silent. Even the distant street-lights far across the back garden seemed to have lost some of their sheen. The shadows on the wall grew less distinct.

I swung in my chair and without switching on the light, I clicked on the Internet. I spent nearly the rest of the night reading up everything I could find on auras. The yellow-golden halo around the head usually denotes a master, or a guru, or what we regard in the West as a spiritual teacher. Those who have the power, or the ability to read auras, can actually diagnose illnesses, or the state of health, of anyone whose aura they are observing. And just then I heard Winston's voice butting into my thoughts. Again.

"You can also learn to consciously control your aura..."

Was this Winston's voice in my head? Was he guiding me onto the path I had been intended to travel? Intended by whom? Or what? A god? I knew of no gods. I knew of no idols. I was alone, deserted. Disgusted with myself.

But, even then, my ego was still fighting back. I wasn't ready to be ridiculed by Winston any time soon, no matter how politely. It is quite absurd, I thought. People spend six, seven years studying law, medicine, a musical instrument, physics or whatever, but they give no time at all to developing the talents that lie dormant within them. I was one of those people. Well, no more, I told myself. I shall do my job as best I can, but I shall also allot time to finding out who I really am. And I shall pursue this journey on my own. I shall certainly not join any teaching, any guru, until I can read his or her aura. If it turns out to be golden-yellow, I shall listen. If not?

I sat up straighter. It's a start, I thought.

And just then I wondered if one could detect the aura of some of those TV preachers who, for the last century or so, claimed that Jesus was about to come down to earth, again, pick up his favourites, presumably those money-loving preachers, and whisk them off to heaven. I had no objection to the singing, stomping, clapping people who called themselves new-born Christians leaving the earthly environs permanently and leaving us alone to fend for ourselves. I only wished they'd do it sooner. What of their aura? It must be impossible to detect, I mused. At least I thought so until somewhere inside my head I heard a deep-throated chuckle followed by a hearty laugh. It was a basso I'd recognize anywhere.

The next morning my mood was back, more or less, to normal. In spite of lack of sleep I got up at the usual time, took an extra-long shower, and was at my desk exactly at eight—a self-imposed regimen. One of the problems of being a boss, a number one, no matter how small a pond one swam in, was that there was no one to create the rules. One led mostly by example, by applying oneself as best one could to the task at hand. Whether such efforts produced results or not was relatively coincidental.

I hoped that my resolve, last night, to make more of an effort to discover my own potential, would bear results. I needed an injection of self-respect.

Neither Ruth nor Cathy had ever complained about my behaviour. For some reason they both regarded me as someone special. I doubt that I had earned such generous consideration, though not for lack of trying. They were both very special people, with great gifts of their own, who thought nothing of putting up with my eccentricities, accepting them as normal, even under the most trying conditions.

According to Socrates, an unexamined life is not a life worth living. I examined things, rather than life itself. My actions consisted mostly of reactions to external occurrences, over which I had little or no control.

Thank God there was Winston.

On my desk I found a photocopy of an article left for me by Captain Morton. He was waiting for me in the anteroom, chatting with my secretary. The two-word headline was followed by a brief report:

STRIKES SPREADING

"The advances in robotics are reported to have left the USA work-force in dire straits. Automatization had already taken so many jobs from so many union members that the economic

> system based on Organized Labour is in danger of collapse. A government spokesman (who asked to remain anonymous) said that the reason behind the imminent collapse is that the wealth of the country is undermined by the fringe benefits retained by the workers long dismissed or retired from their jobs. A spokesmen for Labour (also under conditions of anonymity) said that although the exemplary unemployment benefits were more than ample to sustain the ex-workers' needs, what was lost was the workers' self-esteem."

I've always found it fascinating that when all is said and done, people are quite incapable of doing nothing. I suspect that my own recent frustrations result from the previous twelve months of my life, during which I'd done little to contribute to society. Dr. John Brent, my old mentor, also told me that the reason the medical system in Canada was in such dire straits was because people retired too soon and, subsequently, didn't know what to do with their time.

"Medicine has advanced so much in recent years that we can sustain people in a reasonably healthy condition almost indefinitely," he told me, long ago. "But it doesn't seem to help."

Was it a mental block? Had our genome been programmed to be useful or pay the consequences? Who the devil did this programming? Nature? Nature should have nothing to say in the matter. I know of no organized system that could survive with such a plethora of waste as is inherent in nature. I remember my old biology professor saying:

"Ejaculation is the ejecting of semen and is usually accompanied by an orgasm, which is usually the result of sexual stimulation."

She had a supercilious grin on her face. Her eyes were roving over the men at the back of the lecture hall. I had been one of them.

"Men are wasters," she continued, this time looking superior. "An average male produces between two and six millilitres of semen in each ejaculation. This adds up to between 40 and 600 million sperm cells. An average of 250 million."

She left her lectern and walked up the sloping floor towards the back rows.

"If it wasn't for our restraint, the world would soon become uninhabitable."

The restraint of women producing but a few eggs at a time, no doubt. As if they had a choice in the matter. She sounded so superior, so smug that I became convinced she was a lesbian. My opinion changed somewhat after she had been reprimanded for offering to demonstrate her thesis regarding some biological functions to any young man who was interested.

But even then I have to admit that, at least in some ways, she was right. If not all humans, then at least we, men, were, and still are, perennial wasters. We produced virtually everything in excess, regardless of the consequences such actions might have on the world at large. We've polluted our planet with millions of cars, polluted our oceans with the wash-off from millions of tons of artificial fertilizer we deemed necessary to grow morbidly obese, we even overpopulated mother earth with our insatiable need for sexual gratification. We were definitely wasters.

So what was the answer?

I pressed the button.

"Send the Captain in, please," I spoke into the intercom.

Captain Morton sat in front of my desk for some minutes while my mind performed its usual gyrations.

"Are we affected in any way, George?" I asked him. I pointed to the article he'd left on my desk.

"It affects Solidarity, Sir," he offered.

"Do you think they know that?" I don't know why I was questioning him. With a bit of effort all the answers were fairly obvious. It must have been because of last night. I needed sleep.

"They are not stupid, Sir. Amoral, self-centred, but not stupid in the accepted sense of the word. They know that if the strikes persist, Solidarity International is bound to gain ground in the USA. They wouldn't like that."

"No," I nodded. "They wouldn't like that at all," I agreed. It wouldn't do much for their CEO salaries and bonuses either. Yet, in spite of the Solidarity backing and the clout being placed at my disposal, I had no idea what to do about it. Not right there and then. So, I mused, the Americans would take steps to counteract Solidarity's possible advances. But how?

I never felt so useless.

Just then the viphone chimed on my desk. It was on audio. I picked up the receiver. It was Lena. The line wasn't even secure.

"Peter, my friend, I hope you don't mind, but since Ruth told me about someone following her, I told our people to keep an eye on you, too."

"With a camera equipped with a telescopic lens?" I asked, vaguely annoyed.

"Why, no, Peter. Was it at night? That must have been an infrared monocular. No one is photographing you, at least I hope not! Anyway, I just wanted to set your mind at ease in case you noticed something, and I don't want this to be general knowledge."

She hung up. So, I allowed myself a lopsided grin, I'm so useless that I am not even worth being spied on. And Lena found it necessary to look after me from across the ocean. Am I really so completely innocuous, so utterly hopeless?

When I looked up I saw the back of Captain Morton closing the doors behind him. He'd withdrawn discreetly to give me privacy for my call. A good fellow, that Morton. A nice guy, too. I wondered if he'd ever felt as useless as I did at that moment.

***

13

Christmas

There are a number of things one can do when one is depressed. One can get drunk, go on a trip to far-away places, get a popcorn novel to escape into artificial reality, or make love. You could do all of them, of course, in no particular order. I decided to show restraint. I chose the last. Cathy had returned to Canada for Christmas—the greatest present I could wish for. I wanted her wrapped up with a big gold and red bow and placed under my Christmas tree. I wanted to unwrap her myself. Instead I found her on my bed. An even more preferable location.

It all happened quite suddenly.

I left my office and hurried home. I had been at a meeting when Winston called and left a message with my secretary. She gave it to me word for word.

"It is a matter of some urgency, the gentleman said, Sir." For some reason she sounded a little flustered. "It would be highly desirable if Dr. Thornton could find his way home at first opportunity, he said, Sir. Word for word."

Some dark thoughts crossed my mind. Images of yesteryear flashed before my eyes with painful urgency. The children had been kidnapped, again. Ruth disappeared. They took her... no, she was here, at the meeting. There was a fire? Winston, the invincible Winston is sick? Winston!

"He didn't sound worried, Sir. Just, sort of, well, persuasive..."

I let the air out of my lungs. Poor Miss Dibbs had no idea what Winston usually sounded like. I called back and there was no answer. I put on my coat and ran.

I called out when I got home. Silence. I threw my coat on the chair and ran upstairs to check Winston's room. It was empty. The door to my bedroom was closed. I always left it open. I almost knocked. Silly. I walked in. She was lying on my bed, apparently sleeping. She looked glorious. Just glorious. Like an angel sent from heaven for Christmas. Ready to be unwrapped.

She opened one eye. "Just a quick nap," she said. "I've been flying virtually all day. Then I went directly to see mom and dad. Funny that. I left at ten a.m. and got here at ten a.m., six hours later. Talk of relativity! My parents are both fine. Just fine. I didn't want to bother you in your office. I came here. Winston let me in. Do you mind?" It came out in bits and pieces interrupted only by stifled yawns.

No matter. My mouth was open but no words were coming out. I felt like a teenager on my first date. Cathy is here... it kept going through my mind... Cathy is here. I am not useless, she came to me. On her own.

"Aren't you going to say something?" She propped herself on one elbow.

I didn't. I turned and closed the door. Then I locked it. I hadn't used the lock in many years. I never had anything to hide. Now I did. I didn't want anyone to find us. I wanted to hide her and keep her all to myself. Forever and a day.

Around six we both took a shower. Together. Neither of us heard anyone coming in. From outside, I mean. Winston must have kept the children quiet. If Ruth was back from the office, she also remained hushed. Perhaps she took a nap? Lately, she'd been under a lot of pressure. The USA was none too pleased with the way things were unfolding. Even as they kept reducing their labour force, Solidarity's work on genetics was showing the union members, world-wide, that we could all live longer, healthier, and continue to make a contribution to the world at large. This was in direct opposition to the consequences of the rapid growth in robotics. Something had to give.

I shook my head. The interests of Solidarity were becoming etched into my mind. They vanished the moment Cathy and I appeared at the top of the stairs. To our disbelieving eyes, Mo and Jo displayed a newly acquired restraint admirably.

Just a short while ago, a couple of years at the most, I would have heard, "Did you see the Christmas tree? Did you, Uncle Peter? Did you, Aunt Cathy? Did you?"

This time they stood, practically at attention, with a dignified expression on their ruddy faces. They must have been playing outside. They took Cathy and me by the hand and escorted us towards the sitting room.

"Good evening, Moira. Hello, Jonathan," Cathy muttered, being pulled along.

"Good evening, Cathy. Good evening, Uncle Peter," came a ceremonial reply. But that was as much as they could do to restrain themselves. Simultaneously they pointed to the Christmas tree.

"Look at the angel, up there, on the top!"

"There, there, right at the top!" Mo joined her brother.

Indeed, there was some sort of bird perched just below the ceiling looking like a cross between a young woman and a hen with her wings outspread. Or it could have been a golden cockerel.

"Yes, Mo, yes, Jo, I see it. Her?" Evidently Cathy wasn't sure either.

"So do I!" I confirmed, when both of them let go Cathy's hands and were ready to grab both of mine. "I really do," I insisted.

Only Ruth's stern look persuaded the children to let us go, if only for a short while. Even as the bell rang, Winston was already at the front door. I still didn't know how he managed to do that. To be at the door before the bell made a sound.

Cathy smiled. "That's another surprise," she said.

"Dr. and Mrs. Bartholomew Mondellay," Winston announced gravely.

Ruth, Cathy and I all headed to the hall to welcome them. The children were somewhat taken aback.

"B-b-but..." apparently there were more things to show us.

I was always in awe how young they both looked. The doctor, Bartholomew, must have been in his late eighties. Considerably shorter than his wife, they made a peculiar-looking couple at best. One had an impression that he could carry his wife around as for security. By the time they decided to have Cathy, it had been almost too late. Ever since, they'd doted on her. It was obvious from whom Cathy got her looks. That silky skin, the gloriously lustrous hair, the jade eyes, all came from her father's side of the family. As did a lot of the grey matter. Not that Mrs. Mondellay wasn't a very intelligent woman, but her husband was a borderline genius. Perhaps past the borderline. He *was* a genius. He was the man who had proven that the nucleus of hydrogen could be converted into pure radiation, improving conventional nuclear reaction outputs many times over, and providing a source of energy one hundred times more efficient than fusion energy. He also devised a magnetic field in which the conversion was contained without converting the rest of our dear Earth into a little nova. On the bright side, in the burning of coal or oil, only one billionth of the mass is converted to heat. And on the brighter side still, it seemed apparent that Cathy had benefited from his genes in that department. I meant brains, although heat came a close second.

I had a considerable debt of gratitude, or perhaps a bone to pick, with Mrs. Mondellay. I'll try to cut the story as short as I can. In her relative youth, Mrs. M. had written a novel that adorned the shelves of her literary agent for an extended period of time. She had said, when we first met, or soon after, that manuscripts "gather dust on the agent's shelves for a period inversely proportional to the agent's degree of financial success." Ever since, we, that is my sister-in-law and I, have considered Mrs. Mondellay the expert on all literary and publishing matters.

She very nearly was. When I wrote my Dialogues, a collection of essays on my perception of reality that Cathy helped me put together when recovering from my stint at Gaston's Tavern, she had my book published in no time at all. This was, of course, back in the days before I became obsessed with hiding my identity from the world at large. She'd persuaded the great Dr. Mondellay himself to write a Foreword, and convinced the publishers to forego their usual intemperate editorial scrutiny. Last but not least, she had procured for me a healthy retainer of $100,000. Having, at the time, just lost all means of earning any income, I had particularly appreciated her efforts.

The bone of contention came later.

Unbeknownst to me, and to Cathy, or anyone that I can think of, Mrs. Mondellay took it upon herself to publish yet another book. In it, with a high degree of accuracy and an even greater degree of imagination, she described the last few years of my life. Originally submitted as a biography titled *One Just Man*, it was eventually published as a novel. It hit the bookstores a mere three months ago. By the time I raised my objections, it was too late to change all the names to protect the innocent. However, Dr. Mondellay offered to buy an oversized insurance, in case anyone would sue his wife for excessive flights of fancy. He also offered to indemnify the publishing house. Mr. James Bernhardt Fitzpatrick, the principal editor of Birngham & Birngham, knew better than to argue with the wife of *the* Dr. Mondellay. Lawyers took care of all the details.

To my utter surprise and Mrs. Mondellay's frequent 'I told you sos', One Just Man became an instant best-seller. Strange though it may seem, instead of raising public interest in my story, the book did the opposite. Since the facts were published as fiction, then surely, people argued, they can't possibly be all true. My story became something of an urban legend, and few people were interested in hunting down the details, or me, to see for themselves.

And now, here I was, suffocating in the portentous bosom of Mrs. Mondellay.

"You made me famous, my boy," she exclaimed, holding onto me for dear life. "You made me a literary giant!"

That was pushing the scholarly envelope a little too far, but the royalties were still rolling in. There was no denying that the percentage of royalties that Mrs. Mondellay insisted were my spoils did keep me going without imposing too much on Ruth's generosity. Perhaps, after all, I wasn't as much of a leech as I'd imagined, these last few days.

Taller than myself or anyone present by a good few inches, she delighted in administering a hug that pulled my head into the pulchritude proffered before me, and thus disabling me from any chance of escape. When I came up for air, she looked at me proudly, with a warmth normally reserved only for her daughter.

"I love you, Peter," she declared, "as if you were my own son."

At long last, Cathy managed to disengage me from her doting mother. "It just had to be done this way, Peter. I really wanted to spend some time with you, darling. So I called Winston, and he agreed to arrange dinner for us all. You don't mind, do you?"

I was looking into those jade eyes, still trying to catch my breath. I wouldn't mind if she shipped all of us to the moon, as long as I could string along.

"I gather Winston agreed?"

"He told me to get some rest and said he would take care of things."

And take care he had. The supper was home-cooked, simple, delicious, the sort you cannot get in any restaurant. To this day I have no idea how Winston acquired his culinary skills. After dinner, we retired to the already sparkling fire in the sitting room, while the children walked in an orderly fashion to the bottom of the stairs, and then raced up to their rooms to test the latest computer game. I added another log, and offered to help Winston with the Vintage Porto.

"If I may, Sir, we shall just pass it along."

An old English navy custom. When the seas were rough, the Captain would pour into his own glass and pass the bottle to the next in command. And so around the table. Not a drop was spilled.

We chatted about inconsequential items of everyday life. Dr. Mondellay had already retired and was keen to learn what was new in the world. Ruth brought him up to speed on Solidarity, I mentioned a thing or two about genetics and artificial intelligence, and Cathy expounded about the things she loved but could not see.

"It's simply not fair," she finally declared, pouting. "You all see the fruit of your work. Only I am sentenced to forever dream, imagine, theorize and never give up."

"But you see the trails…" Her father was a physicist himself.

"I wish I could see some pointer in front of me," she said, unsatisfied, "not just the trails they leave behind."

"But you know they are there, otherwise the equations wouldn't work," Dr. Bartholomew Mondellay insisted as though he couldn't understand what his daughter's problem was.

These were physicists talking. They imagined invisible things, they created theories, they defined them with equations, and then worked like mad to prove that their assumptions of invisible things were real. Sometimes I thought that they hadn't discovered anything at all, ever. I thought that their overwhelming desire to find an invisible particle actually brought it into being. Into our reality. I recall the saying, 'be careful what you wish for.' Well, they wished for some invisible bosons and, presto, there were bosons. The word made flesh. Sort of. They thought long and hard about strings, as in the Super-string theory, and strings fit nicely into their equations. Don't we all create our own universe? That's right. Soon they will be telling us not about our Universe, but about countless Universes winking in and out of existence. Just to confirm their mathematical speculations. They sounded more and more like some sacerdotal proselytisers on TV. Only the southern Baptist accent was missing.

"You know, Dad, if we can confirm the boson, the implications are staggering. I imagine they would back up the other dimensions."

"Other what?" Ruth looked up from examining the fire through the crystal of her glass. The rich red of the Porto complemented the rubies she wore.

"Other dimensions, Ruth. There may be as many as thirteen of them. Or perhaps an infinite number, all curled up inside each other. They talked about it at the end of the last century, but it took us all this time to find actual evidence for their existence."

"Are you discussing science-fiction, dear?" Mrs. Mondellay raised an eyebrow. Her expression suggested that the young ones must have their fun.

"No, Mother," Cathy said patiently. She seemed used to her mother's disbelief. "We know of no other way to explain the Universe we live in. We don't make up those things. We observe and draw conclusions...."

"You observe things you cannot see?" Her mother's facial expression was a mixture of compassion and concern.

Cathy looked up at her father. There was 'help!' written all over her face.

"Scientists, Mother," Dr. Mondellay spoke softly, "see the Universe as vibrations. The so-called strings or the super-symmetric strings theory is an attempt to explain all particles and fundamental forces in terms of a single theory. Rather like a symphony that consists of countless scales, arpeggios, beautiful chords and melodies, but really they are made up of individual notes all vibrating in space."

"And gravity or quantum gravity is where I come in," Cathy added weakly.

"Why did you have to ruin it all, Cathy? The music part made so much sense," Mrs. Mondellay scolded. But her eyes said, "Look at my daughter. Isn't she clever?"

"No, you don't, I was first!"

"No, you weren't, I was... let me go!"

We all looked up. Mo was sitting astride the balustrade, Jo immediately behind her, holding onto Moira's waist with both hands.

"Well, I'll get there first!" Jo declared triumphantly.

Suddenly Mo let go and both of them slid down the balustrade by some miracle landing on their feet. I remembered the hours of practice they'd put in under Winston's august scrutiny.

"The children, Madam," Winston's grave voice announced from the bottom of the stairs, "have descended to say goodnight."

Jo and Mo ran to their mother, to me and Cathy, plastering kisses on our proffered cheeks. Dr. and Mrs. Mondellay were accorded a bow and a handshake. I was jealous. I could never get away with just shaking hands with Mrs. Mondellay. Perhaps I should slide down the balustrade or wait till she sat down. It's harder to assault people from a sitting position.

Having carried out their duty, the children walked slowly to the foot of the stairs, and once there, with a scream, "race you to the top," they did just that.

"I won," we heard from upstairs.

"No, you didn't, I won," Mo wouldn't give an inch.

"You were cheating," Jo asserted.

"No, I didn't, you cheated…"

"Good night, Master Jonathan. Good night, Miss Moira." This was Winston's basso followed by a stunning silence. We all held our breath, unsure if we were allowed to speak.

An hour later, Dr. Mondellay rose to his feet.

"Cathy must be awfully tired. Till tomorrow, around noon?"

We agreed to meet at noon at the Mondellay residence with all our presents. The children were already dreaming about theirs. Our guests left quietly so as not to wake them. Cathy gave me one of those long looks that would keep me awake for the next hour or two. It's strange, I thought. She and I have been together more times than I can remember, yet whenever her parents were around, Cathy reverted to the innocent child they pretended she still was. And which, for me, she forever will be. The next few days were a blur of never-ending festivities.

Once again, it was that special day. In the past, it had been men who, on this date, relieved their wives in the kitchen. These days, more precisely for the fourth time in as many years, the ladies gathered and multiplied their culinary expertise, forcing Winston Smith, to his considerable chagrin, to sit back and do nothing. Not that he could do so for long. He soon occupied himself with the preparation of some sort of secret concoction of which we were about to partake. The dinner may not have been quite up to Winston's punctilious standards, but sitting at the head of the table he repeatedly uttered effusive praise for the efforts that Ruth and Cathy had put in.

Later, we were all sitting in the comfort of the living room, caressing the grog that Winston contrived to prepare according to his inimitable storehouse of old recipes. Sweetish, yet with a suggestion of tartness, the vaguely viscous drink that tickled one's throat in a most delectable fashion went well with the crackling cold outside as well as the crackling fireplace.

"This is a long way from the rum-and-water served by the Old Grog," John Brent commented, his face a picture of appreciation.

Our collective eyebrows went up.

"Old, ah... Grog?" Dr. Mondellay spoke for all of us.

"The nickname given to Admiral Vernon, around 1745, I believe. He was so named after the grogram cloak he wore. My great-great-grand Uncle," John added, as if that tidbit accounted for everything else.

The eyes of all present looked startled. Doctor Brent an old mariner? They all stared at John, who rarely, if ever, shared his family's rich past, at that particular moment evidently confused with his own. I, on the other hand, pictured Winston, the ancient sea dog, with sails billowing under driving westerlies, scouring the seven seas for recipes of grog.

"Grogram?" This was Lucy. Even she wasn't up on all of her husband's secrets.

"From the French *gros-grain*," John explained. "As in coarse fabric..."

He was interrupted by a volley of cannons obviously fired by Admiral Vernon's descendants. This was followed by the rattle of machineguns, seemingly all around us.

"It has begun..." I said ominously. "The armada..."

"The war?" Ruth's smile was none too comfortable. After the wine that poured freely at dinner, she was just this side of tipsy.

"The Yanks," I added. "I knew they were up to something."

This was followed by another broadside, this time closer to home. Ruth got to her feet, Cathy started laughing, John Brent looked pleased as punch, the Mondellays looked at each other with questions in their eyes. At that moment Winston walked in with a tray of champagne glasses.

"I offer you, Ladies and Gentlemen, a very happy New Year!" he announced with appropriate flair.

Ruth collapsed into her armchair.

"Oh, no," she whispered, resignation filling her eyes. "More wine...."

The day after New Year's, Cathy and I drove up north to Mount Burton, an old hunting cottage that's been in the Thornton family for generations. At least that was the story I'd heard. Cathy and I wanted to be completely alone, without access to a telephone.

We bought some provisions, en route, to last us a week. We decided that, God willing and weather permitting, we would do some cross-country skiing, or at least some snow-shoeing. Neither of us was in good shape. Cathy and I tended to be bookworms. Not enough exercise.

"If worse comes to worst, we could spend the next week just stoking the fire," I murmured, trying hard to hide the glee in my eye.

The pine-panelled walls, the heavily worn pine floorboards, the windows that looked out on wild, snow-clad firs and cedars held memories for us. Strong, binding memories. It was here that Cathy had nursed me back to health. To life, really.

For a moment I saw myself prostrated on the wooden recliner, waiting for me at the still unlit fireplace. My memories of the early part of our stay there were vague at best, but I must have lain in that chair for a week before I'd gathered enough strength for my first walk outside. All thanks to Cathy. And here we were again.

I reached out and pulled her into my arms. "Thank you, darling," was all I could utter at that moment.

Later I took care of the fireplace. The wood had been piled against the east wall, under the eaves. It looked dry. It was. Ruth had a caretaker looking after the place.

Within an hour or so, the place began to warm up. In another half-hour, we took off our anoraks.

My memories retreated again to the last and only time we'd been here, Cathy an exemplary Florence Nightingale. It had been way back when I was still on the run, imagining that I was going to be chased by hordes of demanding, incurable patients. It's quite amazing, the importance we give to our egos. It is true that some sort of healing energy flowed out through my hands. It is true that I could and still can help some people. What I didn't know, at the time, was that if I removed the symptoms of a malady and did not remove the sickness anchored deep in the subconscious mind, my patients would revert to their previous condition in no time at all. We keep forgetting that everything in this reality is transient. Except our consciousness. This seems to function day and night, during our sleep, even when we're in a coma. Consciousness is life, and life is consciousness. Remove consciousness and we are just a bunch of atoms whirling around until natural decay takes over.

Even as our bodies are renewing themselves, cell by cell, atom by atom, so the Universe is also suspended in an eternal instant of creation. Nothing is as it seems. What we see is only what already was. What has been. What we really witness is the instant of continuous creation. 'I am life,' a great teacher once said. 'Whosoever believes in me shall never die.' If we recognize our self as life, we become immortal. If we think of ourselves as our bodies, than we pay homage to that which is already dead.

A penny landed on my lap. I looked up questioningly.

"For your thoughts," Cathy murmured.

"Nothing much," I said. "Mostly about robots." That was close enough.

She sat next to me. That was stupid. Had I said 'nothing much' and stopped there, she would have ended up on my lap.

"I'm trying to determine the difference between robots and ourselves," I half-lied. But my thoughts were drifting in that direction. "Unless robots develop rudimentary consciousness, we have nothing to fear from them."

"Why would you think otherwise?"

I told her about the latest stuff I had heard about the USA versus Solidarity. Or really versus genetics. The two were on a collision course. "Their robots are made from replaceable parts, we, or ours—from renewable. I prefer our robots."

"Robots as mobile constructs that enable us to find food to sustain the genes that insist on self-reproduction?"

"Something like that." It didn't sound quite right.

"Unless we have relatively little to do with the biological robots we occupy," she mused aloud.

"As in consciousness being independent of the body?"

"I wonder...." We could go on like this for hours.

"Seriously... What if the Americans realize that Solidarity presents a real threat to their survival?" I asked.

"It doesn't. It does though, to their way of life."

"That's what I meant. What then?"

"Then they will take steps to protect themselves." Cathy stifled a yawn. "Don't you think we should give our genes a chance?"

"What?" And then I saw the dreamy sparkle in her eyes. The sort that says I want to sleep but not alone. "I am all for our robots fulfilling their mission. I consider it my duty…."

"Oh, shut up, Peter."

I didn't say another word till our robots took us upstairs and exposed our magnificent structures. Then, and only then, did I dare say anything. It wasn't much. Just a simple, stereotyped, almost trite expression so many robots use in such circumstances.

"I love you," I said.

"I know. But tell me anyway."

I did. Except for some heavy breathing there was relative silence for quite some time.

"I like your robot," she said softly.

"I wonder what the Americans would say," I mused.

"I hope they never change their way of life," Cathy whispered. I heard amusement in her voice.

"I'll drink to that."

With that profound assurance I reached over for the tumbler with Martinis already mixed, biding their time in an ice bucket.

"Here's to robots," she said. I couldn't agree more.

The next three days were almost exactly and gloriously the same. My frustrations were gradually coming under control. The anger that I felt towards the world at large, my feeling that fate had short-changed me, could not be sustained in Cathy's presence. We went for hourly walks, did some cross-country skiing, talked in front of the fire, ate, sipped wine, and finished the days by paying homage to our robots. On the fourth day, I began to feel those stupid hairs on the back of my neck. At first I thought that we might have been followed. I had made sure there were no cars behind us, but there were always helicopters. And some unfriendly character may have inserted some kind of electronic device into the car, perhaps when we were shopping, that acted like a signal for a GPS.

On the fifth day I told Cathy about it.

"That's sort of funny," she said. Her lips were smiling, but there was sadness in her eyes.

"What is it?" I asked her. I hated it when she was sad. It was as if the sun disappeared in the middle of a cloudless day.

"You told me those same words last time... about a year ago. You had been in a motel. You told me that you had just said good-bye to the people. That you had to go somewhere. That you weren't sure why...."

It had been in a motel. I'd been moving from one room to another, changing addresses, never staying too long anywhere. I was learning. I recall saying good-bye to the people. Some embraced me, some just shook my hand. They had also bid each other farewell as if the family had to disperse to far-away countries. I could see those faces behind my eyelids. They weren't asking for much. Just, perhaps, a little hope. They were not lost souls. They just needed a little help along the way.

"I had to go back and see Ruth," I said. "I took a taxi."

"And now?"

"Now I have to go back and... and see Ruth." I was surprised at my own answer.

We packed in ten minutes, doused the fire, and took a last look through the window at the pristine snow, the sort one never sees in a city. Certainly not in Montreal.

"So long," Cathy whispered. "Till we meet again..."

I, too, was hoping that another year wouldn't pass before we returned to this corner of heaven.

We got back to Westmount before dark. I dropped Cathy at her home and sped back to my place. Winston was waiting for me.

"Madam has been missing since yesterday," he said.

"The office?"

"Has been notified," he said. "There is a man in the sitting room waiting for you."

Winston must have known I would be coming. He always knew such things. I peeked through the archway into the living room. There was a man slumped in the armchair in front of the extinct fire.

"He's been there since yesterday lunchtime. In case someone calls," Winston explained.

Obviously the man had little or nothing to tell me. If there had been, Winston would have already said so.

"No word of any sort?" I couldn't help asking anyway.

"Not yet, Sir. Perhaps they are waiting for your return?" Winston wasn't joking.

About then I realized that something else was wrong. I looked around. Nothing was missing. Then I had it. There were no sounds of Mo and Jo performing their usual boisterous greetings. No one sliding down the balustrade. No one screaming joyful welcomes. I looked up at Winston. His eyes were strangely veiled.

"They are upstairs, Sir," he said in a half-tone. "I thought it best to keep them busy. With homework, Sir. Perhaps you could go up and see them?" This didn't sound like Winston. There was almost a plea in his voice.

I nodded. But that wasn't the only thing that bothered me. There was something else that was missing. It was also an absence. Then I had it. Winston had momentarily lost the serenity that I always found in his eyes. Winston was worried.

Now *that* scared me.

***

14

Bionics

There was nothing I could do at home. By the time I got back from Mount Burton it was too late to go to the office. I awakened the detective—I assumed he was a detective—and told him to go home. Frankly, the guy looked utterly miserable. He insisted on staying.

"The boss told me not to leave you alone. I mean not to leave Mrs. Thornton."

"The boss?"

"Miss Walesa," the man said, bowing his head.

So he got his orders from the very top. No wonder he was sticking here like a leech. Apparently he hadn't done a very good job.

"When did you last see Mrs. Thornton, Mr…."

"Morris, Sir. We left her office to go to the cafeteria and she never arrived there."

"We?"

"I mean Mrs. Thornton, Sir. She was going for lunch. I was in the corridor and I followed her. We are told to make ourselves in-consi-cu…"

"Inconspicuous?"

"That's right, Sir. So I took the stairs, not to be seen….

"And when you got to the cafeteria she was missing?"

"I know, Sir. It doesn't make sense."

"So what did you do?"

"I waited, then looked all over, then I checked the cameras, then I notified Mr. Gowan, Mrs. Thornton's deputy, then security, then I called the police, then I came here, then…."

"I get the picture. You feel all we can do is wait?"

"I don't rightly know what else to do, Sir."

Winston was standing in the hall, busily feathering some non-existent specs of dust from the ornate picture frames. I was sure he hadn't missed a word. Not that he could do anything. Not that I could. I could call Cathy, but that would only worry her. Lena must already know, I supposed.

"Did you call the Vatican?"

"Oh, yes, Sir. First thing. I was there when Mr. Gowan called Miss Walesa. Right there, in front of me." The poor man's face was drawn, haggard, and I suspected, not just from lack of sleep. He may also have been worried about his job. With instructions coming directly from Lena, it didn't look good for him. On the other hand, Lena also had her men watching me. So much for Solidarity security.

I nodded. I wanted to call Lena on her private line, but Rome was six hours ahead. There, in the east, it was well past midnight, and I felt sure that Lena had enough to deal with. I decided to get some sleep, go to Solidarity Headquarters first thing the next day, and see if there was anything I could do to help. I found it amazingly annoying how helpless we all were. I should have been used to acting in areas over which I had little or no control. Not so. My fulminating anger that Cathy managed to assuage up north was returning with renewed force. Apparently we never get used to being useless. Perhaps it's our ego?

Cathy called me an hour later.

"Any news?" she asked.

She already knew about Ruth's disappearance. They'd called her from Headquarters, in case she was at the Mondellay residence. Just in case. I told her briefly what I'd learned from Morris, which wasn't much. She listened without interrupting and in the end also agreed to wait till tomorrow.

"After all," she said, "I'm sure there's an army of Solidarity security agents combing Headquarters, and probably all of Montreal. And remember, Ruth has her implant. If she gets anywhere near a scanner, they will know instantly. At least I think so. To my knowledge the scanner cannot be switched off, can it?"

"Not to my knowledge, either," I agreed. It was good to listen to someone intelligent for a change. It had a calming effect on me.

"Sleep tight, darling, and call me the moment you hear anything. Anything. No matter what hour."

We left it at that.

I had flashes of déjà vu. A year ago there had been that convoluted story with the children. They had been abducted, yet it turned out that a persuasive stranger had merely taken them for an ice-cream cone. Their purported kidnapping turned out to be just a decoy. The rest was flamboyant imagination; anyway, you know about it from Mrs. Mondellay's One Just Man. Only now the boot was on the other foot. It was Solidarity who was the abductee, not the abductor. On the other hand, if they wanted to kidnap Ruth in order to procure anything else, for instance my healing powers, then it would surely have been easier to kidnap me in the first place. None of this made sense.

Yet, the more I thought about it, the darker my thoughts became. I decided to stop thinking and spend the rest of the day with the children. They had not been told about the suspected abduction but were beginning to sense that something fishy was going on.

"Who is the worried man downstairs, Uncle Peter?" was the first question Jo asked.

"He is a man who is here to look after us," I told him.

"Why do we need anyone to look after us? Can't you look after us, Uncle Peter?"

So I made a boo-boo. I spoke too soon. "Yes, I can, I mean I do, but tomorrow I have to go to the office, and Mommy had to fly out of town on business. The man can help Winston if necessary."

"He can help Winston do what, Uncle?"

"Shopping," I said, before I had time to think. I was not at my best, either. To make things worse, Lena's man refused to budge from the sitting room. Apparently from the particular armchair he occupied, he could keep one eye on the front door, the other on the window and any movement outside.

No matter. Tomorrow would be another day. I tried to console myself. Perhaps Ruth would return during the night.

The next day, at Headquarters, the wheels had been set in motion, but there was still no news. I was told that Mr. Gowan was in constant touch with the Vatican. They hadn't received any news yet, either. There were dozens of plainclothes sentries posted at all three airports, most of the land crossings between Quebec and the USA, all the long-distance bus stations, though no one really imagined that the abductors, if indeed there were such, would choose a bus to whisk Ruth away. Also, all the Solidarity scanners were under close scrutiny around the clock.

"Madam could be suffering from amnesia," Winston offered, when I got back home.

If that was supposed to cheer me up, it didn't. Winston was usually more careful in his choice of words. He, too, must have his limits. The lingering anger at my own inadequacies, which I managed to suppress while working, was returning once again. I tried to divert my thoughts to work. What if Solidarity had advanced the science of genetics? What if they had succeeded in making people live longer and be more useful? There was nothing to stop the USA from making their own strides in whatever direction they'd chosen.

Ruth kept invading my thoughts. I couldn't think straight. They could put their senior citizens to sleep, for all I cared.

I tried playing with Mo and Jo. I was never particularly good at dealing with the children. Needless to say, neither Winston nor I told them about Ruth, not that there was much to tell. I caught myself keeping a constant lopsided smile on my face. It must have looked phoney. I was afraid Mo and Jo would see through my charade. Children can be very perceptive.

Winston helped. He introduced a question and answer game I'd never heard of. He mentioned a name of a town and we had to tell what country it was in. One letter at a time. Each letter scored a point. I think Winston made the game up on the spur of the moment. He, Winston, was the absolute arbitrator. In time, I was actually drawn in. By bedtime, Mo won, Jo came second and my smile had grown more natural.

The following day I just couldn't go to the Old Vic. My mind wasn't on my work.

I thought about the amnesia angle. Such things happened. But wherever Ruth might have wandered to, even if unaware of her whereabouts, the scanners would, by now, have pinpointed her location. The only thing that would make her invisible to the cameras would be either the distance she kept from the scanners—this would require detailed knowledge of where the countless scanners were located—or a lead barrier of some sort, that would stop the radio waves from reaching the scanners. Either proposition would require some third-party participation.

Dear Ruth. She'd never hurt anyone. She just couldn't. It wasn't in her nature.

The call came at two p.m. Winston handed me the receiver.

"I see you're not in your office, Dr. Thornton, is anything wrong?" The caller did not introduce himself.

"Who is this?" I asked brutally. I was in no mood for cat-and-mouse games.

"We met, Dr. Thornton, some time ago...."

There was a click on the phone. From the corner of my eye I saw that Morris was missing. He must have picked up the extension in the hall.

"Since we are no longer alone, Dr. Thornton, I'll just say that Madame Thornton is well, and there is no reason for you to worry. We are taking good care of her. She'll be back in her office in two days at the latest. Good-bye, Dr. Thornton."

"Damn!" This was Morris. "We didn't get the location," he swore again under his breath.

"At least she's all right," I said.

"And just how do you know that, Dr. Thornton?"

"Because the man...."

"...the man said so." Morris completed for me. He was already on the phone speaking to his headquarters. Then he called the police, and finally the Vatican. He spoke briefly on all three numbers and then shrugged and returned to his armchair.

"Mind if I stay here a little longer?" he asked belatedly.

It was my turn to shrug. "Make yourself at home," I said ironically. Evidently the man already had.

Winston was in the kitchen getting out some cold cuts.

"I'm taking the liberty of serving Mr. Morris some food, Sir. He looks starved. I hope you don't mind."

I shrugged again. I didn't care what Winston did as long as Ruth was all right. And I disagreed with Morris. Why would the man, whoever he was, call, if they intended to harm Ruth? And, there was something familiar about the man's voice. I just couldn't place it. No. There had to be a different answer. But I had no idea what it was.

Sitting around doing nothing drove me crazy. Not just angry at my uselessness—I was getting used to that—but stark raving mad. After the snack that Winston practically forced on me, I walked to my office after all. Frankly, I needed the walk as much as I needed to do something. Anything was better than sitting around and biting my nails. I decided to dip into bionics. Soon my mind would be caught up in my research. It would take my mind off the present dilemma.

I walked faster. The fresh snow squeaked under my rubber soles. Just an inch or so, but it made the street look clean, innocent. Not like the people playing with my sister-in-law's welfare. I was beginning to long for power. Not like my healing gift, but something more concrete, tangible, something that would enable me to control my fate. Ruth's fate.

I shook off the snow from my coat under the canopy. There, the infrared lights would melt it; it would evaporate as if it had never been. Perhaps nothing really ever happens. Perhaps we are all imagining things just to give substance to the reality we live in.

When I opened the door to my office, Miss Dibbs got to her feet, smiled and looked away. She knew about Ruth.

"Anything from Rome?" I asked.

She shook her head.

Stop imagining things, man, and get on with your work, I whispered already in my office. But I had to use my imagination. It was part of my job.

I bit my lip and started pacing. I wanted to grab the viphone and call Lena, or at least Ruth's deputy, or someone who could do something. I held back. Everyone was working hard to get Ruth back.

I spun around, grabbed my coat, went past my secretary without a word, ran down the stairs and went outside. I needed to feel alive, to feel my body moving. I turned towards Mount Royal.

Within minutes I was jogging, my feet making crisp, creaking sounds on the packed snow, my lungs taking deep gulps of cool air emerging in fleeting, foggy clouds.

It helped.

It was bad enough that Ruth was per force unproductive. At least I could do something. Yet, here I was. The months I'd spent doing nothing were catching up with me. It was the indolent inactivity that must have been at the root of my hostility. I stopped to catch my breath. God, I needed exercise. Even as I quickened my step again, the desire to escape returned to me with a nagging force. There was another side to all this. During the last few years of my life, I'd witnessed that everything, absolutely everything that happened to me, followed a precise path. From the day of my leaving the seminary, to my meeting with the late Pope, a year ago, not one item could have been altered without changing the course mapped out for me. In a way not even I could explain, all the peripheral events had led me to my mystical communion with Vincenzo in Saint Peter's, in sight of the Pietà, or before that, with His Holiness bidding the final farewell to the world, the Church, to life itself. At the time, I didn't even know that his name was Vincenzo....

And then again, there were the events of some weeks ago. They, too, must have been preordained.

Yet here I was and, try as I might, I was quite unable to apply the same philosophy to Ruth. Surely, if the tides that govern our life are designed for our own good, then this must apply to everyone in equal measure. By opposing the current, we only delay our destiny, postpone the inevitable, but never eliminate it. I supposed, quite stoically, that should we fulfil what was intended for us, we would die, and wait for another incarnation.

I slowed down somewhat.

I was in no condition to jog. I'd been sedentary for too long. With the bare winter trees on my left, the relatively pristine snow hugging the slopes, I was surprised that the world around me was still functioning as it should. I recalled cross-country skiing on the top of Mount Royal in my youth, an undulating course right in the middle of the city. In those days things were so simple. Which course to take, what wax to use, how to get dressed for any particular weather condition were as grave problems as I had to face. Andrew often came with me. Now he was gone. As was Ruth. Even Cathy was away. The mountain wasn't quite as beautiful as it once had been. Without them, that is. Is beauty still there when there is no one to appreciate it? Would God be God if we weren't here to worship Him? A haven in the middle of a concrete jungle. A haven. Shall I ever find a haven again? Or God?

I was a slave to my destiny. Helpless.

But if so, what of Shakespeare's assertion? What of Cassius's dictum that 'The fault… is not in our stars but in ourselves that we are underlings'? What of destiny in those terms? We definitely have free will to follow our destiny or to delay it. It is not ours, however, to change the course of history for our convenience. Past or future. As I observed my own life, dispassionately, it seemed to me that the history of earth had already been written in minute detail. We all live in a giant aquarium scrutinized by some benevolent being, who seems to have very little interest in us. We can swim freely within the grand plan, but never veer on a new, a different course. It is not our world to enjoy. It was created by someone else for His or Her own purpose. Not for us. Not really. We're just visitors. Migrant workers. We must obey the laws. We cannot step out of bounds. If we do, we come across an invisible barrier that puts us in our place. But if so, then where are we supposed to be going?

For some reason my steps slowed down even more. I felt as if I were winding down. Like an old, rusty watch. Then again, there is no reason to hurry when you are going nowhere. I stopped, looking down at the snow. There was nothing there. As I looked up, I actually smiled at the slopes of Mount Royal. I walked past her slopes every day, but this was the first time I'd noticed the trees as barren of leaves as I was of ideas. Yet there was beauty in their filigree. Perhaps it was just the season. Perhaps we are all dormant in winter. Half dormant?

Still, where are we all going? Perhaps we are not supposed to know. Unless we learn who we really are. And then... are there not other realms? For some reason Winston's face shimmered before my eyes. He seemed to be smiling. Smiling knowingly?

Surprisingly, this little private soliloquy, this walk from nowhere to nowhere, the prolific patterns of fractal complexity hidden in the twigs waiting for spring, helped to settle my wrought nerves. Ruth will be all right, I told myself. All things will be all right, if we could only let them.

My office felt strangely lonely. Miss Dibbs must have gone on some errand. Since before Christmas, a guard had sat just inside the door of her office. He wasn't there. I always worked alone, but today there was emptiness surrounding me. I shook my head and clicked on my computer.

Bionics, I read, from bio as in *bio*logy meaning *life* and electro*nics,* is the application of methods found in nature to the engineering systems in modern technology. It is also known as *biogenesis*, *biomimetics,* and *bionical creativity engineering*. In computer science, bionics resulted in the advancement of cybernetics, artificial neurons, artificial neural networks, and swarm intelligence.

This was not going to be easy.

There was a great deal about the history of bionics, and about the methods of application. It seemed scientists thought of intelligence as a form of energy, or force, that could manifest itself through whatever offered itself for 'exploitation'. Rather like rain feeding the crops, though also causing flooding and destruction. I thought of the St. Thomas dictum, 'Whatever is received is received according to the nature of the recipient.' Artificial intelligence, it seemed, models an intelligent function regardless of whether it is inspired by organic structures or not. In some ways, it could be more applicable to robots. While bionics tend to enhance human functions and proclivities, artificial intelligence, as applied to robots, could reach beyond our inherent limitations.

I let that stew in my head for a while.

Also, I read on, in bionics, copying or mimicking led to another name for bionics, namely *biomimicry*.

Very appropriate, I thought.

There was also some stuff about broader applications of bionics in industry. Water-repellent surfaces of the lotus leaf, hulls of boats imitating the thick skin of dolphins, sonar, radar, ultrasound, and other imaging applications were all derived from imitating attributes developed by bats. Copying nature was definitely the way to go.

Unto the image and likeness… was nature god?

I glanced at my viphone. It remained silent. Stoically indifferent. I forced my attention back to the computer.

I suspected that my particular efforts should be directed at the application of bionics in medicine. For years already we'd had artificial hearts and most other internal organs. What was more, the deaf could hear, the blind could see. In most cases. Since early this century, silicon retinas had been implanted, performing the same function as a living retina. As far back as 2006, the first bionic hand had been produced in which all fingers had individual motion and motor reflexes.

The articles listed a number of new directions that the general public rarely heard about. These included bioimplantronics, biophysics in general, cyborgs, and fatronik that was directed mainly at the elderly and the disabled. These branches of bionics were so advanced that it was theoretically possible to manufacture a 'living' being, virtually from scratch. After repeated substitutions of electronics devised for living tissue, the recipient looked, acted, and seemed like a human being, although if humans are defined by their biology, then they were of a different species.

Was this the portent to the extinction of man? By unnatural selection?

Why doesn't the bloody phone ring?

Automatons, controlled from a distance, came next. I strongly suspected that the USA was much more advanced in this area of research than they admitted. Their incursions into Mgambia, a new splinter republic, and other troubled spots on earth, were living proof of that. I doubt that they could have accomplished the policing of the whole globe without such semi-human entities.

Were they still human? What makes us human? Didn't Socrates ask that very question or something very much like it?

What makes us human?

Who's to decide what human is. If computers superseded their own creators in intelligence, no matter how 'artificial', then were they, the computers, the sole arbiters? Computers had long passed the once famed Turing test, indicating intelligence indistinguishable from 'biological' humans. The human judges were convinced that the uploaded re-creation couldn't be distinguished from the original specific person. Even the human brain's incomparable ability to recognize patterns, our last bastion of superiority, might soon be lost. And then, who would decide who was human and who was not? Who is to be the judge and the jury? Who are the superior beings? Are we to be defined by our limitations? Our stupidity?

Einstein thought so. 'Only two things are infinite,' he'd said, 'the Universe and human stupidity, and I'm not sure about the former.' But also said that *the most incomprehensible thing about the world is that it is comprehensible*.

I wiped my forehead. Apparently we don't need to destroy our species with hydrogen bombs. We shall just wilt into oblivion even as artificial intelligence takes over. Science-fiction has become science. Like magic. The magic of today is the science of tomorrow. Well, it seems that the saying is no longer so trite. I began to understand the problems that Lena and her Solidarity were facing. We have to decide whether or not to survive.

How come I still feel, in a visceral, inexplicable way, that I am immortal?

The phone rang. Finally.

Cathy's voice was carefree yet sympathetic. She evidently didn't want to add to my problems.

"Anything new?" she asked.

"Not yet." How I wished I could have said something else. Anything.

"I've spoken to Winston. He offered to feed us, Peter. I thought of a restaurant, but he thought we ought be at home for the children."

"He's like that," I said, slightly embarrassed. Not that I intended to go out, but I hadn't thought of the children all day. They were in school, of course; but in Ruth's absence, staying at home in the evening was the least I could do.

"I thought you would appreciate it," Cathy replied, apparently not detecting my discomfort. "I'll be there at six, if that's OK." And not waiting for an answer she hung up.

When I got home, there were candles on the table. The Christmas tree lights were switched on and the subtle shimmering lights cast by the fireplace completed the warm atmosphere. It was almost time to put the tree away into storage. We'd used the same one for many years. Less pollution, my brother had said. Seems like ages ago.

Cathy was already there. The candles were her contribution. She thought I might need some cheering up. Less than a minute after my return, the balustrade deposited Jo and Mo at my feet. For them we had to act as if Ruth were just away on business.

"I did trigonometric progressions, Uncle Peter. Shall I show you?" Jo offered to bring me up to date with his schooling. I had no idea whatsoever what trigonometric or any other progressions were.

"I can do them faster," Mo announced.

"Trigo what?" I pretended not to have heard right.

"That's how you format composite video signals in a computer," Jo explained.

"Isn't that a bit advanced for your age?" I couldn't believe what they were teaching children in schools these days. Private schools, of course.

"You can look them up in a table of chrominance information...." Mo wouldn't be left out of the conversation.

For crying out loud, they were twelve years old!

Winston came to my rescue. "I think you should finish your homework before dinner, and then join us," he said in his usual relaxed voice. Halfway through his sentence the children were racing up the stairs. As for their information, I'd heard of arithmetic and geometric progressions but trigonometric?

"Do you have any idea what they were talking about?" I asked him in disbelief.

"Not so that I could explain it to one not trained...."

"...one as ignorant in technology as I am?"

"Come, Peter, your Martini is getting warm." This time Cathy came to Winston's rescue.

"But it's not Friday," I objected.

"Never mind, darling. Sometimes we all need a little extra something." She pulled me by my hand to my favourite armchair. Then she turned towards Winston. "Won't you join us? I know dinner is ready."

Winston bowed and took one of the armchairs. Whereas Cathy and I practically sunk into ours, he filled his to overflowing. "I gather there is nothing new, Sir?"

Something was missing. "Where is Morris?" I asked.

"I sent him home, Sir. He hasn't had a good night's sleep in two days."

I took a sip of Martini. "Winston," I asked, "are we immortal?"

"Yes, Sir." The reply was instant.

"You mean you and I and everybody?"

"No, Sir, not everybody."

"Are we not all equal?"

Winston allowed himself the vaguest of smiles. "No, Sir. No two of us are alike. Not even you and I."

I wondered why he singled out the two of us. Also, why he didn't include Cathy among the happy immortals. "And Miss Mondellay?"

"She's still working on it, Sir."

This time Cathy smiled. She also nodded her head. "I find it difficult to accept some premises without measurable evidence, Winston."

"Exactly, Madam. You start from the bottom and work your way up. Dr. Thornton did it the other way round. He had total conviction in his own immortality, which resulted in the direction his life took."

"And I am still working on it, eh?" Cathy's smile was almost coquettish.

"Very much so, Madam. And if I may say so, you are getting closer to your destination."

"You may say anything you want, Winston, but why did you draw that conclusion?"

"It is in your eyes, Madam."

"That's it?"

"And the pattern of your behaviour. You are pursuing that which is beyond the appreciation of our physical senses."

"Like bosons?"

"I am not conversant with the terminology, Madam. But it is quite evident that if your pursuits lie in infinity, then you are in grave danger of becoming immortal."

"Just what is the difference, Winston?"

"Well, Madam, it is hard to be human if you believe you're a monkey. It is equally as difficult to become immortal if you do not accept immortality as a modus operandi inherent in your state of consciousness."

"According to your faith it will be done unto you," I murmured, citing a verse from the past.

"Precisely, Sir. We cannot acknowledge what we do not believe in. Nor can we manifest it."

"And we can believe in things that are... that are unbelievable?" Cathy sounded very doubtful.

"The evidence of things not seen?" Winston said very quietly.

It was the second time that this phrase had come up in recent days. "The evidence of things not seen." Cathy had said those very words when she discovered in CERN the evidence of exploding bosons, I think. Or something like that. Nevertheless I was flabbergasted that Winston knew enough of the Bible to quote it.

"The Hebrews, I believe, Sir," Winston must have been reading my thoughts, or my facial expression as he called it. He meant Paul's letters to the Hebrews, of course. "Some time ago, Madame Thornton was in need of some assistance in this area, Sir. I took the liberty of reading the Bible I found in your room."

That was true. Ruth was becoming extremely fundamentalist in her beliefs, rather like the rest of the Solidarity movement. Not that I knew that many of its members. But still, to read the Bible once and retain enough of it to quote verbatim was staggering.

"Is Ruth immortal?" I asked out of nowhere.

Winston looked at his hands resting both palms on his thighs.

"I think the children have finished their homework, Sir. Perhaps I should call them to join us?"

I nodded. There was sadness in Winston's voice. I realized that it might well be impossible to be a fundamentalist and an immortal. A fundamentalist believes in power outside himself. An immortal believes the Immortal manifests through him. Or her, of course. In time, to the exclusion of everything else. Like that time in the Vatican, a year ago. It was getting to be more like eighteen months.

Once again, the dinner was simple and tasty. Cathy was a perfect lady of the house; I did my best to be a stand-in father. Not that the children needed any stringent control. They were quite embarrassingly precocious. Like with those trig-progressions, or whatever they were. They certainly didn't teach such things when I was going to school. Or even later. Frankly, technology has left me somewhere between the Neanderthal and the Peking man level. Whatever was not directly related to medicine, I'd studiously avoided. For years. In the meantime, I suppose, progress really has accelerated along an exponential curve. But if so, why do so many people seemingly go backwards? The stupefying computer games sharpening the players' ability to kill or maim, the escapism into the lands of fantasy usually sprinkled if not awash with blood... Why did people continue to escape reality?

Suddenly I felt sick to my stomach. Wasn't this exactly what I was doing? *I wished the viphone would ring. At least Ruth was firmly anchored in the here and now.* I was beginning to get nervous. Beginning?

We sang some carols. Cathy demonstrated a passable mezzo, Mo and Jo provided the treble so requisite for such occasions, and I did my best not to be heard. When the table was finally cleared, we all stopped in mid-note. Reaching us from the kitchen was a powerful basso. Moses, or possibly God Himself.

Gloria, gloria, gloria... in excelsis De-e-o.

This must have been the first time I had ever heard Winston sing. And most certainly the first time I heard him sing in Latin. Was there anything he couldn't do?

And then Winston's voice also stopped in mid-syllable. Powerful as his voice was, it did not drown the penetrating ring of the viphone. I got up and put the receiver on the speaker.

"Hello, my darlings," Ruth said. Her face on the tiny screen looked relaxed, almost radiant. "Just wanted to tell you that I'll be back tomorrow. The day after at the latest. Bye now...."

She waved to the kids, blew a kiss to Cathy and smiled at me. I must have inadvertently set our own lens on wide angle. Normally we could only see one person at a time. How did she know that Cathy and the children were all dining together? She didn't even look surprised.

***

15

The Attack

Ruth walked into her office at 10:37. Unharmed, and looking well rested, she came *down* the elevator. "Morning all," Ruth smiled breezily. The security guards stared at her as she walked passed them. At 10:39 her deputy, Mr. Gowan, a gentleman of proven acumen and unblemished character, took a deep breath, blinked a few times, and pressed the hotline connection to the Vatican. The recording light flashed repeatedly. "Mrs. Thornton is back," he said and hung up.

Ruth phoned me in my office moments after she arrived. Again, she sounded and looked as if nothing had happened. There was nothing wrong with my viphone.

"You'll never believe it, Peter, whom I met!" she began.

"Are you all right?" I couldn't hide the worry in my voice.

"Why, of course. Why on earth shouldn't I be?"

Something was fishy. I decided to take her words at face value. "You were away for three days, and no one knew where you were," I said, as calmly as I knew how. Somehow stating the obvious didn't sound silly.

There ensued a lengthy silence. At last Ruth cleared her throat.

"Peter, I've been away since last night, I called as soon as I could, and said I would be back today. I saw you all sitting in our sitting room. You and Cathy and the children... What is going on,

Peter?" Her previous good spirits had vanished. Her face was drawn if not actually worried. "Are the children all right?" she asked, after I didn't react to her words.

"Yes, Ruth, they're just fine. I think we'd better meet at home and get to the bottom of this."

"But I have work to do..."

"Have you spoken to Lena yet?"

"Why, no. Why should I bother her again?"

"Again?

"I was with her only a few hours ago."

This was getting too complicated.

"Look, if you don't want to go home, then I'll come over to your office. But I would rather Winston were there when we talked."

"What on earth has Winston to do with any of this?" She sounded a little rattled and frustrated.

"Can we have lunch at home?"

"Very well, Peter. But I think you're getting hysterical over nothing, or whatever men do in such circumstances. Not that I know what you think they are!"

In spite of the tension, I felt like laughing. Some time ago I took pains to explain to Ruth that it is biologically impossible for a man to get hysterical. Excitable, irascible, peevish, irritable, petulant, waspish, even acrimonious, but not hysterical. She'd remembered. At least some of it.

"I'll call Winston and meet you in Westmount in one hour," I was about to hang up when I remembered. "Oh, and make sure you're escorted," as apparently I would be. Not that I cared so much about my own safety. I clicked off the viphone.

I wondered if I should call Lena. I felt sure that she, or her office, had already been notified of Ruth's return. At this stage I had few answers and plenty of questions. I decided to wait.

I walked home even faster than I did yesterday. For a moment I felt sorry for my sentry, who must have found my pace irritating to say the least. On the way home I called Cathy on my vicell. The more the merrier, I thought, but only people I knew I could trust. Completely. Who knows what devious plans the ungodly had in mind? I sniggered at my choice of words. 'The ungodly'? Even to my own thoughts such words sounded like an afternoon TV soap opera. In spite of Ruth's return, I still felt nervous. I hated that.

What the devil had happened to Ruth, anyway? Perhaps Winston was right. Perhaps she had had a bout of amnesia. But if so, where had she made that call to us last night? And why would she say she would be back in a day or two and not in the morning the next day?

Winston must have performed miracles to have the table set for four within an hour. I'd already told him that I wanted him present at the luncheon.

"It will be a working lunch, Winston, and I need you there," I'd said, after I told him that Ruth was all right.

I felt detached, annoyed in an unspecified way, apart from the world. Why can't I be like other people, I wondered? Why can't I get deeply involved in some bellicose computer game or other toys that weaken the mind, dilute, dissipate, or even twist reality to sate my senses?

Then I recalled Winston's comment, 'No two people are alike,' he'd said. 'That's why,' I nodded my head in futile understanding, as I turned into my street. Upper Westmount. The land of the rich, the chosen few. I wondered where the chosen lived in Jerusalem. Atop a mountain? On Golgotha—the eighteen-foot-high Skull? Giv'at HaMivtar—the Ammunition Hill? The Mount of Olives? Or the fashionable south-west hill itself known in the time of Simon the Hasmonean as the new Mount Zion. Or perhaps, as in Rome, on any of the Seven Hills. Is that where the Christ will descend in all His glory after the Antichrist has ruled for three and a half years?

False images? Superstition? Futile speculation.

Had any of us been chosen, or do we all do our own choosing?

Vanity, vanity, all is vanity!

Futile vanity, because I've been trying to overcome this state of dissatisfaction for a year now. Apparently the victory is not up to me. Submission? And just then, for the first time ever, my attention rested on the giant oak in our own front garden. It ruled in all its majesty over the surrounding area. It cast a shadow even when denuded of its foliage. I wondered if I would ever cast a shadow. Over anyone. Any part of the earth.

Vanity?

As I opened the front door, I wondered why I hadn't taken a taxi; in spite of the chill, I got home covered in a slight perspiration. Walking got into my blood, I supposed. I am training to be a Nomad, I murmured dejectedly. A passer-by. I'm still good for nothing.

"Peter!" Ruth threw her arms around my neck. I was glad the children were in school. I needed Ruth's attention.

Evidently, she had taken a taxi or probably the company car. I returned her embrace, though with a little less ardour. I was angry at myself for feeling angry at her.

"What's wrong?" she asked, her expression turning into a worried frown.

"You are asking me?" This was nuts.

"Well, of course I am asking you. What is going on, anyway? In the office they wouldn't tell me anything. They said Lena would let me know, eventually I suppose, but Lena was not in her office. I've been out on overnight trips before. In fact, almost each time Lena stops in New York we meet there. It's easier to touch base that way."

"Lena was in New York?" Something didn't fit. "Last night?"

"Why, yes. I just told you so, didn't I?" Now Ruth looked perplexed. She was beginning to sound exasperated with my reactions.

Just then Winston let Cathy in. I told her what Ruth told me in one sentence. "There is only one problem," I added, turning to Ruth again. "Lena thought you'd been kidnapped three days ago and ordered a complete blockade of Montreal airports and other routes of escape. Doesn't quite tally with your story, Ruth."

Ruth let go of Cathy's and my hands and took a step back. Then she turned and sat heavily in the nearest chair.

"B-b-but I spent the evening with her last night. We only had about an hour so we thought we might meet again today. But there was some trouble in CERN and she had to leave early."

"In CERN? What?" Cathy was up in arms. That was her domain.

"Two of her men disappeared. They were her leading liaison officers, geneticists, I believe, in the European... But why are you asking? Didn't anyone tell you?"

"Tell me what?" I asked.

"It seems that the Americans have started an all-out attack against our genetic research team. There were incidents in CERN, in the Vatican, London, Paris and Berlin. A total of seventeen of our key research computer hard disks had been erased. All at precisely the same time. We still aren't sure what if anything was lost. Lena spoke to the UN ambassador in New York to launch an official complaint against the USA. Or the Pentagon, to be precise."

"Is that what, ah... Lena told you? Is there direct evidence that the US is behind it all?"

"We have our people at the Pentagon. We just can't admit it openly."

"Surely, you have duplicate files . . .don't you?" Cathy was shaking her head in disbelief.

"Why yes... I suppose so. I am not on the scientific staff."

I wondered why nobody had mentioned the disappearing files. Of course, I was not involved with security. "And Lena told you all that?" I watched Ruth's face.

"Well, yes. She told me just before she left for the airport."

Throughout all this Winston hadn't said a word. Now he appeared at the door to announce that lunch was ready.

"*Madame est servie*," he said gravely. And then in a lighter tone, he added, "Might I inquire, Madame, what is your recollection of leaving your office before you found yourself in New York?"

We all turned to face him. Ruth didn't reply. She raised her hand to her forehead, seemingly trying to remember. She didn't say anything till we all gathered at the table. No one felt like eating.

"That's what I started telling you, Peter, when I said that you would never guess whom I met." Her tone no longer sounded quite as confident.

"Please, Ruth, do not keep us in suspense. You...." Now I was really getting angry. My sister-in-law was still acting as if the whole affair was a big joke.

"It was Sawicki. Captain Sawicki. You know? Lena had sent him to escort me to New York by a STOLL jet. It was fun, taking off from the middle of..." she stopped when she saw my face.

"Ex-Captain Sawicki was fired by Lena, personally, in my presence, more than a year ago," I said very softly.

"B-b-but, that's impossible," Ruth was gasping for air.

"He was dismissed for the way he'd been operating on her behalf. Using children to assure my services, remember?"

Judging by Ruth's face, the memories were coming back to her. A year ago she must have been under sufficient stress to block out some fragments from her memory.

"And what exactly did Captain Sawicki say to you?"

"He said that Lena wanted to see me in New York," her eyes were getting larger. "He said he would get me there."

"To the best of my knowledge, Lena hasn't left the Vatican during the last few days," I said flatly.

"B-b-but Captain Sawicki was so polite..." Ruth began.

"...as he was a year ago, as I recall." It appeared that Ruth didn't. "Captain Sawicki was oozing charm even as he was organizing the abduction of your children to save his beloved Lena. It appears that love has turned to hatred. Love scorned, and all that."

"That's only true of women, darling," Cathy said, rising.

She walked around the table, stood behind Ruth, and began slowly massaging Ruth's neck. My sister took a deep breath and visibly relaxed. "You are among friends, Ruth," Cathy whispered. Then she returned to her chair.

Winston very pointedly raised a plate of canapés and passed it to me, to pass on to Cathy and Ruth. They both reached for morsels and began eating. We all needed a moment's grace from the hard questions that had to follow. I got up and opened a bottle of Merlot. I thought wine might relax Ruth, as well as myself. My own temper was fluctuating between worry, anger, and frustration. Everybody was doing their thing and I was merely reacting. I felt a great need to do something on my own.

"If I may, Madam, might I ask where did you stay in New York?" Winston asked, after a moment of pensive silence.

"Why, I don't know. We landed on the roof. At least that was what Captain Sawicki said. The cabin windows were drawn for security..." and then she looked up from her plate. "I have no idea where I was, Winston, but I did meet with Lena."

I remembered the photographs of Lena in places she'd never been. "Or her doppelgänger," I murmured, but everyone heard me.

"You don't really believe that, do you, Peter?" Ruth was practically in tears.

Yet no one denied it. It was the only explanation. Then Ruth remembered. "Those pictures... They wanted to test if I'd recognize..." she began but turned deathly pale. "I told her... I mean whoever it was, things that were highly confiden...."

"They were of a highly confidential nature," I completed her confession softly. Lena's doppelgänger had evidently passed its, or was it her, test. "On the other hand," I said aloud, "Ruth did mention that when Lena and she met alone, they seldom talked business. Women's talk?" I offered hopefully.

"Perhaps, Madam should rest for a while," Winston suggested, ending lunch almost as quickly as it started. Winston escorted her upstairs and insisted that she rest a half-hour before joining us again. Ruth obeyed him, even as the children did. As we all did, at times.

"It appears that she was drugged and introduced to an android, or some sort of Lena's double," I offered when Winston got back.

"Androids are creatures of science-fiction, Peter," Cathy said, shrugging her shoulders. "There must be a better explanation."

"Have you read about the advances they've made in bionics?"

"Not lately, but androids..."

"The name is immaterial. We are dealing with people who have made gigantic strides in robotics, in artificial intelligence and also in bionics. If you combine the three, we are facing artificial intelligence that can move around and look human."

"You're serious, Peter? Have they gotten that far?" Cathy was beginning to take me seriously.

"It's not really that far, unless you don't know where you are going. I think for our friends down south it's all a matter of expediency. Whatever they do is no more than a means to an end. And in their context of morality, the means don't matter..."

"And the end? The end is what?" She sounded doubtful.

"How should I know? World domination? Protection of their way of life? Mammon?"

"They've already got plenty of that, and they already act as world police."

"Power, like love, is never fully satisfied. You always want to take more, even as love always wants to give more. We cannot reach perfection down here..." I mused aloud.

"You are beginning to sound like a preacher, Peter."

It was too late to withdraw my previous statement. I tried to veer the conversation back to more scientific rails.

"Don't knock the android," I said. "The word comes from the Greek *andr-* meaning man, and the suffix *–eides* used to denote 'of the species'. At the Osaka University and the Science University of Tokyo, the Hanson Robotics in Texas, the KAIST Research Institute of Korea, and many other places, they've been working on humanoid mechanics for ages..."

"And soon we shall be unable to recognize an android from a human being?"

"Computers passed the Turing test some years ago. Bionics can reproduce artificial body parts, robotics can propel them, what else is there?" I held my ground.

"The soul?" For a change Cathy was venturing into the esoteric.

"And this coming from a woman whose reality is suspended in the Higgs field?"

"Perhaps that is why," Cathy countered, "I can see so much more than one can see with one's eyes."

"But can your eyes tell you if Ruth is Ruth... or a substitute...."

"Peter! Stop! This is madness!" Cathy stood up waving her arms. Very un-Cathy-like. We stopped the argument that wasn't leading anywhere. I no longer felt like talking. It seemed futile.

"Madam is her true self," Winston announced with measured words. "She is exactly who she appears to be. And, if I may, Sir, Miss Mondellay is right. We do have a higher consciousness that is discernible in human beings, if often hidden under a veil of materiality."

I took a deep breath. Now I knew why we needed Winston at the table. He was the only sane person here. Or maybe Cathy, too, after all. As for myself, I had to decide which god I was going to serve. I felt I was being torn apart. Pulled in opposite directions. I'd begun with religion, transferred to science, withdrawn into the mystical, and now was slowly sinking into mechanistic jargon. Something had to give. Probably, my sanity.

"Am I mad?"

Ruth stood framed by the archway leading to the dining room. We all rose to our feet. Cathy reached her first, embraced her and led her to the table. "Am I mad?" Ruth repeated softly.

"We all are, my dear. That's what makes us such an interesting group of people," Cathy assured my sister with a grave face.

"I'm so glad. For a moment I thought I was the only one," Ruth replied.

The quick nap had done her good.

I hadn't even noticed that Winston had cleared the table and brought coffee. As I've always said, the man became invisible at will. Alternatively I am a prize scatterbrain. For now I was glad that Ruth seemed her old self. Seemed or was? I had to stop that, I told myself, if I wanted to remain reasonably sane. Reasonably would do for now.

"So what did you guys talk about?" Ruth asked innocently.

For some reason we all looked down at our hands, then the ceiling, and finally Cathy and I reached out for coffee.

"We were wondering, Madam, if you had been substituted for your real self," Winston offered at last. Cathy or I would never have dared to say it.

"Really? And what conclusion have you reached?" Ruth didn't even blink.

"I took the liberty, Madam, of assuring our guests that you are indeed the Mrs. Thornton that we all hold in such high esteem."

Winston had a way with words.

"Why, thank you, Winston. And did you manage to convince our guests?"

"If anyone calls me a guest again, I'll scream," I snapped.

It wasn't often that I heard Winston laugh. It started somewhere at the tips of his toes, mounted and swelled as it travelled upwards and then filled the dining room to the brim. Ruth joined him, though her contribution could be likened more to a string of pearls being strewn over a crystal plate than to a roll of thunder. I looked at Cathy.

"I think they are laughing at us, Peter. I don't think we should patronize this restaurant any more. Shall we go?" With that she picked up her cup and saucer and walked stiffly, her head thrown back like an offended celebrity, towards the sitting room. I soon followed. It was a little while before the offending duo joined us.

"So what exactly happened to me?" Ruth looked perfectly relaxed. I wished I was.

Apparently Ruth knew even less about the last few days in her life than we did. I looked to see if either Cathy or Winston wanted to speculate on the situation. No such luck. I took a deep breath.

"We do not know anything, Ruth. But as far as we can surmise, three days ago you were hoodwinked by an old acquaintance. I rather think that after leaving your office to go to lunch, you received a call on your vicell. I suggest that you recognized the face of Captain Sawicki, smiling and inviting, who delivered to you a phoney message from Lena. You didn't remember his dismissal. Evidently he was counting on that."

"I most certainly did remember his face. I just didn't..."

"Yes, we know. At any rate, the captain, or should I say the ex-captain, instructed you to go up to the roof where your heliport is situated, and where he was probably waiting for you. If you have your people at the Pentagon, we must assume that the Pentagon has people in your organization also."

"It's all so dirty..." Cathy made a face of disgust.

"They are not scientists, Cathy, they are men and women of emotions and..."

"Are you suggesting that I am a woman devoid of emotions?"

"I love you, darling. Emotionally and in every other way. May I continue?"

She gave me a dirty look.

"From the roof you were taken to a location that was clear of any Solidarity scanners. There, or *en route,* you were probably drugged and either there or somewhere else, you met the false Lena, who fed you a lot of hogwash about the war between the Pentagon and Solidarity, to gain your confidence. Remember that most of the three days you were likely under the influence of some sort of narcotic that affected your perceptions, and your perception of time. You may have been hypnotized to believe that you flew to New York, or that you were away only one night from Montreal. How am I doing?"

I looked around.

Ruth looked stunned, Winston rather pleased with my performance, and Cathy was beginning to recover from my misunderstood suggestion that she might not be a fully emotional being.

"B-b-but the files…?" Ruth blurted.

"If they really were erased, it was all essentially a warning. A series of warnings. Like your disappearance. After all, they must have known that scientists keep copies."

I couldn't but wonder if 'they' kept a 'copy' of my sister-in-law. If there was a pseudo-Ruth conversing with pseudo-Lena somewhere in the bowels of the Pentagon. For now, there was little else anyone could add to the story. Suddenly Ruth got up and ran upstairs. She came back with her handbag. She turned it upside-down on her lap. The usual paraphernalia made a little heap on her skirt. She looked through it by moving the various items around. It was almost comical. She looked frazzled.

"I know I have it somewhere. I saw it this morning… There!"

From a side pocket in the now empty bag she pulled out a piece of paper. She held it up like a prize trophy.

"Can anyone tell me what this means? It wasn't in my bag before... you know, before…"

Once again I took charge. I unfolded the double-folded sheet of paper and held it up to the lamp on the side table. It was a handwritten note, in an orderly, disciplined hand. I read the words aloud.

"Next time it will be more permanent." It was signed Superman. The 'S' being a stylized S used on Solidarity letterhead.

There were no pleasant conclusions we might reach. The relative peace we'd achieved following my *exposé* was once again ruined. I called Ruth's office, as well as my own, and advised them that we would not return to work today. I also told them to advise the Vatican that all was OK, that we would report later. As for myself, I was determined to spend the rest of the afternoon devising a plan of action. I was through reacting.

Cathy returned to her parents' house. It was funny. She had her own *pied á terre* on Sherbrooke Street but never seemed to stay there. She preferred to give what little free time she had to her mother and father. After all, she was the only daughter. She was scheduled to go back to CERN early next week. If I knew my girl, she was looking forward to it. At least there the things she did were clean. Untainted by human depravity.

"I'll go home and have a long shower," she told me. She probably did.

At last I was alone. For some reason my room seemed small and intimate, especially after spending long hours in my office at the Old Vic. I no longer thought of my room as a prison but rather as a quiet place, almost the haven I had been longing for. *Enter into thy closet…* echoed words from my past. A desk, a bed, two armchairs—one seldom used—and bookshelves that lined two of the walls, floor to ceiling. Yes, it was definitely a haven, a place I could escape to. I need not look any further.

It was time for me to employ my particular talents. So far I was only aware of my healing power. What other surprises lurked inside me about which I still knew nothing? Perhaps I wasn't quite as useless as I thought I was.

It was time for action.

After all was said and done, I found a perverse pleasure in remembering some of the ancient scriptures. It appeared that the androids, the cyborgs, or the bionic men and women, robots of any and every kind, were all created in the image and likeness of man, their creator. And let us not forget the clones that even now were fighting for legal recognition. With all those creatures demanding equality with us, or even superiority over us, man still stood alone. There was a reason for that. Only man had been created unto the image and likeness of God. I derived a strange comfort from that thought. Even if it was just a myth.

But would man survive? Was man really immortal?

Whatever happened to Neanderthal man? To the Empire of the Incas? What of Lemuria, Atlantis, the Kingdom of Mu? Did they not all disappear?

***

16

Nomad

Apparently, there are different kinds of action. "*Wu wei*," Cathy said. "*Wu wei er wu pu wei.*" She smiled at me. God, how I loved that smile. "Your Chinese is not very good, is it?"

This wasn't as inane a question as it sounded. During the period before Quebec had rejoined Canada, the Chinese influence had grown enormously. Essentially they'd flooded the Province with capital. The 'sovereign' government just didn't know how to refuse. And cultural influences followed. Still, I continued to lag behind with my Chinese.

"It's attributed to Lao Tsu," she explained, making me none the wiser. "It means, roughly, 'taking no action, there is no not acting'."

Now that made it perfectly clear. Evidently I must have looked at her with exasperation.

"It teaches you to just be. To stop trying so hard, and just be. Just be the best you can…."

That came a little closer to the mark. There was a difference between doing nothing and just being. One is a sign of laziness, or in my case a form of escape from reality that I didn't like, whereas the other is a conscious act of acceptance.

I decided to try it. I sat still, attempting to relax, waiting for something to happen. I must have been doing it wrong. Perhaps I shouldn't have expected anything. Perhaps I should have made myself available to give, as in healing, and not hold my breath to receive something in return. I'd seen Winston sitting with the children apparently not doing anything, but those inner realms into which Winston must have been guiding Mo and Jo were not for me—as yet. I hope it was just 'not as yet', because Mo and Jo seemed to feel very good after such inner communion with Winston. On the other hand, perhaps it was Winston who was the key. The man had something indefinable and, for me, still unattainable. I decided to tackle him at first opportunity. Or it could be that I was still too worried about Ruth, her inexplicable disappearance, and all the shenanigans that the Pentagon seemed to be indulging in.

In the meantime, Cathy was about to leave for Switzerland. CERN was awaiting, and God's particles were exploding in arcs galore. I wondered if she was wu wei'ing while trying to capture the elusive boson. I hoped she would find it.

We found a small café at the airport before she boarded her plane. We kept to the shadows, like two forlorn lovers longing for privacy. We didn't want to be spotted by anyone.

"But, darling," Cathy said, her eyes welling with mystic light, "the Higgs particle is created in collisions every day. The problem is that each lasts less than a thousandth of a billionth of a billionth of a second."

"That's about as long as my medical career," I quipped, but she was off and away.

"The 7000-tonne Atlas detector sits inside a cavern large enough to rival... the nave of Westminster Abbey… or the Duomo di Milano…" She went on for a while, leaving me miles behind. I understood every third or fourth concept.

"So large to capture so small," I whispered, but there was no holding her.

"…all those extra dimensions." I heard her voice but not her meaning. It was like explaining the beauty of Renoir's painting to a blind man. "One of the extra dimensions is gravity," she continued. "If we can wedge extra dimensions open, we might release a tug of gravity powerful enough to compress matter into miniature black holes."

This went on for a little while. I'd heard of some black holes having a mass of a billion suns, madly spinning about their axes as fast as 950 times a second, but mini-black holes? It sounded ridiculous.

"You would never believe how exciting it is..." She was referring, once more, to the invisible, the intangible, the ephemeral. Just like I'd been at the seminary. Is science a religion? They had their dogmas, their mysteries, and certainly their martyrs.

Had I not stopped her, Cathy would have missed her plane. There were kisses and hugs as we parted.

"Did you lose any files?" I couldn't help asking.

"I called the following morning, their time. Not one. I suspect the whole thing was just a hoax."

"You mean the info they fed Ruth..."

"Yes. A sort of cat-and-mouse game. Just to scare us. I mean them, the Solidarity people, I suppose?"

A hoax? Not Ruth's disappearance, I mused, but I kept my thought to myself. There was no point worrying her.

"One day," I said, instead, "we shall both live and work on the same planet, on the same side of the ocean, in the same city." I wanted to add, in the same house, the same home. Dreams are made of such simple things.

"Hopefully, darling, you'll find time to come over for a visit," she pleaded, her eyes gazing into mine.

Those glorious eyes. I felt sure that no robot, not even a bionic clone, could match the fires shimmering in their depths. In that instant I knew, with utter conviction, that Cathy was human. Although I could not even define the term as yet, the humanity was not in her appearance, her behaviour, or even in the things she said. It was hidden yet overt in the depths of her eyes. She didn't look at me *with* her eyes, she looked *through* them, even as I looked at her.

I stood in the departure lounge until her plane left the runway. Those birds were fantastic. Many times less noisy than anything that had flown some years ago. For a moment, once again, I felt lonely. *Wu wei,* I told myself. Even if I don't do much, I shall be the instrument through which great things can be accomplished. On the way to my car I remembered one of my seminary colleagues, a man with whom I shared a room. His name was Stanislas, after the

Polish saint Stanislas Kostka. Once, when I needed an emotional prop, he'd quoted the words of his patron. *Ad majora natus sum*, he'd said. For greater things am I born. I still wondered what they were. Or what they might be. Funny that. I didn't even remember my roommate's face, but I remember the Latin saying.

Ad majora natus sum.

Aren't we all? Are we not all born to do greater things than the mundane, the ordinary? Are we not all chosen people, if only we'd realize it?

When I got home, I looked for Winston. He was out. Through the half-drawn curtains I could just see two men in a grey Toyota parked on the other side of the street. They must have followed me. Lena was not taking any chances.

I went up to my room, sat at my desk, and closed my eyes. I had to learn to do nothing. To do nothing actively. To listen, not to demand. To learn to be grateful, not to allow frustration to guide my emotions. I tried wu wei.

Nothing happened.

Frustrated, I switched on my computer and typed 'aura' in the search engine. I got tons of results. I clicked one at random.

HOW TO SEE AND READ THE AURA

The article that followed claimed that there was nothing 'paranormal' in the Universe. I liked that. Winston had said as much not so long ago. Also, all the evangelists agreed. *For nothing is secret, that shall not be made manifest; neither any thing hid, that shall not be known and come abroad.* And later, ….*it is given unto you to know the mysteries.* There had been days when I believed such words. They were part of my training, conditioning. Now my mind was metamorphosing them into knowledge. Simple beliefs into simple knowledge. The Gnostics of old must have gone through a similar process. Do we really progress toward a greater understanding, I wondered? It seemed that thousands of years ago peoples' knowledge of the true nature of the Universe was greater than whatever we could measure or quantify today, including the fragments detected by Cathy's oversized collider at CERN. The ancients held the big picture in their fingertips; today we play with details. Einstein was right. Tell me the thoughts of God, he said, the rest are details. Yet Cathy, in her special way, was searching for both. She wanted to know the big picture by building it up from its components. Is that what quantum mechanics was all about?

How to see and read auras.

So there is nothing paranormal in nature save for our inability to understand and perhaps accept the truth. What we know today is but a tiny drop in an infinite ocean of Knowledge. Yes, with a capital K. Secret Knowledge. Spiritual—I used to call it. It wasn't. Isn't. It's just knowledge of our inner nature. There is ample evidence that since ancient times people have been able to see auras, depicting advanced giants such as Buddha and Jesus, and many of his disciples, with golden halos. These were not religious symbols, as similar halos had been drawn in prehistoric cave paintings in West Kimberleys, Australia. Prehistoric!

Were we subjects of devolution? Was humanity drawing to its dismal end? Have we fulfilled our function in the scheme of things? But if so, what is that Big Scheme? What are the Thoughts of God?

How did they see the auras?

The article insisted that anyone can see auras. Or at least, train oneself to see them. It is, they said, an acquired skill. The article identified techniques that doubled the energy of the electro-phonic aura in minutes. And there were many colours to be seen, each having a different meaning to an experienced practitioner. The yellow tending toward gold was the highest hue, denoting joy and freedom, a high degree of spiritual development. The word spiritual, however, was not explained. But there were also purples and blues, turquoises and green auras, pink and orange and red. There were also some dirty colours such as browns and greys, the colour of mustard and even white that was not close to golden but rather gave evidence of grave problems, of sickness and disharmony, like noise in most of the music we hear these days. The white aura precedes our death and greatly increases in intensity.

There was a great deal to learn.

There were exercises. For the next two hours I sat staring at various coloured shapes, at circles and segments of circles. Then I looked at the winter trees outside my window. They were asleep, dark grey against the snow. But as I looked, slowly I started to see another colour. A sort of pale yellow surrounded the trees, like a lighted fog at their periphery. They were still alive. Dormant yet alive. Then I looked at my hand. A different colour but it was there. Oscillating between grey and sulphur. Not nice. There was still a great deal of anger, of unclear intentions. I had a long way to go. On the other hand, I shared the same life force that enlivened the trees, or at least the trees of winter. Am I also merely half-alive? Is there but one life that courses through our veins? Through the whole of nature? I am the original fragrance of the earth, and I am the light in fire, Krishna had said. I am the taste of water, the light of the sun and the moon... Such beautiful words came from a young cowherd boy. And what of other Avatars? I am within you even as you are within me. Who was it that said that? Whosoever believeth in me shall never die. Who is the *me*? I am life, he'd said. And life is within me.

I am the Self, seated in the hearts of all creatures.

I was beginning to relax when my viphone blinked, demanding my attention. JR's face grinned at me.

"I thought you might like to know," he said. "It was sodium thiopental. A small dose. That and some other stuff we are still analysing."

"We?"

"The medics. I have a friend there. You know, the labs on the eighth floor."

So Ruth's blood tests were trickling in.

"Thanks," I said and clicked off.

I had a vague idea what sodium thiopental can do to a psyche. Better known as sodium pentothal, it is a rapid-onset short-acting general anaesthetic. Sodium thiopental is sometimes used during interrogations—not to cause pain but to weaken the resolve of the subject and make him or her more submissive to persuasion.

It makes you say the truth. Poor Ruth, I thought. I hope she doesn't know that.

I tore myself from my crowding thoughts. For now, there was nothing I could do for Ruth. I also refused to sink back into religious interpretation of the words that flooded my mind before the viphone interruption. Life was an energy that transformed chaos into order and harmony. Chaos that possessed latent order within itself. A chaos that was omnipresent. Like heaven, with its infinite potential. Chaos that gave birth to beauty. Beauty that is life, the process of becoming....

My head was spinning. I got up, ran downstairs and grabbed my coat. I went outside. The last rays of the sun kissed the very tops of twigs reaching for its life-giving energy.

I walked down the street looking at people's auras. I didn't see much. It took time to really perceive the colour. Yet there were suggestions of many. Weak and strong, mostly weak, none radiated pure colour. Then, from a distance, I saw a minor sun illuminating the street below me. Just that. A radiant halo of pure light that seemed to float some five or six feet above the sidewalk. I found it unbelievable that no one else could see it. Then I recognized the contour, then the massive shape. Winston was coming back. It was hard to believe that only yesterday he would have been as invisible to me as he remained to the masses of people milling on the street below me. For a while I stood transfixed by the image I witnessed. Then, even as he approached, his aura diminished until I couldn't see it at all. Did Winston suspect something? For some reason I was afraid.

I turned and walked away.

The following day I continued to do my work on genetics and artificial intelligence, though my heart wasn't in it. I observed the aura of every person I met. I wasn't good at it. They thought I was staring.

"Is there something wrong, Dr. Thornton?" they'd ask.

You bet there is. A dirty brown aura is clinging to your head, mister. The same was true of women. Only I couldn't tell them that. Winston had never told me about my emanation. Was it really an emanation? Is the colour of our aura a secret that we must carry to our grave? What of other people's?

At noon I left my desk to go to the cafeteria. I walked slowly, to gain maximum time for observing people. I concentrated on their heads, particularly against a light or white background. It paid off. There was such a rainbow of colours. Did saints walk around surrounded by rainbows? Or did this have nothing to do with one's moral standing? Just a characteristic like the colour of one's eyes, or hair? Just a trait like any other.

My head swam.

Everyone had an aura. Some hardly discernible, as if uncertain, just a shimmer, a sliver of light following the contour of their head. But it was there. I continued to walk slowly, pretending to be looking for something in my pockets.

And then I stopped dead. Sitting against the wall was a man, a sentry's insignia on his lapels. He had no aura at all. I sauntered back and returned again, staring at his forehead. Nothing. Nothing at all. And then he turned. Obviously, he wasn't dead. Just his aura was missing. Is that possible? Winston would know, I suspected. There was a slight shimmer surrounding his head, but no more so than I would detect on a stone, a rock. Perhaps a millimetre in thickness, a little less. And the human auras I'd seen pulsated; his, what little there was, didn't.

I forgot about lunch and went back to my work. I still had to file the final report to Lena on the latest stuff I got from JR, our expert on Artificial Intelligence. John Robb was a very thorough man. He didn't leave out any details but refused to draw conclusions. That was my job. I had to make heads or tails of the mass of data he'd supplied me with.

By seven, the office was quiet and the report was finally finished. My report was as up-to-date as it could be. It confirmed all previous suspicions. Artificial intelligence and the resulting technologies were advancing along an exponential curve. AI was about to surpass anything man could do on his own. Already, computers were designing new computers, cyborgs improved other cyborgs, bionic enhancements were embedded in semi-artificial men. *Homo sapiens* had run his course.

I sent my report to Lena and turned my computer off. She could pass it on to anyone she chose. For now, my work was done.

I took a last look at the gentle aura generated by the tree outside my office window, just to make sure it was still alive. I smiled at my thoughts. For thirty years, ten of them studying medicine, including diagnostics, never had anyone mentioned any auras. Not once. I just couldn't believe it.

I walked home.

When Winston opened the door, he looked exactly as he always looked. No matter how I squinted, directly, overtly, or with my peripheral vision, his aura just wasn't there. Perhaps the man was a robot, after all. An android? If so, becoming a race of androids wouldn't be half bad for the human species.

"That's very droll, Sir," I heard his deep laughter inside my head. And then Mo's and Jo's screams demanded all my attention. Two gregarious golden globes sliding down the stairs at full speed. Raucous banter and energy.

The great silence and the boisterous screams. An exercise in duality?

I raced them upstairs and dove into my room. Safe at last.

Children…

We are all capable of the good as well as of the despicable. That's what reality on earth is all about. Duality—in my case a virtual dichotomy. What I needed was to find the exact middle ground. Beyond doing right, and doing wrong, there is a field... I'll meet you there.

Are children the middle ground?

Jalaludin Rumi was so much more than a poet. A poet and a theologian but most of all a mystic. But not of the anthropomorphic gods. He was a Sufi, he served his Beloved... God named Love, and no other. Can anyone do more? To him belonged the enigmatic words; the journey was up to me—beyond the realm of duality.

I spent the next few days sauntering through the Headquarters of Solidarity International in Montreal. I did it under the pretext of getting to know my bread provider. Ruth gave me a pass that admitted me to even the most confidential places. A triple A clearance. The top. She also gave me one of those elusive signalling devices. It wasn't implanted subcutaneously in my head; I carried it on a little chain around my neck. It was feather-light, almost invisible, yet it weighed me down. I felt as though I'd lost some of my individuality. No matter, I needed it, for now. I never realized just how much security was involved in Solidarity's activities. I suppose when you run an international organization of well over two billion people, there were things that you wanted to keep to yourself. Like some aspects of finances, or the latest trends in crowd control—the psychology of the masses, or of security itself.

I never thought I would ever be entertaining such thoughts as were now becoming strangely acceptable.

I was beginning to face facts.

I was becoming an ardent atheist. I say 'ardent' because it wasn't just a philosophical conclusion but also emotional. I didn't recognize any superior beings, superior entities, who deigned to control my life. I and I alone was responsible for my fate. Yes, there was a destiny awaiting me, but no more so than anyone else. It was that field beyond the doing right and doing wrong.

Yet, for now, the Field itself remained as elusive as ever.

I began to identify, with some degree of confidence, the colour and character of people's auras. I could tell liars from the speakers of the truth, the healthy, who pretended some malady to gain time off from work, from those who really suffered.

"Can you tell the character of a person just from seeing his or her aura?" I asked Winston that evening. He allowed me to be aware of his own, though it remained virtually invisible. It felt as though I were detecting an echo.

"Can you, Sir?" came the cryptic reply.

"Why do you ask?" I smiled. "I think so, but only in very general terms. Right or wrong type of thing. Not the nuances."

"It will come, Sir. It is necessary," he added, after a momentary silence.

"Necessary? For what?" I really wanted to know.

"It depends, Sir, what you are looking for," he replied as though discussing items on a menu.

Once cryptic, always cryptic. If there were such a philosophical school of thought, I would call Winston the greatest exponent of crypticism. And if there is no such word, well, that's just too bad.

I called Cathy late that night. I wanted to catch her before she left for work. She was already up. Six-thirty, her time.

"Darling, how sweet of you to call!" She was already full of beans. I wondered what colours her aura emanated. I bet it was a beautiful rainbow crowned by a ring of pure gold.

"I just missed you, darling. Everything OK?"

"Oh, Peter, you just won't believe it. It's like living science-fiction!" Her tone already assumed the euphoric overtones of a passionate believer. "Yesterday we activated new detectors. There are a number of them. Some will study the theory of super-symmetry, perhaps proving that each particle in the Universe is balanced by a heavy invisible twin. This would explain why ninety percent of the material in the Universe seems to be... missing, oh... I am babbling, aren't I."

"It doesn't matter what you say. I just wanted to hear your voice...."

"I love you, you know?" was her next revelation.

"Yeah, I know. Likewise. See you..."

I hung up. There was no point. We may have been going towards the same destination, but we were approaching it from opposite directions. The ethereal thread that kept us together over miles of land and sea was love. How tenuous a link it is, I mused. I also didn't tell her about Ruth and the sodium pentothal. She had problems of her own.

It was later that same night that I reached my first understanding. It emerged from the dim antiquity of my personal experience of about a year ago, and from a deep conviction that demanded to be recognized. I finally understood the word Nomad. A year ago I called myself Simon Nomad. Now, lying in bed, waiting for sleep, I understood why I had chosen that name. For some time now, I'd felt like a stranger in a strange land. I had nowhere to lay my head. My thoughts, my ideas, my longings, searching, the hunger for Rumi's field. With a force that literally made my head spin, I realized that I didn't belong here. That what I saw with my eyes, detected with my senses, was just a thin layer protecting the true reality, yet a reality accessible to each and everyone of us. Somehow…

No. My kingdom was definitely not of this world. Here I would forever remain a nomad. A passer-by. Be passers-by, Thomas advised in his Gnostic Gospel. Vaguely, as with the shimmering auras, as in my unwilling hands that could do more than any physician's could, and most of all that time in the Vatican when the Last Pope was dying, the man I later saw in the Main Apse, at the Triune in St. Peter's, all these provided me with glimpses of a different realm. Perhaps that kingdom belonged to my Cathy, too. My very own Cathy.

If not, I would remain a nomad forever.

***

Nanotechnology

The role of the infinitely small is infinitely large.

Louis Pasteur

The principles of physics...
do not speak against the possibility
of manoeuvering things atom by atom...

Richard Feynman
Joint recipient of the Nobel Prize in Physics in 1965,
in his seminal speech in 1959 in Pasadena, California:
"There's Plenty of Room at the Bottom"

17

The Blanks

While it cannot be confirmed beyond a reasonable doubt, scholasticism which produced such giants as St. Thomas Aquinas, the 13th century Christian philosopher, theologian and a Dominican monk, preoccupied itself, *inter alia*, with the question of how many angels could dance on the head of a pin.

An evangelist of the last and early 21st century, renowned for communal gatherings at which he breathed fire and brimstone at his many followers, assured us that, "Speculation about the nature of angels has been around since long before Queen Victoria's time, and it continues down to the present time." I strongly suspect that the devout proselytiser missed the "speculative period" by at least a couple of millennia, but he was right that there indeed has been lots of speculation. Later the very same reverend alluded to, "The old debate about how many angels can dance on the head of a pin." Regrettably, he failed to inform us of his conclusions.

Some of the present-day philosophers shrug their shoulders, informing us with a degree of contempt that the question cannot be answered without knowing what sort of dance the angels are performing. Also, they say, it depends on what sort of angels are performing the dance. Furthermore, there is a 17th century source that says that the philosophical poser has been misquoted. That it is not a question of angels dancing on a pinhead, but how many can do it on the point of a needle. A much tougher proposition. Yet others scorn all the previous inspired notions, assuring us that the angels do not have to dance at all, and the question is only how many angels can stand on the point of a needle, presumably just minding their own business.

Saint Aquinas, (in his Summa theol. I q.52 a.2) never mentions dancing. His reference to angels refutes those who wish to limit angels to a specific location by saying, *crediderunt quod angelus non posset esse nisi in loco punctalis...* roughly, "who believe that an angel is not able to exist except in a place that is a point," which point *est indivisibile habens sitan*, i.e., that it is indivisible and has a site. The point, as such, refers to Euclidean geometry. No mention of pins nor needles, no heads nor points, neither is there any dancing or other disorderly conduct attributed to angels.

Just as well.

Our present scale, even when applied to a point of a needle, would have made the philosophers stick pins and needles into their own heads. We have now entered into the age of nanotechnology. The size of angels notwithstanding, a nanometre is 40,000 times smaller than the width of a human hair. If we convert this measurement to a pinhead, we could calculate the size of an average angel, if only we knew how many of them performed a fandango or a medieval madrigal. Alas, no such luck.

The scientists in India and China have long chosen to study the very small without the aid of angels. This has made things considerably easier, and presumably accounts in no small measure for their unprecedented success in the field of nanotechnology.

And this is where I come in.

Lena was extremely pleased with my last report. Not wishing to douse my interest, she asked me to do 'my thing' with nanotechnology. I told her that I do not have a thing.

"Believe me, Peter. You do. You have a wonderful thing," she assured me, her eyes lighting up with fire on my viphone, but failing to explain what the devil she was talking about. When I told Ruth about it, the next time she spoke to Lena she managed to extract an explanation.

"She must have been very busy," Ruth assured me. "What she meant was that you have *done* a wonderful thing for Solidarity."

So I was right. I did not have a thing after all. For some reason I couldn't quite understand, I felt just a bit emasculated.

Briefly, the 'n', or more accurately the 'nm', also referred to as nanofabrication, covers a broad range of topics. It bears mentioning that one nanometre (the said 'nm') is one billionth or 10^{-9} of a metre.

A metre is defined by the French *Académie des Sciences* as 1/10,000,000 of the distance from the equator to the North Pole as measured through, of course, Paris. On the other hand, the nms I had been asked to handle where still giants compared to Cathy's bosons.

I suppose Cathy's heaven would be filled with multihued elementary particles, all arranged in angelic order, forming larger alliances with quarks and leptons, vibrating to the tune of equally angelic music. Not so for me. I dreamt I was a dog. It could have been the mutt I had restored to health on my way home. He was hit by an inconsiderate driver, speeding along Pine Avenue. Not a place one should speed. Too many children waiting to cross the street to get to Mount Royal, especially on a sunny day, and too many proud dog owners waiting to spend a day frolicking on the park's snowy slopes, without forcing their owners to pick up the litter. Anyway, he wasn't hurt much, but his leg had been broken. Under the pretext of getting him off the street, I picked him up and delivered him to his owner—a nice girl who wasn't quite sure if she ought to be hysterical or grateful. By then the mutt, benefiting from my mystical gift, had recovered, and I was well on my way before the young owner came to her senses.

Anyway, I dreamt I was in a canine heaven. Somehow I knew that in such a heaven there was, or is, I suppose, an eternal summer. I was running around Mount Royal, just as in real life when I was young and frisky. I was delighted to find that all the lower branches of bushes and even the bark of some trees were made of juicy and tender meat. Each time I took a bite, the bark repaired itself as if touched by a magic healer. I was pleased to see that all the cats were being led on long leashes, which retracted whenever I wanted to pass near one, although I could not see who was holding on to the other end of the leash. Perhaps God, or possibly some invisible angels. That must have been why I couldn't see them. And yes, there were also some people around, but they were all busy just picking up poop after my brothers and sisters. It was a really nice heaven.

When I woke up, I wondered how many heavens there were. Paul had written about some guy he met in the third heaven, but he didn't describe it. Neither the guy, nor the heaven. Cathy told me that there are whole universes winking in and out of existence... maybe some of them are heavens. Maybe we might latch on to them in that split second when they make their appearance on earth, in our reality. I wondered if heavens are very large, or we, once we get there, very small. Like the bits and pieces I've been reading for the past week, about nanotechnology.

Ah, yes. Nanotechnology.

"...a highly multidisciplinary field, drawing from fields such as colloidal science, device physics, supramolecular chemistry..."

This was pure science. Soon, judging by what I was reading, it would be easier to implant biomedical prostheses circumventing areas in the brain, expanding one's memory, accelerating absorption of new knowledge... yes, that, too, was part of nanotechnology. There would also be brain computer interfaces.

In China they had tied nanotechnology in with neurocybernetics. The ultimate goal was to improve and accelerate the processing of information by a biological organism. That meant us. You and me.

Neurology, cybernetics, systemics, biocybernetics;

Neuroprosthetics, brain-computer interface, neurotechnology in general with accent on neurocomputing;

Control theory, mean field theory, pattern recognition...

The list went on. What I found strange about all this was that my past studies in medicine had dealt only with organisms that went astray. With sick people, sick brains, bodies, systems. These people, these scientists were prepared to play around with perfectly healthy people just to make them even more healthy. Isn't health a state of perfect balance? But they didn't limit themselves to healthy organisms only.

Neural cell nanostructure for therapies;

Nanoscale visualization for neurology;

Nano-neural interfaces and prosthesis;

Nano... nano... nano... nano... the world was shrinking. Hello, Cathy! There were about 97,800 entries on just one of my computer servers and that was just on nanotechnology in neuroscience. There were many other disciplines, all dealing with nanotechnology.

I decided that people living through the 13th to 17th centuries weren't such bad sorts. Angels might well have proven to be much more interesting. Whether they danced or not was of little consequence. I didn't feel like dancing myself. My head was hurting. A single cubic millimetre of my cerebral cortex contained around five billion synapses. We all have those. As we advance on our evolutionary journey, we also develop spindle cells that handle our emotional and moral judgment. I needed those the most, yet we only had some 80,000 of them. Could this be why so many of us are so consistently immoral? Unless the spindles were all working overtime, I supposed? Gorillas developed only about 16,000 of them, the baboon about 2,100, and chimpanzees, our nearest cousins, a mere 1,800. Other mammals are missing them altogether.

"If my memory serves me," I mused aloud, "right now the neurons in my head are dancing like no angels have ever danced. My spindle cells are making countless new connections on apical dendrites, new axons on outgoing signals, expanding basal dendrites and axons to allow my soma, the brain of each spindle cell, to make the decisions."

"Did you call, Sir?" Miss Dibbs put her head in the door.

I made a mental note to stop talking to myself. Apparently it makes a bad impression on the staff. I smiled and waved her away. Politely, of course.

I decided to go home.

I wanted to know more about auras. Their colours, their meaning, how to control them—if possible, their intensity. They were all around me, invisible, self-generating, vibrating, like the neurons I'd been studying in the office. Like the nano-objects, like the strings of the super-string theory. Like the strings of a violin in the andante of Beethoven's violin concerto. Soft and warm and gentle.

And enchanting. Like the air above a hot paved surface. Like the Universe.

Does God vibrate?

Did any part of Him explode in the Big Bang? Or Her? We are very politically correct at the MNI. At the Old Vic.

If they catch the god particle in CERN, will they catch a little piece of god?

Am I just a heretic, a pagan, an atheist par excellence?

Or is my God so very different from all the other gods that they are not even related?

I'm an atheist.

I am against creating gods in my own image and likeness.

I love the world, the creation. Both the process and the manifestation. But mostly the process. Is god a process or just its infinite potential? Like chaos. Or heaven. Is there a difference? I still felt like a confused philosopher. Well, confused, anyway.

The children held on to their auras. Near golden shimmers that warmed me as I opened the door. There was no denying that we are all born with golden potential and then we, most of us, lose it along the way. We are gods, but we die as men. Whose fault is that?

"Uncle Peter!"

"Me, too!"

Mo was pushing hard to hang on to my left arm, while Jo was already taking charge of my right hand. Perhaps some of their aura would rub off on me. Wouldn't that be nice? You just rub your head against the little ones and you become as wise as a spiritual master.

Ruth was working late that day so, before dinner, I took the children to the cinema. We saw the 47th version of 007 performing single-handed miracles on a worldly scale. The holographic stunts were breathtaking. Almost as good as in *Marie-Reine-du-Monde*'s performance of The Decalogue. James not only saved our ball of dirt from aliens appearing out of nowhere in our upper stratosphere, but also the moon, the nearer planets and a number of colonies hanging on the asteroid belt. Not bad for one man and his bag of tricks—all in just under 2.5 hours.

I was hardly surprised when both Jo and Mo decided to become secret agents and then to save the world whenever an opportunity presented itself. On the way home they shot down dozens of flying saucers, the moon (twice), and a couple of stars. It appeared that we were safe. For now.

Ruth returned from Headquarters with a frown. She didn't want to discuss anything over dinner, while the children were present. Later, when they went upstairs, she gave me one of those looks that I knew meant trouble. I had to admire her control to have held it for so long to protect her children.

"Peter," she started without preambles, "I am scared."

She'd never spoken to me like this. If fact, she always treated me more like a younger brother, not someone she could lean on. For an instant I felt flattered. After all, Ruth was one of the most powerful people in Canada. She didn't act as if she were, but perhaps the truly powerful people never do.

I waited for her to continue.

"I really do not know whom I can trust. Not any more. After what happened to me..." Her eyes drifted to the fireplace as though looking for solace. "I spoke to Lena. You were right. She never left the Vatican… I have absolutely no recollection of what transpired over those three days. It's... it's like being dead. I'm afraid of what might have happened during that time. Of what I may have said, even done..."

I got up and moved to the armchair next to her. After a little while I put my hand on her arm. I didn't do so in any profound way; just as one friend to another, to show that I cared. But even as I looked at her, a change was beginning to take place in her expression. Her face relaxed, the lines around her eyes faded, her lips that were tightly drawn showed a suggestion of a smile. Just a suggestion and even then mixed with surprise. In the next instant I saw the face of a girl I once met in front of a motel, a girl that was sad and lonesome. It seemed little more than a year ago, when people came to me not to be healed of any physical maladies, but to seek solace, relief from overwrought emotions, from the foibles of everyday life. Those people left consoled, their faith renewed in their own capability. It was almost like creating a new reality for them.

A minute later Ruth looked up at me, her eyes filled with wonder.

"What just happened, Peter?"

How I wished I could tell her. You underwent a change of mindset, I could have told her. You began to see things in their proper context. You saw purpose and reason when previously there was none. Perhaps only at your subliminal level. I could have told her all that, but truly, I didn't know what had happened. I was only vaguely aware of the results, of the trails that the invisible powers left behind them.

"You are not worried anymore?" I asked instead.

She looked at me with those round, now relaxed brown eyes. She gazed at me with wonder, with disbelief.

"I was never on the receiving end of your... you know, of your..."

"Gift?"

I must have looked sad when I said it. Again, I could have said 'of the gift that I do not understand,' 'of a gift that I know not how it works,' 'that uses me as a man uses his hands to drive his car.' Purely mechanical, unthinking, instinctive.

"Your incredible gift, Peter." She continued to examine my face. "At last I understand why Lena loves you so much. It isn't that you saved her life. She told me that you opened her eyes..."

I was about to say that people in a coma always have their eyes closed, but I thought better of it. This was the wrong time to show off my personal frustrations. Anyway, I knew that I was wrong. Perhaps I didn't understand because I was blocking the knowledge from reaching my consciousness. From reaching my conscious mind.

They have eyes yet they could not see, I remembered from childhood. *He opened their eyes... Having eyes, see ye not? The light of the body is the eye...*

The blind leading the blind...

A hundred quotations, a thousand memories. A million years ago.

I saw myself kneeling at the altar, praying. Lord, teach me to help them... I must have been ten or twelve then. Dressed in a short surplice, not long, to the ground, like the priest's. The all-knowing priest who held the keys to the kingdom of heaven. I was just an acolyte. A beginner. The aroma of incense drowsing my senses, the candlelight shimmering up there, inaccessible, holy... Help me to help them, I asked many times over.

I shook my head. I'm still a beginner.

Incongruously, I wondered what other so-called healers felt when the 'whatever it was' passed through them. I felt nothing. Nothing at all.

"I don't open people's eyes," I told Ruth. "I just touch their arm or embrace them. What happens next is not of my doing."

I am you.

"Who are you?"

I am within you. And without you. I am also everywhere and nowhere.

I must snap out of it. That last occurred in Rome, three months ago. Before that, also in Rome, at the Vatican, a year ago. I was sitting in my hotel room, looking out on the Eternal City. The next day I would meet His Holiness. The dying Pontiff. How clearly I remembered that day. What's happened since? I stood still.

"...and I thought I'd better..." Ruth was talking.

"I'm sorry dear sister, could you please say that again?"

"Say what, from the beginning?"

"I'm sorry," I smiled weakly. "I really am."

Ruth was looking at me with newly found compassion.

"You heal others but you cannot heal yourself?"

"Apparently."

She seemed to study my face for a while. Satisfied, she got up, walked to the sideboard and poured two crystals of Old Porto. She gave one to me. It was good. Relaxing, more so because of my disposition than by its alcohol content. Somehow it gave me a sense of well-being.

"I was telling you that there are people I recognize in my office but they are not the people I know," she said. "At least I think so. I can't really be sure."

"People close to you?"

"Yes and no. Mostly among the security guards. They are overly polite. Almost servile. People in Solidarity do not act like that."

"You're all equal, right?"

"There is no need to be snotty, Peter. We try to treat people as people. And that's what's wrong with some of those guards. They treat me as someone vastly superior."

"But you are, Ruth. You are their superior. You are their boss and probably the most powerful person on the North American continent. Save for the Big Shots in Washington."

"Not so much Washington as the Pentagon," she changed the subject.

"And just what do you want me to do about it?"

"I don't know. Something. You have all that data on security..."

"Not security, Ruth. Genetics, artificial intelligence, robotics and now I am just digging into nanotechnology. Not security."

"Lena said it all has to do with security."

"What Lena does with the information I send her is her problem. I simply..."

"We're not going to fight over this, Peter."

"I agree. As long as you don't think of me as some sort of supercop."

She smiled. "I can't think of anyone looking and acting less like a supercop than you, my dear brother."

"I take that as a compliment, I think."

"It is. Anyway, if you think of something, let me know, will you?"

Her eyes spelled out a wondrous, enticing, bewitching 'please?' I knew that Ruth had her own inimitable way of handling people. She wouldn't have been able to run Headquarters without it. But this was the first time that I'd found myself on the receiving end of it. The 'please' could not be refused. I smiled my acquiescence.

The next day I left early, and, using my security pass, positioned myself in Ruth's Headquarters before her arrival. Once inside, I set about becoming invisible, though not to the scanners. I stepped into one of the public washrooms and put on my 'Decalogue' disguise. I hadn't touched it since seeing the opera, and it took some time to make it look natural. I also intended to adjust it from time to time, in case I wanted to follow or watch the same person more than once. As of now, I officially nominated myself the Solidarity Supercop. So there. I hoped the trouble I took would give me an edge. For the first time in years I was feeling my age. I felt young. I felt blood coursing through my veins. I felt the thrill of expectation. I had to restrain my step. It was becoming too jaunty.

"Down, boy," I told myself. "You're on a mission of great importance. The world rests on your shoulders."

Had I allowed such a train of thought to continue, I would have been in danger of introducing myself to the next person I met as Bond. James Bond. License to kill, 007. I wished I had a Vodka Martini handy.

Ruth arrived at 7:55 a.m.

I was already on her floor, pretending to read the memos on the notice board. In fact, I was doing my very best to read people's auras. When I'd started, I had to stare at a person for some thirty seconds before the aura became apparent. Now I started to see colour after only five or ten seconds. I still wasn't much at interpreting the auras, although I thought I could spot very negative auras practically at first sight. Before Ruth came, there were two or three such halos that I wouldn't want to count among my closest friends.

I followed Ruth down the hallway to her office. Her aura was a clear blue. She greeted people as she went. I saw her nod at the security agent stationed at her door and I nearly stopped dead in my tracks. The security guard had no aura at all. Like the last time I was here, all I could see on this officer was a dull grey outline that wasn't pulsing or vibrating at all. For all my efforts, he was a complete blank. I walked on. At the end of the corridor, there were two other guards posted. I also drew blanks on both of them. Either I was losing my touch, or there was something very wrong here.

At nine I left my post, removed my disguise and took a cab to my office. I found work difficult. At noon I called home and asked Winston if he could rustle up a snack for me.

"I want to talk to you about something," I said. Somehow I didn't feel confident enough to talk freely even on my own viphone.

Winston agreed, and a half-hour later I was home. As always, I enjoyed the walk. That's what nomads do, I told myself. They walk. They cross the dunes of shifting sands, deserts of human depravity. Actually, on the whole, people were not depraved. They just seemed asleep. In a state of rarefied stupor. I hoped I was imagining things.

Without telling Winston where I got my data, I told him about the blanks, the people whose auras I could not detect.

"Don't you find it strange?" I asked.

"They must be quite advanced spiritual masters, Sir. A rare occurrence indeed."

"In a guard's uniform?"

"They were sentries, Sir? As in Solidarity sentries?"

I told him the rest. I also told him about my chat with Ruth the previous evening.

"If I may, Sir. Would you allow me to look into the matter myself?"

"Why, of course. But I doubt they'll let you into the building. You look rather imposing, you know?"

"I have been told that, Sir. Leave that problem to me."

And with that Winston became invisible. At least, once he entered the kitchen to get more coffee. There was something very impressive about Winston, and I don't mean his physical size. There was an invisible yet very palpable aura of serenity and confidence. Perhaps that was why I found work that same afternoon no effort at all.

***

18

The Dragon Awakens

There was a delegation from China here, in Montreal, to negotiate the renewal of trade contracts, mostly aimed at equalizing the import and export disparities. They were on a tour—Mexico, the States, and finally us. Ruth had been asked to participate on behalf of the labour force, of which nearly eighty percent was represented by Solidarity International, which had absorbed most of the 'old-fashioned' trade unions. When the once powerful labour bosses realized that there was no longer abundant money to be made from their memberships, they retired on the fruit of their efforts, usually to the Caribbean Islands. Those that really cared about their members continued to work for them under the auspices of Solidarity International.

Ruth was very impressed with the Chinese delegation. They spoke fluent and accentless English, French, and obviously Mandarin. Ruth, who spoke quite decent Mandarin herself, had lost the advantage she had had at some of the previous negotiations. Later on during the meeting, she realized, belatedly, that when there was no unanimity among the Chinese delegates, they switched to other, less known Chinese dialects.

"Not only that," Ruth told me over dinner, "but they seemed to switch into a 'fast-forward' mode, speaking faster than anyone I'd ever heard."

"Nanotechnology," I murmured.

Ruth heard me. "Are you suggesting that the delegates' brains have been enhanced somehow?" She sounded incredulous.

"Without a doubt," I assured her. "Without the slightest doubt." And not just their brains, I felt like adding but didn't want to depress my sister-in-law.

But even so, a month ago I wouldn't have said that much. It was only thanks to the demands Lena had placed on me that I had become aware of the quite extraordinary strides the Chinese were making in nanotechnology. Furthermore, what was publicly available on the Internet was probably considerably out of date. There also must have been some government-sponsored programs that, I felt sure, were on the confidential if not actually the secret list.

"Next thing you will be telling me that they can fly by flapping their arms," Ruth said dryly.

"Not yet," I told her, with an equally straight face. "But don't hold your breath..."

Mo and Jo hadn't seemed to be listening to any of this exchange. About a minute later, however, quite suddenly, Jo came to life.

"Uncle Peter, will you teach me to fly?"

Moira measured her brother with a curious gaze. "Me, too," she said, making sure she would not be left behind.

I was trapped. "I promise both of you," I said, solemnly putting my right hand on my heart, "that the moment I learn to fly by flapping my arms, I shall teach you both immediately."

This seemed to satisfy them, not that I really expected them to take me seriously. At least I thought they wouldn't. After all, they were twelve. But towards the end of the dessert of peaches and frozen sherbet, Jo reminded me of my promise. I'd fallen into my own trap. Children who were dealing with trigonometric progressions assumed that if adults said so, then they would be able to learn to fly by flapping their arms. Or, perhaps, under Winston's daily tutelage, they just refused to accept any limitations.

The next day my ever up-to-date assistant on just about everything of any interest, John Robb, stuck his head round my door.

"Come in, JR," I waved him to a chair in front of my desk.

His arms dangling as ever, his torso looking even thinner than when he'd given me his last input on robotics, JR swaggered in. I didn't mean swaggered because he looked superior or boasting, but there was an air of quiet confidence about him mixed with a dose of *je-m'en-foutisme*. Not that he didn't care. That was just his manner.

"Out with it," I encouraged.

He stretched his mile-long legs and sucked the air into his concave chest. I wondered how come the man didn't fall apart. If he was the product of our early experiments in bionics, then they must have used Krazy Glue.

"The Yanks got shafted," JR declared with a straight face.

I was surprised. The American press had mainly only ridiculed the Chinese for not bringing any computers with them. The daily newspapers in the USA had had a uniform, repetitive headline plastered across their front pages.

CHINA LAGGING BEHIND

Under these headlines had been photographs of the delegates, each sporting a proverbial nondescript Chinese smile, only more so. A smile that was as inscrutable as the old novels had described them, and as even older movies depicted them to be.

"Would you mind explaining?"

JR's lips twisted in a smile that was close to a contemptuous grin. "Those Yanks think they know everything, boss. Just about everything. Well, they don't. I have this friend who is Chinese, see? And he thinks that the Chinese are just about ten times smarter than the Yanks. They are not only better off at birth, but they insert nano bits and pieces into their heads that make them smarter than most computers. And certainly more intelligent."

"There is a difference?"

"The one calculates, the other is a question of survival," JR said performing two enormous arcs with his legs, changing the way they were crossed.

"I'm glad we got that straight," I murmured. JR's definition did not quite meet my criteria. No matter. The man was entitled to his opinion.

"You know, Dr. Thornton, the Americans are very proud of their electronic hardware. And probably to show off a little bit, some of them came to the negotiations accompanied by mobile robots that did their calculations for them. Percentages, delivery dates, net and gross profits, losses, whatever's necessary to arrive at a figure they could use to gain an edge and impress people. They didn't have to press any buttons, you know. The robots listened, on their own, and did the calculations. Now and then a delegate would just tap on his or her earpiece and the answers would just flow in."

It was very apparent from JR's facial expression that my number one supplier of info was not a great admirer of the USA establishment. Hardly surprising. Few, if any, Solidarity members were. Primarily, I believed, because they couldn't stand the astronomical incomes that the Americans still assigned to their CEOs, chairmen, directors, and other executive officers of mega corporations. Or even to their movie stars or professional sportsmen.

"And, I gather, they didn't get it."

"What's that, Sir?"

"The edge. They didn't get the edge?"

"That's right, Sir. They didn't."

"So what happened exactly?"

"I am not an economist, Sir, but I can read facts and figures as well as any man."

Having said that, he reached inside his right-hand jacket pocket and extracted a pile of papers that on a lesser man would have stuck out like the pecs of a professional bodybuilder. He then repeated the procedure with the inside left pocket of his jacket. There were occasions, most of them, when JR liked to play a simpleton.

"These are condensed printouts, Sir, from all the meetings. On page one you will find the conclusions I drew."

I found it amusing how his language changed from when he was expressing his personal opinions, particularly of our friends down south, to a precise statement when he was talking business.

The pages were tightly spaced printouts from a number of sources. Economical interchanges were not my primary interest, but it was evident from even just scanning JR's conclusions that within a very few years, the USA would be owing the China-India Consortium countless trillions of dollars, and getting very little in return.

"How come, JR?" I asked. If JR was right, the Chinese were giving the USA a royal shaft.

"Garbage in, garbage out, Sir. The Yanks expect their computers to do their thinking for them. Well, they can't. It's all a question of the pattern, Sir."

"The pattern?"

"The pattern, Sir. The big picture. What a human brain does is eliminate all the superficialities and only the pertinent facts are taken into consideration. Computers can't do that. They must consider everything. What the Chinese did was feed the American delegates a profusion of biased yet correct facts which make it virtually impossible to arrive at the correct conclusions mathematically."

"A sort of wild goose chase?"

"Sort of, only consisting of a few million wild geese, all flying in opposite directions to each other. Left, right as well as up and down. It's quite funny, really..." JR's eyes grew misty. He was the only man in Solidarity who could reach a draw, repeatedly, with all the computer-run chess programs.

"And you say that the Chinese have those implants?"

"The Chinese and the Indians, Sir. They are in this together. And they are not exactly implants, Sir, I don't mean the Indians, Sir..."

"I get your drift, JR," I assured him.

"Yes, Sir. Those nano-things they are injected with, or something like that, are nanorobots that react on biological input. And vice-versa. They do not do the work for you, they just make you work a million times more efficiently. They cut the edges, round the corners, so to speak. They enhance your innate capabilities. The smarter you are, the smarter you become. But it's still you that does the work. Not the computer."

Most of us tend to reject the new and the untried as something to be kept at bay. Perhaps we are afraid of the unknown. Not so JR.

He had the capacity to accept the new and the untried as perfectly natural. It would be like a new piece of music, a new game to be studied, enjoyed, and only then accepted or discarded. He was a very bright customer, our JR. I was glad he was on our side.

"Thanks, JR," I said looking up from the papers he'd left on my desk. "Thank you very much," I repeated, which he took as dismissal.

He collected various parts of his body from the armchair and in three steps reached the door.

"Bye, sweetie pie," I heard him calling to my secretary.

There was a slight giggle and then the sound of the door closing. The moment he left my office I remembered that I'd completely forgotten to study his aura. The thing about auras is that for the most part you don't see them unless you look for them. Children up to the age of five or so can see auras quite naturally. Watch kids looking up over your head. If they don't like what they see, they avoid you. Anyway, when over the years the children notice that everyone is ignoring the auras, they give up looking for them. I smiled at my thoughts. Was this also part of the instructions to be like little children? To retain access to the invisible kingdom that was not of this world?

Or am I just dreaming...

When I got home, I was determined to pin Winston down on the meaning of auras. After my initial success with seeing them, I seemed to have come to a dead stop. I was not advancing, assuming there was somewhere to advance to. My gut feeling told me that I'd only just scratched the surface.

Winston smiled his usual surreptitious smile.

"Everyone and everything has an aura, Sir," he said. "A rock, a grain of sand, an atom, every electron or any other elementary particle—vibrates. This is why they all have auras. The art is to train yourself to see those vibrations. You might call it an electro-photonic vibration, thus producing light and colour."

"And I can learn to see all those electrophonic vibrations?"

"Electro-photonic, Sir. It implies light rather than sound. Although, with training, one can also hear the aura..."

"You what?"

He did not repeat his sentence. Instead he asked me to close my eyes. "Now listen," he said.

"Listen to what?"

"Just listen..."

We sat in chairs across the kitchen table, eyes closed, listening to I knew not what. And then I heard sounds. An incredible number of sounds all meshed together into a sort of droning that permeated my whole being. It was omnipresent, persistent, incessant...

"That is why it is easier to detect the electro-photonic vibrations, Sir. The electrophonic are much harder to separate."

I opened my eyes. Winston was missing. He was gone. And then I heard his voice behind me. "The photonic can be just as distracting, Sir."

I had no idea what to make of it.

"It has to do with frequencies. We can only see vibrations in a certain range. If we slip into a different range..."

"You become invisible?"

"Not to people trained in the detection of auras, Sir."

My head was swimming. This was bordering on miracles, but, the way Winston put it, they were all natural phenomena of nature. The auras, the music of the spheres, the disappearing saints and avatars, bilocation, it all fit.

"They are all natural phenomena. There is no such thing as an unnatural phenomenon, Sir."

He was reading my thoughts. Next he would claim that this, too, was natural.

"It is, Sir. We can all do it. Only... few people really want to listen. Most of us are busy trying to tell others what we think. It reinforces our illusion that we are alive."

"And we are not?"

"We all project our consciousness on the space-time continuum. We see what we want to see, hear what we want to hear."

"Are you telling me that one of us doesn't really exist?"

"Define exist, Sir. Am I he whom you perceive with your senses?"

Suddenly I realized what a dismal, arrogant, retarded child I still was. When I saw Winston going up the hill some days ago, all I could see was a sphere of light hovering some feet above the pavement. I deemed it to be Winston's aura. In a way it was, I suppose, but in another way perhaps that was the real Winston.

I looked up and saw that once again I was sitting alone at the kitchen table. My head was propped up on my hands, my elbows on the table, my eyes staring straight ahead. I was definitely alone. A moment later I heard Winston's voice.

"Very well, Madam. I shall serve a light meal at six."

Winston was welcoming Ruth who'd just returned from her office. As I turned slowly, I tried to see her aura. It was a beautiful colour of turquoise. I reached back in my memory...

> *People with strong organizational skills, able to do many things simultaneously, are capable of influencing others. Their subordinates love them as they explain their purpose rather than issue commands. The turquoise auras indicate dynamic personalities, popular and capable of inspiring and leading others to their own ends.*

Ruth Thornton was a woman in the right place doing the right thing. No wonder Lena had picked her. I never realized I had such a wonderful sister-in-law. Actually I knew I did, I'd just never fully appreciated why.

"Very good, Peter," I heard Winston behind me. When Winston dropped the 'Sir', that was praise indeed. I didn't even bother to turn to check if he was really there.

Only then did I remember that I'd failed to ask him about the blanks I'd met at the Headquarters. Aural blanks? It would have to wait. I wondered if Ruth was still worried. Too busy, I suspected. Worry is a privilege of those who have time on their hands. She was a woman capable of leading her subordinates by persuasion, not command. I wondered if I could do that. On the other hand, I wasn't leading anyone anywhere in particular. Except myself, lately, around the bend.

I missed the children. They were in a winter camp in Mount Tremblant. The snow was good there. Downhill in the morning, cross-country in the afternoon, swimming in an Olympic-size swimming pool in the evening. Such regimen would probably kill me in a day, let alone in the two weeks Jo and Mo would be staying there.

And then I tapped my head with my knuckles. You are thirty years old, for crying out loud. You are a young man. Two years ago you were picking up nurses to do them favours in linen cupboards; you were planning all sorts of outings the moment you passed the Fellowship exams, and then? And then you became an old man almost overnight. It is time to wake up, my lad. Months ago I managed to lose my neurotic fear of being accosted by people begging to be healed of incurable diseases. I'd had my moment of fame, and no one was interested in me any more. I liked it that way. Isn't that what I wanted? To be free? To be a nomad? But for as long as I officially continued to reside in Westmount, Montreal, Canada, The Earth, I must act as the earthlings do. I must live and let live. I must...

I picked up the viphone to call Cathy. The moment I heard the ringing tone, I hung up. It was 2 a.m. for her. Cathy was fast asleep, her subconscious working overtime and getting ready to create a brand new Big Bang. Not as big as the original one, but still, a biggish bang. Even if it was tiny. Dear Cathy.

I went up to my room to freshen up. Even as I got there my vicell played its melody. Grieg's *La Chanson de Solveig*, the incidental music to *Peer Gynt*. Somehow this forlorn little melody helped fill the void whenever Cathy left.

"Peter? I couldn't sleep," Cathy sounded delightfully coy. "Have you been thinking about me?"

"I never stop," I assured her with a high degree of truth. "I really was. In fact I just tried to call you only I thought you would be sleeping."

"I was, when something woke me up. I think it was you."

"Why me?"

"Whenever I can't sleep I always think about you. So, you woke me up."

There had to be some sort of logic in that declaration. "When shall I see you?" This was becoming a repetitive question.

"It has to be soon," she replied. "I really need some sleep."

I loved hearing her voice. "How are the experiments coming along?"

"We're getting there, and you?"

"I've just learned that the Sino-Indian Corporation is producing super-brained geniuses."

"Isn't that like double trouble?"

"I want to go dancing with you," I said, inconsequentially.

"Here or there?"

"Yes," I gave her a straight answer.

"I also want to go skiing, downhill and cross-country, and then fly south and dive into a warm Caribbean Sea."

"Give me five minutes," she said, her voice smiling.

"Love you." I had nothing more to add.

"Welcome back, Peter," she said and hung up.

It was good to be back among the living. She must have detected signs of awakening in my voice. I've been too old for too long. I wasted a whole year thinking about myself instead of thinking about life. I wasn't that important, life was. Is. Always will be.

Cathy wrote me an email. I loved her emails. As I clicked it on, her face then the rest of her body, shimmered then solidified before my eyes. She was sitting cross-legged on a settee, propped up on some pillows. She came to life when I pressed the action button. I caught her in the middle of a conversation, apparently with herself. She was saying that enhanced brains in the East are beginning to understand quantum mechanics. That if she would ever undergo any sort of enhancement, it would be to understand the Superstring Theory. It's quite different to understand them as equations and to actually feel them. I want to understand all of it. All the imponderables. Did you know that Einstein saw the

Universe as muscular shapes? That's what he said. I want to know the thoughts of God, she wrote, quoting the ancient master.

Einstein's name still carried magic for the physicists of today. They disagreed with a lot of his stuff, but they still loved him as children love their father, even though they surpass him in knowledge.

And then Cathy asked if I would still love her if she were enhanced.

I wondered what sort of aura he emanated. Einstein, I mean. I still had to look up what colour represented intellectual prowess.

I was also curious if I would ever learn to become invisible. It would be fun to creep up on people. Really, just for fun. I needed more fun in my life. More *joie de vivre*. It would be easier if Cathy were here.

I lay down on my bed and closed my eyes. I saw myself floating, up, slowly, until I was just a contour against the ceiling. Then the ceiling was gone and I was looking at the stars. It had been snowing earlier. I'd risen above the clouds. Up, way up against the stars. A myriad of them. Clean, sparkling, spots of icy fire. As I saw them in that little square courtyard at Gaston's, just before I collapsed. I was walking again, feeling the chill in the air.

...twenty paces to the right, twenty straight forward, then back again. A square circle...

It was just after Mavis had given up her cigarettes. Or was it George? There was an accident. A bad one. She'd refused something, George... his breath didn't smell any more... an accident, and then it was over. All over.

I wondered if Cathy could fly. With her I could go anywhere. Anywhen...

I had to learn more about auras. Perhaps then I should be able to help people help themselves. I wondered if I would remain helpless vis à vis the cyborgs and bionic men. And women, of course. Could they also be helped? Or the clones for that matter? Why is there so much progress? Am I really sure that it's progress? It was becoming confusing. Isn't ignorance bliss?

***

19

The Black Horse

A *measure of wheat for a penny; and three measures of barley for a penny; and see thou hurt not the oil and the wine.* Calculators. Computers. That is what men were becoming. Calculators. Mental jigsaw puzzles. If I were still at the seminary, I would call the Americans the riders of the black horse of the Apocalypse. *And see thou hurt not the oil and the wine.* Oil—the biblical symbol of praise and thanksgiving, not the stuff that adds to global pollution. Wine—always stood for secret knowledge. The water of life. So we can calculate all we know, as long as we do not forget to be grateful, as long as our pseudo-knowledge doesn't go to our heads. And the wine? Wine is what makes us drunk. Or at least distorts the distorted reality and makes us forget how very ordinary we are. It also helps us to dream of being more than we really are. Or have aspired to be. Good wine, that is.

So we can only aspire to secret knowledge when we close our senses to the mundane. To that which we perceive with our muted senses. As an ex-seminarian, I could hardly be expected to ignore my past altogether, and my past was, to quite an extent, Bible study. Or at least the ability to recall the parts that might affect my everyday life. I had been a closet theologian. And an atheist by any other definition.

After a whole year, I was once again enjoying the solitude of my study. The books lining the walls exuded a certain peace, the longing man has for the unknown, the mysterious. Wasn't that what I had been searching for initially, when I thought I would become a priest? I don't remember. The memories were gone, only the hunger remained.

I was alone but not lonely. My thoughts kept me company.

I put down the Bible and leaned back in my chair. Lately, the last two weeks or so, I'd picked up the old book, its frayed edges speaking of the uses it had been put to in the days gone by. The days when I still believed there was a Being, up there, a Benevolent Being looking after our every need, rewarding our good deeds, punishing our mistakes.

I found it incredible that there were some two billion people who still took the Bible as the inerrant word of God. Inerrant, complete, infallible.

It was only when I found the key to the book, the key to the symbolism used in this splendid document of human achievement, that I began to treat the Bible in a completely new light. It was no longer an unquestionable regimen to which I had to conform to the exclusion of my free will, but a fascinating testimony of experiences gathered, over thousands of years, by people who dedicated their lives to just such a purpose.

The stuff dealing with the Black Horse of the Apocalypse was a marvellous exposé of the American approach to evolutionary progress. There was a time when the Americans were the inspiration of the world. Then power came into the picture. The next moment the inspiration was gone, and their desire to protect and sustain that which they'd already acquired took over. Every empire the world has ever known has been corrupted by power. The USA is no different. I don't mean all the people—many of them have remained individuals. I mean that for which the USA now stood. The Police. The Wielder of Power. The Master of Life and Death.

There was no room for love in that equation.

But what really caught my eye was one particular sentence. It was a phrase that I could not, as yet, quite digest.

And I saw a new heaven and a new earth: for the first heaven and the first earth were passed away.

So far so good. The earth changes all the time, and if we regard the earth as symbolizing the materialistic mindset, then it changes even more. Genetics, robotics, artificial intelligence, and now nanotechnology left little doubt about the aspect of change. It wasn't that. It was the next sentence that continued to perplex me. *And there was no more sea.*

The sea always symbolizes the mental aspect of human nature, particularly the subconscious. With no more sea, how can biological life exist without the input of our subconscious? In psychological terms, our subconscious is what drives our physical bodies forward. It stores the information that has made us who or what we are today. If we eliminate the 'sea', we eliminate ourselves. There had to be another explanation. The ex-physician in me refused to accept that such a thing was possible, Bible or no Bible.

I wondered if Winston would know. He knew just about everything else!

If the Yanks, in JR's vernacular, were infiltrating the ranks of Solidarity with some kind of robotic-bionic-clones, then Solidarity was losing ground.

The Sino-Indian Consortium stood on firmer ground. The Americans might well emulate a man or a woman, the Homo-sapiens, but they could hardly emulate, for want of a better word, Homo-genius. And the Sino-Indians were 'breeding' geniuses in vast numbers. I was beginning to wonder who would eventually inherit the earth.

And let us not dismiss genetics. The progress in curing diseases, restoring health to the infirm, genetic manipulation to regrow internal organs, the sense organs, injured nerves and such like, even brain cells, and the overall extension of useful life was also making enormous strides. What remained a little questionable was the purpose. What was the point of having a longer life? To serve whoever became the higher species longer, in vaster numbers? Were we, ordinary folks, the throwbacks? The pets of tomorrow?

Ouch...

So what of us, I mused in quiet desperation, what of us the normal people? I was supposed to provide directional input toward solving the dilemma, but so far I was stumped with the best of them.

Cathy was coming to Montreal next week, officially to see her parents, and that was enough to raise my spirits directly to Cloud Nine. And then, the story broke.

SPIES SPIES SPIES EVERYWHERE

This was the headline in the *Ottawa Citizen* and two other national dailies the next morning. They could get only three 'spies' in the width of the page. The article that followed shed little light on their suspicions. It sounded like groping in the dark...

> Since the metal detectors had been installed in the Houses of Parliament, some two decades ago for the protection of its members, there had been a number of arrests. This time, however, the alarms had been set off by a man who had proven to be completely unarmed. The culprit claimed to have had an 'ultra-thin' metal plate installed in his pate, following an injury sustained during a USA Police Action. His papers gave no indication of any military service while the X-rays revealed no metal plate in his head. The man could not explain this discrepancy. Citing security reasons, the RCMP detained the culprit for further examination. Following an in-depth independent inquiry, *The Citizen* has learned that there have been three other men detained in similar anomalies in recent months, each carrying USA identification.

I looked up from the paper and my morning coffee to face Winston. I wondered if they were cyborgs with metal components integral to their cardiovascular, or even cellular, systems. If so, they could be spies, as the *Ottawa Citizen* obviously suspected.

"Do we have a chance against all those humanoid creations, Winston?"

The elusive misnomer we called progress. Surely, one can only define as progress a movement that is going toward a specific goal; that has a specific direction. I wasn't sure that any of the scientific endeavours that Lena had asked me to examine were aiming at a specific destination. With the possible exception of the United States' robotics—but those, surely, had as their aim world domination. As such it was only a matter of time before it would collapse under its own weight.

Winston bypassed my question and cut into my train of thought.

"Progress is defined by human laziness," he said, studiously pretending to be thinking of something else.

"They work round the clock, Winston. They're anything but lazy," I commented instinctively.

"A wise man adapts to the environment. A lazy man tries to adapt the environment to cover his own inadequacies," he said.

I had a vague impression that he had been waiting to be able to put this idea before me. Perhaps I was beginning to read his thoughts as well.

"I met a man in Tibet," Winston said, for the first time divulging of his previous existence something other than meeting my late brother in China, "whose ambition was to enter one of the local monasteries. The man, already a monk, though of a lesser order, was reasonably advanced in the intricacies of Hatha Yoga. He was prepared to prove his worthiness. He had no idea, however, what his test would consist of. You may not be aware, Sir, that in spite of the severe climate, the monasteries do not enjoy the comforts of heating even during the winter months."

It was a rare occasion indeed that Winston would venture into such an extensive tirade. I waited with bated breath for what point he was about to make. I had to make sure I would understand it.

"Isn't Hatha yoga a method of controlling one's body with one's mind?" I asked.

"To a considerable extent," Winston assured me, "if properly used, and if *pranayama* is properly administered."

He was about to continue when he glanced at my face. I must have looked dumb. Winston granted me a smile he usually reserved for Mo and Jo. In a peculiar way I didn't feel insulted. In fact, rather flattered.

"In the West, people understand *pranayama* to consist of breathing exercises. But *prana* cannot move in the nerves as long as they are full of impurities. Like everything, it takes time."

I was reminded of my research into the subject of 'breatharians', people who reputedly forego any intake of food or drink, relying only on the air they breathe. Although I suspect they would call it cosmic energy.

"Which it is," Winston completed my thought for me. "Anyway, the monk was told to sit in subzero temperatures, outside, naked, and to cover himself with six blankets soaked in water. If the blankets were dry by sunrise, he would be welcome to join the monastery."

"Not very comfy," I muttered.

"The man's blankets were dry by midnight. It was a rare achievement. Three other aspirants had frozen to death." With that, Winston got up and left me to ponder his words. I thought of the incredible effort humanity had made to advance control over the environment, when all they had to do was to learn to breathe properly. And then I thought of the three unsuccessful candidates. Well... almost, I added to my previous conclusions. But what was it that Winston wanted of me? When he expanded on any subject even for half the time he had on this occasion, there was always a message for me to uncover. I was not about to sit naked in the garden covered with wet blankets. I suppose one could cover some robot with wet stuff and have them dry it out. Or maybe even cyborgs. Would that make them qualified to enter some Tibetan monasteries? Somehow I doubted it. On the other hand, I could never be that sure of what exactly Winston was trying to teach me. Maybe it was just to think straight, which I wasn't doing right then.

So what was it that he wanted of me?

Obviously I needed to go to Ottawa, but before going I called my friend John Robb into my office.

"Can you fix me up with a microcamera that would not show the person I was photographing that I..."

"There are three types, Sir. The button, the lapel and the buttons on your sleeves. Or, of course, all three. The button operates best with limited light and has a higher DPI. The two others are both good, but they work better on documents."

JR looked down on me from his Olympian heights. The man must have been taller than Winston; but being extremely slim he gave the impression of being twice as tall.

"Doing some hanky-panky, Sir?" His grin broadened even wider.

"Mind sitting down, JR? You give me a headache from staring up," I said only half jokingly.

JR didn't sit down. Instead he leaned over my desk and pressed his right hand with the index finger of his left. Then he moved towards the window, looked out casually and then came back to my desk. He inserted a tiny something-or-other into a USB outlet in my computer. The next instant, I found myself staring at my own face filling the screen. He did a similar thing with the button he took from his sleeve and displayed a perfect image of the papers I had spread on top of my desk. The pictures were so good that I could actually read the typing on the sheet lying on the edge of the surface. I was impressed. I also felt a little uncomfortable.

"Do you carry these with you all the time, JR?"

"Not to bed, Sir. I leave my work in the wardrobe at night."

I felt like a secret agent in a cheap spy thriller. I almost wished Jo and Mo could see me.

The corridors of power in Ottawa do not have that much power compared with the USA. We were the go-betweens. We more or less maintained peace between the Far East and the Far West, the latter represented unilaterally by the USA. South America still kept mostly to themselves, Russia decided to slog it alone, and Australia had become the Switzerland of the present-day political landscape. If anybody wanted to be more neutral than Ottawa, they went to Canberra. There was also the whole of Africa, but no one quite understood what they were about. I thought they were still trying to define what they stood for or, as RJ would say, their thing. Funny that, I thought—hadn't life begun in Africa? Australopithecus africanus or somebody?

In Ottawa I did what I had done at the Solidarity Headquarters in Montreal, minus the disguise. No one knew me from Paranthropus, africanus or otherwise. In direct contrast to every politician who ever strolled the corridors of power, my best disguise was to try to not attract attention to myself.

My purpose was fairly obvious. If they had gotten tabs on an android of some sort with American affiliations, there might be others, not endowed with an equal amount of metal and thus reasonably undetectable.

I spent a few hours sauntering through various departments of our governmental buildings. Not in any particular order, but rather as a tourist would—a tourist who had been granted a special pass, which Ruth had procured for me. That same evening I came back with my cameras fully loaded with snapshots of some eleven people whose auras didn't meet my expectations, and three more who had auras, but I thought them disastrous. Before I handed over my work with an appropriate report to the Solidarity security, I bounced my efforts off Winston.

"You shouldn't, if I may say so Sir, rely exclusively on the auras. Even greater a window to a man's soul are his eyes."

Thank you for nothing, I thought, but wouldn't dream of being so ungrateful to Winston as to say it out loud.

"Don't mention it, Sir," came Winston's instant reply. I decided to pay more attention to my thoughts in the future. Winston told me two years ago to live more consciously. "Can you account for every minute of your day, Sir?" he'd asked me at the time.

Well, I still couldn't. I couldn't even control my thoughtstream. "Remember all those things are already there," he'd told me. We had been talking about time. "You just arrange them in a sequential order for convenience." Winston was hardest to understand when he was explaining things to me.

"And what about the blanks? The invisible auras?" I asked hopefully.

"That was why I mentioned the eyes, Sir. Otherwise we would have to assume that the objects you photographed were either devoid of life force, or had a master's control over their auras. Masters seldom let other people see their auras, Sir. It would be unseemly. Like showing off, if you understand my meaning, Sir."

I understood his meaning and was not any closer to a solution than I had been that morning. "Goodnight, Ruth," I called over my shoulder and slowly walked upstairs. It seemed pretty obvious. Aren't eyes called the windows of the soul?

Lena saw to it that the Canadian government received a copy of my Ottawa report. Over breakfast the day after I submitted my report, Ruth was looking at me a bit the way I looked at Winston—a mixture of admiration and disbelief.

"How did you do this, Peter? How did you know whom to photograph?"

"Just lucky, I guess," I said.

She tsk-tsk'ed me a few times. I shrugged and told her that I was looking at their auras, and the ones I didn't like—I photographed. "As simple as that," I concluded.

"Don't be silly, Peter," she was becoming less and less amused. "You don't have to tell me, but don't treat me as an imbecile, either."

I left it at that. A year ago I wouldn't have believed in anyone seeing people's auras either. One hears, periodically, of miracles, miracle cures, of Lourdes, Fatima, various shrines previously approved by the church, even some gurus in India who did some curing on their own. There were also ample examples of healing in the Bible that Ruth always spelt with a capital B. She didn't question it; she just accepted it in totality. Not only was Jesus, at least part-time, in the healing business, but there were countless disciples who did a pretty good job of restoring the juices in some ailing people. Or something like that. Anyway, this, at least in Ruth's eyes, was different. Nobody in the Bible read auras. Professionally or otherwise. This was just plain silly. One just didn't go around snapping auras of people or, even worse, snapping pictures of people who did not have adequate auras to meet your requirements.

"You will tell me when you are ready," she declared judiciously and left for the office.

Neither my report to Solidarity nor the Solidarity report to the Government specified the source of 'our' suspicions. 'It has been brought to our notice that the people whose photographs were taken (there followed times and locations) had been acting suspiciously, etc., etc.' We couldn't tell them why I chose to photograph these particular delinquents. Had we done so, the report would have been shelved at best, and at worst would have ended up in file thirteen. The waste-paper basket. Their reaction would have been similar to the one I got from Ruth. People at large were still fundamentalists. Things they couldn't touch or detect with their five senses, or at the very least with their technological instruments, just didn't exist. Or had been delegated to Divine Intervention which, though on occasion agreeable, remained always quite unpredictable and thus unreliable. I doubt the secular authorities were even willing to accept the seemingly esoteric evidence as real. The establishment was real, as were the taxpayers under their control. Everything else...

"We shall take appropriate action after your data are confirmed by independent sources." Read: 'By means that everybody can understand. They must be tested under laboratory conditions'.

Good luck. Nevertheless, Ruth's people told her that every person I identified had been quietly removed from their positions. There was no mention in the press about the affair. The USA couldn't complain without giving the show away.

As for the laboratory conditions, I would love them to test Winston. Should he choose, which I am sure he would, to remain anonymous, he would present the dullest, the most ordinary, or what the government called 'normal' face to the scanners. Not even Kirlian photography could reveal his aura against his will.

I was becoming very jealous of our majordomo.

But the matter didn't end there. Solidarity, under the expressed wishes of Lena Walesa, opened a new department of esoteric studies. Few people knew that such a department had already existed in Russia long before the Socialist system collapsed. After all,

Semyon Kirlian, an amateur inventor and electrician of Krasnodar, was a Russian. Sceptics still held that there was nothing spiritual about it. They were right of course. As Winston said many times, there is nothing unnatural in the Universe. I'm not quite sure what Lena hoped to achieve with her new department, but I strongly suspected that the girls had been talking. Ruth and Lena, I mean. Ruth may have ignored my 'aura' stories, but I'm sure she hadn't failed to mention them to Lena. They were close.

On Friday evening I picked Cathy up at Mirabel International. She asked if I had told her parents about her arrival. I hadn't, of course. I seldom butted into other people's business, unless asked.

"I want it to be a surprise. They don't get many surprises these days," she said.

I gave her a long look. Then I snapped open my vicell. A pleasant face appeared on the tiny screen.

"A double for…" I glanced at Cathy, "for two nights, please?"

"You devil, you," Cathy said, grinning

"Yes, Sir." She gave me the code number for my room. I didn't even have to check in at the front desk. Next I called home and I told Winston that I'd been called away on very important business.

"Please give Dr. Mondellay my best regards, Sir," he replied calmly. Was there something in my voice?

The Mirabel Hilton was a little piece of heaven all wrapped up in a plush carpet, a luxurious Jacuzzi, an oversized bed, delicious food, and a band that was strangely reminiscent of the one that played a few million years ago at the Ritz-Xentung. Or it could have been just me.

I was one lucky fellow. And I was feeling young again.

***

20

Miniatures

Quantum Mechanics do not rely on the predictability of facts, only on the probability of possibilities. An important distinction. After making love, continuously I might add, for close to two hours, we came up for air. There was a distinct probability that we might never get out of bed. The possibilities for staying in were endless. Cathy showed me the equations. They were beautiful. After careful consideration, we both decided that a soak in our Jacuzzi might well prove propitious for generating further theoretical theories that theoretically described a theoretical Universe. That was close enough to how she began.

"Unless you make some assumptions, you just can't prove them, can you?" she said, sticking her toe where she oughtn't.

"What you are telling me is that you create a concept and then work your butt off to detect that concept in reality," I offered, inching my own toe towards her.

"Not at all. The concept is reality. The rest just follows."

"Ouch!" escaped from my lips.

"That's what happens when the theory is not backed up by observations under laboratory conditions," she smiled, massaging my own inadvertent toe.

Now that was interesting, coming from a scientist. Not the last part, the one before. The one about the concept of what is reality. It sounded much more like theology than a scientific hypothesis. In the beginning was the Word... the Concept. The Idea came first. And then? I read somewhere that theoretical physicists get their best ideas while soaking in a bathtub. Well, Cathy was doing her level best. She was really good at soaking.

"The idea precedes its manifestation?"

"Well, it depends whose idea it is. It has to be an original."

"God's?"

"Define god," she countered. "Doesn't your own scripture say that you are all gods? Some psalm, I believe."

"You, not we?"

"I am not sure about myself yet."

On the other hand, the last thing I needed from Cathy was to be reminded of the past I was trying hard to escape. Krishnamurti, an Indian sage of the last century, said that freedom comes when the mind experiences without tradition. I've been trying to free myself of everything I could think of. Except for Cathy, of course. After all, I was experiencing Cathy very much in the present.

"There is some such thing," I admitted, just as Cathy was beginning to emerge from the swirling Jacuzzi. "It says nothing, though, about you being a goddess."

Tethys, the daughter of Uranus and Gaia, the wife of Oceanus, still moist from the caress of the water from her marine kingdom. A statue chiselled with great care from warm, pliant marble now stood before me, smiling, accepting homage that must have been brimming in my eyes. I tried to stand up to bow before her... I slipped and slid headlong under the water. I came up spitting.

"I'm hungry," the goddess whispered.

"What, again?"

"No, silly. For the food of mortals."

We ate in the main restaurant. It was there that the band was playing. It was the Ritz-Xentun all over again. La Cumparsita. That very first time I laid eyes on her. On my personal enchantress. It seemed that that day's magic would never cease.

The next day we went for a walk along the indoor botanical gardens the Airways had provided to ease the waiting period for its passengers. It wasn't a large garden but well planned, and it fitted our needs. We both wanted to be down south, and this was as close as I could take her. We sat on a bench under a Royal palm, awaiting the westerlies to fondle our faces. Then we tried to guess how long it would take for the palm to grow through the glass roof.

"They grow pretty big, don't they?"

"Up to eighty feet, I believe," Cathy said. There was a time when she'd travelled south for most winters.

"I wish I had been there," I mused.

"South? Didn't you just say..." She stopped, looking surprised. I could have sworn she was expressing a wish similar to mine. "Do you think we are beginning to think alike?"

"We've always done so. For as long as I've known you, darling. And, yes. I have been thinking how nice it would be if we were down south, just the two of us."

So there is something like equanimity of minds. I wondered if that was how Winston read my thoughts. He tuned himself to my vibrations, and hey, presto, we thought as one.

"We got one," Cathy said after a moment, contemplating the palm tree.

"A black hole?"

"How did you know?"

"We, spiritual masters, know such things," I assured her gravely. "But seriously, have you really produced conditions matching those from the beginning of the world?" It was a commonly accepted theory that at the instant of the Big Bang the gargantuan pressures may have created a countless number of tiny black holes.

"There may have been a dozen of them, but one we are sure of."

"A mini-big-bang? How?"

"Well, all that we do is, of course, photographed electronically. We have one image on which there is a distinct void that grew in size for almost three milliseconds. Then it disappeared."

"How," I repeated, still only half understanding what exactly she was talking about.

"We are not sure yet. But the void could only have been produced by a mini black hole."

"I thought black holes were spheres into which things disappeared, not things that disappeared themselves."

"I know. Funny that, isn't it? Perhaps there was nothing there to sustain it? You must realize that space is mostly void. The ratio of matter to space, at atomic level, is almost negligible." Her eyes drifted to her distant computer screens. "There was more. There was evidence of gamma rays, x-rays, and what seemed to be a sort of mini-magnetic wind. It was all at the sub-microscopic level, of course, but the latest technology enables us to capture even the tiniest and shortest of events. Even at the event horizon. For a few milliseconds there was a void that does not occur naturally in the Universe."

I let that pass. "So what's next?" I asked after a while.

"More of the same," Cathy said slowly. Then she turned and looked into my eyes. "I was there, Peter. I was there when it happened..." she hesitated.

"And?"

"Well, this doesn't make scientific sense, but I felt that those tiny black holes, that all of them were miniature universes. I mean... Oh Peter, I'm a little afraid..."

"Of being snatched up and pulled into one of those black miniatures?"

"No, darling. Of having my... my mind pulled into the event horizon. It doesn't make sense, does it?" She looked down at her hands, fingers interlocked in her lap. "That's really why I flew in. I had to get away. I can't explain it any better."

"As above, so below," I murmured. And then I said louder, "If the black hole can snatch you, can you snatch a black hole? Can you engulf it with your consciousness?"

She looked at me as though I were talking complete balderdash.

Nonsense or not, I pulled her to my side and we basked in the artificial ultraviolet light of the overhead lamps. A balmy breeze barely moved the leaves of the overhead fronds and softly caressed the nearby subtropical plants and bushes. For a transient instant of eternity we were lost in a miniature Eden. It was the wrong place to be afraid.

As luck would have it, there were no other people around. For a blissful while I held her close. We were almost as one. Gradually she relaxed and pulled away to rub her face, as one waking up.

"There," she said. "Now you know that I'm just a hysterical woman in need of reassurance."

"Why didn't you tell me yesterday?"

"One, I was embarrassed, and two, well, we were rather busy last night..."

That we were. I felt rather proud of myself, of being able to divert her thoughts from what was obviously eating her innards. Not that she didn't want to discuss her work—she loved talking about it. Her reticence was limited to just that particular incident, or particular feeling, that unnerved her. When she relaxed, once again, I asked her about the event horizon, a term I was only vaguely familiar with.

"It is a term we borrowed from general relativity. It simply defines the boundary, with respect to the observer, beyond which the observer cannot be affected by the events taking place. Like in gravity. Now it seems that with the black holes there are some other 'events' taking place that we are still unaware of." Her fingers indicated inverted commas on each side of 'events'.

"Such as?"

"Things or events that are not physical. At least, they don't appear to be..."

Even as she spoke, I remembered reading about Bruno Groening, a German healer who astonished a vast number of people towards the end of the last World War. The Second, and hopefully the last one, although with the ambition bubbling up at the Pentagon, we could no longer be sure. At any rate, people came from far and wide to seek Groening's healing powers. There was a peculiar difference in the way he affected people. Usually men endowed with healing power use the sense of touch to affect their 'patients'. Saints and avatars, even little *moi*, did that to some good effect. With Bruno it was different. He emitted some sort of event horizon. When people came within a certain distance of him, healing occurred. Quite spontaneously. People had consistently recovered from their disorders or maladies at a considerable distance. But it didn't affect everyone. It seemed that the power he emanated, or that emanated through him, needed the right receiver to work. Still, the term 'event horizon' struck a chord in my memory.

"...basically, in the case of a black hole," I continued to listen to Cathy with my other ear, "the event horizon describes the boundary within which the escape velocity is greater than the speed of light. To give you a scale comparison, the escape velocity would have to be greater than 300,000,000 meters per second, as against a mere 11,200 meters per second on the surface of our Earth. Perhaps this gravitational attraction alone makes us feel a certain allegiance to Mother Earth."

"Are you suggesting that the gravitational attraction that the Earth exerts on us affects our minds and emotions?"

What of an attraction almost 27,000 times greater? Perhaps Cathy had experienced some sort of emotional allegiance to the mini black hole.

"Have you heard about lunatics? Strange behaviours of people under the influence of a full moon? And that's only a borrowed light. Astronauts used to tell so many stories along those lines that all manned space flights were suspended more than two decades ago, remember?"

"Since your dad..."

"Yes, since Dad put a citizen of China on Mars, even if it was for only two hours to deposit some delicate instrumentation. And anyway, Mars can be regarded practically as a neighbour of Earth. Astronomically speaking it really is next door."

She seemed quite adamant about her observations, about the observation of herself, of her emotions, and none of my prodding over the next hour or two managed to budge her from her stand. She insisted that what she'd experienced was real. Her concern was beginning to shift, not into confirming its veracity to herself, but to measuring the effects under laboratory conditions. To my knowledge one often expressed one's emotions in a laboratory, but no one ever bothered to measure them. A bit unfair, I thought, to those who managed to keep theirs under control.

"Don't you need mass to be subject to gravitational force?" I tried a different tack.

"You are thinking of photons," she picked up on it immediately. "No, photons do not have mass, but, well... they have momentum."

"And that's what the event horizon curbs also?"

"We know a lot less about the black holes than we care to admit."

"Could they be miniature universes, as had been suggested by some..."

"...scientists and science fiction writers. We don't know what they are, and therefore we don't know what they are not. The laws of physics, the physics we *do* know, don't apply within their..."

"...event horizon?"

"Yes, darling."

"If a black hole ever pulls you inside itself, I'll go over and jump right in there with you," I assured her.

"You might have to hurry. You'll have less than three milliseconds."

Joking aside, there was evidence, at present tenuous at best, that there was some sort of event horizon, as in the case of Bruno Groening, that exists right here, on earth, and that does affect not only our bodies, but also our emotions. I wonder where my own healing power fit into this equation. I'd spent a year wondering, to no avail. Yet, for some reason, that seemed as irrational as Cathy's fears. I was deeply convinced that all secrets would be unveiled to us, if only we didn't lose heart.

"Would you mind awfully if we went back today," Cathy asked, looking away from me. Whatever pull I had on her, seemed equally balanced by the pull of her parents. Obviously, my event horizon did not include her parents. I hoped to change that, soon. "They have no one but me," she added by way of an excuse.

"I think I'll just increase my gravitational pull and swallow you whole."

"Sometimes I wish you would, Peter. Sometimes I lose hope that we shall ever learn more about ourselves, about human potential, or more even just about the Universe we live in, than the old Masters already knew, millennia ago."

I understood exactly what she meant. This was one reason why I found it so hard to break away from my own past, from my early studies of the Bible, the Bhagavad-Gita, the Sutras, or even Cathy's favourite, Tao Te Ching. I still found them deep wells of information, provided one did not treat them literally. But we had to move on. Over the years, we have all accumulated such material dross in our subconscious minds that it is a real effort to reach out beyond it.

Perhaps the Indians were right. Perhaps in the age of Kali, the goddess of death and destruction, we, as a species, were retreating into an abyss of ignorance. It seemed that there was no one alive who could enlighten us, who would take us under his or her benevolent wing. Were we a dying race? Has man outlived his welcome on Earth?

I just couldn't accept that; I couldn't justify my faith in the future, either. There was still that seemingly unfulfilled potential. That unshakeable hope that under the debris that diminished our ability to think clearly, to trust the evidence of things not seen, there was still that precious ember that was not wholly extinguished. Time would tell, I kept assuring myself. We were, however, no matter how slowly, running out of this precious commodity. Space-time was shrinking and was being sucked into the miniature worlds, by the inexorable authority of the black holes that have polluted the Universe ever since the Big Bang. And now we have begun creating our own little monsters. What were the scientists thinking?

I drove Cathy directly to her parents' house in Upper Westmount, where people more equal than others lived in their aeries. The eagles of society, the secret powers behind the overt thrones. They were a world unto themselves, a world that Cathy had rejected the day she became infected with the holy fire of science. It hadn't stopped.

Minutes later I arrived at home, moments before Jo and Mo returned from their Mount Tremblant holidays. They looked suntanned, and quite indecently replete with energy. They jumped higher, screamed louder, raced faster than ever before. Until Winston performed his magic.

"I think we shall go upstairs now, Miss Moira and Master Jonathan. We shall wash our hands before dinner." Winston offered this suggestion without raising his voice by a single decibel, as calmly as if declaring the time of day. It was a very clever device. They could as easily have washed their hands in the downstairs powder room, but then the respite from their explosive presence would have been much shorter. I strongly suspect that without Winston, Ruth and I would already have been transferred to the nearest psychiatric ward. We would probably have laughed hysterically all the way there. Weren't they little darlings?

"Yes, Uncle Winston," they both said.

Now that was a new one. To my knowledge they'd never addressed Winston except by his first name, as was proper for the heir and heiress of the estate. I looked at Ruth and raised an eyebrow.

"I thought it best," she said, and left it at that.

Later she told me that it was ridiculous to treat Winston in any way other than a member of the family. He'd lived with us for years, he contributed greatly, the children evidently loved him, and he did his work in an exemplary fashion, which was more than could be said for average members of a family.

"I promise to improve, Ruth. I really will," I assured her.

She looked at me and began laughing.

"Peter, darling, that was not a dig!" She took me into her arms and planted a kiss on my cheek. "You are you, no matter what you do or don't do. I was referring to families at large."

"Nevertheless, I intend to surprise you," I insisted having absolutely no idea how to make good on my threat.

"You already have. What you did with the security people, both at Headquarters and in Ottawa, was nothing short of miraculous. Do you know that Solidarity has been granted, at our discretion, a permanent access to all federal department offices? I can assure you that no 'trade union' or any other organization for that matter, has ever been awarded such a privilege."

I was surprised, but not wholly. They were probably hoping that I would make it a regular practice to visit their dark, dank corridors. Actually they were neither dark nor dank, but I didn't particularly like people who told others what to do. Like various governments. Or politicians at large. Or the police, or the army or... There were quite a few of them. Until recently that list had also included the illustrious members of various Churches. Mostly the Holy Roman Apostolic Church. Other denominations and creeds still existed of course, though they, too, have been shrinking.

With an elegant bow befitting the Mistress of Solidarity International, I said, "We are here to serve and obey."

"If only," Ruth murmured, and pulled me towards the sitting room.

"Do you know this is the first bit of quiet I've had at home since you left? And by the way, weren't you coming back only tomorrow?"

"It's her parents," I said, by way of explanation. "They are OK, but Cathy, well, you know Cathy..."

"She loves her parents? How quaint, these days," Ruth smiled. And then her face darkened considerably. "You know, Peter, you might have to help us again. There was trouble in the Vatican. Serious trouble. I'm not sure we should even talk about it here. This house hasn't been swept by our people for months now. And the opposition is getting smarter."

I nodded. "Will it keep till the morning?" I asked.

"There is nothing we can do right now, anyway. Come, play with the children, and you must have missed your Friday Martini. Let's ask Uncle Winston to teach us how to mix them."

We did. Uncle Winston was a great teacher, even if his new title made him grin from ear to ear. Did I mention that his ears were very far apart?

And then we all heard the swish of two supercharged bodies sliding down the handrail. The blissful quiet was over.

After dinner, I sat in my room, once again in front of my mirror and practised aura reading on myself. Reading your own aura is more difficult, in-as-much as you tend to influence it to make it as 'good', so to speak, as you know how. In other words, your subliminal mind is cheating on your conscious mind. In some ways it was fun, but I did not learn much about myself other than that I was able to manipulate my own aura. For now just a little, but I had to start somewhere.

When I first tried it some weeks ago, I got nowhere. Eventually, I could sit down and see my emanation within seconds. Not in too much detail, but at least it was a clearly defined halo that flowed down, changing its colours progressively until, by the time

I reached my hips, it was hardly visible. In fact, I usually couldn't detect it below my waist. It could have been, at least partially, due to the fact that I didn't actually look at the aura at all. I would gaze intently at my own forehead, and my peripheral vision would take care of the rest. I might mention, however, that my peripheral vision had at least tripled since I began my exercises. My auric sight was improving.

What could Winston see? He could probably examine the aura on your toes and determine what you'd had for breakfast. You could never tell with Winston, and Uncle Winston would seldom if ever tell himself.

I practised for some hours.

I was glad that, manipulated or not, with time my own aura was becoming clearer. When I began on this particular venture, my emanations tended toward medium dark shades. One didn't have to be an expert to guess that that was not a good sign. Over time, for whatever reasons, which frankly I did not understand, my aura had become clearer, brighter, better defined. I had hardly made any spiritual leaps lately, so I could not really account for what I knew was a considerable improvement. On the other hand, I also felt much more alive, and on the whole more determined to reach whatever it was that I was reaching for. I suspected it was something to do with my destiny. Or every one's destiny.

I knew that the aura, like a mirror, is a true reflection of my nature at any particular moment. And, until we learn to control it consciously, the aura cannot lie. But once we gained such control, we probably wouldn't want to lie anymore. There is a strange, almost mesmeric attraction in truth for its own sake. You feel that, somehow, it sets you free.

However, at that stage of my development, if I told myself that I felt just fine but my aura was dirty, then I was lying and not my aura. When I was angry, disgruntled, jealous or generally discontented, my aura would lose some of its luminosity, or the clarity of its colour. It was quite unnerving, if not humbling, which in turn did more harm to my aura, so to speak.

Peace. The secret of the saints.

When I could relax sufficiently to feel a sense of serenity, my aura seemed to pulsate with blues and wisps of purple, that translated lower down into different shades of green. It really was quite breathtaking. When I saw those colours, I felt a peculiar sense of gratitude. And when, on occasion, those emotions reached my deepest convictions, I actually witnessed yellow wisps of joy rising above my head. I wondered, wistfully, what it would be like to transform those wisps into flames.

In time I would learn what all these shades really meant. Suffice, for now, that they made me happy. Happy with an overwhelming sense of peace that I hadn't experienced for more than two years.

About that time, it also struck me as peculiar that I'd never attempted to read Cathy's aura. Perhaps I was afraid of what I might find. She was a very mental person. Driven by her intellect. Yet there was also that inexplicable warmth and kindness that I first experienced up north, in the hunting cabin, when she took the time to restore me to life a year ago. If I were to judge her by that behaviour, her aura would have to be pure gold. Perhaps I was afraid to be disappointed.

I took my eyes off the mirror.

I blinked a few time, then allowed my eyes to wander over the countless books that stood, shoulder to shoulder, at attention, like a long inactive army forgotten on the regimental shelves, on either side of my desk. So much knowledge. Other people's knowledge, other people's realities. Can we really live in knowledge we steal from other people? Or must we create our own earth and our own heaven, as God did when he started it all?

I loved those books. So much effort of human endeavour. Yet I couldn't get rid of the feeling that we, the human race, were all going in the wrong direction. Why should we extend our physical lives by genetic manipulation? Were we really just our bodies that we held in such precious esteem? And what of the clones? Is not an exact copy of the original, indistinguishable from an original man or woman by any means available to us, still unto the image and likeness of God? If a Higher Being created us, can we not, as lesser gods, create other beings lesser than ourselves? And the people whose bionic enhancement exceeds all that originally made us human, are they not all also still human? Perhaps more than human?

Perhaps we should all curl up and die, making room for Homo Superior.

These thoughts did not depress me. They merely refused to be ignored. They also insisted on being answered.

Even as I closed my eyes seeking that blessed state of not-thinking, that state of mental inaction that brought peace and cut down desire... the Wu wei? Was that what Buddha called nirvana? Can we really rise above the noise that our past creates in our brains, our minds, demanding answers, always answers?

Good night, Cathy, my love. Good night, my soulmate. Was there really no such a thing? And if so, why do I feel, repeatedly, that part of me is somewhere, far, yet very close, most tiny, yet wielding enormous power, loving yet somehow deadly? Or am I just afraid for my life?

***

21

The Man Immortal

"The way things are, the world will continue to expand, cool, and over time, we will become little more than black dots in a black sky that stretches out for ever," Cathy mused aloud.

Her eyes drifted far, far away, probably focused on some forgotten star born in the throes of the primeval Big Bang, billions of years ago. Now this lonesome fiery fragment of the Universe, cooling even as it accelerated towards the enigmatic abyss of seemingly endless space, was receding from us at nearly the velocity of light. Speeding along, away from the gargantuan explosion, towards the ever-receding horizon. Towards the barrier that simply wasn't there. Towards nothing.

Oblivion?

Cathy's face held a mood one would expect to see when reading poetry. Though I didn't know it at the time, for a little while now, she had been expounding to me the mysteries of dark matter. Every time we met, I was distracted by her beauty, by the fire in her eyes, by life literally bursting forth from her every word. I saw her floating in space, on a cloud of pristine whiteness that radiated a myriad stars in all directions. "There had to be another way and we found it," she declared, taking credit upon herself.

"I thought you were dealing with the very small, not the..." I had to look away from her face to gather my thoughts. I shook my head.

"I am. But really, we cannot separate the two. Einstein did and look where it got him."

Einstein had been known to resist some of the postulations of quantum mechanics. He needed his world to be orderly, not subject to imponderables.

"The Nobel prize?"

"Don't be flippant, Peter. This is serious. There simply is not enough matter in the Universe to stop it from expanding forever. Actually that was true until some years ago. Then astrophysicists speculated that there must be some invisible matter. Too thin to reflect light but enough of it to provide the big crunch impulse. You see, the nonbaryonic particles that move relativistically and non-relativistically... never mind that."

Just as well. She'd lost me at the nonbary-or-something. I allowed myself a deep sigh of relief. "So you would rather be squashed than spread out?"

"I haven't thought of it in those precise terms," she admitted, looking up at me for the first time. She was talking about dark matter, but there were bright stars in her eyes.

Physicists normally regard non-physicists as something just above a short-tailed monkey—not quite an ape in mental development. Except when they were in bed with you, of course, but then the primitive aspect of you...

"If there is any squeezing to do, I reserve the right to do it myself," I affirmed gravely. I thought it wise to stake out my claim, which did little to dissuade her from her probable assessment of my acumen.

"Are you listening, Peter?"

I constricted my face into an image of acute concentration. "May I ask why you covered us all in this black mass?"

"Black matter, not mass, although it does have mass, and thus gravitational attraction. Which is precisely the point."

Cathy didn't have to tell me anything about attraction. She was oozing it. Probably all over the Universe.

"The point?"

"I already answered that. The big crunch, remember?" She sighed deeply. "And now we have our miniatures. Don't you see, Peter? If we can produce them, isolate them in the Collider, then surely there must be an infinite number of them all over the place, each exerting its pull on the totality of the mass of the Universe."

We were about to sit down to lunch with the Mondellays, and she was about to give me indigestion. When Cathy was in town, we always ate alternately, or almost so, at the Mondellays or the Thorntons. It was invariably a festival, something akin to a carnival, precipitated by her arrival. She was the queen of the ball and strangely enough seemed completely unaware of the royal treatment accorded her. She was a loving daughter, an excellent friend and a great lover. She also did, I've been told, an excellent job at her father's Mondellay Institute, right here in Montreal. There had to be a skeleton in her cupboard somewhere, but to date I have not discovered it.

"So?"

"We cannot see them, Peter. They must be there, but no one can see them. They might be right here, in front of your nose, and you would be none the wiser!"

"Wouldn't it just suck me in?" I had to try something.

"Not if they were winking in and out of our Universe in milliseconds. By the time the mass of your body got polarized, they would be gone."

I could see that that would be a problem. If I wanted to disappear, that is. Could I wink right back, in due course? I thought it best not to ask her.

"It would be all right if only we could wink right back, wouldn't it?" Unexpectedly she helped me out.

"You've contracted the Winston disease," I said.

"What?"

"You are reading my thoughts. Again," I added, after due consideration.

She stopped and looked at me with renewed interest. "I know," she admitted. "What's going on, Peter?"

"People do that after years of married life," I assured her.

I looked up to see Mrs. and Dr. Mondellay regarding us from the open door. The doctor had one arm wrapped protectively around his wife's shoulders. They had that look in their eyes which, I presume, all parents have when they look down at their children. Cathy was still unaware of their presence.

"Do you think we ought to get married?"

"I much prefer wayward women," I said, winking at Mrs. Mondellay, who'd once told me that she and the doctor lived together for years until getting a passport had proven to be more convenient for married couples. "I'd always fancied myself as a wayward woman," she'd said at the time. "Not that Cathy ever believed it," she'd added with a smile. "Sometimes I think she still regards me as a virgin, prone to an Immaculate Conception."

"I don't know. My parents might not like it," Cathy pursued.

"Then I won't marry them," I countered.

As Cathy looked up, she saw her mother, and behind her her father, his other hand pressed against his mouth to hide a broad grin.

"Just how long have you two been standing there?" she asked, her voice combative.

"Long enough, darling. And now come and eat. Luncheon's ready."

They seldom talked 'business' when at home. Dr. Mondellay was that rare breed that combined theoretical physics with laboratory experiments. Perhaps that was how he'd made his millions. Billions, some said. He'd patented his discoveries. Cathy, though emulating her father, tended towards the theoretical, expecting others to follow up on her speculations. Projections, or perhaps theories. After all, she could hardly be expected to build her own atom smasher just to prove her point.

"I'm going back tomorrow," she announced over coffee.

Was this the skeleton? Her announcement came in a voice devoid of emotions. Sometimes I felt like I was dealing with two Cathys. One, a highly emotional, passionate kitten, often tiger, who swept me into a forbidden garden of delights; the other cold, a calculating scientist who discarded emotions as inconsequential. On the other hand, she sounded just as passionate about her bosons. My dear Cathy remained an enigma. Perhaps, under a magnifying glass, we all are at times.

I took Cathy to the airport that we'd left only some forty-eight hours earlier.

"We must stop meeting like this," I said, trying to hide the sadness that must have been obvious on my face.

"What will people say?" she quipped.

I followed her plane with my eyes until it was but a dot in the eastern sky. And then even the dot was gone. And so was Cathy.

"Immortality is a serious business," Ruth announced at the opening of the conference. She was sitting at her desk, which faced an oblong table that was designed to extend her personal surface.

The gentlemen sitting in a semicircle were the top brains Ruth could gather at a moment's notice. Three were university professors, including Dr. Brent, my old colleague and mentor, and two men who had flown in from the Vatican specifically for this occasion. They would later report our conclusions directly to Lena.

It wasn't often that I saw my sister-in-law chairing an international conference on any subject. The previous occasions had dealt with security, in Canada, at the Vatican, and generally throughout the offices of the world. She was the same sister and exhibited the same grace, but that was as far as the similarity went. Her tone now was commanding not only attention but, in a certain way, obedience. While Lena seduced her listeners, Ruth imposed her personality on them, but in such a way that the listeners were flattered to be in her presence. I was reminded of an old definition of a politician. 'It is a man,' it said, in this case woman, 'who can tell you to go to hell in such a way that you are looking forward to the trip.' Ruth was no politician, but her lieutenants would follow her to the ends of the earth.

To each her own, I thought. She and Lena were indeed a very strange pair. I often found it hard to accept that women so young could develop such a following. And then I thought of Alexander the Great. He was thirty-three when he died. He had ruled for a mere thirteen years, and he left an empire in his wake. Perhaps it was women's turn.

"Also," Ruth continued, "it is a business that begins to affect our everyday life. We cannot function in a vacuum, gentlemen. I expect you to guide me, and by inference all of us, in the direction that Solidarity International should take in the light of the latest research."

She was talking, of course, about my earlier reports on genetics, AI, robotics, and my latest report on nanotechnology.

The reports had been tabled, analyses examined, proposals presented. Only one thing was missing: Conclusions. I, for one, wasn't sure there could have been any conclusions. Each branch of science had its advantages, each produced diverse results. What was best for one group, or even for one nation, would not necessarily serve the interest of another. The problem was that Solidarity International, as its very name implied, was an organization that covered the globe. We, meaning the SI, had to have its fingers in all the pies.

"Would one of you gentlemen define for me the term immortality?"

Professor Darwich very studiously removed the glasses from their perch on the top of his bald head and rubbed them with his handkerchief. When he felt ready, he turned and faced Ruth. "The condition of not dying, Miss Thornton."

Ruth smiled. "Thank you, Professor Darwich. And in future I think Miss would be best used for my daughter. Mrs. Thornton or Ruth will do fine."

Professor Darwich turned his attention, once again, to polishing his glasses.

One of the Europeans stepped in and saved him. "There is a method of recording all the memories and storing them for later introduction into a new brain. This supplements the partial memory loss we envisage even in the latest cloning techniques. One could regard this as a form of immortality."

"But your body is gone?" Dr. Brent put in with a shrug. He'd spent his life preserving bodies, not swapping them for others.

"An exact replica still exists. After all, we are little more than the sum total of our memories," said the men from Europe.

I die daily, I mused, thinking of Paul of Tarsus. What would he have to say to such a premise, I wondered. Or Krishnamurti, for that matter.

"We cannot limit life to a machine that stores memory. Life is a process, not a status quo," Dr. Brent said, looking keenly at Ruth. "Nor can we limit the definition of life to a complex process based on the chemistry of the carbon atom. If anything, we would have to come up with a pattern that, when applied and repeated, would manifest the characteristics that we associate with life."

Now that sounded like my old professor. Nothing is as simple as it seems, he used to say in my old days.

"Whata of cyborgs? You call zem androids, yes?" This was the other professor who had flown in from the Vatican. "We grow zem from fetus, improve zeir bodies, metabolism and such and eventually make all zeir parts replaceable. Woulda they nota live forever?"

"If you define them as life to begin with. If you grow a replacement organ, you do not call it life, just a replaceable organ. And cyborgs are just a lot of such replaceable parts put together," the other man from the Vatican said, showing a marked improvement over his colleague's accent.

Even as I sat there, my eyes wandered over the foreheads of all present, seeking their auras. They were all human, but only Dr. Brent and Ruth passed the litmus test. The other professors had only limited claim to humanity.

"Isn't the whole greater than the sum of its parts?" I asked quietly. Frankly, I was playing *l'avocat du diable*, just for fun. Also, I was beginning to hear echoes of the good, or not so good, Doctor Frankenstein and his monster.

For some reason they all looked at me. I tried to slide under the table but it was too late. "Would you care to expand on that, Dr. Thornton?" someone asked.

No, I wouldn't, I wanted to say. Alas, all eyes were still on me. I took a deep breath and asked a question instead. "Has anyone checked if cyborgs dream? Do they have rapid eye movement when at rest? Are there big differentials in their Alpha, Delta, and Theta rhythms? Are their cycles similar? And if so, are such rhythms in any way similar to human rhythms? And if not, are they, our creations, really an extension of our immortality, or just a new race altogether that might, just might one day take over from us? To my knowledge, albeit limited, the creators of cyborgs, or androids for that matter, were using the human model for convenience only. There was nothing better around. It was never their intention to make a human, but rather, if at all possible, a superhuman creature. And don't kid yourself. When the androids take over the creative process from us, they will not base their next model on us. We are already passé."

I could see from their expressions that nobody liked my questions. Nor suggested conclusions, for that matter. Only then I realized that they all, with the exception of Dr. Brent, who was surreptitiously smiling at me, wanted to become immortal. Immortal even in their old, tired, dilapidated bodies. They were afraid of death. Of the unknown.

After a lengthy silence, Dr. Brent came to my rescue—if indeed such was needed.

"When we describe life, we describe the process of change. Our immortality would depend on the degree to which we could sustain changing our pattern. Our gene pattern, our molecular structure, the replacement of our trillions of cells, but also our concepts, our ideals even our very thoughts. We cannot define life as a thing or even a being. It is more like becoming. We can only decide whether or not such an entity as we are discussing is alive, if the above attributes continue to take place."

All the time he was talking, his eyes never left my face. I loved my old mentor.

Ruth, seemingly in slow motion, began to gather her papers. The conference came to an abrupt stop. No one wanted to offer counter-arguments to Dr. Brent's opinion. Finally she looked up, and her gaze swept all present.

"I shall expect your written comments on this meeting, with such additional information as you choose to add. And now I must remind you that there are trends developing in the world that do not have the best interests of Solidarity International at heart. You, with the exception of Dr. Brent, are not to share our present conclusions with anyone. As for you, John," Ruth turned to my old friend, "I can only hope that we can rely on your discretion. The meeting is adjourned."

After the meeting broke up, Ruth asked me to stay behind. I felt a little like a schoolboy who was asked to stay after school. Had I said something I shouldn't have? And then the doors closed.

"Peter, we must talk about security. I told you about our new problems that we assumed must be from our friends down south. Do you have any ideas?"

"It would help to know why the USA suddenly decided that Canada was a threat to them," I told her.

Ruth looked unconvinced. She fell against the back of her chair, then bounced forward again leaning over her desk. "We've gained a foothold in San Francisco, Detroit and Chicago. Even as we speak, our ranks are swelling in those three cities. I suspect it is in direct response to the success we had there that they decided..."

"...to take counter-measures. That would explain it very well indeed. Why would you push for membership in the US of A? Aren't two billion people enough?"

"Two-point-three, as of yesterday," she threw in, dismissing the number with a wave of her hand. "No, Peter. We did not venture into the States. People in the States have applied for membership in Canadian SI. We never refuse an application. It is our fundamental policy."

"But they can never agree to your terms..."

"They? You mean the elite. I know. That's part of the problem."

For a moment we both withdrew into our own thoughts. Then I felt a wisp of a premonition. Not a vision, or anything as pronounced, but a sort of feeling that I may have found at least a partial answer.

"In Europe, Solidarity grew slowly. After its first tentative steps in Poland, it extended its influence to other European countries, but it took years, many years, and considerable metamorphosis, before it grew into its present international status. In the meantime, the rest of the world continued on its own established path."

"I do not see where you are leading with this, Peter." She sounded dismissive.

"Bear with me. After Canada followed in our European cousins' steps, America, or more precisely the USA, became isolated not just in terms of social structure but, at least in part, in terms of trade."

"So?" Now Ruth sounded impatient.

"If Solidarity were to sweep the USA, the change to their system would be too abrupt—probably catastrophic. It would be revolutionary, not evolutionary as in Europe and to a lesser degree in Canada."

"Peter, you must get to the point," Ruth glanced at her watch.

"Throughout history, revolutions have been bloody. Do you want that blood on your hands?"

"I didn't start the trouble," she almost barked. This was a Ruth I'd never seen before. A moment later my dear sister-n-law sounded defensive, but her impatience waned. She was beginning to calm down. "You are beginning to talk like Winston," she murmured.

"I should be so lucky," I smiled. Then I asked her point blank, "Do you still want to play hardball?"

"As hard as I have to," her stubbornness was already returning. "Do I have a choice?"

"Have you ever read a book called Atlas Shrugged, by some woman, I believe..."

"By Ayn Rand, Peter. What is your point?"

"I would suggest that you propose to big business people south of the border that they play that card. Insinuate to them, very quietly, that to defend against the influx of Solidarity—that happened against your best judgment etc., etc.—that the CEOs, or the management in the United States, should go on strike."

"You are not serious!" Ruth was not amused, but also she did not kick me out of her office. "Surely, you don't mean... this would be against our own best interests!" She stared at me with fire in her eyes. This was a very different Ruth. Yet, almost in the same breath, she added, "Wouldn't it?"

Once again she fell back against the back of her chair. She looked at me with a mixture of horror, smouldering anger, and just a smidgen of admiration. "You don't really think that they would go for such a ploy, do you?" she asked, her tone tenuous. "And I very much doubt Lena would. She is terribly straight, you know."

"I know. Perhaps this should not be initiated by SI, by you, but how about by the Federal Government?"

I could see her grey cells working overtime. She was right. Lena would never sanction such a ploy, but, perhaps, it was time for SI Canada to stand on their own feet. After all, we were playing for big stakes, and we were most likely to pay the piper. I wouldn't be surprised if the Yanks, to use JR's expression, wouldn't turn quite nasty if pushed against the wall. There had been signs of this already.

The following week, Ruth and I had an appointment with the Right Honourable John McPearson-Jennings, the current Prime Minister of Canada, and his nanotechnologically enhanced secretary, Joan Brown, Ph.D. (followed by a hodgepodge of most other letters of the alphabet). The two became inseparable from the day Miss Brown had applied for the job in the Prime Minister's office. They made an odd pair. He—short and stubby, the sort that needed power to justify his masculinity; she—a tall, lanky, willowy woman, cast from the same mould as John Robb. When they walked together, which they invariably did, the Prime Minister took two steps to every one of Joan's. One had to wonder who was following whom. Yet, in spite of this, Joan managed to retreat into the tiny shadow the PM cast behind him. Oddly enough I also heard that she was a high grade black-belt in Aikido, 'The Way of Harmony and Spirit,' which, I'd also heard, in her interpretation was not as gentle an art as its name implied.

Since my visit to the capital a couple of weeks ago, there had been further instances of unsavoury characters, whom I was asked to look over. Just before the meeting, I visited the 'holding area', as it was called, a sort of maximum-security luxury suite in the basement of the Supreme Court building. Two out of three gentlemen held there were just that, unsavoury, and in the third I couldn't detect any aura at all. The unsavoury could be handled easily by the RCMP, but the blank had to be removed with caution. I made up an appropriate story without giving the RCMP the actual reasons for my selections. They'd already been warned about me and been told to act on my recommendations.

Apparently the PM had also already been notified of my descent into the governmental Hades, by the time Ruth and I were received in his offices.

Ruth explained to the PM the problem Solidarity International was encountering in the USA. She also found a way of suggesting the Ayn Rand fantasy, if not fantastic solution that, she hoped, would forestall any difficulties the Government of Canada might encounter with their US counterparts.

"It is a question of good relations, Prime Minister," she explained. "A question of trade, of good security, of mutual cooperation. If such a suggestion came from the highest levels of the Federal Government, there would be a good chance of success."

The PM glanced at his assistant, who seemed engaged in a deep sleep with her eyes wide open. After a moment or two she nodded.

"We shall certainly take your suggestion, Mrs. Thornton, very seriously," the PM said, rising.

The meeting was over. It took all of fifteen minutes. All of Ruth's meetings took about that long. She was a very well organized lady.

Three days later, two of the Canadian delegates to the US disappeared in the Washington Department of International Trade and Commerce. The delegates reportedly went to use public washrooms and never re-emerged. It was an isolated incident, probably a tacit tit for tat after their secret agents 'disappeared' in the basement of the Supreme Court building. Or perhaps some minor functionary at the Internal Security Office was playing maverick, taking it upon himself to initiate tough play against Canada.

Following the PM's chat with the VP, they were released some miles outside Washington. Perhaps our counterparts were just flexing their muscles. The following week, a series of vaguely amusing headlines appeared in the American national press.

ATLAS SHRUGGED

The articles that followed stated that in the light of the demands the workers placed on their employers, the following companies (there followed a list of conglomerates in alphabetical order) in San Francisco, Detroit and Chicago, have closed their doors until further notice.

Actually, no demands had been placed, as yet. This was strictly pre-emptive action to dissuade other workers from attempting to join the Solidarity movement.

There were no other comments on page one. On the business pages of the same dailies, however, there were extensive analyses of possible repercussions the closings might have on the Stock Exchange. A day later, the consequences were obvious and most unpleasant—an ill wind that blew directly at the Solidarity International.

Ruth read me the article aloud.

"Hopefully the wind will stop at the border," she said after she finished reading. "Not that we had much choice, did we, Peter?"

Apparently I have been included in the Solidarity nucleus. I was now a policy adviser and a general factotum. A little like Uncle Winston at home.

***

22

Musica Universalis

About a month after that meeting, and a few days after I began to fast, I heard the music for the first time. I suppose I should spell it with a capital M, even though it was little more than a scintillating, multi-chord legato spread over the crowns of trees that surrounded me. A wondrous feeling of peace.

A girl had broken her leg, falling. Before she realized it—she was whole again and walking away. I looked around and there was no one. Only the tops of the oaks and maples seemed awash with fire. Auras of trees partaking in the healing act. Whether it was God, or just one of his magic harps, I guess I'll never know. What I do know is that I heard it. There have been many sages who spoke of the Music of the Spheres, a sound that seemed quite unattainable to ordinary mortals. Even Leon Lederman, the director of Fermi National Accelerator Laboratory in the latter part of the last century, and Cathy's demigod, suggested that God may turn out to be a beautiful melody.

There was also that phrase I'd read, somewhere, probably the Bhagavad-Gita, that kept tugging at my memory, "I am the sound in ether and the ability in man."

The *Musica universalis* has been known to man since ancient times. It cannot actually be heard. No more so than auras can actually be seen. Yet, under the right circumstances, both choose to raise the veils protecting them from our senses. Philosophers have marvelled at it for centuries. Perhaps millennia. Pythagoras spoke about it. In Sanskrit they called it Shabda, or Shabd. It has many names.

The adherents of the teaching of Eckankar believe that the Satguru, the Eck Master, can merge with the Sound Current in such a manner as to become a living manifestation of it at its highest level. The echoes of the "Word made flesh".

It was the Naad, the Akash Bani and the Sruti of the Vedas. The Nada and the Udgit of the Upanishads. The Logos and the Word of the New Testament. The Sraosha of Zoroaster, and even the most recent Kalma and the Kalam-i-Qadim of the Qur'an.

And I heard it.

Saint Baljit Singh used the term Light and Sound Current. The link between the human and the divine. Between man and God.

I've heard it and I've seen it. What would be next?

I now had the evidence of the invisible and the unheard. Both had been made manifest to me. I had increased my understanding of the auras, and now this. The invisible and the inaudible. Yet real. So very real. The sound filled me to the exclusion of every other perception. And the auras filled my music with colour. There was something going on in my life that reached far beyond my understanding. Perhaps like the Breatharians, I would never eat again unless I had to just to be polite.

On the other hand, quite frankly, I was getting a little discouraged by aspects of humanity that the last few months had revealed to me. First there were the 'pure' scientists, or the scientists that dealt with pure science. Science for the sake of science. Like pure art. They'd invented the Big Bang and decided that it answered their need to account for an expanding Universe. Some time later they realized that if the Universe they defined by their expectations would continue to expand forever, or even for an unpredictably long time, such a supposition would make them grow cold and lonely. Our Earth, our ball of dust, would grow cold, though from a distance it would more likely resemble a frozen drop of water. Our sun would ultimately burn up and die, and we would drift forever into the ever-receding cold, unfriendly darkness. Not a nice prospect at all. A long, lonely, lingering death. Even for the immortals.

The equations they pulled out of their scientific hats did not allow for sufficient mass within the Universe to stop it from expanding. Yet in their minds there was a beginning and thus there would have to be an end. They needed a Big Crunch. The countless black holes Steven Hawking proposed during the last century might provide sufficient mass, but they were uncomfortable. The scientist couldn't see them, measure them, and anyway, by their own definition, the laws within those little monsters defied the rules of the universal laws as they knew them.

Knew them or created them, I asked myself?

Then there came a tenuous ray of hope.

At long last, Cathy had finished her stint in CERN and was back in Montreal. She said there had been some ten thousand applications for her post. They had to spread the goodies around. I didn't care. I was delighted that at long last she was back.

At long last winter was behind us. We were sitting on the freshly cut grass in Mount Royal Park. Have you ever smelt freshly cut grass all around you? There were the auras and the music and now the smell of springtime. The smell of life. The days were already turning into summer. They always do in Montreal. The bare trees turn green practically overnight, and then there is that lazy part of the year when everybody leans back and relaxes. Yet at that time we still breathed in the aroma of springtime, the greens still fresh, the air carrying the equally intoxicating scent of sunshine flirting with the newly sprung shoots just sprouting with fresh buds. I was in my shirtsleeves; Cathy had given up her working suit for a flowing skirt. A definite improvement, not that there was much one could improve in Cathy. And by the way, we'd set the date.

We will stand under the oak tree we once christened ours, on the top of Mount Royal, and promise each other to do the best we can. The trees, the sky, the stars, though invisible in a blue sky, shall witness our intention. Then we shall join our families, at Cathy's parents', or at Ruth's or even in our new condo, and ask our loved ones to bear witness to our commitment.

And then? And then we will live happily forever after. Or even longer... For now we were still discussing Cathy's unresolved science.

"After all those experiments," I said, "can't you just accept the Universe as a beautiful place made just for you and me to enjoy?"

"A nice theory," she countered, smiling. "But a scientific theory must lend itself to laboratory experiment," she added.

"So?"

"Well," she said, "now with the collider that can generate 10 Tv, that's 10 billion times more energy than we need to study an atom, darling," she explained, "we have high hopes of observing not only the behaviour of the Higgs particle, but the mini-universes as well."

"TV? You generate Television?"

"No silly. Capital T small v stands for trillion electron volts. T stands for tera. To study atoms we need only 1eV." And then she jumped an invisible fence again. "You should see those voids left by the mini-universes!"

I gave up. I should see, she told me, the invisible voids left behind by the invisible universes. It all still sounded like double Dutch to me. Or an invisible Swiss cheese.

"God's Universe seems much bigger, but, well, you've got to start somewhere, I suppose?" This didn't come out right, but I was beginning to warm up to the idea.

"Start what?" Her green eyes reflected the fresh green of springtime.

"Creating your own universes," I said. At last that made perfect sense to me.

"We are not creating universes, Peter. Mini or otherwise."

"Then what's the point of it all?"

"You sound like Weinberg," she countered.

"Who?"

"He said that the more the Universe seems comprehensible, the more it seems pointless."

"I'll drink to that!" I said triumphantly. "So there are bright scientists after all." I hoped she wouldn't take this personally.

"He's been dead a long time," she said quietly.

Just my luck, but it was time to go. I dragged her home for a Martini. Only she had a Sherry.

I was gradually loosing touch with Cathy's world, as well as with the world of Ruth and Lena, and just about everybody else's, I suppose. I was still involved, I had to be, but inside, inside myself, I felt as though I were vibrating in different dimensions. At home Cathy returned to her favourite subject. I listened, learned a little, and then tried to finish the conversation before it drove me crazy.

"So now that you can produce all those black holes, you'll have enough mass for the Big Crunch?"

"No, Peter, they only exist for a millisecond."

"Three," I proudly corrected my resident expert. "But the mass must still be there," I said, surprised at my own genius.

"No, darling. It transforms itself into energy."

"So no Crunch?"

"We still have the black matter."

"It wasn't there before?"

"It was, but we couldn't see it. It was black."

"We've been through that before, haven't we?"

"Yes, darling, we have."

For a moment I thought that I had it at last. Each time something isn't there that scientists need—the theoretical scientists, that is—they write down an equation and then wait until someone confirms their suspicions. That way, atom by atom, bit by bit, they create a Universe that is gradually more and more acceptable to them. To their concept of what a Universe should be. What a marvellous way to create reality, I thought. Bit on the slow side, but still, it actually sounded like fun. As long as you didn't take it too seriously.

And then there were those scientists determined to extend the functions of our bodies. They called it life, I suppose. Yet in spite of their efforts and, indeed, quite profound successes, people didn't seem to be happier. They lived longer, they retained their autonomy, they remained ambulatory longer. What no one told them was: why. No one told them what they were to do with all those extra years of life. Their days grew longer, they found it difficult to fill their time with excitement between meals. They were old people in relatively young bodies.

I didn't like that, either.

At least there was relative peace on the political front. In the American press, after the obligatory ten days of sensationalism and speculation, Solidarity International had slipped to the inside pages and then was dropped altogether. The Rt. Hon. Prime Minister had managed to convince the Americans that the Federal Government was not behind the Solidarity encroachment. "I often find Solidarity as inconvenient as I expect the President would, in my shoes."

Yet, since 'Atlas Shrugged', the word Solidarity was no longer a dirty word, except among people who had their life's savings invested in the companies that remained, for the moment, closed. Pro tem suspended. I wondered who would give up first—Atlas or the workers. I forget how Ayn Rand had worked it out.

For now there was peace.

Cathy left shortly after dinner, and with a small sense of guilt for not playing with Mo and Jo, I went directly to my room. The call of celestial music was just too overpowering.

I breathed deeply as I closed the door. At last, I was alone.

First I did my stint in front of the mirror, attempting to control my own aura. Over the last few weeks, I had managed to make my emanation weaker or stronger at will. It was tough in the beginning. But once the idea that not all is as it seems took hold, the reality of other dimensions, for want of a better word, took on almost palpable actuality. I was growing. My definition of life was progressively changing. The more I ventured into the 'unknown', the less important the biological construct I occupied became. Not that I neglected it. I was fully aware that the only time I was likely to have to uncover that which still remained hidden was by using my body. I walked to work, both ways; I often played with the children; and I did my best to discharge my duties at the office. I needed my body, my mind and my emotions to develop my inner potential, whatever that might prove to be.

And Cathy would soon keep all three of my facets busy. Isn't life wonderful?

I was still baffled by the need in the Universe for order and harmony. The more we tear the world apart, the more it seems to unite in its effort to come together again. If God is not a beautiful melody, then he is the most fantastic conductor.

During the years when Quebec had been quasi-independent, that is to say, when it strung along on money that flowed abundantly from China, Sherbrooke Street, particularly around the Atwater junction, had become dotted with a number of multi-story residential towers. Originally designed for the immigrants from China, they'd since been remodelled—two or three apartments combined into luxury suits—and the occupants, over time, had become a very cosmopolitan mix. In the lobby or around the swimming pool of each tower, one could hear a dozen languages. Mostly political representatives of international commerce, visiting dignitaries for whom the embassies kept an array of ever-ready apartments, as well as well-to-do local people who didn't want the trouble of maintaining their own, individual houses.

On the minus side was the absence of anonymity. There was a certain feeling of entering one's domicile through a market place. And, of course, there was the absence of a fireplace. For years now, only houses sporting at least six mature trees were allowed to retain their wood-burning hearths.

"Too much pollution," explained the estate agent, pointing out that there was always the alternative of a gas fireplace that both, Cathy and I regarded as a poor substitute for the real thing. No matter, neither Cathy nor I had time to really enjoy a garden at the expense of the affiliated maintenance chores. We thought the parks, Mount Royal and Westmount Summit, which had been considerably enlarged in recent years, would serve our nature needs sufficiently. An apartment, preferably with a far distant view, was more to our liking and the main reason for our choice.

Thanks to Dr. and Mrs. Bartholomew Mondellay, Cathy and I moved into our own forty-ninth-floor apartment the week after. While on our own we could easily afford the first twenty or thirty floors, the top stories were beyond our reach. But my in-laws insisted that it was our wedding present. And now we had our heads in the clouds; we lived among the angels, should they ever decide to get off the pinheads and come down to earth. Our very own eagle's nest on the forty-ninth floor with a large living room overlooking both mountains. It was awash with sunshine, and the view was breathtaking. There was also one nearly as large master bedroom, and two other rooms that served as studies for each one of us. These rooms could also double up as guestrooms, should the need arise. At that stage we were not actively thinking of children of our own. If and when they came anyway—accidents will happen—Cathy said that she would gladly forego her study.

"As I am sure you would too, darling, wouldn't you?"

I nodded dutifully.

La Chanson de Solveig on my vicell saved me from having to verbally express my acquiescence. I needed my study where I could spend time alone. I'd grown attached to my singularity of existence, my privacy, where I could contemplate, study my aura and venture into the, as yet, incomprehensible realm of the newly discovered Celestial Music. This last drew me the most. I'd spent many nightly hours placing my attention around my pineal gland, just listening, in the hope of catching the sweet strains. I wasn't always lucky.

And now, with the master bedroom looming over my future, I was having doubts if I would ever advance my hearing even as far as my vision. Which wasn't that much, either. Also, I was going to miss Winston. And Ruth and the children, too. We'd been together for a long time.

Still, I loved Cathy and, in so many ways, I needed her.

Two weeks after we'd moved in, Cathy was called to CERN. Apparently the latest results were confirming her theoretical prognostications. She was ecstatic.

She had been offered the rare privilege of partaking, electronically, in the latest research in CERN. But it wasn't the same as being there.

I knew that the mini-universes were her secret passion.

For a moment after she got the call, I thought she'd forgotten all about me. I was trying hard to partake in her joy. It wasn't easy; we'd only just moved in together.

"I'm sorry, darling," were her parting words at the airport. "I'm really sorry."

I believed her. I was beginning to understand the biblical statement about serving two masters: 'for either he will hate the one, and love the other; or else he will hold to the one, and despise the other.' Right now I hated CERN, science, and even all the worldly knowledge. And I wasn't even going away. Yet Cathy didn't hate either. I knew she loved me, though she served her science. A lover and a master, worlds apart.

As she walked away toward the departure gate, I followed her with my eyes. For some reason I began watching her aura. 'Mixed up' was as close as I could describe it. It confirmed that my Cathy was torn between two allegiances. Her work and myself. Perhaps the Bible was right. But if so, were we all destined to be forever alone?

The next moment I felt ashamed. It struck me that, of late, I've been complaining a lot. Even to myself I've begun to sound like a whining baby. This had to stop.

That evening I ate dinner with Ruth and the children. Although we saw each other at least three times a week at work, Ruth prepared a minor celebration on my account. The children acted as if I'd never left, and Uncle Winston was his usual reserved, studious, semi-invisible self.

"Welcome home, Sir," he said as he opened the door for me. I still had my own keys, but, well, you know Winston. He can see through walls. Or, possibly, he saw me walking up the footpath from the street.

"Thank you, my friend. I missed you, too," I replied.

He accorded me a stiff bow. I wondered if Winston knew, or guessed at, the traumas that resulted from Cathy's scientific success. For trauma it was. I felt more alone than I'd ever felt in my life. More so than that time at Gaston's. At least there, people had been waiting to see me. I had been needed. Now, even Cathy sated her needs elsewhere. Perhaps it was a childish reaction, but I'd never been married before. Not even in the modern sense of the word that really meant little more than a commitment to live together and, with luck, love one another. You didn't need a certificate for that. Even if Jesus didn't come to our wedding. Or even stand with us under the oak tree on the top of Mount Royal. That would come later. Not Jesus—the wedding. At least I hoped it would.

We had planned to have the celebration on her return. Just her parents, Ruth and the children, and Winston, of course. John and Lucy Brent had to be there. They were family, too. I had a good mind to ask Winston to officiate. I'm sure he would perform the rites with his usual efficiency, if not originality and good taste.

We still weren't sure where the celebration should take place. Our new condo still felt more like an aerie than a home.

Ruth went to change. I joined Winston in the kitchen. The children moved about on some quest of their own.

Winston was watching me from under his thick eyebrows. Usually he would wait passively for me to initiate direct eye contact, a conversation or even a casual word. Now he seemed to be waiting for such to begin. I felt there were things he wanted to tell me.

"I've been listening to the Shabda," I said when I saw that we were alone.

"Yes, Sir. I know."

Now how on earth would he know, I wondered?

"Your aura has changed substantially," he said, stirring something in the pan.

I must say he looked like anything but a spiritual master. His spiritual insignia was limited to his apron and saucepan.

"It is a good disguise, Sir. Don't you like it?" was his next comment. He had his back to me. He would have made a magnificent psychiatrist. Reading his patients' minds would be an easy task for him.

"I tried that, once. It didn't satisfy me, Sir. People expected me to cure them, not to cure themselves," he continued this ridiculous conversation with my unspoken thoughts.

"How do you do it?" I asked at last.

He turned to face me. "Try closing your eyes, Sir."

I did as he asked.

"Now listen to my voice," he added, after which he fell silent.

A moment later I saw shapes, contours of what I can only describe as unmanifested ideas. This must have been what Einstein called muscular shapes. Then, superimposed on that loose pattern there were sounds. First disjointed, then formulating words, in gibberish, then in English, words discernible but not yet arranged in phrases. I opened my eyes with a start.

"What was that?" I asked.

"It takes time, Sir. We all live in a vortex of energies eternally swirling in space-time. It is up to us to extract and affirm order out of that chaos. That is our destiny."

"That's it? Just to understand..."

"...who and what we are, Sir. Yes. That is all. We are, what Einstein called, the thoughts of God. After that we can do anything we want." There was that smile on his face again. A smile of an adult looking at a child, at a babe in arms.

"You will have some free time, I understand, Sir," Winston said, obviously referring to my evenings with Cathy away. "Perhaps we could exchange some ideas?"

Very funny, I nearly laughed out loud. The flow of the ideas would be strictly in one direction.

"Not really, Sir. We all create our universes and within their confines we are absolute rulers. It cannot be otherwise," he affirmed sternly.

My look must have indicated, somewhat, a lack of understanding.

"If it were otherwise, our universes, would collapse, Sir."

I made a strong effort not to think any idiotic thoughts, in fact not to think at all. It would be futile to try and hide them from Winston.

"I would like that very much," I said, instead. I could hardly believe my good luck. Winston wanted to shoot the breeze with me. In the evenings. Alone. God, there is so much I can ask him, I thought. So much...

Perhaps there was more than one reason why Cathy had been called to CERN.

And then for just a moment I held my breath. I distinctly felt a gust of wind. Only it wasn't a breeze. It was more like a gale.

***

23

War

There were no guns firing rounds of ammunition, no smart missiles killing the invisible enemy, no bombs dropping on women and children. There weren't even any armed soldiers crossing borders. Yet there was a palpable, undeniable state of war. The US versus the World. Versus everybody. No one was to be spared. Not now, not until the US of A emerged victorious.

The way of the Empire.

I was sitting with Ruth, one other woman, and three other gentlemen in her office. We all sat with our faces screwed up in expressions of incredulity.

"Surely, Ruth..." one man began. He looked elderly. He remembered the old wars.

"There is no doubt," Ruth interrupted. She'd never interrupted anyone in my presence before. "There is no doubt at all."

Ruth and I were the only under-forties present. The others carried experiences of some sixty to seventy years each. They were departmental heads who no longer had much to lose other than their posts, which at their level of employment would result in a comfortable pension. They all looked at Ruth with wide eyes, their mouths wider and their hands nervously moving across chair-arms or faces.

I was really glad that I did not have Ruth's job.

The trouble had started simultaneously in Canada, all over Europe, including the Vatican, as well as in India, China, and even Russia which, for whatever reason, hadn't done anyone any harm for two generations. So far the South Americans, Australia, and Africa were exempt from the US attack; but this could be only a question of staging, or of phasing, the illicit war.

It had all begun with an announcement on all the American Satellite TV channels that unless other countries ceased and desisted all anti-American activities, defensive counteraction would be taken immediately. Just to illustrate the case in point, the US had stated that, under the United Nations Charter, the US of A had been granted the duty of policing the world as a preventive measure against possible terrorist attacks anywhere. They also pointed out that the US of A, in order to be able to carry out its designated missions, had military bases everywhere.

"As Britain once had in the good old colonial days," I said, thus defining the extent of my knowledge of politics.

Ruth was still fuming at the announcement.

"We have the means to back up our demands with force," she read to me from the US press release, lowering her already low contralto, sticking out her chest and sounding vaguely pompous. "The General was in his best uniform and announced these words in all seriousness," she almost giggled. "As if anyone had the necessary clout to attack the US. All *intelligent* nations have already destroyed their nuclear stock of missiles."

And then she smiled, evidently at her thoughts.

"His chest," she continued, "was literally plastered with medals of all sizes and descriptions. He must have served in at least a dozen wars from the time he was two years old to have earned them. Except that there have been no wars for the past three decades. Not really," she concluded with a mixture of pleasure and something akin to disappointment.

She must have read surprise in my eyes.

"Wars are terrible crimes perpetrated against humanity," she said, "but few people realize that they often also bring out the best in man."

There was also no mention that there had not been a single certified terrorist attack in the last eleven years, Ruth continued her exposé. There had been attacks, but of the home-grown variety. The so-called Mafia and other competitive organizations. But not terrorists as defined by the UN charter #47, §11 to 24, and those other attacks did not fall under the responsibility as defined by the UN #49, §... There were many such paragraphs, she said smiling again. "Some 348 pages of them. In the days when those rules and regulations were drafted, the UN took its work very seriously." She should know. She was working at UN Headquarters at the time.

"It was a little like the work carried out by the scribes of ancient scriptures," Ruth explained. "It was a little bit like holy work. Work that would assure that the last war was really the Last war. The last of the last."

Presumably we were to conclude that it was only thanks to the US efforts that such a dull, uneventful peace reigned for more than a decade. Who knows, there may have been some truth in it, though my own opinion tended more to the fact that everybody was too busy doing their thing to be bent on destroying other people's efforts to do exactly the same. What the US of A also failed to note was that terrorism seldom flourishes when the majority of people have a great deal to lose. And since the discovery of virtually free energy by our own Dr. Mondellay some fifteen years ago, and the elimination of diseases by the progress sponsored by Solidarity International in the field of genetics, people had plenty to live for and a great deal less for which to die.

Life was good, death bad. And who could tell? Perhaps immortality was just around the corner.

Nevertheless, the US of A discovered too late that they'd bet on the wrong horse. While artificial intelligence was nice and convenient, it was not tangibly human. You couldn't cuddle up against it. You couldn't really make love to it, either. It did not increase your sexual prowess, your personal charm; it did not even give you whiter teeth, nor increase the number of pints of beer you could down watching Sunday night football. Definitely the wrong horse. Meanwhile, people who opted for genetics were healthier, had better skin tone, women had larger breasts, rounder buttocks, longer legs, and they lived longer, to boot.

As for the nanotechnological enhancements, similar benefits were available to its supporters, genetic benefits also notwithstanding, though few cared enough to take advantage of such. They had other interests and, well, often just couldn't be bothered. The nanotechnologically enhanced people were definitely too smart. According to the Americans, almost as smart as their robots.

The consequences were obvious. There had to be a war.

What wasn't quite clear, immediately, was who was going to fight whom and with what.

"I'm sure the President will enlighten us in due course," said the newly elected Secretary of the United Nations, hailing from the Kiribati Islands, deemed small enough to assure his impartiality, to a gentle applause of the gathered fraternity.

"Hear! Hear!" followed from the ex-British, now UE&GB contingent. "Hear! Hear!" picked up the Canadians, Australians, Indians, and even some Americans, by mistake.

It was nice to hear a British accent on the TV recorded meeting.

The rest of the news wasn't so good. There were eleven more companies that had shrugged their shoulders. Eleven chairmen, CEOs, CFOs, presidents, executive vice-presidents, and even managers had resigned. Eleven of each. They were all playing Atlas Shrugged. It must have cost them billions. It was becoming serious.

The whole affair would have been little more than an improvised farce if it hadn't been for the fact that a number of leading politicians of various countries, men and women of power and discrimination, disappeared overnight. A sort of universal outbreak of selectively contagious amnesia or, perhaps more likely, a case of mass kidnapping. There were no threats delivered, no ransom notes. In fact, no one claimed responsibility. To start with, no one even imagined that this could be part of the officially declared war.

The gentlemen, and some ladies in question, had retired into the security of their bedrooms only to be missing the next morning. At first, at least some disappearances were dismissed.

"But he usually returns within a few days," private secretaries would whisper, their faces hiding a conspiratorial grin. "He's been visiting her ladyship for two weeks now..."

The ladyship was also nowhere to be found.

"They will be back with broad smiles," someone threw in.

Only they didn't come back. Not even after a week. It was a sort of Atlas Shrugged, only this time Atlas was not necessarily a willing party and the shrugging was strictly political. The disappearances continued. A handful every day. For now, the world held its collective breath.

There are stories that describe the events preceding the collapse of many an empire. History is replete with them. There was the Elamite Empire, the Akkadian, the Ur III Empire, the Babylonian, Egyptian, Hittite, and even the Israeli Empire from 1050 BC to around 920 of the same era. They'd all collapsed. Mostly cases of acute debauchery.

My computer proudly displayed centuries of debauchery. I never realized how popular a sport it had been over the centuries.

Then came the Assyrian, the Achaemenid, also known as the Persian Empire. They were followed by the Magadhan, Macedonian, Mauryan, Seleucid, Chinese and the Parthian, the Armenian, and the Roman Empires. And these came and went before the new era had even begun. Carousals and over-exploitation of the conquered people lay at the heart of most of the collapses.

Starting from the first millennium came the Sassanian, Palmyrene, Teotihuacano and nineteen others. They all collapsed before the first century was over. Over-indulgence and moral dissipation?

This was becoming fatuous. Boring.

Couldn't they do anything right? They came and went like the wind that blows in the desert. I took a drink from my private stash of purified water. A Scotch would have been better.

I looked back at the screen.

Hungarian, Hoysala, Seljuk, Kongo, Danish... and again nineteen other empires that had their starts in the second millennium.

I couldn't pronounce some of the names. Hoysala Empire? Wasn't that one of the original banana republics in India? No matter. It was long gone with all the others.

In the later part of this same millennium there had been eighteen more that included the Swedish, the British, the Dutch and the Russian, as well as the Austrian, Mexican, Brazilian, and the Austro-Hungarian Empires. Reasons for their demise? Similar to all of the above.

Who needs empires, anyway, I wondered?

Finally we came to the American or the USA Empire that was reported to have began around 1898 and was now showing unmistakable signs of decadence too numerous to list. I'd never heard of any American President declaring himself an Emperor, though, admittedly, some sure acted the part. Remember Korea, Vietnam, Iraq?

I looked out at Mount Royal basking in the setting sun. Who needs empires, I asked again.

In the meantime, the 20th century saw the fleeting onsets and even faster dissolutions of the Belgian, the Soviet, the Nazi and the Central African Empires. That's what my computer said. Surely, I rebelled, you can't rate Nazis as an empire. They were more like a breath of stale air. A deadly fungus.

Whatever they were called, they all came and went even as the wind that blows in the desert. They came and went like thieves in the night. Lining their pockets, seldom leaving anything behind.

They were all transient. *Sic transit gloria mundi* my friend Vincenzo would have said.

None of this made any sense. The world wasn't *becoming* insane. The world had always been crazy. It whirled within a reality, spun in futile circles, like whirlwinds, like devilkins that spun across the Canadian prairies. It denied all rules of logic. It was like a dream, a nightmare, from which, surely, we would all wake up at any moment.

My kingdom is not of this world, said the man of Galilee. Of course not. Our kingdoms are little more than fleeting experiments devised to test human credulity. Or just simply—stupidity? Have you had enough, they seemed to ask? How long will you act like immature upstarts? Like spoiled children? You had despots, dictators, tyrants, absolute monarchies, caliphates, depraved popes, emirates... do you really want more?

Do you really want more?

I swivelled my chair. That last question was enunciated in the unmistakable voice of my friend Winston. I looked left and right. I blinked repeatedly. There was no one. I was completely alone. Now that Cathy wasn't here, more so than ever. I was sitting in front of my computer looking at a long list of World Empires. It took me a moment to remember what I had been reading. Reality was bending.

The world empires, I mused. Symbols of temporal power. Doesn't temporal also mean transitory, ephemeral?

Vanity, vanity, 'tis all vanity...

King Solomon. He knew. He'd lost it all.

There had been a countless number of men who'd placed their faith in the transient, the illusory. Countless empires, countless emperors. They all came and went. Had any of them been real? Is anything real in this world? I wondered what Cathy would say. Are her mini-worlds also just figments of someone's imagination? They are ephemeral enough. Aren't we all?

So we were at war.

Or at least a farce-like conflict that was supposed to resemble war. It was conducted by invisible players, asserting their invisible presence. Were they at least real? The invisible ones?

I was back in my office. Too large to do so little, yet how much larger than Cathy's mini-universes... My mind was wandering through infinite possibilities. There was so little I could do. When I still practised medicine, there had been rules of engagement. That's what the Pentagon would have called them. Rules of Engagement. At least, there had been rules. I was still a visible, tangible subject to human foibles. Not like the robots or cyborgs, or whoever conducted the abductions. They didn't seem to cast shadows, even at night.

I dialled JR's number. His face was smiling. I wished it weren't. I was tired. Tired of futility on so many fronts. In two minutes he was in my office. First his arms, then legs, then the rest of him. He was still smiling. Was I missing out on something? He brought me a coffee. It made me smile. The world was at war and JR thought of coffee. Perhaps he had the right idea. Perhaps at least he was real.

"So how do you like the war, Sir?" was his opening salvo.

He took his usual chair without waiting to be invited. He was a very logical man. He must have concluded that I wanted to discuss something with him, probably the war. Still, I found his lackadaisical air a trifle annoying.

"You don't take it too seriously," I commented dryly. I was worried about Ruth.

"When it's all talk and virtually no action, we don't have too much to worry about, Sir." At least he was always polite. No one else called me Sir, except for Miss Dibbs, of course.

He had a point there. So far the disappearances had taken place mostly in Europe and were hardly limited to the Solidarity ranks. In fact, the very opposite. Most had been politicians, some of whom, I suppose, may have been Solidarity members. A very different story. We still weren't sure what was really behind those disappearances. I said as much.

"Well, Sir," JR did his usual orbits with both arms, "it seems a question of mathematics," he said. "Mathematics and pressure."

It sounded like statics and dynamics. He was also beginning to sound like my imaginary Winston talking about Brahma and his longevity.

"Care to say that in English?" I encouraged as calmly as I could.

"Well, Sir, it stands to reason." The smile didn't leave his face. "For each CEO or chairperson or manager that no longer creates wealth for their country, they remove one politician," he said. "It seems almost fair."

"And the pressure?"

"Well, Sir," his grin broadened still wider. "There would be little point in kidnapping the managerial classes in Europe or in Canada, for that matter. When they make a multiple of five times average income, they are too easily replaceable. No, Sir. The only way they can hope to effect pressure is through the highly overpaid politicians."

"They'll nit-pick at the governments till the countries themselves take the necessary action.".

"Precisely, Sir. It seems to me to be that simple. The Yanks must have infiltrated the domestic staff of the political households. It may have taken them a year or two. The British, or the French for that matter, never really look at their servants. They don't... matter, the servants I mean, as long as they do their jobs."

After a moment's silence, I shook my head. "Thanks for the coffee," I said.

He took that as a dismissal, which it was. I had to talk to Ruth. I think she should benefit from JR's perception. He still was one helluva bright guy.

Ruth was out and I didn't feel like waiting for her. I left her an e-note. I decided to walk home. It was too early to barge in on the Thornton household. I would see the children later, and maybe ask Winston how he manages to be in two places at the same time—assuming my imagination wasn't playing tricks on me when I was studying the empires. Which it probably was.

The view from my forty-ninth floor continued to take my breath away. I wished dearly I could share it with Cathy. The next moment I could swear I could smell her perfume. It's amazing what tricks your mind can play on you. I went to my study.

"Brahma sleeps for one hundred years and then wakens," Winston said.

"That's a long snooze..." I probably sounded flippant. I was tired.

"Some say the opposite. Some say that Brahma is awake one hundred years and then falls asleep. It doesn't really matter."

It would matter to me, I mused, forgetting that my thoughts were not hidden from Winston. Elegantly, he chose to ignore my meandering mind. I began wondering if I was fully awake, or still asleep.

"Indeed?" as usual Winston was restrained in his comment. "One day of Brahma consists of a thousand cycles of four ages: the Satya, Treta, Dvapara and Kali. For the last 5,000 of our years, we have been immersed in the Kali yuga. In the age of Kali. It is the age of abject ignorance. We have another 427,000 years to go. But, we don't have to wait for stupidity to overtake us."

I was beginning to waken to his words.

"The four ages, rotating a thousand times, make up one day of Brahma. The same number comprises the night. The going out and the coming in. The Big Bang and the big crunch, Miss Mondellay would say."

"If she studied mythology..." I muttered wistfully.

"We all travel our chosen road, Peter. We do not judge others." He glanced at me and returned to his subject. "By earth calculations Brahma's sleep or the waking state add up to three-hundred-eleven trillion, forty billion earthly years. A lightning flash in eternity."

A lightning flash in eternity, I heard myself repeating. The futility of it all?

Now I was sitting up staring at Winston's face. It was quite expressionless. At times, the words he spoke seemed to fill the room as though he were speaking through a stereophonic system. At other times, his words seemed to be born inside my own head. I knew I'd read all that he was saying some time ago. When I'd first come back from Rome. When I was determined to understand with my mind things that were beyond the mind's reach.

"Is Brahma God?" I had to ask.

"Aren't we all?" came the answer.

Ye are gods, I remembered. I and my Father are one. Am I asleep? Each man is Buddha, not as yet awakened. The maid isn't dead, but sleepeth... In the Old Testament people never died, they just slept. David slept with his fathers, so did Solomon, Rehoboam, Abrijam, Asa, Banasha, Omri. There had been many others. How come I remembered all this? They all slept with their fathers, yet they were all buried. What was going on? Are we all asleep?

Are we all asleep?

Winston was smiling at me. There was a question in his eyes that he failed to enunciate. But I heard it as clearly as if it were spoken aloud. "Are you?"

This sounded like a call for me to wake up. Wake up from what? Am I dreaming even now? I was about to ask this question but I no longer could. The Winston that was forcing me to re-examine the ancient wisdom once again had vanished. I seriously doubted he was ever in my room.

I walked to the bathroom, splashed some cold water on my face, and looked up at the mirror over the sink. There was luminosity around my head that I'd never seen before. It seemed to shimmer; little flames jutted out as if my head were on fire. Even as I looked, the effect diminished. I tried to recall my last thoughts, but they receded the way a dream recedes when you awaken from deep sleep.

Only one question kept coming back with nagging regularity. It echoed in my head, reverberated inside my cranium with a mind of its own. Only I had no idea what it meant. There, I hear it again...

Are you really awake?

The children looked at me without moving. It had never happened before. Seconds later I realized that they were looking just over my head. I cringed. Winston must have taught them to see auras. Or maybe they had just not lost their ability as they grew up.

Then I noticed something even stranger. They seemed to be looking at me the way they usually looked at Uncle Winston. They needed to see permission in my eyes. To do what—I had no idea. Then I smiled.

The next moment they were all over me.

"Uncle Peter! Uncle Peter!" the pandemonium was in full swing.

I really had to learn to control my aura. Unless it was just that I was no longer living in the house. Winston was bound to know.

"Madam shall be back within the hour, Sir. Would you care to visit your old room to discuss some matters of mutual interest?"

I've known Winston for a number of years. This was the first time he'd made such an offer. I thanked him and before going upstairs decided to make a little tour of the house. After all, I'd spent a number of years there. It was my home, apart from the seminary, the only home I really remembered. Before that the traumatic events connected with my parents' death had erased all earlier memories.

I looked at the walls, the small but precious collection of paintings. A little bronze statue of a girl stood, lonely, on the low side table next to the reading lamp. I spun it on its base. It became a happy statue. I looked at the fireplace, now dormant, waiting for the first signs of winter. The tulle curtains were drawn, but it was still light enough not to draw the heavy drapes. I remembered how afraid I had been to approach them. In that reality I was a fugitive. A man afraid to show his face in public. Or anywhere. I lived in the company of shadows, of chimerical creatures that seemed to persecute me. Only they weren't really there. Just images, constructs of my imagination. For a while I stood by the windows, those facing the garden and the street. I caught sight of one of the two security guards posted at the house. Just waiting and watching. And then, in my mind's eye, I saw people gathered there, waiting for Peter Thornton, or was it already Lazarus, to come out and lay his hands on them. Or just to be there, among them, to share his presence.

"I'd been something better in those days," I mused in undertones. There must have been a little bitterness in my voice. "I paid dearly for my generosity. Or was it just ignorance?"

"We are here to learn, Peter. Do not despair. Nothing is as serious as it seems." This was Winston's voice. I didn't bother to turn around. I knew he wasn't there, behind me. Not in the flesh I recognized as real.

I went upstairs.

"...and in that instant it congealed into, what people later called matter and antimatter, and became torn apart. The matter fell into the creative process of the Universe we observe with our senses. The rest became fragmented in countless nuclei where the original freedom continued to prevail. Nowadays, people call them black holes. Over billions of years the damage is being slowly repaired. Only under extreme pressures can the polarization be reconciled. Slowly and carefully, lest the two become united too quickly. It is the process where consciousness must be stronger than either of its expressions. Gradually the matter returns to its source with its accumulated wisdom gathered over many lifetimes and becomes unified, rejoicing in its original freedom."

Mo and Jo were sitting cross-legged on the carpet. Winston seemed to be hovering about a foot above the floor, likewise in a posture of great expectation. A trick of the light, I'm sure. No one looked up when I came in but Winston shifted to make room for me.

So there are black holes in the other realms also, I thought. So Cathy isn't that far from the true reality.

"A minute portion of our consciousness descended into the world of duality. A small part of us was torn away, entwined with the universal matter. Over countless aeons, evolution leads us back to self-realization. In time we shall liberate ourselves and join our true Essence that is one in the many."

I felt that the next words were directed only at me. "Soon you will understand all this. Soon we shall be as one."

Just then I heard Ruth coming into the house.

"I'm home!" her voice reached us from the hall.

At that precise moment Winston's image dissolved. I'm sure that he was standing downstairs closing the front door behind my sister-in-law. And then I heard his sonorous voice.

"Good evening, Madam. I hope you had a pleasant drive."

Even as Winston greeted Ruth, I heard the swish of children taking their usual shortcut along the balustrade to greet their mother. Nothing had changed. Perhaps, nothing really ever does. Just the appearance of it, but not the essence. Someone once said that evolution advances at a pace somewhere between dead slow and dead slow. The rest doesn't matter. Not really. In this reality we all play our parts, act our banal roles, to justify our existence. But somehow I felt that it was only a game. A little diversion, a pastime, to sate our primitive senses.

"Hello, Ruth," I embraced her. It seemed proper.

"Why, Peter! I didn't know you were coming. How very nice."

"I have a few things to share with you," I said. I already seemed to need an excuse to invade her house.

"You don't need a reason to drop in on us, Peter. This is your family home, it always will be. Yours and Cathy's as well," she added.

She led me to the living room, her arm intertwined with mine. Like old friends, more than just brother and sister. The children retreated upstairs to do their homework. I told Ruth about my discussion with JR. She listened attentively, asked a few pertinent questions, and sat back.

"So there is little we can do, at present?" she asked, in the form of affirmation.

"You cannot change the course of history, or make the river run upstream. Wu wei is the answer."

"Wu wei? That sounds like Cathy's expression."

"Do by doing nothing, or something like that," I explained feebly. "In our language it corresponds to wait and see, but keep hoping."

"And play your cards close to your chest, I suspect."

"We don't have that many cards, Ruth. But there again, nor do they. They cannot really start a real war with the whole world. They also cannot continue on the path that leads them away from the global village. All we can do is wait."

"Wu wei?" she smiled.

For some reason I suddenly needed to assure myself that Ruth would continue to receive reliable advice. Maybe I was just being paranoid again. But who knew what might happen to me? I might go to Switzerland on a moment's notice. I might be kidnapped like so many people these days, though I doubted I was important enough.

"JR is a very smart man, you know," I said. "Both you and Lena can benefit greatly from his expertise." I did my best to sound convincing.

I imagined that JR could easily take over my job and possibly make a better job of it. Usually people who specialized in any one field lose the big picture. John Robb evidently didn't. He was a very good man.

"I'm glad to hear it. You have a habit of evoking the best in the people you meet," she said.

"I'm pretty sure JR was pretty good well before I met him," I assured her. "It's just that he's never pushed his weight around. I suspect he likes to remain in the shadows—not easy with his six-foot-four frame," I smiled. "I hope you'll put him in the organization where he belongs."

Winston announced dinner. It had an air of finality about it. Not the announcement—the dinner. I wondered why. I stole glances at the children. They seemed perfectly relaxed. Ruth was warm and friendly, as always. Uncle Winston smiled enigmatically. He always smiled enigmatically. It must have been something I ate.

***

24

Elohim

I knew that something momentous was about to happen. I just didn't know what. Cathy was still away. I'd already bid farewell to people I knew and held dear to me. Except for Cathy. People kept disappearing. Perhaps I would be next. There are many ways one can disappear. Just ask the politicians in England. Or anywhere in Europe. People would probably assume that I'd returned to my nomadic life. That is, if anyone bothered to think about me at all. I felt just a little nervous. Most of the time I was just sitting, listening. Listening to Winston. Even when sitting alone in my apartment.

"Shall I ever be able to come back?"

"Aren't you forgetting, Peter? Ye are gods."

Masters and minions. Gradually his words were sinking in.

"So there is nothing I cannot do?"

Winston smiled. I had a feeling that he was still looking at me as though I were a promising child not quite ready to stand on my own feet. At the same time, there seemed to be, in his eyes, a good measure of approval that served to fill me with confidence that I was on the right track.

"But what of the time...?"

"There is no time. You decide in what order events take place. For some people, Buddha occurs only now, some two and a half millennia after he visited this reality. Others are having visions of the Christ, today, at this very moment. Those visions are very real to them. They build their realities on them."

"So we don't ever leave? Not really?"

"Are we really ever here?" was his cryptic answer.

Somewhere at the back of my mind I observed a dot of light that grew, intensified, became a wondrous sunrise. It blazed to an inferno and then receded. Nothing was real, everything was real. We had to choose. I suppose that had something to do with this business of free will.

"You are where your attention is."

I knew that. He told me that way back when I got back from Gaston's. Funny how memory can become as clear as spring water. I could see, hear, sense even the minute details, even the grains of sand at the deepest end. I liked that.

"I remember. It was also Carl Jung, the man I studied ages ago, who said that the self is the only reality. He was a very wise man."

"He was also right," the deep voice replied in my head. Dear Winston, was he still playing with the children?

"They show great promise. They were adopted so that you and they could live under the same roof."

"You're kidding!"

There was stifled laughter. "Everything has its purpose. Even your brother's death."

I gave up doubting anything that voice said, wherever it originated.

"I hardly knew him," I said. I heard myself saying the words, yet was hardly aware of opening my mouth. Things were becoming hazy. I felt I didn't have much time to ask my questions.

"Where are you, Winston?"

"I am everywhere I choose to be."

"Simultaneously?"

"I am also everywhere you choose me to be. I am my servant's servant. That takes some practice. Time only exists as it is perceived and you have to learn to manipulate that."

"By humans?"

"We are all human, depending on what you mean by this expression. I am that I am. I am also this I am. I am any I am I choose to be."

"Am I you?"

"I am any I am I choose to be," the voice repeated in my cranium. Funny that. It sounded as though I were talking to myself. I suppose his answer would be 'I am and I am not.'

"There is only one reality," the voice sang, this time reminiscent of the bassos atop Mount Sinai in the Decalogue. I had to smile. There is no time, I remembered. It all happens at once. Time is only to separate events for the convenience of perception.

"You are not Moses, are you?"

"Before Moses was, I am," came the reply from the very top of my head. Perhaps higher. Yes, definitely higher. I couldn't reach that high.

I had to start from scratch. In the beginning God created heaven and the earth, I remembered. I wondered if Cathy would let me have one of those tiny black holes, those tiny universes for me to play with.

I must concentrate.

And the earth was without form and void. And darkness was upon the face of the deep. Not any more. I could see light. A smidgen. A spark. But the spark grew. I was going to create my own heaven and my own earth. For them it would be billions of years, but for me just a fragment of infinity. There was no hurry.

A time will come when they, the little ones, those recognizing my earth and my heaven as their own reality, recognize me as their God. They will write their scriptures and say that in the beginning God created the heaven and the earth...

They will make up stories about me.

My children.

I shall create them in my own image and likeness. I shall plant a seed in their consciousness that will enable them, in the fullness of time, to create their own heaven and earth. And so forth. Forever.

I shall visit my children under different guises. They will make up stories about those images of me, and so create religions. They will distort my image, not knowing that we are all one and the same. It is only our perceptions that differ, not the essence.

I and my children will forever be one. For ever. Even when they become fully cognizant of the beauty of the creative process. Eternal, sublime, infinite, omnipotent.

Even when they realize that they, too, are gods. Even when they create their own planets, galaxies, universes.

I shall reveal for them a world of splendid, blinding beauty, and their mind's eye will open to the splendour, the blinding beauty. To my kingdom.

Let there be light...

Hold on. I want my children to have stars to look up to. A firmament they can rejoice in, a universe they can admire. Yes, it is my job. I want to surround them with beauty. And I want to give them music, that's right, light and music. I'll make them part of me, even as the children truly must be. Then, in due course, I shall give them skins to cover their bodies. I shall give them eyes to see and admire my creation, the beauty I brought into their life. They were just tiny vibrations, then an assembly of atoms, then molecules, later cells, organs and skeletons. Finally, whole independent entities. They'll rise to their feet and look up at the sky. My children. Millions and millions of them. Perhaps billions?

I wonder when they will transpose their matter, the matter they are made of, into a semblance of order and harmony and then, only then, into the mirror for the light and sound. And then we shall unite again. And they will create a new earth and a new heaven, and there will be no mind. Just consciousness. As I am even now. They will probably call it spirit, but these are just words.

And I shall shower gifts upon them, and gradually they'll learn to accept them.

And then, suspended beyond all time and all space, I felt an instant of inexplicable joy. For that brief moment, I was no longer looking at my Universe. I *was* the Universe. I felt the vibration of every atom. I surged up the tender capillaries of plants and trees, as though reaching for the sky. I pulsated in the blood vessels of those born and those who have not yet come to life. I became, or I suspect I always have been, an integral, inseparable part of this Universe.

The moment passed. The next fraction of eternity flung me into the depth of agony. Of pain unmitigated by human emotions.

Do gods feel pain?

Is there Divine Pain and Love?

Do gods suffer?

I felt the void of separation, a great sorrow at having to leave, to step outside and look at my creation from without. A great sorrow that lingered for a time that was no time, even as I admired part of me evolving into new heaven and a new earth. I knew that, in essence, I never left that particular world. I neither would nor could leave it. Yet I also knew that I could not limit myself to just one reality constrained by time and space, even if it remained an inseparable part of me.

And then, once again, I ceased to be....

All that I'd ever read in ancient scriptures, all that I'd ever heard of arcane myths, caught up with me. The knowledge surged in me even as sound catches up with one in a supersonic aircraft. Silence.

Light seemed to originate within me. It came as a burst so intense as to erase the countless stars and galaxies. In that single instant I knew that, even as time doesn't really exist, this is the eternal now of the Big Bang in which this and all the other universes have been created and will continue to be created by the countless entities who, but for an ephemeral moment, reach this sublime awareness wherein they encounter the Face of God.

And then, for one that cannot sustain such sublime consciousness, time returned to its rightful place. Almost shyly I looked at the incipient universe of my creation.

One day, I mused, one day I shall embody my consciousness there, down there, forever. My self-awareness. I shall leave my progeny to abide among them, my children, to show them my way.

***

Cathy is walking through the arrival gate at Mirabel. She looks glorious. For the briefest of moments I ask myself whose child she is, and then I remember. It is not easy to juggle realities. Winston is so good at it. He's been doing it for millennia. His worlds are already on their own. Order and harmony inherent in the Light and Sound have taken over the new realities and will continue to unfold themselves into what people will call, one day, evolution. A gradual, yet inexorable journey towards their inevitable destiny, towards home. He injects his presence into them, periodically, and then lets nature take its course. I know. I, too, am Winston. Or else, he is me. He is I am. We are one. We all are, only most of us don't know it. Not yet.

"Good flight?"

"Missed you, darling. I missed you terribly."

She snuggles under my arm, making driving difficult. No matter. There is no hurry. There is no time. We just arrange things in a sequential order. I must keep repeating that. I must metabolize the concept that all is up to us. Up to me. How difficult it is to remember this premise from within a material body. Perhaps it's just some sort of test? Or it could be all those bosons fighting for recognition.

"Anything happen while I was away? Anything interesting?"

"Well, we are in a state of war."

She laughs. "Yes, I heard about that. I said something *interesting*."

I love those eyes gazing at me. Those pools of jade filled with promise. If only people knew that paradise is wherever you find it. It can be anywhere. Literally anywhere. I swerve. Must keep my eyes on the road. Each reality has its own rules that must be obeyed. I know. I created them. Some of them.

"How's mother and father?" she asks.

"They are fine, darling. Just fine," I assure her.

She's happy to be back. Can I do something to make it more *interesting* for her? No. That would be cheating. I am not allowed to cheat anymore. Gods don't cheat. It is against their nature.

Against their own laws. When will people learn that each time we allow a miracle to happen, it breaks the universal laws? We can repair the damage, of course, but it shouldn't be necessary. If people do not like their reality, they can change it. We all wield that power. Every one of us. We always have—it is just a question of realization. Of acceptance. There is nothing we cannot do. Only it takes total commitment. And effort. Or faith as big as a grain of mustard seed.

"Wait till you see the view from our floor. There is just nothing like it."

I was going to add 'on earth', but that would have been presumptuous. And anyway, there are probably a great many views on earth that I haven't yet seen. Then I feel silly. Cathy has already seen the view from our forty-ninth floor. From our private heaven.

I blink my eyes. I was lying. I know there are incredible views on earth I haven't seen. On the other hand, none are as beautiful unless Cathy is standing right there next to me. So I'd said the truth, after all. I don't have to strike myself with lightning.

I smile at my thoughts.

"What's so funny?" She is watching me.

I must watch myself. As I said, I cannot lie anymore. "I was thinking of you standing at our window, looking out, and me looking at you." This was close enough.

"And that's funny?"

"Only if you knew the rest of my thoughts at the time. But tell me. Anything new on the mini-universes front?"

"Plenty. There is preliminary evidence that there are countless numbers of them. And that there must have been virtually an infinite number following the initial Big Bang. Literally infinite."

One for every human being that will ever live, I assumed. I couldn't tell her that. At least, not yet.

"Have you learned anything else about them?"

"Well, that's still a bit of a mystery. But there is some evidence that they may well consist of antimatter."

How on earth could Winston have known that? And then I remember that Winston could know anything he put his mind to. Winston is so much more than a man. Winston is an idea personified.

"The strange thing is that they expand and then just wink out. As if there were nothing to sustain them. There seems nothing rational about their behaviour." Her eyes are turning dreamy and then a subtle haze enwraps her into a luminescent sphere. Of course...

I am looking at my own Universe. It needs to expand. It needs to be supported by divine intervention, by an act of will. It is my consciousness that has to expand. It must span the Universe I've created. And I must continue to create it. I see countless galaxies coming into being and then moving away to make room for others. There is a centre to my Universe and it provides motive power for its vitality. I am that centre. I am watching myself expand. I am the observer and the observed. We were one... on the way to infinity.

It is a cycle. Ongoing. Eternal. There is so much gods have to learn.

I am that I am.

"It was almost as though they were all in abeyance, waiting for something. It's so hard to speculate on such things. They are so small yet they seem to have an enormous potential inherent in them. I really can't explain it. You had to be there. You must feel it rather than think about it..."

Her voice reaches me from afar.

Again I blink my Universe away. We are at the window of our apartment, the city beneath us, the sky closer. Cathy's luminescence subsides, shimmers, then disappears. Only her aura remains. Ah, yes. Her aura and her potential universe waiting to be filled with her presence. With her consciousness.

"Yes, darling. They do have infinite potential. They really do."

She looks at me with eyes filled with wonder. Her mouth opens, then closes again. Whatever she wanted to say must have seemed inadequate to her. I want to ask her if she would like to see my Universe. The world I've created. She must have read my thoughts. She smiles and nods hesitantly.

I hold her close.

The stars shimmer all around us. We hold hands in this boundless expanse, feeling no fear, expecting naught, accepting all. It is a two-way exchange. What I did before is already solidifying into its own reality. But there is a peculiar disorder. A sort of chaos. Some stars are whirling, others seem almost static. There is no order to them.

"You need time," I hear her voice in my head.

"I have eternity," I answer glibly.

"No, darling. You need to create time. To set things in order."

Of course. Young gods are stupid, inexperienced. They need help. Of a woman?

"YHWH. Yahweh. It is not a name, it is an acronym. A tetragrammaton. It stands for the universal masculine and feminine principles. You need the two. One to create, the other to sustain."

"Dear Cathy. Will you be my goddess?"

"I am," I hear her voice filling infinity. "I am that I am."

"We are, they are only becoming..."

'They and we are one," she whispers, yet her sweet voice is like celestial music. Is that what it is? Is that *Musica Universalis* — the whispering of the gods?

I hear the familiar vibrations I first heard some weeks ago, when I listened with Winston. Electro-phonic vibrations, he'd called them. How incredibly inadequate a description. How inadequate it all seems in the material reality. It's all unreal there. On Earth.

"The Music of the Spheres. They whisper to each other. You and I are also whispering. We are all one."

"There is nothing outside you and me?"

"There is only one god; you and I are its expressions. In each one of us rests his and her potential power. Power and love that stimulates us to share that which is within us. A never-ending cycle."

We are thinking as one. It did not matter who said what, out here. Out here? We are everywhere. Here is where my attention is. *For where two or three are gathered together in my name, there am I in the midst of them...* That is where duality is no more.

Beyond the doing right, and doing wrong....

The galaxies are retreating from each other in an orderly fashion. They were created in the name of order and harmony, and they are sustained by love and beauty. The view from the forty-ninth floor is still fantastic. We stand, arms about each other's waists, motionless, spellbound. There is a slight whirling of atoms all around us. Then they, too, subside, recede into the silence of the gods.

"That wasn't real, was it?"

Cathy is first to break the silence. I didn't want to talk yet. It is painful to bring myself back to this glorious earth, so beautiful yet so diluted in its intensity. It is like looking at an old sepia film, with hardly any colour injected into its images. This isn't real. Not nearly.

"You're right. This isn't real... not nearly," she whispers. Then she looks up at me, her eyes still filled with wonder. "Can we be here and there, simultaneously?"

"We are," I reply. "Only our attention wanders. We are still just beginners."

"There is no end to learning, is there." This wasn't a question. She already knew. And even as she asks, she pulls me closer to herself. "Can we ever go back there?"

"We are there, even now. I am as sure of this as I am of holding you in my arms."

She nestles her head on my shoulder. "We can't do this there, can we?"

I have to laugh. Here she is, a goddess who introduced order into a brand new universe, and she is asking me if we can cuddle up within our own creation.

"Out there, that is also here, we are one. There is no need. This is just a mere image... a projection."

"But I like it, Peter. I like it here, too." I do too. I've been human for thirty years. Old habits die slowly.

"I know. This is why we are here and there. In a way, we are omnipresent. We are gods, remember?"

"Is this what they meant? You know, those ancient scribes...?"

"You will have to ask them yourself," I murmur. "I suppose, being in charge of time, you could really do that. You could really reach back to when they lived and ask King David what he meant when he wrote all those beautiful psalms."

"I know, they are beautiful," she agreed. "They are like poetry."

"What, no Tao?"

"They do not negate each other. There is only one truth, but there are countless paths towards it."

"As many as there are people?"

"As many as there are people in all the universes. You cannot place limits on gods-in-waiting, either." She smiles at her new understanding. "I didn't know that yesterday... there were so many things I didn't know yesterday."

"And yet all knowledge rests ever within us," I muse aloud. "It really is a wondrous Universe. Worlds without end..."

"That's not as yet established," Dr. Catherine Mondellay states firmly.

We both laugh. "I dare say it never will be. It would be so dull to place limits on the infinite."

"That doesn't make mathematical sense," she almost snaps.

"I know, isn't it wonderful?"

That makes her quiet again. We stand looking out at Mount Royal again, the tops of the trees at our own elevation. Even then I feel his presence. I don't have to turn to know that Winston is standing right behind me.

"I'm here to congratulate you, Sir, Madam," his voice reaches us from somewhere.

Cathy doesn't move. "Wasn't that Winston?" she asks, hardly needing an answer.

"And he still calls us Sir and Madam. Winston," I turn to face him. "Do you want us to call you Master, Guru, or just a Wondrous Friend?" I ask, unable to hide a broad grin.

"I rather fancy the latter, Peter. So, what are your first impressions?"

"Staggering would be the understatement of the ages. Beautiful is closer. Infinity best describes it. It places no limits on our impressions."

He smiles, nodding. But before he has a chance to speak, I ask him, "Winston, why didn't you ever tell us?" How silly of me. I know the answer.

"Would you have ever believed me?" I am sure he said it for the sake of Cathy.

"Not in a million years. Yet..."

"I know, Peter. You accomplished with Cathy more in a single second than I did in years..."

My mind is flooded with all the statements Winston has made to me over the years. If only I'd known how to listen. He led me through the straight and narrow. It is I who wandered off course. So many times.

"The healing... was that also you?" I asked.

"It seemed like a good idea at the time. You had the potential but were too anchored in—pardon me, Cathy—in science."

"So you destroyed my career just for this?" I make a sweeping motion that embraces this and all the other universes.

"Guilty as charged."

I let go of Cathy, walk up to my old friend and embrace him. There is no need for words. We both know what true love means. And I've experienced an abundance of it.

"Will you stay with Ruth?" I ask after a little while.

"The children are most promising. It would be a pity to withdraw too early."

"Really? Jo and Mo... how wonderful," Cathy comes to life. "They're such wonderful children."

"Particularly Jonathan. Moira tends to look up to her brother a little too much. She must gain her own balance. But I am sure it will come."

I don't dare to ask about Ruth. We both know that Ruth is still anchored in her own brand of fundamentalism. She's attached to things that are temporal. Transient. She thinks them important. She abides in the world that she can perceive with her physical senses. Perhaps it was her upbringing. I'm not wise enough to know.

Many are called, but few are chosen, I hear a voice inside my cranium. Winston just smiles while Cathy looks surprised. She's probably never heard him inside her own head before. And then he opens his mouth.

"When in Rome..." We all laugh. Then he looks into my eyes. "Do you know, Peter, that of our seven billion people, right here, on earth, only a handful have crossed the great divide, as you two did just today?"

"A handful?"

"Maybe a hundred. I've tried to do my level best with you and the children. And they still have a way to go..."

"How fortunate that time is but a figment of our imagination," Cathy says.

"Not when you're waiting your turn at the dentist's," I put in softly. This was getting too serious for me.

"Quite right, Peter. There are times when time seems very real. And also, we're in the age of Kali. We don't have that much time to go..."

I am not ready to dispute that. The age of Kali, some four-hundred and twenty-seven thousand years...

"A twinkling of an eye," Winston assures me.

"Are there many such as you?" I ask as Winston's silhouette is just beginning to shimmer.

"There are two more of us as of today," I hear him say from some distance away. I close my eyes and see the children coming back from school. "In this reality," I hear, inside my head yet somehow from afar.

"I wish you luck, Peter. And you Cathy. We need all the help we can get..." and Winston's image dissolves into the filigree of shadows the setting sun casts on the wall opposite the windows. My last thought remains unanswered. Who is *we*, I wanted to ask?

"He is a wonderful man," Cathy says after a while. "Do you know that I saw him in my dreams, in CERN, at least a dozen times?"

I spin on my heels.

"So you were under his..." Of course... How else could she possibly have joined me on my universal jaunt. How else could she have become a goddess. And yet he'd assigned all the credit just to me.

"You never told me," I say when Cathy remains silent. There must have been a little angst in my voice. Gods, too, can be angry. And gods can hurt.

"Did you ever tell me of *your* relationship with him?" she asks.

"There was nothing to tell... not really. Anyway would you have believed me?"

"I don't know. Would you? That's what real love is all about, isn't it, Peter? Giving and expecting nothing in return."

"Divine love," I say, my head still spinning from this new revelation. "For how long have you been sensing Winston's influence?"

"More or less from the time he arranged for our stay at your great-grandfather's hunting lodge, up north, remember? But I saw some evidence of it even in my early years. When I was little."

"I'll never forget." I'm still thinking of the hunting lodge. Winston is an old scoundrel. That's the wrong way to speak about a god. And such a wonderful god. A god that chose to be a butler for the sole purpose of raising four people to a higher level. Is that the real measure of love?

I heard that... a distant voice murmured in my head. And then I only felt a warmth.

I am beginning to understand.

Carpe diem.

Heaven, the new universes, is the reward. They are creations of our limitless mind. They lie within us. They are moments of being that lie beyond time. Within that realm, within heaven, we are the source of all becoming. Of all creation. Here, on earth, we were involved in the divine process of becoming. Here, I am life. The process.

In but a few billion years Cathy and I and Winston will fall asleep, only to awaken again, aeons later, to a new Golden Age. Like Brahma.

In the meantime, we can rejoice in the state of becoming. In the infinity of the present. In fragments of forever.

Carpe diem. Each day a fraction of eternity.

Tomorrow, I shall do my best in the office. If I meet someone who needs my help, I shall offer it gladly. Without judgment or reservations. And one day, when I learn a lot more than I know today, perhaps I shall become a butler. A majordomo, to guide someone to the edge of eternity. In the meantime, I shall rejoice in my becoming.

Carpe diem.

I put my arm around Cathy and pull her towards me. For a little while we look, silently, as the sun's red beams try vainly to pierce through the ripe summer foliage atop Mount Royal. The whole mountain shimmers with ripples of the dying sun. The crowns are alive with tiny flames, reaching ever up, towards the limitless space. And then we both hear the music.

Cathy looks up at me. I feel her sweet breath on my face. We turn towards our bedroom. There is no law that prohibits heaven from descending to earth. Even as we approach our private Olympus, the music intensifies. Soon, we are one.

And then time stands still. Again.

*****

Acknowledgments

I would be remiss were I not to thank Madeleine Witthoeft for her diligent editing. My thanks also to all my many friends for their proofreading, none more so than Kate Jones, whose meticulous attention to detail and exemplary knowledge of the intricacies of the English language edify us all. As always my gratitude to my wife, Bozena Happach, who, having put up with being a grass widow for weeks on end, offered me her inimitable insights.

Sincerely,
Stan I.S. Law

A Word about the Author

Stan I.S. Law (aka **Stanislaw Kapuscinski**), architect, sculptor, and prolific writer, was educated in Poland and England. Since 1965 he has resided in Canada. His special interests cover a broad spectrum of arts, sciences and philosophy. His fiction and non-fiction attest to his particular passion for the scope and the development of Human Potential. He authored more than thirty books, twenty of them novels.

Under his real name he published seven non-fiction books sharing his vision of reality. He also composed two collections of poems in his original native tongue in which he satirizes his view of the world while paying homage to Bozena Happach's sculptures.

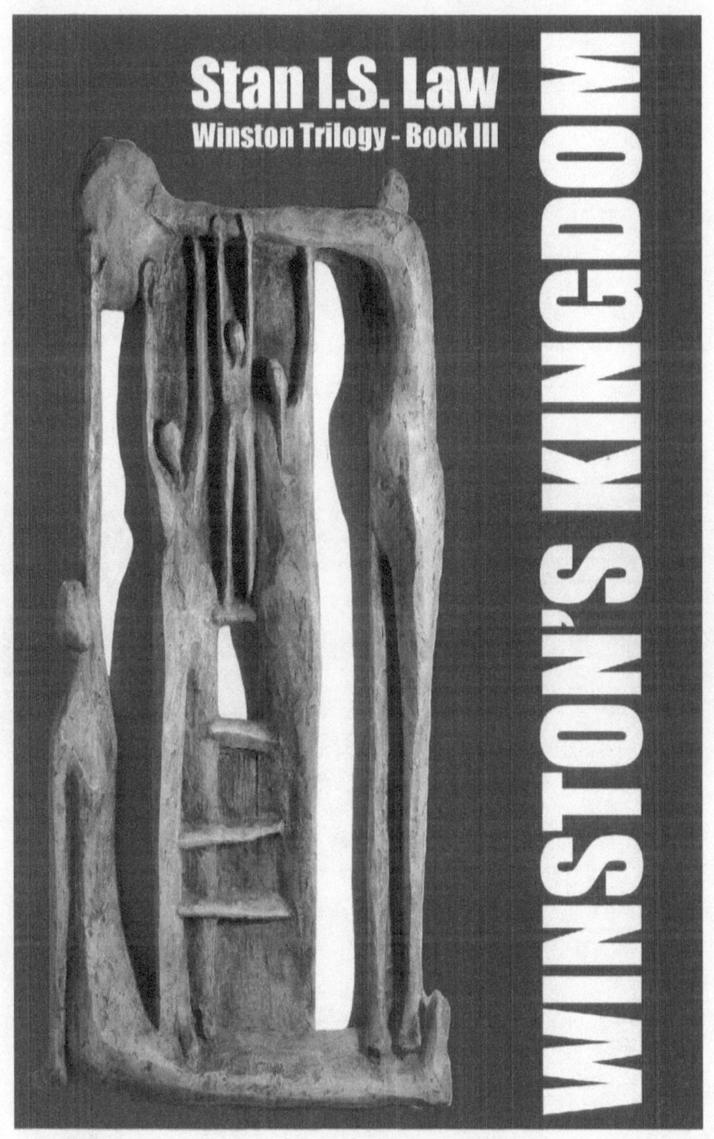

INHOUSEPRESS presents WINSTON'S KINGDOM
Book III of Winston Trilogy
109769

www.ingramcontent.com/pod-product-compliance
Lightning Source LLC
Chambersburg PA
CBHW020903200626
46814CB00001BA/157

* 9 7 8 1 9 8 7 8 6 4 0 4 5 *